Grudges and Grace

Trial and Triumph

Volume 1: Grudges and Grace

Volume 2: Reclaiming Love

TRIAL AND TRIUMPH

Volume 1

GRUDGES AND GRACE

B.J. SALMOND

Frontier Mountain

American Fork, Utah, U.S.A.

Hardcover ISBN: 978-1-7366053-7-0
Paperback ISBN: 978-1-7366053-8-7
E-Book ISBN: 978-1-7366053-9-4
Library of Congress Control Number: 2021904814
Cover design by: Virtually Possible Designs
Edited by: Kathy Jenkins Oveson

Printed in the United States of America 29172-3300
10 9 8 7 6 5 4 3 2 1

For my dear
beautiful wife
Stacey.

Chapter .5
Discovery

Jefferson brought the chair down hard against the wrought-iron stove. Splinters of wood flew in every direction.

His stepfather had just left the house but came running back in when he heard the loud noise through the front door. As he surveyed the scene all the muscles on his face tightened. He saw Jefferson holding the remains of the chair. "What do you think you're doing?"

Sarah, Jefferson's mother, quickly intervened to calm her husband, then turning to Jefferson said, "Go to your room, *now.*"

Jefferson dropped the pieces of the chair that were still in his hands and went straight to his room. He could hear Jean yelling at his mother about what he had just done, upset that she wasn't letting him take more severe action. Jefferson slammed the door to his bedroom, stomped his way to his bed, and flung himself onto the mattress.

"Jefferson Chestnut Slade! Don't you dare slam doors in this house," his stepfather shouted.

He heard his mother talking to his stepfather, unable to make out what she was saying. Then he heard her forcefully say, "Just let me talk to him first."

After a few moments, the door opened a crack, and a soft knock followed.

"Go away!" Jefferson called out.

He heard the voice of his stepfather from across the house, "Don't you talk to your mother like that."

"Jean, please let me handle this," Sarah called back as she walked into the room, shutting the door behind her.

Sarah pulled a chair next to the bed and sat down. She stared at Jefferson in silence, considering how best to help him.

"Jefferson, blowing up about what your father told you and smashing the kitchen chair to pieces is not going to make things any better for you. You need to control your anger."

Jefferson scrunched his face. "He is not my father."

"He provides for you, feeds you, gives you a bed to sleep on, and a home to live in. He is your father."

"I can't stand him," Jefferson said, his speech hurried and strained. "I try to do what he asks, but every time he sees me, he wants me to do another chore. I never get to play, then he whips me when I try to do something fun. I hate him."

"He's just looking out for you. You can't get into much trouble when you're working."

Sarah tried to meet his gaze and smiled. Jefferson folded his arms and stared at the floor, refusing to look at her.

Sarah touched his knee. "Come on now, other ten-year-old boys have just as many chores."

Jefferson raised his voice. "Then how come they're always outside playing, and I'm always working?"

The voice of his stepfather boomed from the other side of the door. "Don't you raise your voice with your mother."

Sarah lifted her eyes to heaven and in a sweet voice said, "I've got this, dear. Please let me talk to him without interruption." She looked at Jefferson. "Jefferson, those boys out there playing, likely put their shoulder to the wheel and got all their chores done."

"Well, Jean is just plain mean, and I hate him."

"Maybe you wouldn't hate him so much if you tried doing what he asks of you," Sarah said, speaking slowly and deliberately. "He wouldn't be as mean, and you would be a lot happier."

Jefferson was silent. Sarah considered her son for a moment. She saw the anger in his eyes. Her heart ached to see him like this. She came to a decision. She opened her mouth to speak, but no words came out. She closed her eyes, swallowed, then pressed on.

"You know, my father struggled in much the same way. Not with his father, but with his anger."

Jefferson blinked, and his jaw dropped. "You've never mentioned your father before."

Sarah glanced down, her eyes moistening. "I lost him in the most painful way. It is hard for me to talk about him without remembering that awful day."

Jefferson had never heard about any of his mother's immediate family and was eager to hear more. He spoke softly. "What was he like?"

Sarah noticed the change in her son's demeanor and smiled. She looked at her hands, then wiped away the tears that threatened to spill down her cheeks, "His name was William Albert Chestnut."

Jefferson's eyebrows rose. "That's why my middle name is Chestnut."

"Yes. He grew up on a farm, but he didn't like farming. He was finally able to get out of it when he had an accident with his horse."

Chapter 1
First Shot

St. Louis, Missouri
April 20, 1832

The horse fought against the reins as William tried to get it moving in the right direction.

"Move, you dumb animal!" he hollered.

He had to finish getting this field plowed in the next few days, but at the rate he was moving, it would take weeks. William set down the plow and walked over to the horse so he could look it in the eyes. "Come on!"

William slowly shook his head, then in a softer voice said, "I can't get this done without you."

He grabbed the reins and gave them a hard tug. The horse resisted and pulled against him. William pulled harder but to no avail. Finally dropping the reins, he walked back toward the plow. As soon as he passed the horse, it turned a little and kicked. William felt a sharp pain as the hoof rammed into his side. The air completely gone out of him, he fell to the ground. William struggled to breathe for several agonizing seconds then everything went black.

~ * * * ~

William opened his eyes. He stared at a white ceiling. A soft, plush blanket covered him, and a cushy, down mattress pressed against his aching body. His mother sat in a chair by his bed.

She put her hand on his forehead, testing his temperature. "St. Louis boys weren't meant to fight horses."

William moaned. "I don't want to farm anymore."

William's mother blinked, and her lips parted, "You no longer want to work for your father?"

"It's not working for Father that I don't like—it's farming. I'm no good at any of this . . . besides, Wilford died plowing, and I almost suffered the same fate today."

The image of his brother collapsed on a plowed field forced its way into William's mind.

His mother's eyes dropped. "You and your older brother were very close. His death was more getting sick from the ague, and him ignoring it than from plowing. Even so, I can see how that memory would turn you away from farming."

"What I really want to do is own and run one of those mercantile stores."

William's mother stared into his green eyes. "I know you keep talking about that. You are twenty now. Perhaps it's time for you to explore that option. I'll talk to your father."

"Thanks, Ma!" William tried to sit up and hug her, but as soon as he moved, the pain in his side reminded him that he should stay put.

William's mother ruffled his thick, brown hair, and she admired the light freckles on his face and arms. "Right now, you need to save your strength and stay down. The doctor said you cracked a rib and have some nasty bruises. You need rest so you can heal."

"All right."

As his mother left, William gazed out the window. He saw his father's prosperous farm and the hired hands finishing the work he had left undone. Tall stalks of corn had grown there the previous year. His father tried to teach him how to plow the field that year. He made it look so easy, but William was more accustomed to taking care of the animals. His father had told him that he could plow this year. William hadn't looked forward to it, but he didn't want to let him down.

William's father had been able to sell much of what they grew in the St. Louis market. The city had three miles of riverfront, and was where the Missouri and Mississippi rivers converged. Because of this, ships of all sorts were regularly stopping at St. Louis to drop off passengers and to resupply. It was the last major city in which anyone headed west could get needed provisions for their journey.

After the death of their firstborn, William's parents devoted more money to helping him. When he turned twenty, his parents had given him his own horse and wagon.

As William lay resting on his bed, his father came in. "How are things going, Son?"

"Good. I haven't seen you in a while."

His father sat down on the chair by the bed. His plump cheeks puffed up as he blew out the air, then he rubbed his thick mustache in thought. "I've been busy talking to Governor Dunklin. He wants to start up a standardized public education system in Missouri. But I think it will kill the free-market education, making it a slave to the whims of the government and a select group of people who think they know what's better for our children than we do."

"You going to try to get him voted out?"

"Maybe." His father stroked his chin. "A fellow by the name of Boggs seems eager to take his spot. He might have some promise."

William's father always liked to meddle in politics. When William was nine years old, President James Monroe began his second term in office, and Missouri had just become a state. He remembered that his parents left home to celebrate frequently during that time, leaving William in the care of his nanny.

When he was sixteen, his father kept going on about the Democratic Party, a new political party that had recently formed. William didn't care much for politics except once when, in that same year, the war hero, Andrew Jackson, became President. William was excited about that, as he had grown up on stories his father had told him at bedtime about how "Old Hickory" drove the British out of our country and saved the nation. William figured someone like that deserved to be the President of the United States.

~ * * * ~

After several weeks, William was feeling much better and was finally able to walk around. He heard the cook call out that dinner was ready and made his way downstairs to eat.

After his father blessed the food, as he did every meal, he looked at William. "How are your ribs feeling?"

"Hurts if I move the wrong way, but otherwise I'm feeling a lot better."

"Your mother and I have been talking. I know your heart has been set on owning your own store for some time now. I was hoping you'd take to farming and run our farm someday. But I've been thinking that maybe I ought to let you spread your wings a little. I've decided—"

Williams's mother cleared her throat and stared at her husband with raised eyebrows.

William's father looked to his wife, then back to William. "Excuse me—*we've* decided that if that's what you really want to do, we'll support you. I've talked to Andrew Burnham, who owns Burnham General Store in town, and he is willing to take you on and teach you the business."

William's eyebrows shot up, and he smiled from ear to ear. "Thanks, Pa! That is so macaroni! I can't wait. When does he want me to start?" He sat up straighter and instantly regretted it, flinching with the pain.

William's father lifted his chin and creased his brow, "I told him about your injury, and he said you can start just as soon as you're all healed up."

Chapter 2
Last Straw

By the time William turned twenty-one, he had eight months of clerking experience behind him. His father surprised him on his birthday by getting him his own shop and giving him a loan so he could buy the goods he would sell.

William was able to keep his store going successfully for three months. He even paid his father back some of what he had borrowed for the start-up costs.

In the fourth month, the business started struggling. The bank gave William a few loans to keep his store stocked, though his business continued to fail. William felt compelled to go back to the bank and ask for another loan.

The banker shook his head at the request. "I hope you understand, Mr. Chestnut, I'm hesitant to give you any more loans until you've paid back what we've lent you already. Why do you think you need more?"

"I have more than a few customers who are not paying their accounts. I just need one more loan until I can get them to pay me back. I've also had a problem with theft, but I've rearranged my store. Now I can see anyone who tries to slip something away while I'm at the register."

"I've been to your store, Mr. Chestnut. I like to shop around and compare prices, and I've noticed that your competitors are selling what you do for a better price. Just some friendly advice: you may want to price your goods a little more competitively."

William looked at the ground and bit his lower lip. "I have noticed that, but there is not a lot I can do about it if I want to make any profit at all. I don't know how they get away with selling things at those prices. I'd be out of business if I sold goods at those prices."

"From what you've told me, that may happen anyway." The banker shut his book. "I'm sorry, Mr. Chestnut, I just can't afford the risk of giving you another loan. If you can't pay your debts by the end of the month, I'm sorry to say that we'll be forced to foreclose and confiscate your store and your assets to pay your debts."

William could feel the blood rushing to his head. He tapped his thumb on the desk and narrowed his eyes. *I don't have to listen to this.*

William grabbed the papers on the desk and threw them into the air. Papers rained down around them. The banker tried to seize him, but William dodged, and pushed the banker out of the way, sending him flying head first into a desk. William left the bank, slamming the door behind him.

~ * * * ~

A week passed, and William's situation hadn't improved. He had to pay a large fine for what he'd done at the bank. He knew he should not have reacted the way he did, but the banker had made him so angry.

He walked down the street, his hands in his pockets, his head down. He stopped in front of Burnham General Store. The familiar yellow sign that advertised the store's name stared down at him. William remembered when he looked forward to seeing that sign. Now it represented the mean-spirited man who oppressed his ability to thrive in this business.

As he walked into the store, the familiar, musty smell of dry goods greeted him. Mr. Burnham sat behind the counter giving change to an old farmer. Two other men milled about the store, critically eyeing the goods. After the old farmer left, William approached the counter.

Mr. Burman's lips went tight, and he nodded in greeting. "William."

William slammed his fist on the counter. "Why are you working so hard to drive me out of business? What did I ever do to you?"

Mr. Burnham considered William for a few seconds, then smiled. "You opened a store and drew away my customers. So, I decided to compete. A little competition is healthy. Drives free enterprise forward, you know."

Then, looking into the sour expression still on William's face, he leaned his body over the counter and whispered, "If you can't handle the plow, then stay off the field, Mr. Chestnut."

William thought of his brother, who had died while plowing the field, then of his own failure at plowing. William looked at Mr. Burnham through silted eyes, then hit him in the jaw.

Mr. Burnham stumbled back, eyes wide. He shook his head, and quicker than William expected, came around the counter and hit William square in the forehead. The blow sent him reeling back into the shelves. They toppled like dominoes, goods of all kinds lay strewn across the floor.

William got up and charged straight for Mr. Burnham. Just before he could make a connection, the two other men in the store grabbed him.

Mr. Burnham rubbed his jaw. "Hold him tight, boys, while I go for the sheriff."

~ * * * ~

William stood in front of the judge, waiting for him to speak. The judge ran his fingers through his black, curly hair, then licked his finger as he thumbed through the papers in front of him. He glanced up.

"Well, let's see . . . we have William Chestnut here. I would say welcome back, but a court is not a place where one should feel welcome." Pointing at William, he said, "You shouldn't be wanting to come back after even one visit. So why is it, William, that this is the sixth time I've seen you in this courtroom?"

William stared at the judge, his lips tight and his brow lowered. "Judge, none of those were my fault."

The judge raised his eyebrows. "No? Well, let's go through them, shall we?" Holding up a finger, the judge continued, "You assaulted your teacher for giving you a bad grade five years ago." He raised another finger. "The year after that, you threw a rock at a man who had dealt dishonestly with you, and the rock hit the horse next to him, sending a carriage on the run through the streets without a driver. The sheriff broke his arm trying to stop it."

The judge raised a third finger. "Last year, you pushed over a public outhouse because you claimed the man inside had stolen some flowers you had purchased for a lady friend."

The judge threw up a fourth finger, then a fifth. "Seven months ago, you broke the window of a cooper shop because you were fighting a boy who insulted you. Just last week you made a mess of the bank, flinging their important loan documents about the room because they wouldn't grant you a loan. You pushed the banker over when he tried to stop you; his head hit the desk, which knocked him out. And now you attack your former employer in his place of business." The judge now had six fingers raised and slammed his hands on the table. "What do we do with you now, Mr. Chestnut?"

"Those things weren't my fault! In each one of those cases someone made me angry; it wasn't my fault."

The judge shook his head, and squinted. "Mr. Chestnut, William. Those folks likely did do things that aggravated you, but no one can *make* you angry. No one can force you to hit someone else. That is a choice that you made on your own. I know other men who have been turned down for a loan, yet somehow, they don't choose to destroy the bank's papers and assault the banker. That is a choice you made. You could have chosen to take it like a man and walk away, but if you had made that choice, we wouldn't be here for the sixth time, would we? Anger is a choice, Mr. Chestnut; it's not forced on you. You chose to be angry, and you chose to do those things that kept bringing you back to this court."

William stared at the floor. "I'm sorry, Your Honor. I'll try harder to control my anger."

The judge removed his glasses. "I'm sure you will, because now, *I'm* going to make a choice. I'm going to choose to not see you in this court again. At least not in the next six years, one year for every time you've graced this court with your presence. Because you're still young, William, I'll give you a choice. You get to choose whether to spend those six years behind bars in a state prison, or to leave the state and live far enough away that you won't be able to plague this court any further with your presence. What do you choose, William?"

In a voice that was barely audible, William mumbled, "Leave the state."

The judge leaned forward. "Speak up so I can hear you."

William straightened his back and said in a crisp, loud voice, "Leave the state."

"Good. I thought you might choose that. You've got until the end of the month to be gone. And let me just warn you: if I even so much as hear that someone has seen you in this state in the next six years, I will put a warrant out for your arrest and a bounty on your head. And I'll put you away for the maximum time allowed. You don't want that, do you?"

"No, sir," William said.

"Good. Now get out of my court," the judge said with a pound of his gavel.

Chapter 3
Getting Ready

The next morning as William sat at breakfast reading the local newspaper, he read a story that reported an uprising on the western end of the state. The locals had expelled a group of religious folks to a neighboring county.

Another article noted that President Jackson had signed the Force Bill to get more taxes out of imports just before being sworn in for his second term.

His father came in the dining room while William was wading through the news of the day. He walked over to the table and called out to their cook, "Bessie, make me something I can take on the road this morning."

"As you say, Mr. Chestnut," Bessie replied.

Bessie had broad shoulders, a wide forehead, and always kept her hair in a bun. She was an immigrant from Germany who had lost her husband and children to cholera when they traveled to America.

When William's father found her begging on the streets ten years ago, he asked if she knew how to cook. She took the job and had been the family's cook ever since.

As William's father sat to wait for Bessie to bring him his breakfast, he glanced through the newspapers William had left on the table. Then he turned to his son. "Looks like attacking Mr. Burnham didn't help you none. Now you have to close your business and leave the state."

William lowered his head. "I would have lost my business anyway. My competitors were playing dirty, selling the same goods I did but for way less than I could afford to buy them. I swear they were in cahoots trying to drive me out of business."

His father looked him in the eye. "Well, they're just trying to keep their businesses alive the same as you, son."

"No!" William said, pounding his fist on the table. "They're no-good cheats! I had problems with theft, too. Wouldn't be surprised if they sent people to steal from me just to make things more difficult. I won't forget what they've done to me. They'll—"

"Come on, William. Even if they did do that, holding a grudge will only hurt you and hold you back from becoming your best self. It won't bother them none. You'd best get on with your life, forgive them, remember the lessons they taught you, and learn from those lessons."

"You say that like it's easy. How can I forgive someone who has intentionally hurt me?"

"You have to make a decision, and it has to come from your heart," William's father said, putting his hand on Williams' shoulder. "Sometimes it takes involving the Lord in your struggle. But if you let your grudges consume you, it could lead to making the wrong choices—like going into Burnham's store and punching him in the face. If you let that line of thinking go too far, you'll end up doing things you'll regret for the rest of your life."

"Maybe. But I just know my business would have been successful if they hadn't been so underhanded."

Williams's father shook his head and looked away. "Maybe it's best you take a break from all that anyway. Go east to Kentucky, and start a farm. Farming is honest work, and folks will always need to eat."

William thought for a moment. "Farming's not what I want to do with my life, Pa. The mercantile business is my passion, and I can be successful in it. Since I have to leave the state, I was thinking I would go north to Illinois."

"You think you won't run into more competitors like Burnham and Charles in another city?"

William considered his words. "Perhaps I can find a town that's further from the river, that won't have as much supply coming into it, I could make long trips to bring in better supplies. My business will take off. Before long I'll be able to pay you back the rest of the money you've given me to get my last business up and going."

"Maybe," his father said, "but this time I'm not going to finance your business."

William's jaw dropped.

His father held up his hand to stop William from saying anything, then continued, "You'll be gone for six years—maybe longer. You need to start figuring out how to fend for yourself. You can use the $60 you were able to salvage from the store and whatever is left in your savings to get things started."

His father paused, staring at the ceiling with his finger on his lips. "Although, if you want to start a farm, I could leave my farm to the hired hands for a few months and help you get started. If you're going to try this mercantile idea, I'm afraid you're on your own."

William's face reddened. "Father, I can't stand farm work. I'm fixin' to start a store. This time I'll make a name for myself. This will be the investment that pays off."

"We'll see," his father replied as Bessie walked into the room and handed him a bag.

"Here's your breakfast, sir."

"Thank you, Bessie." William's father put his hat and coat on. "I've got to go into town. When your mother gets back from visiting with her friends, William, you can let her know your decision. When the maid comes in, tell her I left her wages on my dresser. I'll be back tonight. In the meantime, you can start getting ready for your trip."

~ * * * ~

"William, your father told me about the judge's decision."

William dropped his eyes. "Maybe it's for the better, Ma. I need a fresh start. This will kind of force me to make one."

"I'll miss having you around."

William embraced his mother. "I'll write regularly, Ma, I promise."

William booked a steamboat heading up the Mississippi River to Illinois. Over the next few days, he got his affairs in order and said his goodbyes.

Before he left the house, his mother came to him and said, "William, look up my brother when you get there." She handed him an envelope. "Give this to him if you see him."

William examined the envelope. It was addressed to Peter Meier of Springfield, Illinois. "This is your brother?"

"Yes. I haven't seen him in more than ten years, but when my father visited last winter, he said Peter had moved to Springfield." She reached out to William and embraced him. "Please be careful."

"I will," William replied, giving her one last hug.

"Remember to write us often to let us know how you're doing. One more thing, William," his mother said, looking at him straight in the eye. "I want you to remember something as you go out on your own, trying to build your business and wealth. It's not the material things that make us truly happy—it's the people in our lives who we hold dear and the relationships that we form with them that make us truly happy. Look for that kind of happiness in your life. Everybody has relationships. Not everybody has material things, yet everybody can be happy because they have relationships."

"I will, Ma, and if I go to Springfield, I'll seek out your brother."

~ * * * ~

William's father took him to the docks. As he eased the horses to a stop, he said, "I'll miss you son. Be careful, and be wise with your money. Every now and again you'll get a feeling in your gut when you hear something or when you're thinking through things. Sometimes you'll get that feeling as you pray. Listen to your gut, William; it won't lead you astray. That's been the secret of my prosperity, and it'll be the secret to you unlocking yours. If you start listening to other people when your gut says different, you'll be digging around in the dirt like a prairie chicken."

William embraced his father.

"Be sure you remember that," his father said.

"I will, Pa."

"Take care of yourself, Son," his father said, his eyes moistening.

William boarded the steamboat, waved goodbye to his father, and was on his way.

Chapter 4
New Acquaintances

The steamboat moved slowly as it made its way up the river. The rhythmic whacking of the paddlewheel made it difficult for him to get much sleep on the two-day trip.

When the boat finally docked at Quincy, Illinois, William disembarked. It was a thriving, bustling town with a train station, plenty of taverns, and other beautiful buildings housing numerous businesses. Trees adorned the city. A variety of riverboats, tied to docks, rested in the water along the river's bank. *What a gem of a city*, William thought.

William knew he needed help if he was going to get a new business going, so he decided to take his mother's advice and look up his Uncle Meier. He found a stagecoach that was going to Springfield and bought passage.

Springfield was a larger town with a theater, large banks, and lots of businesses. The buildings and roads ran in a block pattern, which made the city easier to navigate.

Finding a place to take lodging, William walked into the wide foyer of the Carpenter Street Inn. A well-worn rug covered the floor. At the far end was a hallway leading further into the building. To the right of the hallway was a staircase leading to the upper levels; to the left of the hallway was a tall counter. A skinny bald man, who looked to be in his forties, stood behind the counter writing something in a large book.

William cleared his throat a few times, trying to get the clerk's attention. The clerk continued writing.

"Excuse me," William finally said.

"Can I help you?" the clerk asked as he continued writing.

"I'd like to board here for a time," William said.

The clerk put his pen down and closed the book. "Thank you for your patience. I'm Alfred Nancy, the owner of this establishment."

"I'm William Chestnut."

"How long would you like to stay?"

William shrugged, "Not sure exactly. Maybe a week, maybe two."

"Well, let's start with a week, and if you stay longer, you can pay by the week," Mr. Nancy offered.

After William negotiated a room and a price, he made his way up the stairs with his luggage.

The first thing he noticed when he entered the room was that it wasn't large. It had one small window, a bed, a washbasin, a chair, and a desk. Striped, yellow-and-brown wallpaper covered every wall, and a framed painting of fruit hung above the bed.

After getting settled in, William went down to the front desk. A cute young woman had replaced the bald clerk. She was thin, with long auburn hair that curled at the bottom. She had green eyes and a beautiful smile. William guessed she was a few years younger than he was.

He approached the desk, "Well, howdy."

"Howdy yourself," she responded, smiling.

"Looks like I picked the right place to stay. Is every girl in this town as pretty as you?" William asked.

She blushed slightly. "I'm just fillin' in for my pa. He's out buying groceries down the street. Is there anything I can help you with?"

"I'll say," he whispered to himself.

"Excuse me. I didn't quite catch that."

William leaned slightly forward. "Pardon me . . . what did you say your name was?"

"I didn't. My name is Johanna," she replied, lifting the corners of her mouth into a smile.

"Johanna," he repeated as if testing the name on his lips. "Even your name is pretty."

Her smile got bigger, and she tilted her head. She was about to say something, but William pressed on, "I'm William Chestnut."

"Pleased to meet you, William," she replied.

William put his thumb on his chin and bit his lip. "Johanna, I have a question for you."

Johanna leaned forward. "Go ahead."

"Where would a man go to find someone who lives in this city?"

"If I were looking for someone I knew who lived in the city, I would first ask some of the locals—perhaps someone running an inn, who is likely to know most people in town."

William grinned. "Would you be referring to yourself?"

"I do know a lot of the people in town. Who is it you're looking for?"

"A man by the name of—" William paused, furrowing his brow, trying to remember his uncle's name.

"What's wrong? You don't know who you're lookin' for?" Johanna teased.

"I forgot his name!" William explained. "He's my uncle, but I've never met him, nor even heard of him until my mother mentioned his name a few weeks ago."

Johanna raised an eyebrow. "Well, you've given me quite the challenge helpin' you find a man without a name."

"I've got a letter for him up in my room with his name on it. I'll go get it and be right back," he said as he turned to leave.

"I'll be right here," Johanna responded cheerfully as William ran up the stairs and out of sight.

It took William a while to find the letter as he couldn't remember where he had stashed it. After rummaging and digging through his things, he finally found it in a pocket of the trousers he was wearing the day he left home.

As he rushed back down the stairs, he tried to think of something clever to say. He stopped dead in his tracks when he spied a man standing behind the desk. The innkeeper was back, and Johanna was nowhere to be seen.

"Why do you look so surprised to see me? And what's your hurry?" the innkeeper asked.

William took a step back and blushed. "Oh . . . uh, sorry, sir. I was just . . . uh, I wanted to know if you have ever heard of a man by the name of—" he looked down at the envelope, then back at the innkeeper— "Peter Meier?"

"Can't say that I have. You might want to try the postmaster. You'll find his office down the street three blocks to your left."

"Thank you, sir," William replied. He put the envelope in his pocket and left the hotel.

~ * * * ~

People and wagons abounded on the dusty streets of Springfield. The sidewalks and streets in town were made up of black soil; sticks and stones were laid for crossings. As William made his way to the postmaster's office, he thought that this town might be a good place to stay as he looked for a place to set up shop.

The postmaster's office was a fancy building. A porch stretched across the front. Eight large pillars stood like sentinels, framing the double doors in the center.

As William walked in, he could hear the booming voice of a tall, homely man behind the counter. William guessed he was the postmaster. Speaking to a customer at the counter the man said, ". . . then the man pointed his gun at me. So, I asked him, 'what seems to be the matter, sir?'

"'Well,' the stranger replied calmly, 'a few years back I swore an oath that if I ever were to come across an uglier man than I, I'd shoot him then and there.'"

The man behind the counter paused and noticed William. "I'll be right with you in a moment."

The man listening to the story prompted him to continue. "What did you do after he said he would shoot you?"

"Well, I was a little relieved after hearing what he said and told him to go ahead and shoot. I stared him in the eye and said, 'If I am an uglier man than you I don't want to live.'"

"Did he shoot?"

"Well, I'm still here, aren't I?"

They both laughed. "I guess so," the customer said. "I best be on my way so you can get to your other customers. Nice talking to you, Abe." He put his hat on and made his way to the door.

William stepped up to the counter. "I suppose you're the postmaster."

"Actually, I am the postmaster of a nearby town. The postmaster that works here is away on business, and I'm filling in for him while he's out—just for the day."

"I take it then, that you don't know much about the people that live around here?" William asked.

"I wouldn't say that," Abe responded. "You're not from around here, are you?"

"No, I just came in from Missouri."

Abe rubbed his chin. "Seems like Missouri is a good state to move from."

"Now, why would you say that?" William asked.

Abe raised a finger. "There was a man in Menard County just to the north of us who was acting as a witness in a court hearing. The man was asked his age, to which he replied that he was fifty.

"Of course, it was apparent that the man was much older than that, so the question was repeated, as was the answer. Upon hearing this, the attorney said, to the man, 'The court happens to know that you are much older than fifty!'

"The man replied, with an air of arrogance, 'You must be thinking of the ten years I spent on the western end of Missouri. Well, that was so much time lost, it doesn't count.'"

William smiled. "Well, thank goodness I haven't been to the western end of Missouri."

"Indeed," replied Abe.

William stuck out his hand. "I'm William Chestnut."

Abe took his hand to shake it. "Abraham Lincoln. You can call me Abe. Now what can I help you with, Mr. Chestnut? What brings you to town?"

"I came here to start a general store. But I need financing to get it moving forward. I have an uncle here in town that might have the means to support me. But I don't know where he lives."

"Well, Mr. Chestnut—"

"Please call me William. I don't feel old enough to be called Mister."

"Fair enough, William. You came to the right place, and not just because I might be able help you find your uncle. I just became postmaster in a village about twenty miles to the southwest of here, right along the Sangamon River, called New Salem. I have two general stores there that I'm not having much success with. I'm now trying to divest myself of one of them. If you've done that kind of work before, you may be just the man to buy it, keep it moving forward, and turn it into a success."

"Is New Salem a big city?" William asked.

"It's not particularly big, but it has promise. There is plenty of opportunity for growth."

William thought back on his experience with the Burnhams. They had helped him too, until he started competing with them. Then they had driven him out of business. The memory made

William's blood boil. How could he trust this man? He might do the same.

"Actually, I was thinking Springfield might be a better place to start," William said, forcing a smile.

Abe considered William for a few seconds. "You know, there once was a visitor who came to this town to deliver some lectures. He soon learned he needed permission from the city's mayor, so he arranged to meet with him. The mayor asked him what he was going to be lecturing about.

"'My lectures will be focused primarily on the Lord's Second Coming,' came the reply.

"'Don't bother wasting your time,' the mayor said, 'If the Lord's seen Springfield once, He ain't gonna return.'"

That brought a genuine smile to William's face. *This guy certainly knows how to disarm a man. Smooth as a snake-oil salesman.*

"Point is," continued Abe, "you want to start your business in a nice, wholesome place. One that doesn't have a lot of competition, yet has a lot of opportunity for growth. That place, my friend, is New Salem."

"That's definitely worth thinking about," William said.

"Opportunity's knocking. You just have to know when to open the door. Wait too long, and she'll move on without you," Abe said, grabbing a paper and pen and handing them to William. "If you'll write a letter to your uncle and include where you're staying, I'll leave it here for the postmaster to deliver. Then your uncle can contact you."

William wrote the information, and gave it to Abe Lincoln with the letter his mother had given him. "Can you make sure he gets both of these?"

"I'll let the postmaster know," Abe replied. "You can find me at the New Salem postmaster's office if you decide to take me up on that offer."

"Thank you, Mr. Lincoln."

Abe smiled. "Don't call me Mister. I don't feel old enough to be called Mister."

"All right then. Thanks, Abe," William replied, smiling.

Chapter 5
First Date?

The next morning, William sat at the Carpenter Street Inn's breakfast table with other guests waiting for breakfast to be served. He sat with both elbows on the table, his fingers interlaced, and his head resting on his fingers.

"Didn't your parents teach you any manners?" a familiar young voice said from behind him.

He smiled and took his elbows off the table. He looked into Johanna's eyes as she put a plate of food down in front of him.

"That's better," she said with a smile and briefly met his gaze before pausing.

"I was wondering when I might see you again," William said.

"I better get back to work," Johanna said, and walked back to the kitchen to grab more plates of food.

William smiled as he watched her leave and as she almost collided with another server bringing out food.

After breakfast, William saw Johanna leave the kitchen and head for the foyer. He got up and rushed to catch up with her.

~ * * * ~

Remembering she had left a book in the kitchen that she wanted to read, Johanna turned around to go back. She was surprised to see William standing inches from her face as he almost ran into her.

"Oh!" She stood on her toes trying to halt her forward momentum. "Mr. Chestnut, is there anything I can help you with?" she asked, landing on her heels.

"Please call me William," he said.

She blinked a few times and said, softly, "All right, William."

They both stepped back a pace, and William continued, "I was just wondering if maybe, perhaps . . . I could . . . call on you tonight?"

She smiled, meeting his eyes, then looked around to ensure nobody was watching. Satisfied, she let her gaze return to William. "Well . . . I suppose that would be all right."

"All right. Would four o'clock work?" William asked, more confidently.

"Sure, but let's meet out in front of the bank," Johanna said as she played with her hair.

"Are you sure? That's several blocks from here."

"Yeah, I will be in that part of town already," Johanna replied.

"Well, I'd best be off," William said.

"All right," Johanna said, winding her hair around her finger.

As William walked away, Johanna remembered she was on her way to gather her book from the kitchen.

~ * * * ~

William walked over to the courthouse to apply for his business license. It was a large red brick building. He asked for the paperwork needed to start his business, and was handed a stack of papers.

After filling out the paperwork, he handed the stack to the clerk. William paid the $4 fee and got his license.

As he walked toward the door to leave, he noticed a name block on a desk at the side of the room. The word *Meier* was burned into it. William turned back to the clerk. "Excuse me, sorry to bother you again, but I noticed you have someone by the name of Meier working here."

"You mean George Meier? What of it?"

"He might be a relative of mine. Is he here today?"

"No, he's off on a trip with his father to visit some relatives in New York. Been gone several weeks. Don't expect him back until next Monday."

William glanced at the name plate. *This George might just be my cousin.* "Thank you, sir."

William pulled out his pocket watch and saw he only had twenty minutes before he had to meet Johanna. He had spent most of his day trying to get licensed. Now he needed to get ready for his date.

William rushed back to the hotel to put on nice slacks and a casual shirt. He double- and triple-checked his hair before leaving the hotel. On his way to their meeting spot in front of the bank, he realized he hadn't gotten anything for Johanna. Then he remembered that there were some nice-looking flowers growing by the courthouse.

All these beautiful flowers—they shouldn't mind if I borrow one, he thought before picking what he considered the nicest one.

As he approached the bank he spotted Johanna and caught his breath. She was dressed in a light-blue dress trimmed with lace and white gloves. She was talking to another girl who was nodding her head a lot as she listened to Johanna.

Johanna noticed William and stepped toward him as she finished the conversation with her friend. As she drew closer, gazing at him, a branch caught her foot and she started to fall. Seeing that she was losing her balance, William ran to catch her, but in his haste, he also tripped, falling onto the road. They both lay sprawled in the street, their faces inches apart. As their eyes met, Johanna was on the verge of tears. William laughed.

Johanna's tears turned to anger. "Why are you laughing?"

"We must be quite the spectacle," William said.

As she thought about it, Johanna also laughed.

William jumped to his feet and offered his hand to Johanna. She took it and stood up.

"Thank you, William," Johanna said. "This is so embarrassing."

"Nonsense! You still look as beautiful as ever, and it doesn't appear many people saw us." William knew that last part was not entirely true, but he wanted to help calm Johanna so she wouldn't leave. He picked up the flower, which still seemed in good condition, and handed it to her.

"I got this for you," he said.

"Thank you," Johanna said as she took the flower. "Now, if you'll excuse me, I'm going to go into the Wagstaff Inn over there, and freshen up. Come on, Savanah."

William called after her, "I'll wait here for you." As he brushed himself off, a man with a metal star pinned to his leather vest approached. William figured he was the local sheriff.

"I'm going to have to ask you to come with me," the sheriff said.

William's eyes widened, and his eyebrows shot up. "What? Why?"

"I got a complaint from a city official that you were defacing public property," the sheriff replied.

"Wha—oh," William remembered the flower, "you don't mean you are arresting me for picking a flower, do you?" William asked, shaking his head.

"I'm afraid so, son. That was city property and didn't belong to you. Come along now—and it's best if you come peacefully."

"But I'm waiting for someone important. I promise I'll pay for it."

"Sorry, son, you'll have to tell that to the judge." The sheriff grabbed William's arm and tied a rope around his wrists then led him back to the courthouse. William felt a pit in his stomach as he glanced back at the Wagstaff Inn. *How am I going to explain this to Johanna?*

As William climbed the steps of the courthouse, Johanna's father emerged through the courthouse doors, complaining loudly to the man next to him, "But that's my money, and I deserve every cent."

The innkeeper glanced in William's direction and stopped talking. He quietly said, "Good evening, Sheriff Taylor. Excuse me."

As Johanna's father walked away, William groaned inwardly and wondered if his day could get any worse.

Sheriff Taylor left the room and closed the door behind him. After what seemed to William an excruciating amount of time, Sheriff Taylor returned with the judge and a third man.

The third man announced, "All stand. The court is now in session, the honorable William J. Allen presiding."

William stood for the judge as the third man pulled out a pen and paper.

The judge took a seat on the other side of the desk. "Please be seated."

The third man sat at the end of the table.

As William planted himself in a chair, the judge asked, "What do we have here?"

"Charges of defacing public property," Sheriff Taylor said. The man who announced the judge was busy writing.

"I only plucked a single flower. That can't be a crime," William complained.

"So, you admit your guilt," the judge said, with a raised voice. Then whispering to the third man, he muttered, "This should be a clean-cut case." In a louder voice, he said, "According to ordinance 07-11, I hereby fine you $10 or one night in the city jail. Which will it be?"

William was dumbstruck. He couldn't believe they would charge so much money for a single flower. "Was that flower made of gold? That's almost two weeks' worth of wages. This is highway robbery!"

"What's your name, boy?" Judge Allen asked

"William Chestnut."

"Well, William, it is not robbery; it is the law. You would do well to remember you can choose your actions but you do not get to choose whether there are consequences. There are always consequences. Right now, I'm giving you a choice. You need to decide which you value more, your time and freedom or your money. Either way, the law will be satisfied. So, either you choose or I will choose for you."

William hesitated. He didn't have much money and couldn't afford to lose so much if he wanted to get a new business started. He couldn't afford to lose almost a sixth of what he had. He would have to bear the night in jail.

His thoughts went back to Johanna and what she would think coming out of the inn after being embarrassed and then seeing him gone. He'd been at the courthouse so long already that she had probably already given up on him if she had waited at all.

"I can tell you right now, I'm not giving up $10," William said with an air of stubbornness.

"So, you prefer the night in jail? Is that your decision then?" the judge asked.

William steeled his expression, stared into the eyes of the judge, and nodded his head.

"So be it. Sheriff, take him away," the judge said, gesturing to the door. As William rose to leave, the judge added, "If you're caught doing this again, the fine and penalty will be double."

"Noted," William said with the same steeled expression.

~ * * * ~

The sheriff escorted William into the jailhouse, up some creaky stairs, and into a dimly lit hallway. One side of the hallway was a wall of iron bars with three iron-barred doors, a jail cell behind each one. Each cell appeared to be a single room with barred windows, a cot, a small table, a hand towel, a chair, and two buckets. One bucket was filled with water, and the other was empty. As William passed the first cell, he noticed a man inside wearing overalls and boots.

William muttered, "He must have spit in the street to make it in here."

"Quiet," the jailer said as he escorted William into the last cell, then shut and locked the door behind him.

"What are these buckets for?" William asked.

"One is so you can wash up if you need to, and the other is your privy. We replace them once daily. If you want any food, it will be thirty cents per meal."

"Is your food that good?" William scoffed. "Those are restaurant prices."

The jailer ignored his comment. "Holler if you need anything."

As William sat in the lonely cell, resentment started building up in his heart against the sheriff and the judge. They had cheated him of his time with Johanna and were exercising authority over him to extort him of his money. He pounded his fist on the bed and threw the pillow against the bars. A few feathers billowed out of the pillow and glided to the ground.

The next morning the jailer woke him and asked if he wanted breakfast. William *was* rather hungry. "What's on the menu?"

"Porridge."

"You're gonna charge me thirty cents for porridge?"

"Do you want it or not?"

"No thanks." He focused his thoughts on getting a better meal, at a better price in a better place as soon as he got out. He didn't want to make his stay here more unpleasant than it already was by having to use that empty bucket and stinking up the room.

It felt like an eternity before the jailer came to let him out.

"All right, you've served your sentence—time for you to vacate."

William passed the jailer and headed down the stairs. "What'd you do to get in here anyway?" the jailer asked.

William's face tightened as he turned back and replied, "Picked a flower."

The jailer smiled, then laughed. "You must have picked one from in front of the courthouse. That's the judge's wife's special flower bed. Everyone knows you don't touch those."

"Well, I guess now *everyone* knows," William replied as he continued down the stairs.

"You ain't from around these parts, are you?"

"Not quite." William walked through the door and squinted into the sunlight.

Chapter 6
Old Tricks

A stone skipped several times across the river followed by a stone that plopped straight in.

"Come on, Otto. One point for every skip," Rupert said.

Rupert threw another stone that skimmed the river's surface, dancing across the top. Otto threw another that immediately sunk.

"This is stupid," Otto said. "Let's do something else."

"Wait a sec, Otto. Here comes a river rafter. Watch this." Rupert threw a stone that skipped across the water until it hit the side of the raft.

The man on the raft turned his head when he heard the noise. Rupert threw another. The man cursed at the boys.

Rupert gestured toward the skiff. "See if you can hit it, Otto."

Otto picked up a rock and threw it. The rock traveled over the river and barely missed the man on the skiff, who pulled out a pistol and fired multiple shots over their heads.

Rupert turned and ran. "Let's get out of here!"

Otto followed him as they ran away from the river.

Rupert and Otto had grown up as neighbors in New Orleans. Rupert had rich parents and a nice home. Otto had only his father, who was drunk most of the time, and his home was in disrepair.

As they walked home, Rupert asked, "You got anything for dinner tonight?"

"Likely not. My pa doesn't like to cook, and ever since my mother passed away, I usually just find something."

"Why don't you come over to my house for dinner? My mom's making fried chicken."

"No thanks, my pa will be expecting me home. I usually find something for him to eat, too. See you tomorrow at school."

"Not me—I'm too old for school now," Rupert said. "I'll be turning seventeen in a few weeks."

"Did they kick you out for when you threw that rock through the school window?" Otto asked.

"Yeah, though I meant to hit that little know-it-all, Tim. I just missed him because he ducked. The school won't let me back in now. My parents got me some tutors to finish out my education—though if you ask me, they're wasting their money. Half the time it seems the tutors don't know what they're talking about."

They stopped in front of a run-down, two-story, log cabin. One of the windows was boarded up, and the porch had broken railings.

"When's your pa going to fix up your home so it looks decent again?" Rupert asked.

"It protects us from the wind and rain. Besides, after the food and liquor is bought, there ain't no money for doing any kind of work like that."

"You're welcome to camp out in our barn if you ever need to."

"Thanks. I appreciate the offer."

"I'll come by the school about recess time. I'll be done with my tutors by then. We can go up to the Mississippi and get some fun in."

Otto thought about it for a minute. "Won't I get in trouble for skipping out on school?"

"Who's going to get you in trouble? Teacher don't care, and your pa don't care."

"I suppose you're right."

"Of course, I'm right," Rupert said. "See you tomorrow."

~ * * * ~

"What we doing today, Rup?" Otto asked.

"You know that abandoned old house on Chartres Street with a purple roof?"

"Yeah."

Rupert smirked. "I've got a way to get back at Tim for getting me kicked out of school."

On Chartres Street, they found the house with the purple roof. In front of it was a dirt pathway with a thick row of bushes on one side and a wrought-iron fence on the other. Another thick row of bushes stood just behind the fence.

"See these bushes?" Rupert asked.

"Yeah."

"Tim passes by here to and from school every day. Next week, we're going to scare him good. We'll set off some gunpowder by those bushes as he walks by."

"Why not do it today?" Otto asked.

"Because it's going to take some money, and we'll need the weekend to earn it."

"How we going to earn the money?" Otto asked.

"Old man Benson bought a field he needs cleared. I talked to him and got us hired to work this weekend helping him clear it."

Otto's eyebrows shot up. "That's hard work, Rup."

"Otto, you're one of the strongest guys I know; you'll handle it fine. Knowing you, you probably won't even break a sweat until mid-day. I'll be there right alongside you. Not that you need my help. You could probably clear that whole field in one day if you were let loose on it."

"I am pretty handy with a shovel and pickaxe."

"Yes, you are. With what we make we'll be able to afford the supplies we'll need to get back at Tim."

~ * * * ~

Rupert and Otto worked two days over the weekend and cleared a little more than half of Benson's field. He gave each of them twenty-five cents and asked them to come back the next weekend.

As soon as they walked away, Rupert held out his hand. "Give me the twenty-five cents he gave you, Otto."

"Why? You've got enough to buy a horn of powder."

"I'll be our banker. I know different ways to help our money grow. Besides, you won't miss it. If you ever want to buy anything, just ask me, and I'll buy it for you. If you keep it, it will run out quick, and you'll miss out on the extra money you could have had by letting me be the banker."

Otto's brow lifted, "Sounds good, but . . . how you going to make our money grow?"

"I've got my ways. My parents are rich, aren't they? Don't you think they passed their secrets for accumulating wealth to me? Of course, they did. I can almost double our money. You leave it to me, Otto."

"All right, Rup," Otto said, nodding his head and handing Rupert his money.

After the field had been cleared and they got their last bit of pay, Rupert took all their money and spent it on a keg of black powder.

"That was everything we earned, Rup. I wanted to buy some jerky."

"Didn't I tell you I'd make our money grow, Otto?"

"Yeah."

"Well, have some faith. I invested it and made it grow. So, we still have some left over for spending."

"You got extra?"

"Of course, I do, Otto. I'll go and get you some jerky and be right back."

Rupert went into the store and waited until the shopkeeper was busy with another customer. Then he grabbed a handful of beef jerky and stuffed it under his shirt. His heart raced with adrenaline as he left the store. Smiling, he ran across the street to where Otto was sitting and handed him the jerky he had stolen.

"See, Otto, our money grew so much I got you all of this. Now come on, we've got a trap to set."

With the black powder in hand, Rupert and Otto headed to the house with the purple roof.

Rupert set little sacks of gunpowder every foot along the fence side of the pathway. He poured a line of black powder to each sack, then up through the fence.

"How we going to get into the yard? The gate is locked," Otto said.

"We'll have to jump the fence and hide behind the bushes on the other side until he comes along. Then we'll light the powder with this flint and steel," Rupert said.

After hopping the fence and laying a trail of powder to their hiding spot behind the bushes, they sat and waited. Almost an hour had passed when they finally spotted Tim.

As he walked by, Rupert struck a spark and the powder ignited. The trail of powder was quickly eaten up by the fire. A loud boom rang through the air, and an invisible wave of force pushed Rupert and Otto back onto the ground.

Tim screamed before everything went silent, except the ringing in their ears from the blast.

"Let's get out of here," Rupert said.

"What if he's dead?" Otto asked.

"Then we definitely don't want to be anywhere near here," Rupert said. "Come on—we'll jump the fence at the back of the house so no one sees us."

"Whatever you say, Rup."

~ * * * ~

The next day, when Rupert went to the kitchen for breakfast, his father walked in the house. "That boy, Tim, from your school, got caught in an explosion walking home from school that knocked him unconscious."

Rupert shrugged, "Oh, that's too bad."

"He has some pretty bad burns. You wouldn't know anything about that, would you?"

"Why would I?"

"I know you've been harboring a grudge against that boy ever since you were expelled."

"I'd never do something like that, Pa."

"If you know anything about it, you have an obligation to share what you know with the sheriff."

"If I ever do hear anything about it, I'll come straight to you."

Rupert's dad nodded and left the room.

Chapter 7
Hanna

Johanna still felt stung from being left alone at the inn. She lay on her bed, brooding, thinking of all the things she would say when she saw William. When she heard a knock on her bedroom door, she was sure it was William coming to apologize. She braced herself, ready to tell him off and send him packing.

Johanna's father raised his eyebrows as the door was flung open. Johanna looked angry, then surprised.

"Everything all right, Sweetie?"

Johanna couldn't let him know she had been trying to date a patron, so she tried to hide her emotion. "Sorry, Papa. I'm just tired of being cooped up here in this boring town."

"Well, I think I have just the thing to cure you of that. Follow me."

Her father led her to the kitchen, where a letter sat on the counter. He picked it up. "Sit down, Sweetie."

Johanna pulled up a chair. The serious tone in her father's voice and the somber look on his face prompted her to ask, "Is everything all right, Papa?"

"I just got a letter from your Grandma Nancy. My father has passed away."

Johanna clapped her hand over her mouth. "Oh, no!"

"I need you to go and stay with her. Help her along, and keep her company. I'll send for you in the fall. By then, I'll need you back here to help at the inn."

To Johanna, this couldn't come at a better time. "Of course, I'll help Grandma."

"Thank you, Johanna. I'll have a stagecoach ready to take you tomorrow."

~ * * * ~

Johanna's grandmother, Hanna Nancy, lived in Kirtland, Ohio. Johanna had been named after her and had always felt a close connection with her. As she made the three-week trip from Illinois to Ohio, she thought about how lonely it must be for her grandmother to lose her companion of forty-two years.

Even then, she couldn't stop her mind from drifting back to William, wondering why he would have left her like that. Savanah had left her there to wait for him after they came out of the inn, convinced that perhaps William had run to the outhouse or maybe gone to buy Johanna something in a nearby store to cheer her up.

Johanna had waited quite a while for William to return, thinking that any minute he would come out of a building, or walk around the corner apologizing for keeping her waiting. But her wait was in vain. She returned home upset and disappointed.

The long, jostling roads did not help cheer her up, though she did look forward to spending time with her grandma. The roads were in such a state that the wagon jerked and swayed most of the way.

By the time the carriage finally pulled up to her grandmother's home, Johanna was tired and worn. The teamster opened her door and helped her to the ground. As he unloaded her luggage, Johanna's grandmother came out of the two-story frame home, greeted her warmly, and put an arm around her shoulder. Hanna was a shorter woman with long gray hair that she always wore in a bun.

After getting her things unpacked, Johanna rested a little bit before finding ways to help. Hanna sat in her rocking chair staring into the corner of the room as Johanna busied herself.

Johanna went about dusting and finding different ways to tidy up.

"Stop fussing," Hanna finally said. "I've got some soup on the stove that is nearly done. Come help me set the table, and we can eat."

"All right, Gran."

As they set the table, Johanna asked, "Do you miss Grandpa much?"

"He has been gone four weeks, but I do miss him something awful," Hanna replied. "Since he passed, I've spent a lot of time making cloth with my loom. It helps keep me busy and takes my mind off things. If you don't mind, perhaps tomorrow you could get me some supplies in town."

"I don't mind, Gran. I'm here to help with whatever you need for a while."

"Bless you, child. Thank you for coming."

~ * * * ~

After lunch the next day, Johanna headed into town. Kirtland was a beautiful town surrounded by forest. Its winding roads were peppered with taverns, churches, hotels, and stagecoach stops. Log cabins and large frame homes dotted the landscape. On the edge of the city were various clusters of smaller, unadorned cabins.

As Johanna walked, she noticed a large foundation was being built along the main street. She stopped a lady who was walking toward it, holding in her hands a jar half-filled with pennies.

"Excuse me," Johanna asked, "what is that big structure being built?"

"Oh. That is going to be the Mormon temple."

"What's a Mormon?" Johanna asked.

"You must be new in town."

"Yes, I just arrived yesterday," Johanna said.

"I'm Eliza Snow."

"Pleased to meet you. I'm Johanna Nancy."

"Mormons are a religious group devoted to following the Savior and the teachings from His prophets, both the living prophet and the ones who have left us scripture."

"Living prophet?"

"Yes. Joseph Smith," Eliza said, smiling as if it were an everyday, well-known fact.

"How did he become a prophet?"

"He talks to God and to God's angels, and he receives revelation."

Johanna lifted her eyebrows. "Well, that sounds very interesting—but I'm on an errand for my grandmother and must be on my way. Can you point the way to the clothing store?"

"Yes, it's just over there," Eliza said, pointing.

"Thank you."

~ * * * ~

The following week after Johanna had finished her usual chores, she found her grandma in the sitting room working on her loom. Johanna sat beside her and watched as she moved a weaving shuttle back and forth through crisscrossing threads.

Johanna picked up the yarn and wound it into thin spools. The cloth they wove would be sold to the local store, and the money made from the sale of the cloth helped her grandmother buy food and supplies. As they worked side by side, they heard a knock at the door.

"Come in," her grandmother called out.

Three well-dressed men, likely in their early thirties, entered the room. She didn't recognize them, but they looked friendly, were well-groomed, and had pleasant demeanors.

Johanna brought three chairs in from the kitchen. She took their hats as they sat down and introduced themselves. "Thank you," one of the men said. "I'm Brigham Young, and these are my companions, Heber Kimball and my older brother, Joseph."

"Pleased to meet you. I'm Hanna Nancy and this," she pointed at Johanna, "is my granddaughter, Johanna."

"We're just passing through on our way to New York but wanted to meet a few people before we left so we could share a message of the Lord's gospel with you," Joseph Young said.

"It's always nice to visit with fellow Christians," Hanna replied.

Brigham smiled at her. "The Lord has restored His true gospel to our friend, a prophet named Joseph Smith. An angel came to him and revealed the location of some gold plates that he translated by the gift and power of God through revelation."

As they spoke, Hanna quietly kept weaving at her loom. The men testified that they had been called of God to preach the gospel one last time before the Second Coming of the Lord Jesus Christ.

When they finished their message, the rhythmic clatter of Hanna's loom came to a halt, and she turned to face the men. She stared at them for a few seconds then in a firm, angry whisper declared, "I do not wish for any of your damnable doctrine to be taught in my home. Please leave at once!"

The man named Heber spoke up. "But, ma'am, this message is God's truth! He has sent angels to restore His priesthood to the earth. And we hold that authority."

"Well, I'm done listening to your twisted truths. I will ask only one more time. Leave now, or I'll send for the authorities."

"We're leaving. You won't hear from us again," Joseph Young replied. Johanna, who silently listened to the whole exchange, stood up, fetched their hats, and saw them to the door while her grandma kept weaving.

Johanna came back and picked up the yarn to resume winding. Pondering what the missionaries had said, she asked, "Do you think it's really possible that they saw angels?"

"I've never heard anything more absurd in my life. There are no such things as angels visiting people anymore. That all ended in the times of the Bible, as did revelation. People will say anything to get you to join their religion nowadays," her grandmother said.

"I heard they are going to build a temple; they already have the foundation laid. I saw it, and it looks like it's going to be bigger than any other building around these parts," Johanna said.

Hanna continued weaving. "They must have plenty of wealth if they're planning a building of that size. They have convinced a lot of good people to their side. Even Pastor Rigdon got swept up with that nonsense. Though I just can't see how someone so brilliant and bright as he could possibly be fooled by that absurdity. He was a good man, Pastor Rigdon, but I guess even the strongest and brightest can be swept up in their own pride and greatness once they let their success go to their head."

"I suppose so," Johanna said, winding the yarn deep in thought.

Chapter 8
Bargain

William went back to the Carpenter Street Inn, where he noticed the innkeeper at the front desk talking to a customer. William headed for the stairs when he heard the innkeeper call after him, "Hold on there, Mr. Chetnut."

"That's *Chestnut*," William corrected.

Mr. Nancy pointed a finger at him. "I saw you yesterday being taken in by the sheriff. If you're in trouble with the law, it's best you find a new place to stay. We don't have a tolerance for troublemakers at this inn."

William hoped Mr. Nancy hadn't yet learned he was trying to court his daughter. "It's not what you think, Mr. Nancy. I was taken in for picking a flower for my lady friend."

The customer standing in front of the counter laughed. "You must have picked one from in front of the courthouse."

"It might be helpful if they put a sign up about that," William said.

"All right, young man, just make sure you mind what you do, and you should be all right," the innkeeper replied.

William never was able to find Johanna again over the next week. He spent his time scouting out potential locations to set up shop and reviewing his potential competitors. There were four general stores in town, and all of them were very well established and much bigger than the one he had in Missouri. He found this somewhat discouraging, as he wasn't sure he could raise enough capital to buy a big enough store and the supplies he would need to compete.

He stopped by the courthouse a few times too, hoping to meet George Meier, the man who was likely his cousin. Though, George still hadn't returned.

After a week of seeing no sign of Johanna, William worked up the courage to approach her father that evening as he was going over his books and ask what had happened to her.

"What can I do for you?" Mr. Nancy asked, still writing in his book.

"I was just wondering—that young lady who was working here, Johanna, isn't she your daughter?"

Mr. Nancy stopped writing, put down the pen, and closed the book. "Yes, she is my daughter. Why do you ask?"

"If you're all right with it, I would like to court her, but I haven't seen her around lately."

"Absolutely not," came the response. "We have strict rules against carrying on such relationships with patrons. Absolutely out of the question."

"What if I weren't a patron any longer? Would you consider it then?"

Mr. Nancy eyed William carefully, "Maybe, though I much prefer your money. What is your age, occupation, and standing with God?"

William had never been asked such direct questions before, but thought if he wanted a chance with Johanna, he had better be honest. "I'm twenty-one, a soon-to-be general store owner, and I think I'm square with God. I don't prescribe to any particular religion but have a strong faith in what is taught in the Bible."

"Soon-to-be general store owner? What does that mean?"

"I used to run a general store in Missouri, but I wanted a change of venue, so I came here."

"And you have the capital to open a new store? Enough to compete with the four that are already here?"

William searched his mind for something he could say to help convince Mr. Nancy that he could be successful. Then it dawned on him. "I don't plan on competing in this town, Mr. Nancy. I recently talked to a man by the name of Abraham Lincoln, who offered to sell me a general store he had been working on. He became the postmaster in New Salem, twenty miles from here."

"I know Abe. He's a good, honest man, about as good as they come." Mr. Nancy paused for a moment to consider and finally said, "My daughter is away until winter, living in Ohio with her grandmother. Go start your store, Mr. Chestnut. If you can get it up and running successfully, come back in the winter, and we'll talk. If you haven't been able to get it going successfully then that will tell me what kind of man you are, and you needn't bother coming back."

After a brief pause, William came to himself. "Thank you, Mr. Nancy. I'll show you. You'll be hearing good things from New Salem."

"We'll see," Mr. Nancy replied. "By the way, a Mr. Meier stopped in and asked about you earlier today. Said you was kinfolk and left this message for you." Mr. Nancy handed him an envelope.

William took it, thanked him, and headed up to his room.

Sitting on his bed he opened the letter and read,

Dear William,

> I got your message from the postmaster. I just came back from a long trip. Would love to meet you. Come see us any time.

Peter Meier
217 Willow Lane
Springfield, Illinois

William thought about his predicament. He was eager to meet his uncle, but it had been a week since he talked to Abe Lincoln. He still wasn't sure if he could trust him, though Mr. Nancy seemed to think him good and honest.

He needed to make this work if he wanted to see Johanna again, and Abe's offer was the closest thing he had to getting started. Not seeing any other options, William figured that he ought to find Abe right away and see what he could do about buying Abe's store before it could be sold to someone else.

~ * * * ~

William found passage on a wagon headed to New Salem. As he arrived, the sun was about to set on the western horizon, and there was a slight, chill breeze sweeping through the village.

There didn't seem to be much to New Salem. It wasn't a big town. There was an inn that was also a restaurant and a tavern, a butcher shop, a blacksmith shop, a cooper's shop, a sawmill, and a few other buildings down the main street. Even though the town seemed quite simple, the Sangamon River ran nearby—and with some development, ships would eventually be able to come in and spur the growth of this budding village.

William immediately sought out the postmaster's office but was disappointed to find it closed. He walked down the main street toward the tavern. It appeared to be one of the nicer buildings in town. It had two stories with a wood rail that surrounded the porch, which stretched all the way down the building. As William entered, he felt a rush of warm air. A low hum of chatter filled the room. More notable was the smell of smoke, mixed with sweat, stale beer, and spit.

It was a large room with a fireplace off to the side, a bar at the far end and tables dispersed throughout the room. A staircase led to an upper level. Lanterns flickered as the wind rushed through the opened door.

"Come in and have a seat," a man said to William, as he set several plates of food down in front of a group of patrons. As William shut the door behind him, he heard the distinct voice of Abraham Lincoln laughing as he was telling a story to a man in the corner of the room. William couldn't help but focus in on his voice, as it carried quite well.

"The preacher kept going on about how Jesus was the only perfect man, and then stated that there never was a perfect woman.

"Then a persecuted-looking woman at the rear of the church rose as the parson stopped speaking and said, 'I know of a perfect woman, and I've heard about her every day for the last seven years.'

"'Well who is this woman?' The preacher asked.

"'It's none other than my husband's first wife,' replied the afflicted female."

As Abe finished the story, both he and the man laughed heartily, then noticed William approaching their table.

"Mind if I join you?" William asked.

Abe smiled and stood up, towering over the table. "Not at all. Come, have a seat." He shook William's hand. "I'm glad you've come. Isaac, this is William Chestnut, and William, this is Isaac Cody, a good friend of mine."

Isaac rose and shook William's hand.

Abe paused momentarily, then continued, "Isaac here was just trying to convince me to steep myself into politics. He was explaining how I could use the strategies of other successful politicians. I was just telling Isaac, if I ever go into politics, I'm going to approach it from a completely different tack than what has been tried before."

"Suit yourself," Isaac replied, "but when it comes to politics, I've found that you have to learn the system and then figure out how to use it to your advantage."

"Or," Abe replied, "you can learn the system and use it against itself to overcome it, by exploiting its weaknesses."

"It would take a clever man indeed to pull that off," Isaac responded.

"Yes, indeed it would," Abe said, reflectively. "Anyway, last time I saw William, I made him an offer." Turning to William, he said, "I'm guessing you're here to follow up on that offer?"

"I am indeed," William responded. "If you don't mind showing me the store in the morning, I'd like to take a look at it and possibly make you an offer."

Abe nodded. "We'll do that. In the meantime, let's order some dinner."

The evening passed pleasantly with Abe telling more stories, of which he seemed to have an endless supply, and Isaac expounding on the politics of the day with a keen focus on the injustice of slavery. After dinner, William said goodbye to Abe and Isaac and negotiated a price for room and board with the innkeeper.

~ * * * ~

The next day Abe met William for breakfast, then walked him over to his closed-down store. It was a plain, flat-faced building with a tall façade and a sign that read *Sangamon Supply and Goods*.

Abe stopped and gestured toward the store. "Here it is. As you can see, it's a nicer-looking building, and there are still some goods inside that I wasn't able to sell. Come in and take a look around," Abe said, unlocking the door.

It wasn't a large store but had enough room. Shelves lined the walls, and there were two aisles about eight feet in length. Unsold merchandise hung on the walls and sat on the aisle shelves. A barrel half full of salt, an empty barrel for sugar, and another empty barrel for flour sat on the plank floor. Shovels and hoes hung on the walls.

Gloves, chains, and a few other miscellaneous items rested on the shelves. William rubbed a finger against the counter and found a thick layer of dust.

"Going to take some work to get this place ready for business," William said.

Abe looked around and picked up a pair of gloves. "Yes, but as you can see, there are still a few items left that will come with the price of the store. I think it a fair price, what with the goods that are already here and the size of the building. You give me $100, and you can be on your way to starting a successful business."

"It is a nice building," William replied. "But it is going to require some maintenance to fix it up and get it back to a proper state for doing business. How about you give it to me for $60, and I'll use the other $40 to get this place fixed up properly."

"Come now, William, I'm a reasonable man. It may take some effort to fix it up, it surely won't require $40 dollars. I guess I could let it go for about $90."

"Well, I reckon you're right, Abe. Perhaps it wouldn't cost a full $40 to get this old place back up to working order. Though, surely it will need a new coat of paint and other repairs. It's going to take a lot of my time to do all that, and time is money. I think a fair price for that kind of effort would be about $30, if you'd be willing to give me the store for $70."

"I'll concede the point that it will take some doing to get this building back up to working order, William. I'd be willing to let it go for $80 and not a penny less."

"You drive a hard bargain, Abraham Lincoln, I'll take it for $80."

William extended his hand. Abe shook it slowly. "Pleasure doing business with you, William Chestnut."

William gave Abe the $60 he had as a down payment and promised he would give him the rest by the end of the month. This left him with barely enough money to get through the end of the week. Abe took the money. “The key to the building will be waiting for you when it’s paid in full.”

Chapter 9
Lucky

William found the carriage he had chartered for Springfield sitting in front of the tavern. He wanted to go see his uncle in hopes of convincing him to lend him $30. With that amount he could pay off Abe Lincoln and fix up the store. He wouldn't have any money left for living expenses until he could start turning a profit with his business, but he figured he could sleep in the store until his goods started moving, and he could afford a nicer place.

As he approached the carriage, the driver wasn't sitting on the perch. The carriage looked like a big black box on wheels and had only one door with a giant square hole for a window. A white see-through material hung like curtains covering the opening. Two muscular horses, one black and the other a dappled gray, stood tied to the carriage.

A man walked out of the saloon with several bottles of whiskey. He proceeded to climb up to the driver's perch.

"What's with all the whiskey?" William called out to the driver.

"Oh, this? This isn't for me. It's a special order I'm fillin' for a friend in Springfield, who loves this particular brand. It's made right here in New Salem."

"I see," William said as he opened the carriage door.

Another passenger was already aboard reading a newspaper. William sat down opposite the man and greeted him.

As the other passenger lowered the paper, William instantly recognized the face of Isaac Cody.

"William, wasn't it?" Isaac asked as he folded the paper.

"Yes, Mr. Cody. This is an unexpected surprise. You headin' up to Springfield?"

"Please, call me Isaac. I am stopping in Springfield only for a few days. I'm scheduled for a speech at an abolitionist convention there tomorrow, then I'm headed back home to Ohio."

William remembered Johanna had gone to live in Ohio for the summer. "You don't happen to know a family by the name of Nancy out in Ohio, do you?"

"Not that I can recollect. I'm from the Cleveland area," Isaac replied.

"Why so far from home?" William inquired.

"I work for the Whig Party promoting the abolitionist cause. Party leaders send me to all different places to give speeches, and help convince folks to stop the spread of slavery. Every man ought to have the freedom to do what he sees fit with his life without the fear of oppression from any group of people."

"It's a noble fight," William said. "My parents have always been against the practice as well. They have plenty of servants, but they're all well paid."

"How did your business go with Mr. Lincoln? You end up buying his store?"

"We came to an agreement . . ." William paused as they felt the carriage rattle and shake. William looked outside and noticed they were veering off the road.

"Driver, you fall asleep up there?" Isaac shouted.

The carriage bumped off the road and jolted violently. William pushed the curtains aside and stuck his head out of the carriage, trying to see what was going on. The carriage veered back onto the road. He saw a wagon coming from the other direction, pulled by a single horse, running straight toward him. William feared it was going to hit the carriage. He pulled his head back in. The carriage suddenly jolted in the other direction. He fell backward onto the floor. The horse and wagon zipped by the window.

"He almost collided with that wagon!" William exclaimed.

Isaac froze, gripping his seat with all his strength.

William stuck his head out again. The driver was standing on the perch holding the reins in one hand and a bottle of whiskey that was nearly empty in the other. The carriage veered off the road again.

William called out, "You fool! Are you crazy? Stop the carriage!"

The carriage lurched back toward the road and hit a giant rock. William stumbled inside the carriage, and landed on Isaac's lap. Isaac pushed him off. The carriage continued to pick up speed.

William stood up. "I think the driver was thrown!"

Isaac turned pale. "At this speed? We're dead men!"

"Just hold on." William opened the door of the carriage. He climbed onto the door and tried to swing himself toward the driver's seat. Another rock jolted the carriage. The forward motion of the door stopped, leaving it sticking straight out. William tried to reach the carriage as he clung to the door, but it was just out of reach.

As he gripped the door, he noticed some tree branches about to hit his head. He ducked just in time, but the branches hit the top of the door, scraping his knuckles and sending the door swinging back. William's back rammed against the carriage as the door tried to close. Pain seared through his body, but he held on.

The carriage shook violently as the horses raced along the forest road. William thought he might be thrown any minute. He cleared his mind and pushed through the pain, focusing on swinging the door all the way open so he could get to the driver's perch.

William kicked off the carriage, this time making a full swing. He grabbed the roof. Pulling himself up, he hung on as it continued to jostle sharply along the bumpy dirt road.

He hoisted himself over the top. Broken glass and whiskey covered the driver's bench. William cleared the glass with several swipes of his boot and hopped down onto the bench. Whiskey soaked into his trousers as he sat. He gripped the edge of the bench, looking for the reins and spotted them flapping wildly behind the horses.

With one hand still holding tightly to the bench, he stretched out, reaching for the reins. They were just within reach of his fingertips. He caught hold of them and pulled back, shouting "Whoa!" to the horses. They slowed down and eventually came to a stop.

Isaac stumbled out of the carriage onto the ground. He turned, staring at William. "My goodness! I can't believe you actually pulled that off. I thought for sure you were a goner. You saved us."

"Stupid driver," William said, his trousers still wet and stinking something awful.

"Looks like you wet yourself in the process," Isaac chuckled. "I probably would have done the same."

"That wasn't me," William explained. "The driver was drinking whiskey up there. He said it was for a friend. I should have known better. He should have put it with the luggage instead of by his side. Most of the bottles broke on the bench, that's what's soaking my trousers."

"I see," Isaac replied. "I'll go back and check on the driver."

Forty minutes later, Isaac returned. "Driver's neck snapped when he was thrown. His body is on the road about half a mile back."

"We don't have any tools to bury him. We'd best go back and get the body and take it into town," William replied.

William climbed to the carriage perch and wiped off the remaining liquid and broken glass. They drove the carriage back until they found the mangled body on the side of the road.

William ducked and turned his head when he first saw the body. "Let's put him in the carriage. We can ride up on the perch," William said, dropping down from the driver's bench.

Isaac vomited off to the side as they tried to lift the body. On the second try they put the body in the carriage and were on their way.

As the horses plodded along the winding dirt road, after a long period of silence, both men lost in their thoughts, William spoke up. "It's too bad he died, though it wasn't very smart to be drinking when he needed to be focused."

"Some people just don't take the time to think. I've run across a few like that in my day," Isaac said.

"You mean to say you knew others like this man?"

"Well, none who would try anything like this, but there is one who wasn't the brightest. It was the way he acted to convince others to listen to him. He was this pompous preacher back home teachin' the most flowery sermon with a high, shrill voice. He shook and trembled and waved his Bible in the air all around him. It was the silliest display of false piety I'd ever seen. I saw an opportunity to make a little money and humble him a bit."

"How so?" William asked.

"After he finished preaching and people were socializing, I walked up to him and introduced myself. As I expected he would, he asked how I liked his sermon," Isaac said, then paused.

"Well? What did you answer him?"

"Well, I thought his sermon was the worst I'd ever heard. But instead of saying so, I said, 'Oh, it was all right, even if it wasn't original.'

"My comment had the desired effect. He asked, 'How could you say that?'

"'I've got a book at home that has every word you used,' says I.

"'That can't be—I just came up with that this morning,' says he.

"'You seem so confident. Are you willing to put in five dollars that I wouldn't be able to produce such a book?' I asked.

"The preacher confidently pulled out five dollars, handed it to a man listening to our conversation, and said, 'Five dollars!' He asked me to give the man my five dollars and if I produced the book within the hour the man would give me the money. If I couldn't, then the preacher would get the money. I borrowed a horse from my friend and off I went."

"Don't tell me you had such a book?" William asked

"Indeed, I did. I got home, grabbed it, and raced back to the church with five minutes to spare. The preacher was incensed when he saw the book and knew he had lost the wager."

"It had every word from his sermon?" William asked.

"Every word."

"What book was it?"

"It was none other than Webster's dictionary. It had every single word," Isaac said, shaking his finger in the air, trying to keep from smiling.

"No wonder he was upset," William replied.

~ * * * ~

When they got to town they went straight to the undertaker's office. "I'll go in and explain to the undertaker what happened, and you wait here," Isaac said. "I'll be back soon."

Soon the undertaker and Isaac returned. William hopped down and opened the door.

"Sounds like you boys had a wild time," the undertaker said as he nodded to William.

"I guess you could say that," William replied.

Sheriff Taylor came by as they were unloading the body. He sniffed and smelled the strong odor of whisky on William. "What happened here?"

William's hands started to sweat. He had a feeling this was not going to go well.

Isaac and William told the sheriff what happened. Sheriff Taylor listened and finally said, "I'm afraid I'm going to have to take you boys in until we can have the body checked and ensure your story checks out."

William could not believe he was headed back to jail. He was afraid they might not be able to prove their innocence.

Sheriff Taylor escorted them to the jailhouse and turned them over to the jailer, who took them up the stairs. He put Isaac in the center cell, and William in the same cell he had been in before. "Twice in the same week," he said to William. "You're starting to become quite the regular."

"I was starting to miss it," William replied.

After the jailer walked away, William said, "Well, Isaac, it appears we weren't meant to part ways quite yet."

"You're not wrong. Listen, William, I wanted to thank you for being so brave back there. I thought for sure we were goners. I was afraid I'd never see my sweet wife again."

"Wait, you're married?" William asked.

"Yes, it's almost been a year now. My wife, Martha, is here in Springfield awaiting my return. She's in a nearby hotel—the Carpenter Street Inn. I hope we can get out soon so she won't have to worry too much."

"That's where I was staying," William said. After a few minutes, he said, "I'm not sure there is a way out of this one."

"The Lord will provide a way," Isaac said.

William looked up. "You really believe that?"

Isaac nodded. "He always does . . . just wait. You'll see."

"I guess I will," William replied.

A few hours later the sheriff came to see them with the jailer and a tall man in nice clothes. "I'm Keith Steinecker, the state defense attorney," the tall man said.

"Looks like part of your story checks out," the sheriff said. "Undertaker verified he died from a snapped neck and had a considerable smell of whiskey on him. But for all I know, you could have forced the whiskey on him at gunpoint and thrown him off the carriage to finish him off."

"That's not what happened!" Isaac exclaimed.

"Sheriff, you've got to believe we'd never do that," William insisted.

"Doesn't matter what I believe. Besides, I don't know you. I'm afraid we'll have to take this to a jury."

Both Isaac and William stood speechless.

William remembered the wagon that passed them and almost took his head off. "Wait! There was a wagon that passed ours when our driver was swerving all over the road. Our carriage almost collided with it. The man driving that wagon can verify that what we've told you is true."

"That's right!" Isaac exclaimed.

"Well, that's worth looking into," Keith said. "I'll see what I can find."

The sheriff was less optimistic. "Unless you can identify the driver, I don't see how that's going to help."

The sheriff left, but Keith stayed and listened to their story. After they told him everything that happened, Keith said, "Don't you boys worry. I'm going to figure a way to get you out."

Keith left, and silence permeated the air. A feeling of hopelessness settled in William's chest. Instead of being hailed as a hero, he would be condemned as a murderer. He sighed, staring at the floor. He knew he was stuck, doomed to a fate he did not deserve.

~ * * * ~

The next morning when William awoke, he heard someone calling his name. He opened his eyes and saw Keith Steinecker holding the door to his cell open.

"Come on out, William. You boys must have someone upstairs watching over you. My brother Garrett went to the New Salem tavern last night and overheard a man describin' a scene similar to what you told me, to a group of friends. Since your story matches his, I took him to the judge. After hearing the case, the judge says you're free to go."

William and Isaac left their cells and headed down the stairs. As they walked away from the jailhouse, Keith said, "By the way, Judge Allen wanted to talk to you two before you left."

William and Isaac walked to the courthouse and met the judge, who said, "I just wanted you to know that the driver who died didn't have a family or anyone to leave his things to, which means his property will be sold at auction. Since you two had a traumatic experience at his hand, I thought I'd give you gentlemen first dibs on those two horses and the carriage."

"How much?" William asked.

"Well, like I said, they have to go to auction, which means you tell me how much you're willing to pay. It then goes to the highest bidder," Judge Allen explained.

Isaac smiled and whispered into William's ear. William pulled out fifty cents and handed it to him. Isaac told the judge, "I bid one dollar."

"I hear one dollar for a carriage and two horses. Is there anyone present willing to pay more than one dollar?" Judge Allen asked in a mock auctioneer voice. He looked at William, who just smiled back at him. The judge continued, "Sold to the gentlemen standing in front of me for one dollar."

Isaac pulled out fifty cents and added it to what William had given him and handed it to the judge.

Later that week William and Isaac were able to sell the carriage for $40 to an eager young entrepreneur. After finalizing the sale, they met at the stable where their horses were being kept.

The stable smelled of manure. Flies darted in all directions and hay was scattered about the dirt floor. The horses William and Isaac had bought occupied two of the six stalls in the stable. Harnesses and saddles hung on the walls. Isaac peered into the stall where the black horse was, admiring its shiny, black coat. The dappled gray horse looked just as healthy but was not as pretty.

"They're both fine animals. What do you think?" Isaac asked.

William smiled. "It seems you've taken a liking to that black one. You take it, and I'll take the dappled gray."

"You sure?"

"Heck, I don't need anything fancy. I just need something that will take me where I need to go," William replied.

"Good enough," Isaac said as he opened the stall and stepped inside. He reached out and ran his hand along the horse's mane, then paused. "You're a good man, William Chestnut. Good from the heart."

"Good is what makes the world turn round. I think you've helped the world make a few revolutions yourself," William replied.

Isaac smiled. "I don't know about that. How about you let me buy you some dinner?"

"I won't say no to that," William replied as he walked over to his new horse. Looking him in the eye, he said, "I think I'll call you Lucky."

~ * * * ~

As they sat waiting for their food, Isaac took out a cigarette and was about to light it. "Do you mind?" Isaac asked.

"Can't stand the smell of the stuff, but I won't stop you," William replied.

"It's probably not a good habit anyway," Isaac said as he stuffed the cigarette back into his pocket.

Isaac pulled out the money they had made from the sale of the carriage and divided it between them.

"I suppose that man's stupidity was a blessing in disguise. Here is your share," Isaac said, as he handed William $20. "Didn't I tell you the Lord would provide a way?"

William thought about that. "You did indeed, Isaac. It was hard for me to see a way forward at the time, but when you said that to me, I had the feeling just for a moment that maybe you were right. I guess I should have trusted my gut."

"Mr. Chestnut, if you ever come to Cleveland, look me up."

"Please, call me William. I'll stop by if I'm ever out in that direction. Though I reckon Illinois will be my home for a while yet."

"Good enough, William. It has been a pleasure getting to know you these last few days. Good luck with your business."

William nodded. "Thanks, Isaac; perhaps our paths will cross again."

Chapter 10
One Step Back

With the money William got from the sale of the carriage, he could afford to buy the store from Abe. But he wasn't sure he had enough to stock the store with goods. As he walked down Main Street thinking of different ways he could get the money he needed, the thought came to him that perhaps he could invest the money he had into something. Just then, he walked by a street vendor who was selling perfume.

The vendor waved. "Hello! Are you in the market for some perfume?"

There on a silk cloth stood ten beautiful glass bottles, each about three-quarters full of liquid, each a different color.

"Perhaps. How much does one cost?"

"In New York, these are selling for fifty cents each," the man said, "which is what I usually sell them for, but these are on sale today only for thirty-five cents each."

William eyed the bottles with interest. "How many do you have?"

The man raised his eyebrows. "About fifty."

William picked one up, uncorked the top, and held it to his nose. As the sweet-smelling scent filled his nostrils, he did some quick math in his head.

"That's nice," William said, then set the bottle down. "How about I give you $18 for the bunch?"

"What? I could get $30 if I went back to New York and sold them!"

"Perhaps, but that is assuming you could get free passage back to New York," William said. "It's also assuming you could sell every bottle. You'd likely spend a dollar or two, plus the time it takes you to travel, not to mention the hours you would spend in the streets looking for buyers. That's also assuming you don't get robbed. New York does attract all kinds. On the other hand, you could avoid all that hassle and instantly have a profit on each bottle."

The man eyed William for several moments. "Throw in an extra dollar for the silk cloths, another dollar for the box, and you have yourself a deal."

They shook hands. The man packed up the bottles in a wooden box, closed the lid, and set it on the table. William pulled out the money Isaac had given him from the sale of the carriage and handed the man $20. He knew he was now $9 short on the money he needed to buy the store, but figured he would make triple that by selling these bottles. He picked up the box and headed to the hotel.

William set the box by his bed and opened it. He counted the bottles and found there were only forty-seven bottles. His first thought was that he had been lied to about the number of bottles. Then he remembered that the man said he had about fifty bottles.

William figured he had spent about forty cents per bottle, and the man was selling them for thirty-five cents. *I guess that man was quicker with math than I was.*

William took a few bottles out of the box and headed outside. He walked to one of the general stores in town and approached the owner. "I'm William Chestnut. Pleased to meet you."

The shop owner narrowed his eyes and crossed his arms, "All right, well, I'm busy right now. Is there anything I can help you with?"

"Well, Mr.—"

The owner let out a sigh. "Carpenter."

"Mr. Carpenter, I want you to smell this, and tell me what you think." William pulled out a bottle of perfume and handed it to Mr. Carpenter.

Mr. Carpenter furrowed his brow and looked at William, then at the bottle. He raised his brow as he studied the bottle. He uncorked it and sniffed. "That's a pleasant smell. How much are you selling these for?"

"Forty-five cents a bottle."

"Such a high price?"

"It is the finest quality. And I'm actually giving you a discount—in New York, I understand these are selling for fifty cents per bottle. You could sell them for forty-eight cents."

Mr. Carpenter shook his head slowly. "I couldn't sell very many of them. Only the well-off would buy them at that price."

"Think of your wife; don't you think she would be worth spending that kind of money on for a gift?"

Mr. Carpenter put his hands on his hips. "What makes you think I'm married?"

"I mean, don't you have a special someone you might gift something like this to?"

Mr. Carpenter put his hand to his chin. "Possibly." He shrugged and threw his hands in the air. "But still, my average customer won't buy these at that price."

He handed the bottle back to William.

William paused, his thoughts racing. "How about I discount them for you even further? I have forty-seven bottles I'll sell to you at thirty-eight cents a bottle, and I have a nice box and some silk hankies I'll give you for another $2."

Mr. Carpenter eyed William. "I'll take twenty bottles. No need for a box or hankies."

William was unsure what he should do. If he agreed, he would be selling them at a loss. But he did offer them at a lower price in hopes the box and hankies would make the sale worth his while. He knew he couldn't take back what he had said. He looked at the floor. "I'll go and get them."

"Excellent; I'll be here," Mr. Carpenter said with a slight smile.

William left feeling a little dejected. I can't sell any more of these at that price.

He returned to the hotel and grabbed the box of perfume. As he headed back to the store, William tried to think of ways he could change the deal or maybe convince Mr. Carpenter that he needed more. As he walked across the street deep in thought, a horse's nostril passed inches from his head.

A man yelled, "Watch where you're going!"

William froze.

"Get out of the way!" the man yelled.

William tried to jump back but was too slow to dodge the kick as the man's foot caught the side of the box, wresting it from his hands and sending it tumbling to the ground.

Bottles lay scattered and broken across the ground. William looked in dread at the scene before him.

"What do you think you're doing!" he called after the man on the horse, who picked up his pace into a gallop.

He surveyed the scene, scouring the ground for unbroken bottles. The air reeked with a mixture of scents coming from the liquids seeping into the ground. Some of the bottles had broken inside the box. William did his best to clean out the broken glass and liquid inside the box with the silk hankies.

He found that eighteen of the bottles had not broken. His heart sank. He didn't know how he was going to get the money he needed to pay off Abe. He wished he had gotten a better look at the man who had kicked the box. He punched the ground, silently cursing. His anger percolated.

After he packed the unbroken bottles back into the box, he continued slowly toward the store, pensive and angry. He had hoped the sale of the perfume would give him enough to not only buy the store from Abe Lincoln, but to also restock the store. After selling what he now had, he would be more than $2 short.

He thought that maybe he should try to sell them somewhere else at a higher price. But he pushed that thought aside—he had made a gentleman's agreement, and it didn't feel right to break it.

William went into the store and set the box down on the counter. He opened the box and took out the eighteen surviving perfume bottles and set them on the counter. The clerk counted them. "You're two short."

"Turns out I didn't have as many as I thought."

"Fine," the owner said, then paid him for the bottles.

William thought long and hard about what he could do to get more money. He supposed he could work for a week or two as a farmhand. He cringed at the thought. Then he remembered his uncle. He had planned all along on going to him for help. It was time to go pay him a visit.

Chapter 11
Running Ruff

Rupert and Otto sat on the bank of the Mississippi, poles in hand, waiting for a nibble on their lines.

"Hey, Otto, what do you think about building a raft?"

"Sounds fun."

"I'll go get some rope from home, and we can use those fallen trees over there. Can you get your dad's saw?"

"Sure, he won't be needing it anytime soon."

Rupert and Otto worked on the raft over the next two days. When it was completed, they found two long sticks to steer with and headed out onto the river.

As they floated downriver, several ducks flew overhead. They passed several steamships that were taking on passengers.

"Wouldn't it be something if we could own our own steamship?"

"I guess it would be," Otto said.

"We could go anywhere, do anything. That would be true freedom."

"How would we ever get enough money to buy a steamship?" Otto asked.

"We'll have to save up for most of it. Perhaps try for a loan for the rest. We'll have to educate ourselves on how to run a steamship, then find one for the right price."

"How are we going to save up for it?"

Rupert rubbed his chin. "There are only a handful of wealthy farmers in New Orleans, so we need to target them. We'll go to work for them as farmhands."

"How is that going to get us the money we need? It would take years."

"Since they're rich, they pay better than most others. After we get fairly established, we can wait until they're not home, and then we'll find all sorts of stuff that will grow our wealth."

"I'm not sure about the stealing part," Otto said.

"Remember Billy and his family from across the street?" Rupert asked.

"Yeah."

"It was the rich folk who stole his house and kicked him out. How do you think the rich get so rich anyway? They steal it from others—that's why they're rich. I don't see anything wrong with takin' back things they got with money that wasn't rightfully theirs to begin with, do you?"

"If you put it that way, I guess you're right. It almost seems like it should be our duty to take that money from them," Otto replied.

"That's right, and I think I got a way for us to do it that won't get us in trouble with the law," Rupert reassured him.

Rupert always ensured that their wrongdoings would be nearly untraceable back to them. He had turned getting away with things into an art.

~ * * * ~

"I'm glad you boys turned up. I was about to put out an advertisement. When can you start?"

Rupert shook his hand. "Well, Mr. Temblor, I reckon we can start tomorrow."

"Excellent! My oldest boy, Jimmy, will meet you over by that barn," Mr. Temblor said, pointing. "Be here at five in the morning."

A few days later, Otto gazed at the field where they were working. "Why don't we just plow every other row and get done in half the time?"

"Because if we try to take shortcuts like that, don't think he won't notice. How long do you think he'll let us work for him if we do work like that?"

Otto nodded slowly. "I suppose you're right."

"Of course, I am. Otherwise, we'd never get the chance to pilfer his goods."

Rupert knew it was important for them to do a good job so they'd make a good impression on the farmer. He motivated Otto regularly to pick up the slack. On more than one occasion he even did Otto's share of the work. Rupert would be sure to use that later to pressure Otto into doing what he wanted him to do.

~ * * * ~

Late one night, Rupert woke Otto. "Otto, get up."

"What is it, Rup?"

"I just found out that the Temblors are visiting family. Now is the perfect time to see what treasures they have in the house."

Otto crept up to the back door of the house, dressed in his darkest clothes, a hat and a bandana wrapped around his face so that only his hands and eyes were exposed to the cool night air. Rupert was behind him in similar garb. Otto put his hand on the knob and twisted.

"It's locked, Rup."

"Of course, it's locked. You think they'd just leave it open? Break the glass on the door and open it from the other side."

Otto broke the glass with his elbow and let himself in.

As they searched the house, they found Mrs. Temblor's jewels and a lot of cash under the mattress. They bagged it all up in some bedsheets and headed for the stairs. As Rupert put his foot on the first stair, he heard someone unlock the front door. He turned to Otto and put his finger on his lips.

Otto froze and whispered, "What we going to do?"

Rupert made a fist like he was going to hit him and then put his finger to his lips again. He pointed down the hall to one of the doors. They silently made their way to the Temblors' bedroom. As they did, they heard the door open downstairs, then heard the raised voice of Mr. Temblor. "I told you your brother couldn't stand us for even one night."

"Well, if you hadn't argued with him all night about politics, we'd be sleeping soundly at his house right now instead of traveling home at this ungodly hour," Mrs. Temblor said.

Otto leaned close to Rupert and whispered, "How we going to get out of this one, Rup?"

Rupert's eyes were wide as he stared off into the distance.

Otto raised his eyebrows. "Rup?"

Rupert focused on Otto. "Hurry, get a dress and bonnet on and keep the bandana. Throw your other clothes out the window. We'll pick them up on our way out."

"What?"

"Just do it, and hurry."

Rupert and Otto started undressing, and each of them donned a dress and bonnet. Rupert looked at Otto and made some adjustments to his outfit.

"Good thing she's a larger woman," Otto said. "This just barely fits."

"Quiet. Now we'll wait here. Soon as he comes through the door we'll try to knock him out and make a run for it. Now listen, this is important. We're covered up enough he won't be able to tell our gender unless your voice gives us away, so don't let out a peep until we are well away from here," Rupert whispered.

Rupert grabbed a large, thick, black book and waited behind the door. Otto stood beside him. Sweat glistened on their foreheads as they waited.

They heard Mrs. Temblor scream, then heard Mr. Temblor running across the house. There was a period of silence and soft discussion. Then they heard heavy footsteps coming up the stairs.

The door flew open, and Mr. Temblor rushed into the room. Rupert jumped and, with all his weight, brought the heavy book down on the back of Mr. Temblor's head.

Otto jumped onto him and they fell to the ground. Mr. Temblor did not move. Rupert dropped the book and pulled Otto off Mr. Temblor. "Let's go," he whispered.

Rupert and Otto made their way down the stairs and ran to the kitchen. Mrs. Temblor saw them and screamed then yelled, "Those are my clothes!" She grabbed her rolling pin and chased after them. Rupert pulled Otto in the other direction and ran out the front door and into the night. Mrs. Temblor stopped at the front door, hollering threats and insults.

When they had run a safe distance, Rupert stopped. Otto stopped beside him. Rupert gave the bundle of goods to Otto. "Take these to my house, and I'll sneak back and grab our clothes."

"Are you sure that's a good idea, Rup?"

"If they find our clothes, we might as well turn ourselves in."

Otto nodded. "All right. I'll see you back at the house."

~ * * * ~

Rupert and Otto showed up to work the next day as if nothing had happened.

Mr. Temblor met them as they approached. "Rupert, Otto, I'm afraid I'm going to have to let you go."

"Is there something wrong with our work?" Rupert asked.

Mr. Temblor felt the back of his head. "No. Your work has been great. I'll give you a good reference for your next employer. It's just

. . . we had a break-in last night and lost a lot of our money. That's what I get for not using a bank. At any rate, we can no longer afford your services."

"I hope they catch those criminals," Rupert said.

"Me too. A pair of women we think. Don't know what they came dressed in, but they were wearing my wife's clothes when they left."

"You saw them?" Rupert asked.

"I didn't. My wife did. Said they were big women. It was dark, so I don't know how good of a look she got."

Rupert slowly shook his head, suppressing the urge to smile. "Sorry to hear about that. We'll start looking for other work."

~ * * * ~

Rupert and Otto sat in Rupert's room counting their money.

Otto looked at Rupert. "What we going to do now, Rup?"

"We'll keep targeting the rich farmers in Louisiana, and before you know it we should have all we need. If we don't have enough by the end of the summer, we could take out a loan for the rest. With my father's prominence, it shouldn't be hard."

Chapter 12
Uncle's Surprise

William got up with plans to go out and meet his long-lost uncle. He pulled out the note his uncle had left him and checked the address. He mounted Lucky and rode out to find his uncle's home.

When William got to the address on his note, he tied up his horse and examined the large, red-brick house in front of him. As he walked up the steps to the porch, he noticed the front door was slightly open.

He called out, "Hello! Is anyone home? The front door is open! May I come in? Hello?"

He pushed the door open a little wider. Poking his head in the door, he looked around. It was a nicely decorated home. To his right he saw a sitting room, and next to its entrance was a staircase with a shiny, cherry-wood rail leading to the upper floor. Next to the staircase was a hallway leading into the kitchen. As he looked at what he could see of the kitchen, he noticed a leg on the floor.

"Hello," William called out, "are you all right?"

He pushed the door open all the way and made his way to the kitchen. His stomach churned, and his face went pale as he saw the leg attached to an older man's body in a pool of his own blood.

William guessed this must have been his uncle. *How could anyone be so brutal?* Wanting to look away, he kept staring at the bright-red blood.

The man's eyes were open, and they seemed to be staring across the floor. William followed the dead man's gaze and was horrified to see another body on the floor. It was an older woman in a yellow dress, bloodstained at the stomach. She lay near the back door. Her mouth was wide open as if in the act of screaming. Her eyes were also open as if staring at the ceiling. William hunched over feeling nauseous.

In the pool of blood next to her was a brown book that had a bullet stuck in its cover. William inched closer to get a better look. The title read, "The Book of Mormon."

William saw a table covered in a white tablecloth. A candlestick stood in the center, and a few opened envelopes were off to the side. He recognized the one on top as the one his mother had given him to deliver to his uncle. Stepping toward it, he was careful to avoid the blood on the floor, and picked it up.

He turned back around and surveyed the bloody scene before him. As he walked toward the hallway, he noticed someone had stepped in his uncle's blood and tracked it across the kitchen and out the back door. The smell of death lingered in the air. William knew that if he didn't leave soon, his bile would add to the mess and the stink. He headed toward the front door.

I'll never get to meet them, William thought, sad that he had been robbed of the chance. His sadness turned to anger at the thought that someone would be so ruthless to his own kin. Stuffing the letter in his pocket, William reached the front door, determined to go straight to Sheriff Taylor.

As he walked out the front door, he almost ran into a man who was walking into the house. As soon as he got over the initial shock of almost colliding, William recognized the face of Sheriff Taylor.

The sheriff stared at William, then shook his head.

"Sheriff! The people who lived here have been murdered!"

"You don't say," the sheriff replied, as he drew his revolver and pointed it at William. "What are the chances that immediately after I get a report of murder, I come to the house where it took place and find you, of all people, walking out of the home?"

"What?" William exclaimed. "No! Sheriff, this is not what it looks like! I was coming to visit my uncle and saw the door open. I went in to investigate and found them dead," William said, in frustration.

"Is that so?" Sheriff Taylor looked unconvinced. "Seems like you are drawn to dead bodies, Mr. Chestnut. Either you're just plain unlucky, or I caught me a serial killer."

"No, Sheriff, I swear—"

"You can swear all you like. I'm taking you in," Sheriff Taylor said as he pulled out a rope. He made a circling motion with the tip of his gun to prompt William to turn around.

~ * * * ~

"You must really like it here, Mr. Chestnut," the jailer said as he escorted William up the stairs of the jailhouse. "I think you set a record for the most visits in the shortest amount of time."

William didn't say a word. Instead, he walked to the last cell, shut the cell door behind him, and lay down on the cot.

He laid there a few minutes in frustration, thinking back on the horrible sight he had witnessed. He then remembered the letter in his pocket. He pulled it out and opened it up. Five dollars fell out of the letter onto the ground. William picked it up, surprised, and read the letter.

> Dear Brother,
>
> My son William is coming to live in your area for a while to try to get a business going. I'm concerned for him as he has tried to do this already and hasn't been able to get it to work out. Please watch over him, and if he falls on hard times, give him the enclosed money, and help him in any way you can.
>
> I miss you dearly and hope you will come to visit us in Missouri as soon as you are able.
>
> Love,
>
> Your sister, Sarah

William smiled. *She's always thinking ahead,* he thought. If he could somehow get out of this mess, he wanted to create his business and move forward, but now that seemed like an unreachable dream.

It wasn't lost on him that now that he had enough to buy the business from Abe, he had lost his freedom to do so. With no way to prove his innocence, he figured he was likely to spend a long time in this situation.

Later that night, the sheriff came to see him with two other men.

Sheriff Taylor turned to the strangers. "Mr. Meier, Mr. Prosecutor, this is the man who was found in the Meier's home after Mr. Meier reported finding his parents had been killed. His name is William."

William sat up. "Are you George Meier?"

The prosecutor replied, "I'll be the one askin' questions here. For starters, where you from? Why were you in George's parents' home? And how did you know George's name?"

Addressing George, William said, "Listen, I was just coming to visit them because your dad is my mom's brother. When I got there, the door was open, and they were already dead."

"I knew it. Sheriff, this must be a cousin from Missouri. They have no religious toleration out there. You've heard from the papers what the Missourians are doing to the Mormons. They can't stand to even live by them. His family was outraged when they learned about my parents became Mormons. They sent him to take my dear parents from me," George said breathing heavily.

William couldn't believe his ears. "No! It's not true! My family doesn't know anything about yours. I'd never—"

"That will be enough out of you," the sheriff said.

As they walked away, William noticed the bottom of one of George's boots was stained red.

"Sheriff Taylor! I need to ask you just one thing," William said.

The sheriff turned to George and the prosecutor. "You two go on. I'll be right down to take a statement from you."

"What is it?" the sheriff asked impatiently as he walked back to the cell.

"When I was at the home, I noticed someone had stepped in the blood and tracked it across the house. Just now as you were walking away, I noticed that blood covered the bottom of George's boots."

"Really?" The sheriff paused in reflection. "I did notice those tracks when I investigated the house. I guess I had assumed they were yours." The sheriff looked at William curiously. "Show me the bottom of your boots."

William sat down on the cot and showed him the bottom off his boots. "My soul's not the one stained with blood."

Sheriff Taylor turned and went back down the stairs. William listened intently. He heard muffled talking, then a shout. Then he heard furniture banging and boots thumping hard against the floor in rapid succession. Two gunshots several seconds apart rang through the building. For a few tense minutes, everything was silent.

William heard more muffled voices then the noise of boots thumping against the stairs. Sheriff Taylor came back to the cell and faced him.

"Soon as I confronted him, he ran. I saw the blood on his boots, too. Gave him a warning shot, but he didn't stop. The second one took him. The Jailer and prosecutor witnessed the whole thing. I'll get Keith on your case. It should be cut and dried."

William wasn't sure he would ever be able to forgive George for murdering his aunt and uncle, and trying to frame him for it. He was glad George was gone. He had gotten what he deserved.

William's day in court came, and Keith Steinecker represented him well. During the trial, the sheriff was asked what possible motive George could have had for murdering his parents.

The sheriff gathered his thoughts. "Best I can figure, there might be two reasons, or maybe a combination of both. There was a bullet in a religious book they had at the house, so it may have been because he was against their religion. More likely, it could have been that he was an only child and was hoping to inherit their wealth and property. Either way, the innocent don't run—or have blood on their boots."

The sheriff explained that he was able to match the bloody footprints in the house to George Meier's boots. Also, since George ran when the sheriff confronted him, the court decided William was innocent.

After the trial was over, the sheriff approached William outside the courthouse. "Well, William, I don't say this to most honest folk, but I hope I don't see you again."

"I'm hoping the same, Sheriff."

Chapter 13
Parley

February 25, 1833

Travel-stained and weary, William rode into New Salem and went straight to the Sangamon Inn and Tavern. His legs ached, and his knees were worn out from the long ride. He checked into a room and reflected on all he had experienced since he had arrived in Illinois. He wrote a letter to his parents then fell asleep.

The next morning, after a hearty breakfast at the tavern, William mounted Lucky and rode to the postmaster's office. There he found Abe in a good mood and happy to see him. "William, how have you been? I was starting to think you were going to change your mind."

"Sorry I took so long getting back. I went to Springfield to secure more financing and got tied up in some unexpected business that kept me longer than I would have liked. I did get the financing, however."

William handed Abe the rest of the money for the store.

Abe took it, "You've got your store," Lincoln said, handing him the key. "Now you need the important part—the goods."

"Those will come in good time," William replied.

"Pleasure doing business with you," Abe said. "I hope you have better luck with it than I did."

~ * * * ~

William spent the next few weeks cleaning up and restocking the store and getting it ready for business. He did a lot of traveling as he searched for places to get his goods at bargain prices. Abe had let him borrow a small wagon that he harnessed to his horse to haul the goods. It took him longer than he thought to get the store ready. Finally, he needed just a few more bags of flour and sugar to be ready for business.

He rode Lucky into Springfield and stopped by every shop he could find to get the most competitive prices. As he traveled through the streets, he noticed a crowd gathering around a man who was preaching on the corner, standing on a soapbox.

He got close enough to hear a little of what the man was preaching. He couldn't catch all of it but heard something about a new book of scripture and Christ's church newly restored to the earth. That caught his interest, and he dismounted from his horse to ask more about this new book of scripture.

He caught the attention of a man standing near the speaker.

"Excuse me, sir," William said. "I'm William Chestnut."

"Hello young man; my name is Parley Pratt."

"Pleasure. You from around these parts?" William asked.

"No. In fact, I'm from New York; how about you?"

"I'm from St. Louis."

Parley smiled. "I was just there three years ago, passing through to teach the Indians about their heritage."

William raised an eyebrow. "The Indians?"

"Yes, I taught a lot of them, but I remember one in particular who embraced our teachings. Okara, I think was his name. He was a pure soul. Anyway, you had a question?"

William pointed at the man on the soapbox. "I was wondering about what that man said, about another book of scripture. Is he talkin' about another Bible?"

"Let me ask you something. Do you believe God loves all His children?"

"Yes, I believe so," William said.

"What about His children that lived on this continent anciently? Does He love them?" Parley asked.

"Well, I suppose so," William replied.

"God loves all men because we are all His children," Parley explained. "He wanted all of His children to have access to His gospel. Just as He called on prophets to teach His word on the other side of the world, He also called on prophets to teach His gospel in this part of the world. They were the ancient ancestors of the American Indians."

"Now, *how* would you know that?" William asked.

"The ancient prophets of this continent wrote their testimonies down, just like the prophets of the Bible did. We have their words in another book of scripture, called the Book of—"

"Wait a second!" William interrupted. "How come Jesus never talked about these other prophets?" William had read the first four books of the New Testament once, and he didn't remember Jesus talking about another group of people.

Parley pulled out his Bible. "He did. Right here in John 10:16—'Other sheep I have, which are not of this fold: Them also I must bring, and they shall hear my voice, and there shall be one fold and one shepherd.'

"The 'other sheep' that He had to visit were the people living on this continent at that time. And He did visit them. That event, and the testimonies of the prophets of this continent, are all recorded in the Book of Mormon. It's another testament of Jesus Christ."

William's eyes widened as he remembered his uncle's home and the book with a bullet in its cover in a pool of blood next to his aunt's body. The memory was almost too much. William felt queasy. "I'm sorry, I need to be on my way."

~ * * * ~

William got the supplies he needed at a nearby store, and started the twenty-mile journey back to New Salem. He thought about what Parley had told him about prophets on this continent and the Savior coming to visit them. His words made sense in a way, but William had so many questions.

Where did the Book of Mormon come from? If it's about Jesus, why is it called 'Mormon'? He had heard of the Mormons only in a negative light from the newspapers and a few conversations he had overheard now and again. *If the Mormons believed in Jesus so much why did no one seem to like them?*

William stopped his horse. These and other questions kept circling his mind, and were starting to nag at him. He turned his horse around and headed back to Springfield, looking at the sun's position in the sky. He figured he had enough light to go back and spend some time in town. William wanted to see if he could find Parley again and get some answers.

As William rode Lucky down the street of Springfield, he searched for Parley and his companion, but they were nowhere to be seen.

William patted Lucky's head. "Well, Lucky, looks like we are out of luck this time."

William was disappointed but knew he needed to get going back to New Salem soon or he'd be riding through the night. He turned his horse around to get back on the trail when he thought he heard someone calling his name. He looked around and saw the sheriff running toward him, waving his arms and calling after him.

"Sheriff!" William hollered. "Whoever it was, I couldn't have killed him. I only just got here!"

The sheriff stopped dead in his tracks and then smiled. "For once, William, I'm not here to arrest you."

"Well, that's a nice change."

The sheriff stopped a short distance from William. "You're needed at the courthouse."

"What do they want with me there?"

"Your uncle left a will that said his estate was to go to his next of kin. Since the entire family is now dead, you're probably the closest next of kin there is."

William smiled. "Hear that, Lucky? Looks like we're not out of luck after all." His smile faded as he thought of his uncle's untimely death. He followed the sheriff solemnly to the courthouse.

It was night by the time William left the courthouse. Turned out his uncle had only $20 in the bank, but William also received the deed to the house. He knew he wouldn't want to live there after what he'd seen, and it wouldn't be convenient anyway, since his business was in New Salem. He would put the house up for sale and use the proceeds to buy or build a home in New Salem.

Chapter 14
Reunion

William got a good price for his uncle's home. He spent most of the summer and fall building a home in New Salem and running his store.

The people of New Salem were good to him. It wasn't unusual for someone to stop by while he was working on his house and offer to help him for the day. He got to know the residents well that way. Even Abe came by a few times to help him.

His business was just barely making a profit. He finally had a breakthrough one day when he went to Springfield to buy some goods. He had come across a traveling merchant who was selling beautiful shawls and trinkets from Asia. He bought most of what the man had to sell. The new merchandise attracted customers to his business from other cities. The influx of business had gotten him through the summer and most of the fall season. He even earned enough that he began sending money to his parents. He wanted to repay his father for all that he had borrowed from him over the years, and his new success made that possible.

After having sold all of his Asian goods, William's business dropped rapidly. He knew he needed to find more specialty items to keep his business running. The village didn't seem to have grown much since he first moved there. He thought about the various trips he made to Springfield and the new businesses and buildings that popped up all around town there. In New Salem, no new buildings or houses had been built since he built his little home. Even so, William thought the small village still had a lot of potential for future growth. He hoped others would see that as well. More people would mean more business.

William went back to Springfield for supplies. The nine-hour ride was tiring, but Lucky didn't seem to mind the long trips. William always put some apples and carrots in her oats after long rides like this.

After he brushed down Lucky, and she started feeding, William walked toward a nearby tavern to grab some dinner before finding an inn for the night. As he approached the corner of the building, a young lady came from behind the corner, apparently in a hurry, and nearly walked into him. William caught her by the arms as she started to fall backward.

"Whoa! You all right?" William asked

Simultaneously they both said, "I'm sorry."

Recognition instantly dawned. Both of them, caught in a moment of surprise, stood staring at each other, faces inches apart.

"We've got to stop meeting like this," William said.

Johanna smiled.

"When did you get back to town?"

"Just yesterday," Johanna replied. Then she frowned and stepped back, asking, "Why did you leave me last time we were together?"

"Someone, who thought I owed him a debt, came and took me away; otherwise, nothing could have moved me from that spot until you got back. Once I got it all straightened out, you had already gone. Let me make it up to you by taking you on a carriage ride around town."

A smile slowly spread across Johanna's face. "All right. Where are you staying these days? I noticed you're not at my father's inn anymore."

"I looked for you for a long time after that day. Finally, I asked your father about you. He told me you were gone to Ohio for the summer and that you couldn't court patrons, so I haven't been back to his inn since. I have been looking for you ever since summer ended. I've been buildin' a successful business in New Salem, twenty miles southwest of here. I also built a house there. I just came into town for a few days to get some supplies. But since you're back, maybe I'll extend my stay."

"That would be nice," Johanna said, smiling.

After he walked Johanna home and said good night, he spent the rest of the night looking for a carriage that he could hire for their morning get-together.

It was getting dark, and most places were now closed. William found a carriage parked in front of a tavern. It was an open, black carriage with big, red, spoked wheels and gold trim. There was a red, cushioned bench inside that might fit two or three people. The whole outfit was drawn by a single horse.

As William walked toward the tavern, he heard some loud noises. The sounds of glass breaking and people yelling were followed by a gunshot. Then all went quiet.

William stopped to listen. Suddenly, the tavern door swung open. Sheriff Taylor walked out dragging a man who had been shot in the arm. His hands were tied, but he still struggled. The sheriff kneed him in the gut, and the man fell.

“Now you can come along peacefully, or I’ll get a group of men to carry you,” the sheriff said.

The man stood up slowly, no longer struggling.

The sheriff finally noticed William. “Oh, hello, William.”

He grabbed the man by the uninjured arm. “If you’ll excuse me, I’ve got to find a doctor to sew this man up before I take him in.”

“By all means,” William replied.

The sheriff’s attention was back on the man. “Thought you could get away with murdering Tim.”

“Shariff it was his fault he made me so angry.”

William shook his head as he walked past them into the tavern. The air was musty and reeked of stale beer and tobacco smoke. A bar with stools wrapped around the room. Most of the patrons were older and overweight.

“Who owns the carriage out front?” William called out.

A rather large man with a long beard stood up. “You have a problem with it, boy?”

William smiled patiently. “No problem. I was just interested in renting a ride for tomorrow morning.”

“What makes you think I want to rent it?”

“Two dollars makes me think you might want to rent it.”

William knew his offer was triple what he should have been paying for a carriage ride, but he didn’t have any other options. He really wanted this to work out, and since this man didn't seem willing, he thought the higher price would make it worth his while.

The man smiled. "Two dollars, huh?"

William nodded.

The man stuck out his hand. "Deal. Meet me out front of this tavern 8:30 a.m."

"Pleasure doing business," William said, shaking the man's hand. Suddenly he got a strange feeling in his gut that maybe he shouldn't trust this man. He pushed the feeling aside as he thought about how nice it would be to spend the next day with Johanna after not seeing her for so long.

~ * * * ~

The next morning, William went to the Carpenter Street Inn and had breakfast. He was hoping to see Johanna during breakfast, but she was nowhere to be seen. After breakfast, William found Johanna's father.

"Good morning, sir," William said enthusiastically.

"Oh, hello. William, wasn't it?"

"That's right," William said. Then after an awkward pause, he said, "I've been successful in my new store."

"I know, I know—my daughter won't stop talking about you. She is in her room getting ready. You're going on a carriage ride with her this morning, I hear."

William smiled. "Yes, sir."

"Well, William, you best treat her right, or you'll regret having ever met her. Are we clear?"

William swallowed. “Yes, sir, I’ll make sure she’s treated the way a lady deserves.”

“See that you do,” Mr. Nancy replied with a nod.

Just then Johanna came into the room. She looked amazing in a velvet-red long-sleeved dress that had an intricate lace-like pattern sewn into the top half.

“Father, are you pestering him?” Johanna asked.

“No more than I need to,” her father replied.

William smiled at Johanna. “We’d best be on our way; the carriage leaves in seven minutes.”

He offered her his arm, and they walked through the door of the inn. “Is that our carriage?” Johanna asked as they approached the tavern.

“That’s the one.”

“It’s nice,” Johanna said, admiring the woodwork.

The carriage driver came out of the tavern and looked at them. “Welcome to my ride. Go ahead and climb on in, and we’ll get started.”

The driver helped Johanna into the carriage then climbed up to the drivers’ perch. William climbed in and sat next to Johanna. She smiled at him, and the carriage started moving.

“Did you ever find your uncle?” Johanna asked.

“Yes. His son had killed him, then tried to frame me for the murder, but we found proof that he had done it.”

“Oh, that’s awful!” Johanna said, covering her mouth.

William nodded. “You never know what life is going to throw at you. How was your trip to Ohio?”

“Uneventful. I just tried to keep my grandma company and help her as much as I could. She is awfully lonely since Grandpa died. Nothing exciting ever happens to me.”

"Well, what about—" William stopped speaking as he noticed a man with a rifle staggering through the street. The man stood in the street blocking the path of the carriage.

The driver stopped the carriage and yelled, "Get out of the way, Billy."

Billy slowly leveled the rifle, aiming at the driver, the gun just above his waist. "Billy, what do you think you're doing? Put the gun down," the driver demanded.

"My wife told me everything you did to her Russ. Now you're going to get what you deserve." Billy fired at Russ.

William felt a rush of air and heat near his right ear as the bullet whizzed by. The horse took off at a run as the shot rang through the air. Billy jumped out of the way of the carriage, barely dodging the horse and carriage as it hurled toward him.

William held tight to Johanna with one arm and gripped the seat with his other hand, trying to keep from being launched from the carriage as it rumbled forward, racing through the streets. Russ almost fell out of his seat but finally regained his composure as the carriage bumped and shook. After several minutes, he got control, and the carriage slowed and finally came to a stop.

William looked at Johanna, his arm still around her.

"You all right?" William asked.

"Well, I am now," she said, looking into his eyes.

"Get out," Russ said in a gruff voice.

William and Johanna turned to look at him. "What? You want us to get out right here?" Johanna asked, surveying their surroundings. She saw several brothels, a bar, and some other run-down buildings.

"Listen, I paid you well. The least you could do is take us to a better part of town," William said.

"I said, get out. I've got more important business to attend to. I'll show him. Shooting at me like that," the driver said.

"You're not being reasonable," William replied.

The driver reached down behind his seat, grabbed his shotgun, and set it in his lap. "I've got to be quick, if I'm going to get back at him. I'm not takin' you folks anywhere else today. Now get out!"

Johanna stared up at him. "Returning anger with anger will only make things worse."

Russ put his hand on the gun. "If I want to hear a sermon I'll go to church. Now get out."

William got up and helped Johanna out of the carriage.

As soon as they were clear, the driver yelled, "Heeyaw," and took off down the street.

William and Johanna walked briskly back the way they had come.

"On the bright side, now you can't say nothing exciting has ever happened to you."

"Very funny," Johanna replied.

"Let's go and find some food. It will help us calm our nerves," William suggested.

Johanna took William's arm, her fingers shaking. "That sounds nice."

They passed the time quite pleasantly. They found out they had read many of the same books, and faced many similar challenges with their parents.

After lunch, William walked Johanna back to the Carpenter Street Inn. "Can I call on you again some time?"

"I never know what's going to happen when I'm with you," Johanna said, as she leaned in closer to him.

"The feelin' is mutual." William pulled her close and kissed her.

Chapter 15
Separation

February 1834

William spent the winter attending to his store during the week. On the weekends, he went to Springfield and courted Johanna. They enjoyed ice-skating and going for walks through the snow-packed streets as they talked about the news of the day and about their likes and dislikes. When indoors, they loved to chat as they enjoyed a myriad of board games, including Nine-Man Morris, Fox and Geese, and checkers. Once William even ventured to teach her how to play chess.

As the snow melted, so did William's profits. The people in New Salem were more willing to buy his goods when it was cold because his store was convenient.

There was little for William to celebrate in 1834 other than Abe's election to the Illinois state legislature. He ventured out on many week-long trips to find new specialty goods in different locations, like the Asian items he had purchased the previous year. He needed to get something nobody else had and in which everybody would be interested to keep his business going. Sadly, those kinds of things were not easy to come by.

William continued to court Johanna, but her father always asked how his business was doing. His news was seldom good, and Mr. Nancy steadily grew to oppose their continued courtship. He never told Johanna directly that she couldn't see William, but his veiled disapproval of William became regular.

By February 1835, William decided if he wanted his business to stay afloat, he needed to travel to a place likely to have the kind of items he was looking for. He decided Cleveland, Ohio, was that place. It was a major port on Lake Erie that received goods from all over the world. If he had no success there, he could try New York. He could also stop in and see how his friend Isaac Cody was getting along.

~ * * * ~

March 5, 1835

Johanna and William walked down the street hand in arm bundled in their warm coats, hats, and mittens, admiring the wintry landscape of the countryside.

"How long will you be gone?" Johanna asked.

William started thinking, making mental calculations. "I'm not likely to be back until sometime in the fall."

"I'll miss our weekend get-togethers."

"Me too," William replied. "New Salem hasn't grown at all since I set up shop two years ago. Lacking that, the only thing I can think to do to keep my business going is to find and sell things that will capture people's interest—things that nobody else has."

As they walked back to the Carpenter Street Inn, Johanna asked, "Are you going to ride Lucky all the way to Ohio?"

"Yeah, she has been a good horse. She'll get me to Cleveland."

"I wish I could go with you," Johanna said.

"I would enjoy that, but it wouldn't be proper to be travelin' together like that while we're courting. Your father wouldn't allow it."

Johanna raised one eyebrow and glanced at William. "Maybe we could do something to make it proper."

William stopped and stared at Johanna. "Johanna, I love you, and I think making it proper would be the greatest thing that ever happened to me. But I need to prove to your father, my father, and ultimately to myself that I can support a family with my business. Right now, I'm barely breaking even."

Johanna ran her hand down William's arm. "Well, you don't need to prove anything to me. I know you'll work hard and figure things out."

"Thank you for believing in me, but I don't think your father would see it the same way."

"Isn't what *I* think more important than what my *father* thinks?" Johanna asked.

"Yes, of course. I just don't want there to be any obstacle for us as we move forward," William replied.

After a few moments of silence, William said, "President Jackson just paid off the national debt. I need to follow suit and get rid of all my debts and get my business out of the red."

Johanna was quiet until they got closer to the Carpenter Street Inn.

"Why so somber?" William asked.

"I wish you wouldn't go," Johanna replied. "It's just that I will miss you so."

"I'm doing this for us Johanna, so we can have a brighter future."

"Do you promise to write to me every week?"

"I promise," William replied.

Johanna still did not look very happy.

"Hey," William said softly as he lifted her chin to look into her eyes. "I'll be back as soon as I can."

"All right," Johanna said, then gave him a kiss goodnight and went inside.

~ * * * ~

March 1835

William packed everything he needed for his long trip into his saddlebags. It took William and Lucky about four and a half weeks to get to Cleveland, where they arrived in late March.

Cleveland was a busy city, and the Cuyahoga River wound through the center of town like a snake. As William arrived, he saw several notices around town, posted by a Michael H. Chandler, inviting the public to the Cleveland House to see mummies and other

Egyptian artifacts. William noted that Chandler's collection was for sale.

William stopped by the exhibition and paid twenty-five cents to see the mummies and other artifacts from Thebes, Egypt. There were four mummies, several ancient lamps, and some pottery. William made an offer for the lamps and pottery, which Mr. Chandler readily agreed to. He tried to push the mummies in with the offer, but William didn't think they would be a worthwhile investment.

After checking into the hotel and dropping off his things, William sought to find his friend, Isaac Cody. He had to ask only a few times before he ran into someone who knew him. Active in local politics, Isaac was well known throughout the city.

As William walked in the direction of Isaac's house, he saw Isaac walking down the road toward him. Isaac recognized William and waved at him.

"William. So good to see you! What brings you to Cleveland?" Isaac said, shaking William's hand.

"Came looking for goods for my business. How have you been?"

"Doing well, thank you. When did you arrive in town?"

"Only just this morning," William said.

"Why don't you come over tonight for dinner? Rebecca is an excellent cook. My home is that two-story house down at the end of the street," Isaac said, pointing down the road.

"Thank you! I could use a good dinner."

"I've got to run a few errands around town. But come over about five o'clock, and we'll do some catching up," Isaac said.

"Sounds good. Good to see you again, my friend."

That night Isaac welcomed William into his home. "William, this is my wife, Rebecca."

William shook her hand, noting that her belly was big and round. "It's a pleasure to finally meet you. When is your baby due?"

"About mid-July. If you'll excuse me, I've got to finish preparing dinner."

Isaac and William sat by the fireplace chatting while the final preparations for dinner were being made.

"I didn't know you were expecting. Congratulations! What happened to Martha?" William asked.

"She passed away last year."

"I'm sorry to hear that."

"Life has its way of kicking you when you're down. But God did bless me with another beautiful wife. So what kind of things are you looking to get for your store while you're here?" Isaac asked.

"Things that you don't usually see anywhere else. I ran into a man today who had some artifacts from Egypt, and I bought some pottery and oil lamps from him."

"You mean that man displaying the mummies?" Isaac asked.

"That's the one."

"Let me take you around town tomorrow. I know several stores in town that have unusual things for sale that might interest you."

"I don't have a lot of money."

"I'll help you out. It's the least I can do."

"Thank you, Isaac. I really appreciate that," William replied.

"It's the least I can do for the man who saved my life," Isaac said.

Over the next few weeks, Isaac fulfilled his promise, and William was able to purchase a variety of interesting things. Among them were a few globes, some wood-and-ribbon Jacob's ladder toys, a variety of patterns for modern dresses, several items of jewelry, shawls, and hats, and an assortment of other interesting things William had never seen before.

After two weeks of successful shopping, William decided it was time to return home. Isaac invited him to a local tavern to have drinks and say their goodbyes.

As they sat at the bar together, Isaac commented, "Looks like you've got plenty of things to keep your business going for a while."

"Yes, I do. Thank you for all your help the last few weeks."

"No problem at all," Isaac said.

A man from the other side of the room yelled out, "Isaac Cody, how you doing?"

Isaac and William turned around and saw a short, portly man with a thick mustache and wearing fancy clothes walking toward them. William and Isaac stood to greet him.

"Hello, Philo," Isaac said. "William, this is Philo Scovill, an associate of mine. Philo, this is William Chestnut, a friend from Illinois."

"Nice to meet you, William. Welcome to our humble town. Isaac, I want to thank you for all you've been doing to move the abolitionist cause forward. You really are a champion for all mankind."

A little embarrassed, Isaac responded, "That's kind of you to say."

"Can you repeat some of your speech from last week?" Philo asked.

"I don't know if this is the right time or place," Isaac responded.

"Nonsense, nonsense; it'll be just fine. Go on. Go on," Philo prodded.

"Well, all right—perhaps just a small bit."

"That's the spirit," Philo said, with a smile.

Isaac began with a booming voice. "It is well known that one of our founding documents clearly states a universal truth that all men are created equal. No man, being equal to all other men, should ever be in bondage to another. It is an abomination in the sight of God."

Several men gathered around to listen as Isaac continued. "It stands to reason that any new states introduced to the union ought to be free states, to stop the practice of slavery."

At that moment a man lunged forward. Intent on stabbing Isaac, he held out a knife and yelled, "Damn abolitionist!"

William instinctively kicked the man in the stomach before he could reach Isaac. The man doubled over and fell to the floor, the air knocked out of him. Instantly Philo and other men nearby grabbed the man and restrained him. One man yelled he was going for the sheriff and ran outside. Isaac stood white-faced and turned to William. "Thank goodness you were by my side, William."

"I'm glad he didn't get another few inches closer before I stopped him," William said. "The world would have lost a heap of talent in your skill with speaking."

Philo used his weight to restrain the man. "Hear, hear! We'll make sure this scoundrel gets justice."

The man swore and struggled, but there were enough men around to keep him in his place until the deputy sheriff finally arrived to take him away.

Isaac sat down. "That's enough excitement for one day." Then looking at William, he said, "That's the second time you've saved my life, William. You must be my guardian angel."

"I think angel is a stretch. I was just doing what anyone would have done."

"Indeed, our state owes you a great debt saving this man's life," Philo interjected. "Isaac has been the means of much good here."

Bidding his friends farewell, William headed back to his hotel.

Chapter 16
Struggle

William hadn't forgotten his promise to write Johanna, he did so faithfully every week while he was in Cleveland. He had already written to her this week but decided it was time to write to her again. He picked up his plume, dipped it in the ink bottle, and wrote:

> May 25, 1835
>
> Dear Johanna,
>
> I have had an interesting time of things here. It seems there are a lot more folk here who are pro-slavery than in Illinois. I have an abolitionist friend who nearly lost his life for speaking out against that horrid practice. With that friend's help, I have had a great deal of success in finding unusual and rare merchandise here in Ohio. I've been able to procure things from all over the world. I expect to be coming back

sooner than I previously thought. I just need to get a luggage cart for all the stuff I got and should be headed home within the next week or two. I miss being with you and look forward to the time when I can wrap you in my arms and caress your sweet lips with mine.

All my love,

William Chestnut

~ * * * ~

Mr. Nancy sat by the fire going over the day's mail. He saw yet another letter from W. Chestnut. He picked it up and threw it in the fire, just like he had every letter William had sent.

~ * * * ~

"Wait a minute. He burned Grandpa's letters? What a jerk!" Jefferson said, interrupting Sarah.

"Jefferson Slade, you be more respectful."

"Sorry. But . . . how could he do that? Didn't he love his daughter?"

"He thought he was doing what was best for her," Sarah said.

"If someone did that to me, I don't think I could ever forgive them."

"Oh, I'm sure Papa resented that for a long time. Though sometimes life has a way of helping people overcome some of the worst offenses."

Jefferson raised his eyebrows. "You mean Grandpa forgave him?"

Sarah looked at Jefferson and smiled. "You want to know what happened next?"

Jefferson rested his head in his hands. "Well, yeah."

"Like I said, he thought he knew what was best for his daughter, but he didn't want her knowing that."

~ * * * ~

Johanna came into the room and nodded at the pile of mail. "Anything in there for me, Papa?"

"Nothing yet, Sweetie," Mr. Nancy replied.

Johanna dropped her gaze to the floor. "I wonder why he hasn't written to me yet."

"He must not care enough to write. I wouldn't be surprised if he is out there chasing after another woman."

"Why would you say such things, Papa? William loves me and would never do that."

Mr. Nancy narrowed his eyes. "It might be better for you to leave your options open and start dating other men before you put all your eggs in that basket. There are plenty of good men around here. The fact that he hasn't written to you should be a sign to you of where his heart really is."

"He did promise he would write to me every week before he left," Johanna said.

"I have a friend in the state legislature, Abraham Lincoln. I was askin' him the other day if he knew any young men that were well off and single."

"Oh, Papa, you didn't."

"Now, just hear me out. Mr. Lincoln told me about a man named Jacob Hamilton—says he's got a strong character. He's a banker and a fine man. I've asked him over for dinner tonight so you can meet him."

Johanna widened her eyes, staring at her father, then clenched her jaw. "Papa, how could you?"

Her father held up his hands. "I'm not asking you to marry him. I'm only asking you to have dinner together and talk."

"Oh, Papa!" Johanna exclaimed as she stormed out of the room.

Johanna pretended to be sick at dinner time and would not come out of her room. Her father apologized to Jacob and sent him home.

The next evening Johanna was up and about doing her chores. Her father saw her. "I'm glad you're feeling better. Jacob came by this morning and asked if he could take you out for dinner tonight. Since you wouldn't come out of your room when I knocked this morning, I told him that you would love to go."

"Father, how could you agree to that for me? I don't even know him."

"That doesn't mean you can't get to know him."

"I will not!" Johanna said as she stormed out of the room.

~ * * * ~

Johanna sat across the table from Jacob Hamilton. Her father had threatened to take away her books and double her chores if she didn't go on the date he had arranged. She left the house determined that she would have a miserable time, but Jacob was so funny and charming it was hard for her to keep up a sour mood. When he walked her home, he asked if he could call on her again. Johanna thought about it. "Maybe."

"Well, that's not no," Jacob said.

Johanna smiled and went inside. Her father was at the front counter and saw the smile on her face as she walked in. As soon as Johanna saw him she dropped her smile. She didn't want to admit that she had a good time.

"How do you like Jacob?" her father asked.

"Who? Oh, Jacob—he was all right, I guess," Johanna replied.

"He was all right?"

Johanna strolled past him. "Yes, he was all right."

Over the next few weeks, Jacob "just happened" to be at places Johanna visited around the city—probably, thought Johanna, because her father was tipping him off as to where she would be. Jacob was very charismatic and always knew what to say. She did think about William now and again, but figured that since he had not written, he had lost interest in her.

She courted Jacob more regularly as they got along so well together. She loved his wit and his charm, and she knew he could provide for a family when he was ready to take that step.

They continued seeing each other over the next month and grew closer. Johanna's father liked Jacob and regularly invited him for dinner and evening chats.

One morning after getting ready for the day, Johanna left her room to see a trail of rose petals leading from her room out the back door of the hotel. She followed them until they led her to a garden bench, where Jacob sat dressed in his finest suit. Johanna smiled and walked over to him. As she approached him, he stood up.

"Johanna, over the last few months, I've enjoyed being with you more than anyone. You make my soul shine with happiness when I am with you. I don't think I could stand it if that light ever dimmed."

He pulled out a ring and knelt. "Johanna Nancy, will you marry me?"

Johanna covered her mouth and cried, "Yes, of course I will!"

Jacob stood up and slipped the ring on her finger, kissing her.

~ * * * ~

June 30, 1835

William rode Lucky, pulling a luggage cart packed full of goods, down Springfield's main street. He had been gone almost three months, and was eager to see Johanna again. He pulled up to the Carpenter Street Inn, tied off Lucky, and gave her an apple.

As William opened the door, he saw Johanna's hand on the knob; she was coming out at the same time. William smiled, but Johanna stood there staring in shock and surprise. William's smile faded when he noticed how she was looking at him.

"Johanna, don't you recognize me? It's me—William."

Johanna stood there staring, unsure what to say.

"Well, say something. I'm back. I thought you'd be a little more excited to see me," William said, confused as to why she was acting so strange.

"William," Johanna finally said, as she hurried and pulled the door shut behind her. "What are you doing here?" Her heart fluttered.

"What am I doing here? I'm back from my trip to Ohio. I know I've been gone awhile, but—"

"William," Johanna said, her face looking stricken, her eyes wide. "I'm engaged to be married to someone else."

William's heart sank to his stomach.

"After all the time we spent together, all the letters I sent you, you got involved with another man? Didn't any of that mean anything to you?"

"Wait—what letters?" Johanna asked with a puzzled expression. "I checked the mail every day and never saw a single one. I thought you had lost interest in me."

"You checked the mail? And didn't get a single one? I wrote you every week—sometimes more often!"

"Well, I didn't actually pick up the mail," Johanna said. "My father always got the mail. I regularly asked him if you'd sent anything, and each time he told me you hadn't."

Understanding started to dawn on Johanna, and a feeling of anger toward her father crept into her chest.

William rolled his eyes. "Come on, Johanna, you know he doesn't like me. How could you not check the mail yourself?"

Grief was evident in her expression. "I'm sorry, William, I didn't know. He must have burned the letters. He told me you didn't write. But . . . now it's too late. I am sworn to another man."

"Did you find someone else as soon as I left?" William said, anger evident in his voice.

On the verge of tears, Johanna said, "Of course not. I looked forward every day to hearing from you, but never knew that you had written. My father arranged for me to meet Jacob, and I tried to avoid him. He eventually forced me to start dating him. It's just that, that—"

"If he *forced you*, then you don't have to go through with this," William said with a glimmer of hope.

"But I've fallen in love with him. I'm sorry, William," Johanna said, tears falling down her cheeks.

"Fine. You don't need to worry about me getting in your way." William turned around and walked away, hurt and angry.

Johanna called after him, but William just kept walking, tears flowing down his cheeks.

William walked a long while through the city. The hurt ran deep. He had looked forward for so long to being with her again. He should have known her father would try something. He just never imagined it would be anything like this.

He realized he would have to go back to the Carpenter Street Inn to get his horse and cart. He figured he would visit the tavern first and hopefully get something to help him feel better.

William entered and sat at the bar. "Give me the strongest thing you have."

The bartender reached behind the bar. Pulling out a bottle of clear liquid, he poured it into a tiny cup.

"I'll take a pint," William said.

"This is expensive stuff," the bartender replied.

"Fine. Give me half a pint," William replied.

William paid the bartender, then took the drink and walked to a table in the corner of the room and sat down.

~ * * * ~

When it was time to close, the bartender approached William. "Is anything wrong?"

"Why would anything be wrong?"

"I gave you the best stuff in the house more than three hours ago, and you haven't touched it."

"I guess I'm too depressed to drink," William said.

His mind had been swimming over his conversation with Johanna again, again, and again. He wondered what he might have done differently. He thought about how she said she wanted to go with him before he left for Ohio and practically proposed to him so that she could. He kicked himself for not marrying her when he had the chance. Every thought just made his depression deepen.

"Thanks for the drink," William said, standing up and leaving the tavern.

William walked away, unsure if he could ever forgive himself for letting Johanna slip through his hands. He wondered too if he could ever forgive Johanna for leaving him for someone else.

Chapter 17
New Beginnings

July 8, 1835

Johanna's wedding date was set for April 1 of the following year. After seeing William, she was inconsolable for weeks. She was angry at her father for lying to her, and she knew that a part of her heart would always be with William. She also didn't dare talk about her meeting with William. She didn't have anyone to talk to who would understand.

She knew it wouldn't be fair to Jacob if she kept dwelling on William. She had to focus on trying to give Jacob her heart and figure out a way to get over her feelings for William—even if she had no idea how she would do that.

Jacob kept trying to comfort her and find out what was wrong. Johanna knew she couldn't tell him. As a result, she always kept her answers vague. Jacob didn't understand, and he resented her for not sharing her feelings with him. She tried to act more pleasant, and that seemed to improve things between them.

During the winter months, Johanna started to notice things she didn't like about Jacob. He started spending a lot of time at the taverns, and Johanna had heard from one of her friends that he was seen coming out of one of the brothels in town. It disgusted her when she heard that, but she convinced herself it wasn't true. She decided that her friend was just jealous and trying to drive her away from Jacob.

However, Jacob became more unbearable as time passed. One weekend, when Jacob came to pick her up for the evening, he was a perfect gentleman while in front of her father. When Jacob walked Johanna to the carriage, though, he grabbed her bottom and shoved her in.

"Oh!" Johanna growled. She squinted her eyes and glared at him as he got in. "Next time you get in first, then pull me up."

"Why?"

"Oh, never mind." Johanna was unsure how to address what had just happened. "Where are we going?"

"I thought we'd go see a show at the saloon," Jacob said.

Jacob hardly talked to her the whole time they were at the saloon. He seemed more interested in what other girls were doing.

"Why do you stare so much at other girls?" Johanna finally asked.

"There is God-given beauty all around us. You can't hold it against me if I admire the beauty of God's creations."

"I cannot stand being here another minute. I would like to go home."

"Relax, will you? I'm not marrying them—I'm marrying you. Come on, let's go for a carriage ride around the city. The fresh air will do you some good."

As they rode down the city's main street, Jacob said, "You'd be so much prettier if you lost weight, except for up top. Your breasts are very nice—probably the nicest thing about you. How about giving me a peek before I take you home tonight? We'll be married soon enough anyway; why wait?"

"Because we are not married yet!" Johanna exclaimed. "You will have to wait until we are married before we start doing anything like that. I am starting to feel sick. Please take me home."

By February, Johanna was starting to dread spending time with Jacob. When she approached her father on the matter, he downplayed her concerns and told her she was just getting pre-wedding nerves.

About mid-March, Johanna was having more doubts about Jacob but was feeling increased pressure to go through with the wedding. It was only two weeks away, and a lot of money had already been spent on preparations. They expected Johanna's grandmother, Hanna, to arrive in a few days from Ohio.

Depression started to set in. She missed William dearly and was saddened to know that he would probably never want to see her again.

~ * * * ~

March 30, 1836

When Hanna arrived, she greeted Johanna warmly, took one look at her, and said, "Let's go talk, dear."

They went to Johanna's room and sat down.

Hanna asked, "Now, why is it that you are so unhappy so close to your wedding date?"

"What? Why do you think I'm unhappy?"

"I'm your grandmother, dear. I can see it all over your face and in your eyes. Now tell me—what's the matter?"

Johanna had been holding it all in for so long that she broke down and started bawling. "My life is so horrible!" she sobbed.

Her grandmother got out a handkerchief and wiped Johanna's tears. "There, there, tell me what happened."

Johanna unloaded the entire story about William and her father and her father's deceit about the mail. Then she described her relationship with Jacob—how she tried to avoid him, then slowly started loving him, and how nice he was in the beginning. Then she described the awful things he had done since then and what her friend told her about him.

"My goodness, dear. What a story! You can't marry Jacob. You need to marry William."

Johanna stopped crying and looked confused. She never considered that not marrying Jacob might even be an option. "What?"

"It's obvious you don't love Jacob anymore, and you never really stopped loving William. So, the solution is simple. Dump Jacob, and go back to William."

"Can I do that? I don't think I can do that."

"Why not?"

"Papa has already spent so much money on the wedding, and, well, we are engaged. That means we have to get married. Doesn't it?"

"*Engaged* is not the same thing as *married*. Your father's loss of money is his reward for tricking you into this horrible relationship. Besides, most of that stuff can be resold or used later. Anyway, it's better to break it off now rather than be married to that rat-bag who would make you miserable the rest of your life."

"I would rather be with William, but he probably hates me now," Johanna said.

"Nonsense. It's more than likely that he thinks about you as much as, or more than, you think about him."

"You think so?"

"I know it, if what you told me is true. Now, I'll help you break the news to your father, then you can go find William and make up."

Johanna gave her grandma the biggest hug she could. "Thank you, Grandma!"

Hanna smiled. "Easy, child, these bones are still frail."

~ * * * ~

Johanna's father didn't take the news well at first, but Hanna knew how to handle her son. The more Hanna spoke to him, the more he started to come around. Eventually, he agreed that Johanna should not marry Jacob.

Johanna didn't want to see Jacob again, so her father offered to take care of calling everything off.

"Thank you for understanding, Papa," Johanna said.

"Are you sure William is the right one?" Mr. Nancy asked.

"I've known it for a long time, Papa. I just let my head take over my heart. I've never really stopped loving William. I need to find out if he feels the same," Johanna said earnestly.

~ * * * ~

William spent the fall and winter of 1835 focusing on his store and trying to advertise his new products. No matter how hard he tried, he just couldn't get enough sales to keep his business from sinking.

By the beginning of March 1836, it was evident to William that not only was New Salem not going to grow, but the village was starting to lose residents. Several shops had closed, making it necessary to travel long hours to get basic services. The small village was shrinking, and William was confident that it would be a ghost town after another year if this trend continued. With the town slowly dying like it was, William didn't see any reason to stay in Illinois. He knew he still had three more years before his exile from Missouri was over, but he missed his parents and had nowhere else to turn.

It was time for William to go home and figure out what his next move should be. He would have to travel during the night to avoid being seen, but if everything worked the way he planned, he would be back with his parents by the first week of April.

~ * * * ~

April 1, 1836

Johanna borrowed one of the horses from her father's stables. She was determined to find William and make things right. She had never been to New Salem but knew the general direction, and there were some signs along the way to guide her.

Johanna had never ridden a horse for so long and at such a brisk pace. She rode up to the New Salem tavern and dismounted. As she did so, she could feel every muscle aching from the long ride.

As she walked through the door of the tavern, the rank smell of men and tobacco assaulted her nostrils. It took a few seconds for her senses to adjust, then she entered the room. The hum of talk subsided a bit as she entered. There were mostly men sitting at the tables. Some merely glanced at her and carried on their conversation, while others stopped what they were doing and watched her walk from the door to the bar.

"Good evening, sir," Johanna said to the man behind the counter.

"Good evening, ma'am. How can I help you?"

"Do you know where I might find a man by the name of William Chestnut? He owns a store here in town."

"Of course, I know William Chestnut. Helped him build his house down the road."

"Can you tell me where that is?" Johanna inquired.

"I can, but won't do you no good."

"Why not?"

"He closed up his business, packed up, and left town about a week or two ago. Said he was going back home to help his parents."

"Oh." Johanna put her hand to her mouth. She was on the edge of tears. She knew William was from Missouri, but she never heard him say what part of Missouri. A feeling of hopelessness started to overtake her.

"Excuse me, young lady," a man behind her said.

Johanna turned around. Before her stood a tall, homely, lanky man in a nice suit. "I couldn't help but overhear you were looking for William Chestnut."

"Yes."

"I just happen to be the postmaster of this little town. He left me an address where I could forward his correspondence."

Johanna's heart rose. "Is there any way I could get that from you?"

"I think there might be," the man responded.

"Oh, thank you!" Johanna exclaimed.

"But first I need to know why you are seeking him. I could get in a lot of trouble for giving this information to you. Privacy is an important thing to protect in my business."

Johanna wasn't quite sure how to say it without appearing too forward, so she just blurted out, "Well, I need to find him, because, well . . . because I'm going to marry him."

Both men's eyebrows shot up at her proclamation. The postmaster said, "I think that reason is as good as ever I heard. Come by my office in the morning, and I'll get that for you."

Johanna was so happy, she started crying, "Thank you, Thank you so much."

~ * * * ~

April 10, 1836

William's father opened the door and saw William dismount from his horse. "What are you doing here? You could get sent to jail if anyone sees you."

William tied off his horse and looked at his father. "My business failed, and I don't have anywhere else to go."

"Well, get in the house before anyone sees you. We'll figure something out."

As William walked in the house, he saw his mother making her way down the stairs. She stopped, and her jaw dropped. "William!"

She rushed down to him and embraced him.

"What are you doing home? Does anyone know you're here?"

"The sun is nearly set. I don't think anyone recognized me. I came home because my business failed, and I have nowhere else to go."

"What about that nice girl you wrote us about? What happened with her?"

William still hurt too much to talk about it, but he managed to say, "It didn't work out. I'm kind of tired. I'm going to go up to my old room to rest."

He had lost everything he cared about. His business, the girl he loved, and his independence. He now had to rely on his parents to hide him. He felt that God had forsaken him, or turned on him—either way, life was miserable.

He arose early the next morning and read the papers. The headlines featured a detailed account of the battle of the Alamo in Texas, which had taken place two months earlier. It described Santa Anna's cruelty during the battle, which occasioned the deaths of more than 180 men who defended the Alamo, including the famous Americans Davy Crockett and Jim Bowie. As William read about the fall of the

Alamo, he felt the need to stand up to injustices like this. In his mind, it was clear what he needed to do.

As his father walked in and sat next to him, William put the paper down. "Father, I want to join the military."

"You want to join the military? Why not try to build yourself a farm across the river in Illinois, or even start up another business? Why the military of all things?"

"Freedom has to be won at the end of a bayonet. Grandpa knew that—it's why he fought with General Washington for so long. There are still battles that need to be fought today to keep this country free, and I want to help fight them."

"Now wait a minute, William," his father replied. "There are skirmishes going on all over the place, and most of those have nothing to do with the United States. Take the fighting going on in Texas, for example. That's not part of the United States and has nothing to do with us. We don't need to go sticking our noses in other people's business. What we need to focus on is feeding and caring for our own families."

William put the papers down. "This is an opportunity for me to make a difference and to get out of Missouri for a while. Just let me enlist once, and when my exile is over, I'll come back and do everything you need me to on the farm."

"Enlist for what? The United States is not fighting anyone right now."

William shrugged. "Well, I thought it might be worth looking into."

"Listen, there may come a time when the government asks for our help to overcome some force threatening our way of life, but until then, let's keep our focus on what matters most."

"All right, Pa," William said, continuing to read.

William's mother walked into the room and saw William reading the paper and her husband picking through his food. "Why are you two so quiet? You'd think you could find something to talk about after being apart for so long."

"Here it is!" William exclaimed.

"What are you so excited about? Here what is?" William's mother asked.

"The country is calling on us to fight off a force threatening our way of life," William replied.

"What're you going on about?" William's father asked.

William paraphrased the article. "It says right here that another war has broken out with the Seminole Indians, who are threatening to take Florida.

"They signed the treaty of Payne's Landing two years ago, saying they would move west, but have since refused to move, and have started attacking the residents of Florida, including mail couriers and sugar plantations.

"Just last December they massacred 107 troops under the command of Major Francis L. Dade. The Seminoles continue murdering plantation owners and their families in the area and harassing the military.

"The United States is asking for Missouri volunteers to help fight the war and put down the Seminole uprising. They're paying eight dollars per month, with an extra forty cents if you have a horse, which is way more than I could make anywhere else, especially considering the hard economic times this country is facing."

"You want to go fight Indians?" William's mother asked, worry evident in her face.

"Are you sure that's what you want to do? Indians are bred for fighting. I hear they're really good at it," William's father said.

"They're killing innocent residents and their families. The government can't ignore that. People have the right to life and shouldn't have to be in constant fear of being attacked or of losing their lives," William said.

William's father stood to leave. "I won't tell you what to do, William. You're your own man. The decision whether to join the army is yours. Just know this: war is a serious business; it's not just shooting guns for fun on a range. It's shooting real people who have families, just like you have us.

"If you join up, you'll be forced to kill people. You won't have a choice, and that's something you'll have to carry with you for the rest of your life, whether you like it or not."

He then turned and left the room.

William's mother met his eyes and could see he wasn't listening to his father. "William, it's a matter you should take to the Lord. He won't lead you astray."

William blew out his cheeks. "The Lord has done nothing to help me in the last year. I don't see any need to involve Him."

"You have gone through some hard times, William. But if you turn to the Lord, He will help you make everything right."

"I'll think about it," William said.

Chapter 18
Seminole Indian War

May 1836

"I'm Colonel Richard Gentry. Have you come to sign up to fight in my cavalry?"

"Yes sir, Colonel. I'm William Chestnut. I'm ready to sign up."

"Nice to meet you, William. Looks like you have a fine horse. It will fit right in with our cavalry horses. Come right this way, I've got the papers ready to fill out in my office.

"We've got special permission from President Jackson to form this regiment. You'll be among the first to join. This crew will go down in history as one of the finest regiments. You've made the right choice. I'm sure you'll make a great contribution in supporting us in our efforts to suppress the Seminole Indian uprising."

Colonel Gentry led William into a red-brick building. The doors opened into a large room filled with business desks covered with books, papers, and files. A man with two joined silver bar pins on each shoulder sat behind one of the desks.

"Captain Gilliam, this is William Chestnut. He will be in your section of cavalry men. He just needs to fill out all the proper paperwork to make it official. I have other business to attend to. So, if you'll excuse me, good day to you gentlemen."

Captain Gilliam nodded to Colonel Gentry. "Thanks, Colonel." He turned to William. "Welcome to the army. Do you have any prior experience?"

"No, this will be my first time, but I'm no stranger to a gun, and I ride well."

"Sounds like you're qualified enough." Captain Gilliam handed William some papers. "Can you read?"

"Yes."

"Just read the first few pages, fill out the requested information, and sign right here," he said, pointing to a place on the last page.

"We'll send you to Columbia, Missouri, where you will have some basic military training and drills. We'll keep you there until we are able to raise enough volunteers to make up a regiment."

"The training is here in Missouri?" William squeaked, then bit his lip and cleared his throat. "How long do you think that will take?"

"Hopefully no more than a few months," Captain Gilliam replied.

~ * * * ~

When William got to Columbia, he discovered there were only fifty cavalry men. He was glad he didn't recognize any of them.

William walked in one of the barracks and picked a spot that looked available. As he unpacked his things, two men came in and sat down next to the bed William had selected. One of them eyed William. "You a new recruit?"

"I am. Just arrived from St. Louis. I'm William Chestnut."

"Nice to meet you. I'm James Frost, and this is Joe Binder. We've been here a few weeks."

"You guys know where I could get something to eat?"

"We were headed to the mess kitchen anyway. We just stopped by here to get our meal cards. We'll show you where you can get one."

"Sounds good," William said.

~ * * * ~

William spent his days drilling on his horse, learning tactical ways to attack an enemy from horseback. He was issued a sword and two dragoon pistols that he was instructed to keep clean and serviceable at all times.

William, James, and Joe spent most of their time together. James offered to do Bible study with them, which Joe didn't seem too excited about. William was also hesitant, he didn't feel the need, but James seemed so eager to have someone to study with he agreed to join him in the end.

After a few months of training, word came that they needed to get 600 cavalry troops before they would be ready. They already had

200. It was just a matter of months before they would be at full strength, then they would be able to head for Florida.

Winter came and went, and they were still 150 men short. It wasn't until September 1837 that they finally received the last of the troops they needed, bringing their strength to 600 men and horses.

William entered the barracks and saw Joe and James resting on their cots. "I just heard we reached full strength," William said. "We'll be headed to Florida within the month."

Joe set down the knife and wood he was carving. "We finally get to go kick some Injun butt!"

James nodded, "We're just lucky to be a part of the United States Cavalry at a time like this."

"What do you mean?" Joe asked.

"Don't you keep up with the news?" William asked. "Banks all over the place are failing. People are rushing to withdraw their money in nearly every state, but the banks don't have enough backing to give everyone all the money they deposited."

"Shouldn't the banks have on hand what they took in?" Joe asked.

"They should, but the banks spend it almost as soon as they get it," James explained. "Sure, they keep a reserve so that if one person wants to cash out they can. But they can't handle everyone cashing out at the same time. That's why we're lucky to have this job. There's a lot of unemployment going around with people losing everything."

"I hope my family is faring well," Joe said.

"Why don't you write them?" William asked.

Joe looked down at the ground. "Never learned how to read or write."

"I'll help you write them a letter after lunch," William offered.

Joe lifted his head. "Thank you, I'd appreciate that."

~ * * * ~

Preparations were quickly made to get the troops underway. By October 15, 1837, they all gathered for a grand farewell. A silk banner flew that read *First Regiment of Missouri Volunteers, Gird, Gird for the Conflict, Our Banner Wave High! For Our Country We Live! For Our Country We'll Die!*

The troops sat on their horses waiting as they listened to speeches. Colonel Gentry throughout the training had continually reminded his men about keeping their military bearing, which meant when in formation or when given orders they were expected to act with the utmost dignity and respect. He repeated that theme again in his speech.

After the ceremonies were over, the Colonel asked William to formally accept the regimental colors from several local girls. William rode over to them and took the flag. He was so nervous he could only think to say, "Ladies and Gentlemen." As he did, some two hundred Osage, Delaware, and Shawnee Indians who had been hired as scouts burst out in laughter.

Slightly embarrassed, William bowed and nodded his head, then rode back to his place in line, passing the flag to the standard bearer.

They trekked on horseback for five days westward to St. Louis and encamped at Jefferson's barracks. William covered his face with a handkerchief while they were there, afraid he might be seen by someone who knew about his exile. Before long, they loaded onto steamboats that took them to New Orleans.

When they got off the boat, Colonel Gentry gathered all the troops. "The locals are saying that there is an outbreak of yellow fever here in New Orleans. We'll find a campground near town until we can charter the next group of boats or steamboats. As much as possible, stay in camp and don't mix in with the locals. We'll send a team of five men into town to get the provisions we need, and they will be very careful about how they interact with the local population."

The men started murmuring after they were dismissed. William overheard one man say, "I didn't come out here to die of yellow fever!" Many of the men were scared of the possibility that yellow fever might enter the camp and take its toll on the group.

"What do you think, William? You scared of catchin' the fever?" James asked.

William looked at him, then at Joe. "As long as we stick to what the colonel said we should be all right."

"That's what I think too," James said. "I think all these men are so afraid, they can't focus on anything but their fear. I hate to see how they react in battle if they can't handle the pressure of a virus outbreak."

"I heard a few of them talking about returning home," William said.

Joe shook his head slowly. "Deserters aren't fit for much but hanging. I can't believe there would be men so cowardly that they would abandon their country."

"There's a sizable group of them. Not sure they'll be here much longer," William said.

When they loaded onto the next group of boats, Colonel Gentry counted 450 men and horses. "We've already lost 150 men to desertion," Colonel Gentry said, shaking his head.

William led Lucky to the docks. Hundreds of other horses surrounded them, waiting to be loaded onto the ships. The boat Lucky would be loaded on bobbed in the water next to them. Lucky stepped back as the big ship bumped into the wharf.

William pulled on the reins to urge her forward. "Easy now, easy; it'll be okay, Lucky, it'll be okay."

A wide gangplank lowered at the end of the pier, and a few sailors came down from the ship and started loading the horses one by one. The cavalry men followed their horses onto the ship. Three other ships were also loading horses and men for the journey.

When it was William's turn, he found himself hesitant to let the sailor take Lucky.

The sailor motioned for William to move forward. "You just going to stand there all day? We're on a schedule, you know."

William nodded and handed him the reins. He followed Lucky onto the ship and watched as the horse was taken below deck. After several hours, the men and horses were all loaded, the gangplanks were raised, and the ships were on their way.

The second day on the water, William stared out and saw a big, black wall of clouds and rain. The wind blew fiercely. Sailors rushed to lower the sails. As blackness met the ship, waves crashed over the bow. William and other passengers ran to the ship's cabins. The ship rocked so violently many got sick and threw up. The smell spread in the cabin area, causing more passengers to get sick.

~ * * * ~

James woke William. “Get up; the storm is over. Hurry and come up to the main deck.”

“Why? What’s the hurry?

“It’s the horses. One of the crew just went and checked on them. It’s a mess in the hold. Most of the horses have broken legs.”

William drew a sharp breath. “What?! Lucky!”

“They are asking for all men to assemble on deck to help clean up the mess from the hurricane.”

William threw off his covers and followed James to the ship’s deck. Men were moving in every direction, getting the ship back in order. Colonel Gentry walked up to them. “You two have assignments yet?”

James and William responded in unison, “No, sir.”

Gentry nodded and pointed at William. “All right, Chestnut, you go over there and help clean up the deck.” He pointed at James. “You, soldier, go help clean up the cabins.”

William asked, “Sir, would it be all right if I helped with the horses?”

Colonel Gentry considered William for a few seconds, then nodded. “Go wait by the ship’s hold entrance. They’ll give you instructions from there.”

William approached the small group of men at the hold entrance. He needed to know how Lucky was doing.

The sailor directing the group addressed William as he approached. “Are you here to help with the horses?”

William nodded. The sailor reached into a box by his feet, pulled out two revolvers, and handed them to William. “Take these.”

William took the guns and stared at them before closing his eyes and taking a deep breath.

The sailor addressed the whole group. "Most of the horses have broken bones, and they are suffering. Out here on the sea we have no way to care for them. We're going to have to put all the injured ones down. One bullet to the head between the ears should do it."

William's eyes widened as he prayed Lucky was okay.

The sailor opened the doors that led down into the hold, which was eerily quiet. The silence was unnerving. Many horses lay on the ground. The sailor approached one of the horses with a broken leg, aimed his pistol, and pulled the trigger. The other men started doing the same.

William searched for Lucky and found him at the back of the hold in a corner. Lucky was lying down, one of his legs twisted in an unnatural direction. William knelt by his horse. He looked into Lucky's eyes and whispered, "Hey, Lucky. Looks like your leg is messed up. I'm supposed to shoot you so you don't have to suffer, but I don't know if I can."

The sailor walked up behind William. "I didn't tell you to talk to them—I told you to shoot them."

The sailor aimed his pistol and pulled the trigger.

"Nooo!" William screamed as he charged into the sailor, ramming his shoulder into the sailor's gut. The man lifted into the air and fell to the ground, momentarily unable to breathe. William aimed one of his pistols at him.

One of the other men saw William pull back the hammer on his pistol and ran straight into him, tackling him to the ground.

~ * * * ~

William stood, with his hands tied, in front of Colonel Gentry and the ship's captain. The captain sat behind a wide, oak desk. Colonel Gentry sat in a chair next to him.

Colonel Gentry spoke first. "What do you have to say for yourself?"

William glanced at the captain, then at the colonel, then at the ground. "I'm sorry. I was assessing my horse when the sailor came and shot him. I lost control of my temper. I apologize. It won't happen again."

The captain slammed a knife on his desk. "You nearly shot my sailor. I'll see you walk the plank."

Colonel Gentry raised his eyebrows at the captain. "Now hold on one second. He didn't actually shoot anybody. He may have wanted to, but he didn't pull the trigger."

The captain raised his voice. "We don't know that he wouldn't have, had someone not intervened."

The colonel turned to face William. "William, you wouldn't have shot the man, would you?"

William glanced up, then back at the ground. "No, sir."

"Be that as it may, I will not risk him putting my crew in danger again. To the brig with him," the captain demanded.

Colonel Gentry nodded, then looked at William. "That will be your punishment. We should arrive in Florida in three days. Use that time to reflect on your actions. I don't want to see any incidents like this from you again."

"Yes, sir," William said.

William sat in the ship's brig, a murky jail cell that smelled of rotten fish. He had told Colonel Gentry he wouldn't have pulled the trigger, but in truth, William was not sure what he would have done, and that bothered him. He remembered something his father told him before he left home: *If you let that line of thinking go too far, you'll end up doing things that you'll regret for the rest of your life.*

William buried his head in his hands. *I almost murdered a man.* The realization of this truth sunk in deep. He knew he needed to figure this out. But he wasn't sure how or where to start.

Chapter 19
Welcome to Florida

When the ship arrived at Tampa Bay, Florida, they took inventory of men and animals. The hurricane had made it necessary for the hatches to be closed on several of the boats, which ended up suffocating more than 200 horses. Those, combined with the horses that were shot and thrown overboard because of injuries from the thrashing ships, represented a huge loss. Of the 450 horses they boarded in New Orleans, only about 150 survived the trip.

William was glad to be on solid ground again and out of the cramped brig. He found Joe and James and marched with them toward the fort.

When the company arrived at Fort Brooke, in Tampa Bay, most of the men, having lost their horses, had low morale and started to talk about going back. Colonel Gentry called the men together the next morning.

"This trip did not quite go as planned, I know, but we must press on; the United States needs us to defend our people. Many of you have lost your horses, and I am sorry. Those of you who have lost your horse will become infantry, as we have no means to replace them."

One of the men spoke up from the group of soldiers. "This is not what we signed up for. We were supposed to be cavalry, not infantry."

Many other men echoed the complaint.

Colonel Gentry held up his hand to silence the crowd. "I know you signed up to be cavalry, and not infantry. Therefore, those of you who wish to be discharged can report to Captain Gilliam, and he will issue you your discharge papers. That being said, I do wish you would each consider staying with us. Our country desperately needs us. The more men we have, the more effective we will be in overcoming our enemy. The battle is in Florida today, but if the Indians win in Florida, do you think they will stop there? No, they will not. Before you know it, they will be at your doorstep. I implore you to stay and defend your home and your country."

William, James, and Joe stood together.

"What do you guys think? Should we go?" Joe asked.

William stared into the distance. "I do miss Lucky, but I can't go back to Missouri for a few more years, and I don't have any other place to go. I'll stick it out here."

Joe turned to James. "What about you?"

"Horse or no, I'm staying. Our country needs us, and I'm not quittin' on it."

"I'm staying too," Joe said. "Guess I was always one to pile on the agony."

The line at Captain Gilliam's desk formed and then grew. At the end of the day, 150 men had walked away with their discharge papers. Most of those who left had lost their horses.

With three hundred men left in their company, they prepared to leave Fort Brooke. Colonel Gentry formed them into lines; about half were mounted on their horses, and the other half formed into marching lines. William watched as Colonel Gentry's son, a sergeant, was playing with his pistol and trying to draw and twirl it. William shook his head in disgust. *Whatever happened to military bearing*?

Colonel Gentry saw his son twirling the pistol and yelled, "Sergeant Gentry! Put that away and go help Captain Gilliam onto his horse!"

Sergeant Gentry raised his eyebrows and ran over to Captain Gilliam, his pistol still in hand. As he tried to help lift Captain Gilliam onto his horse, his pistol fired. One of the troops standing in formation next to William dropped. William and others around him instantly went to his aid.

Colonel Gentry immediately rode his horse over to his son and demanded his firearm. After the Sergeant handed over his gun, the colonel slapped him in the face and told him to get back into formation.

William put pressure on the man's wound to stop the bleeding. The private, flinched in pain then his whole body went limp. William stared at him, his eyes widened. He gasped. "He's de…, He's dead!"

The men around him echoed his words, "He's dead! He's dead!"

The men broke formation and crowded around the body. A few men started calling for court-martial for Sergeant Gentry. Many others, shouting obscenities, called for him to be hanged. Colonel

Gentry had the officers clear a path and made his way to the body. After examining him, he called for his son.

The two moved out of earshot from the soldiers. The soldiers could see Colonel Gentry yelling at his son, and pointing at him then at the troops. His son hung his head low and nodded every now and then as he listened. The colonel ended his conversation, slapped his son, and stormed back to the troops.

A funeral service was held for Private John Davis. Colonel Gentry gave the funeral sermon, saying during his remarks that he regretted the tragic accident. William leaned over to Joe. "I can't believe his son didn't get anything more than a slap in the face. If it were anybody else, there would have been a court-martial."

"When you're in charge, you make the rules," Joe replied. "He's not about to court-martial his own son. It's not fair, but it's just how it is."

~ * * * ~

When they left Fort Brooke and made their way inland to Fort Gardner, they found themselves slogging through the forests and swamps. Several hundred more volunteers had refused to continue through the swamps and demanded to be discharged. Gentry granted their leave. When they finally arrived at the newly built Fort Gardner, where Colonel Zachary Taylor was in command of the forces, they had only 153 men.

The next morning, James, Joe, and William were sitting together eating their morning rations.

"Say, Joe," James said.

"What?"

"You read the Bible?" James asked.

"No, I can't read, remember? But I've heard some of the stories," Joe said.

"You ever heard of the story of Gideon?"

"Who?"

"Gideon."

Joe shook his head.

James turned to William. "How about you?"

"Yeah, I know the story," William replied

"Well, doesn't our situation remind you a little of that?" James asked.

"Who was Gideon?" Joe asked.

"Gideon was one of the judges in the Old Testament," James explained. "He had to defeat what appeared to be an immense enemy. The Lord told him to go and fight. So, he gathered the troops and got a whole bunch of men, but the Lord told him he had too many. So, he told the group that if they wanted to, they could go home. And he lost half his army. The Lord told him he still had too many, so he told them to drink water from the river. All who drank in a certain way were dismissed. In the end, they had only about three hundred men to fight off an innumerable host. The Lord guided them, and they won."

"How did they win with only three hundred?" Joe asked.

"Through a miracle," James replied.

"I see how that fits," William said. "Contrast where we started with 600 mounted, proud, and ready cavalry men to now 153 men, only about half of them with horses. Wouldn't that be something if the Lord protected us like He did Gideon?"

"He'll be with us," James said. "I know He will."

Combining their strength with Colonel Taylor's forces made them 1,400 strong.

On December 18, William went with a group of scouts that captured a Seminole warrior who had been guarding cattle and horses. The man had a very nice rifle, a powder horn full to the brim with black powder and a hundred lead balls in a pouch. This made them uneasy; they had assumed they would be fighting against bow and arrow, not powder and ball.

Under threat of hanging, the warrior reported there were 2,000 Indians and escaped slaves waiting, armed, and ready to fight near the northern tip of Lake Okeechobee. Colonel Zachary Taylor sent the Missourians to check the story.

On their way to the lake, Colonel Gentry stopped the column and called for a fifteen-minute break. He made the rounds, checking on every group of soldiers to see how they were doing and to make sure they were drinking plenty of water. When he got to William and his friends, he said, "How are you boys doing? Make sure you take a few sips from your canteens."

"We're doing fine, thanks, Colonel," James responded.

William spoke up. "Why does Colonel Taylor seem to be using us for every undesirable detail there is?"

"He doesn't think volunteers are as good as regulars. But we'll show him that we're not only as good as the regulars, we're better! Won't we, boys?"

"Yes, sir," they all responded.

After the colonel went on to the next group, William said, "I'm not sure how much of this proving ourselves I can take."

"We'll make it through this, then they'll see us differently when they see we're every bit the warriors they are," James said.

“If you say so,” William responded.

As they approached the lake, a few gunshots rang through the air, and bullets splashed into the water around them. Colonel Gentry called a retreat. They went back about a hundred yards, and Colonel Gentry sent some men to sneak up and see if they could get a good look and verify their numbers.

The men came back and said they couldn’t tell the number—they were all holed up in a forested knoll, but the trees looked like they were crawling with Indians.

They returned to Colonel Taylor, reporting that the captured Indian’s story was true.

Chapter 20
In the Thick of It

On December 21, they left the safety of Fort Gardner and started their march toward Lake Okeechobee. They trudged their way through the muddy swamp for several hours. The terrain was covered in jagged-edged saw grass that cut through clothing and slashed at their hands and legs.

As they continued their journey they came across about a hundred Seminoles. Seeing they were outnumbered ten to one, the Indians surrendered. Colonel Taylor directed that a fort be built to keep the prisoners; he commanded all officers to help, and he pitched in as well. As a result, his men started calling him "old rough and ready." The quickly constructed fort was dubbed Fort Basinger. Colonel Taylor instructed all sick soldiers to stay at this new fort and left enough men with them to guard the recently captured Indians. None from the Missouri company stayed at the fort.

They arrived at their destination on December 23rd and set up camp. The next day Colonel Zachary Taylor held a war council proposing his plan for a frontal assault. Colonel Gentry listened intently then recommended they try flanking the Indians, but Taylor insisted on a frontal assault and ridiculed Gentry for his suggestion.

On Christmas Day, Colonel Taylor sent the Missourians to the front line. Their force of 153 was further depleted as they had to leave 21 men behind to care for the horses, which were unable to traverse this portion of the muddy swamp.

They were situated about half a mile north of the Indians, who were holed up on a mile-long knoll just north of the sandy beaches of Lake Okeechobee. The knoll was raised slightly above the swamp; it was thickly covered in pine, cypress, and palmetto trees that provided plenty of cover. The Seminoles had found plenty of nooks and had cut notches into the trees in which to rest and aim their guns as they waited for the Americans to approach.

"Why did they put us at the front of the charge?" Joe asked. "You'd think they would want the more experienced soldiers up front."

William slowly shook his head. "Colonel Taylor is using us as cannon fodder so we can clear the way for his men. It's downright disgraceful the way he has treated us."

Overhearing them, Colonel Gentry said, "All right, you two, quiet up; there will be time for socializing after the battle."

Three other companies lay in wait behind the Missourian company in intervals of forty yards each. Colonel Taylor's regiment was the last of the groups. The sound of drums and bugles cut through the silent swamp.

The terrain between the Missourians and the Indians was covered with waist-deep marshy water. Five-foot stalks of saw grass grew thick out of the water. They would have to traverse the swamp water and muddy fields to get to the forested area where the Seminoles were hunkered in.

As William surveyed the terrain in front of them, he leaned over to James and whispered, "Looks like these Indians knew what they were doing when they picked that location. Trying to reach the Seminoles looks like it might be a suicide mission. They're all under the cover of trees, and you can see they've cleared a wide swath of land for twenty yards in front of them so they'll have a clear line of sight on us when we clear the swampland saw grass."

"We'll be sitting ducks for them to pick off," James replied. "Hope they're not good shots."

"You hear that noise?" Joe asked.

The Seminoles started chanting a song that floated across the swamp in an eerie undertone, putting the soldiers on edge as they waited for their commander's next instruction.

"Creepy," William said, staring at the forested knoll, seeing nothing more than faint shadows among the trees.

Colonel Taylor approached the Missouri company. "All right, men, this is our chance to rid ourselves of this nuisance once and for all. You will advance forward as long as you can bear the fire, then draw back behind the regulars and reform and return to the fight. Any questions?"

Colonel Taylor's instructions were met with silence.

At high noon, Colonel Gentry, in his white shirt, drew his saber and yelled, "Come on, my boys!" The Missouri volunteers waded forward through the murky swamp water while hundreds of regulars around them stood unmoving and silent.

Colonel Gentry continued to repeat his initial command, yelling, "Come on, come on!" The water got deeper as they moved forward.

The shorter men had water up to their shoulders while the taller men had it up to their elbows. The men were careful not to let their muskets and powder get wet as they moved forward.

As they reached the point where the Seminoles had cleared the brush and grass, Colonel Gentry stopped the column's march and reformed them into straight lines, then called for them to keep moving. As they got within a hundred yards of the tree line, the first volley erupted from the trees in front of them.

As William ducked closer to the water, he hollered over the sound of the gun fire. "No matter what happens, the three of us need to stick together and protect each other."

James and Joe nodded their agreement.

Indians and escaped slaves popped out from behind the trees and brush, fired with deadly accuracy, then disappeared again. The bullets tore into the front ranks of the Missourians' line, and men fell into the water. Those who were not shot had to help their wounded comrades so they wouldn't drown. Many of the officers dropped first.

All who could, returned fire with limited success as the Seminoles disappeared as quickly as they appeared. Colonel Gentry held them together with his commands to stay low and continued to urge them forward. Having lost nearly 20 percent of their force was discouraging, but they pushed on.

Joe and James were so low in the water their heads were barely visible. James pulled William down. "You trying to get yourself killed? Stay low!"

Colonel Gentry hollered, "Keep pushing forward, boys! Let's go get them!"

William, James, and Joe continued creeping through the saw grass, occasionally firing when they saw any movement in the trees.

The company moved as one under the urging of Colonel Gentry, who rushed to the regiment's left, where casualties were heaviest. The forward progress of the Missourians was steady but slow. Gentry yelled as he waved his sword, "We're almost there! Come on, boys, get onto the knoll."

Men dropped into the water all around William. A few men retreated, and others helped the wounded get to the medical tent. The majority of the group pressed forward.

Gentry and a small group of men finally reached the edge of the forested knoll and plunged into the trees. As his men saw his bravery, they increased their determination and surged forward, many of them reaching the knoll. As Gentry charged forward, an Indian popped out in front of him and shot him point-blank in the stomach.

William watched from 40 feet away as Colonel Gentry fell. He couldn't believe his eyes. William and those around him stood still trying to wrap their heads around what they just saw.

The group of men that were with Colonel Gentry were successful in driving back the Indians in that section of the forest, though they made no forward progress as they stayed near where the colonel had fallen to provide cover.

"Stop gawking and lift me up," Gentry commanded.

"But sir you've been shot!" Captain Gillam said.

"Never mind that, lift me up so the men can see me."

The captain lifted him with the help of Sargent Gentry, who did his best to wrap the wound.

Through the debilitating pain that coursed through his body, he yelled, "Fight on, boys, till the foe retreats!"

William, Joe, and James saw Gentry stand, and hollered, "He's okay!"

Their resolve strengthened, the men continued forward. As they advanced onto the knoll, a volley of fire came from behind them as the regulars finally joined the fray.

William and his two comrades did not see their unit move in a different direction as they climbed onto the knoll. They found a good defensive position twenty feet from where a group of Seminoles were obscured. After surveying their surroundings they found they were alone. One of the Indians snuck up on them and shot Joe in the arm. William shot the Indian at point-blank range and killed him.

When Seminoles realized the three men were alone, they sent a group of ten men to their rear. Thus trapped, and receiving fire from both sides, William and James reloaded their muskets while Joe took out two dragoon revolvers.

William turned to Joe and James. "We are going to run straight at them and yell, 'Come on, boys!' If we're lucky, they'll think they are outnumbered."

James got down and helped bandage Joe's wound, using a torn off piece of his shirt to tie around his arm to stop the blood flow.

"And if we're not lucky?" Joe asked.

"Then we're dead anyway. Don't worry, the Lord will protect us!" James said.

William helped Joe to stand. "We're trapped, Joe! We might as well give it a try."

Joe firmed his resolve and nodded his head.

William said, "Ready?" James and Joe nodded then he continued, "We'll go on the count of three."

Unsure if he would live or die in the next few moments, thoughts began racing through Williams' head. His mind fixed on a memory. It was of the time he had spent with Johanna, and how happy he was when he was with her—though his fond memories turned bitter as he realized she was married to someone else. A tear escaped his eye.

James tapped him on the back, "You going to count?"

All of his muscles tightened as he said, in a horse whisper, "One. Two. Three!"

All three of them ran forward at full speed, each of them repeatedly whooping and yelling, "Come on, boys!" The Indians scattered right and left to let them pass. The feint had worked. They scrambled down the knoll and ran to find their regiment.

They found Captain Gilliam and their group still dodging bullets from both the regulars and the Indians. Returning fire as much as possible, they ducked down into the tall grass, maintaining their ground before the knoll and avoiding being shot from either side. After nearly an hour, Colonel Gentry collapsed. His troops ran past him and drove the Indians out of portions of the knoll.

A group to their left charging toward the knoll, then stopped as they came under fire. Except one young man, who didn't seem to realize his group had stopped and charged headlong into the knoll. The Indians overpowered him and scalped him on the spot. William adverted his eyes.

Eventually the regulars reached the position where the Missouri volunteers had hunkered down. The Missourians joined the ranks of the regulars, pushing forward to drive the Seminoles out of the trees.

The fight went back and forth for three hours, losing and gaining ground. Finally, all combined forces under Colonel Taylor's command charged and overran the knoll. Confusion set in as several Seminole defenders claimed they were Delaware Indians. Many troops had a difficult time distinguishing their Delaware friends from their Seminole enemies. Eventually all enemy forces had retreated, and the American forces won the day.

~ * * * ~

The army regrouped back at their camp, where Colonel Taylor asked for a casualty report. "We lost 150, they lost 25," came the reply.

William and James stopped by the infirmary to see their friend. Joe's arm was in a sling. The doctor told him it should be healed in a few months. In the meantime, he couldn't use it. He needed to rest in the infirmary for a week or so before having limited use of his arm.

William tapped Joe on the shoulder. "There were a lot who didn't make it. Gentry is gone, and I think only ninety or so from the Missouri company made it out alive."

"But we did win the battle," James added. "And it was the Missouri volunteers who made the win possible. Though, it was hard to lose so many that stuck with us when we've been abandoned by so many others. We were lucky to have made it through. I think the Lord was with us."

The Missouri volunteers were praised for their bravery in battle from all except Colonel Taylor, who had falsely reported that they had retreated to their baggage and couldn't be convinced to return. Angered by their commander's lack of appreciation and false representation of their efforts, many in the Missouri unit asked to be discharged and headed home.

William thought about leaving but then remembered all he had lost in Illinois. He reflected on his thoughts of Johanna during the battle, and was frustrated that he couldn't let go of her memory.

Combine that with the judge's mandated exile, his inability to keep his business afloat, and his having to return home to his parents with his tail between his legs fed William's resolve to stay in the army.

As William and his friends lay on their cots in their barracks, Joe asked, "Are you two thinking of going back home?"

William shook his head. "I have nothing to go back to. I lost everything I really cared about except my parents, and I can't even go back to them for over a year. This place suits me for now. At least here I'm doing something meaningful, and I can keep my mind off all the hurt and disappointment I left behind. What about you two?"

James dug his heel into the ground. "I don't know. I don't like serving under Colonel Taylor. I wouldn't mind staying if we didn't have to stay under his command."

"I'm with you on that," William said. "I spoke to Captain Gilliam last night. Everyone who stays will be put in for a transfer to General Jesup's command. He is confident Colonel Taylor will sign the order. What about you, Joe?"

Joe was silent for a few seconds. His eyes were drawn to his arm, then to his friends. "Well, if you two are going to stay, I'm not going to leave you. Someone has to look after the pair of you."

After a few days, the transfer request was successful. The thirty-five remaining Missouri volunteers were sent to General Jesup's command, and assigned with the Tennessee volunteers at Fort Pierce.

Chapter 21
Fit to Fight

February 1, 1838

The Tennessee volunteers turned out to be a friendly enough group. The Missourians stayed with them for several weeks before word finally came that another group of Seminoles were preparing to fight near the Loxahatchee River. General Jesup commanded his regiment to prepare to fight off the impending threat. They gathered their gear and horses and started the march.

As they approached the area, they could see the tree-filled knoll in the distance that was peppered with the Seminoles, who were hiding in the trees and on the ground, waiting patiently for the coming battle. The Loxahatchee River lay just behind it.

Beside the river, the forested knoll was surrounded by the muddy swamp covered in slough. Cypress roots jutted out of the water like stakes planted in the ground to ward off enemies.

William stood next to Captain Gilliam; James and Joe were just behind them. They surveyed the landscape. William turned to Captain Gilliam. "The Seminoles are employing the same strategy they did at Okeechobee, except this time they have the Loxahatchee River instead of a lake to their rear."

"This time we have bigger guns," Captain Gilliam said, pointing to a line of cannons.

"What are all those little pieces of wood jutting out of the water all over the place?" William asked.

"Those grow from the roots of the cypress trees; they're called 'cypress knees.' It's bad news if a horse slips while walking among those; it could severely injure the horse. That's why those who had them left them behind," Captain Gilliam said.

The command to move forward was given. A bullet hissed through the grass. They ducked, searching for the source of the shot. They crept forward cautiously. Suddenly hundreds of bullets whizzed past them. Not knowing exactly where the gunfire was coming from, everyone went to the ground and returned fire, shooting blindly into the tall saw grass.

Eventually the return fire ceased, and the American forces pushed forward. The Seminoles had all retreated into the knoll. The American forces waited in the tall grass until the cannons were in place and started firing into the knoll.

Unable to bear the brunt of the attack, the Seminoles retreated and crossed the Loxahatchee River. William charged forward with his platoon, and chased after them, cheering.

They sprinted up the knoll and into the protection of the trees. When they got to the other side, William suddenly stopped. James and Joe nearly ran into him.

"What?" Joe asked.

"They're not running anymore," William said, staring across the river. "There is another stand of trees on the opposite bank of the river. They're regrouping."

They ducked and ran for cover as bullets whizzed by.

Captain Gilliam was hollering at them about fifty feet to their left. "Over here, boys. Follow me!"

They dodged through the trees until they caught up with Captain Gilliam. "We've got to go join the Tennessee company. I saw them taking cover on the west side of the river where the Indians crossed behind a thick bunch of trees. Follow me."

They went deeper into the trees to avoid the bullets of the Seminoles, running until they came to the edge of the knoll. A clearing opened between them and where the Tennessee company was hunkered down.

They didn't dare cross, knowing that if they did, they would be exposing themselves to the Seminole line of sight. As they hunched down, they saw General Jesup approach the Tennessee volunteers and heard him say, "Follow me, boys!" The general then trudged his way to the river.

When he reached the riverbank, he turned and looked for the men he ordered to follow him. He discovered he was all alone. As the general turned back, a ball skimmed his face hitting him just below the left eye, breaking his glasses. He ran back to the volunteers and swore at them.

"Why do you think they didn't follow him?" William asked, as he watched the scene unfold.

"Not sure. Maybe fear," Captain Gilliam responded.

The Tennessee volunteers now moved forward and trudged into the river. As they did so, many of them fell under the rain of bullets coming from the Seminole lines.

"Look!" Captain Gilliam said. "Colonel Harney is taking their flank with his dragoons!"

The Seminoles ceased firing as they were caught by surprise from Colonel Harney.

William charged forward, yelling, "Come on, this is our chance!"

The other three followed him. The Tennessee volunteers charged forward as well. After crossing the river and climbing into the knoll, they discovered it was empty of Indian forces. The Indians had escaped into the swamp. The conflict was over.

~ * * * ~

General Jesup marched his troops east and built Fort Jupiter. A few weeks had passed peacefully there. William sat eating his evening rations with Joe and James, who ate in silence. Captain Gilliam approached them. "How you boys doing?"

"Well enough," Joe replied.

"Any news of the Seminoles?" William asked.

"As a matter of fact, there is," Captain Gilliam said. "And it's good news."

William motioned for him to sit down. "Sit here and let us hear it! We could do with a bit of good news."

Captain Gilliam sat down by the fire. "Two days ago the Seminoles sent a delegation of two chiefs proposing an end to the fighting."

James spoke up. "That *is* good news! Are they finally agreeing to head to Indian country?"

"Not quite," Captain Gilliam replied. "They said that if they were allowed to stay in the land south of Lake Okeechobee, they would stop fighting."

"Oh," James said, less enthusiastically.

Captain Gilliam continued. "Jesup was agreeable to those terms and sent a letter to Washington asking to be allowed to end the war and give the Seminoles the southern tip of Florida."

"Doesn't that defeat the whole purpose of what we're doing?" Joe asked. "They would still be around to harass the settlers!"

Captain Gilliam shook his head. "General Jesup said that it might be easier to round them up later when the land was needed for settlers. The Indians are camped about a hundred yards outside the fort. They'll be staying there until we hear back from Washington."

"That means we might be done and headed home in a few weeks!" Joe said.

"Maybe," Captain Gilliam said. "In the meantime, the Indians have been pretty friendly." He dug into his pocket and pulled out an arrowhead. "I went over to their camp this morning and traded a small knife for this arrowhead. One of the other officers got an Indian hatchet."

Over the next week, William traded an old pair of boots for some moccasins. Joe was able to trade one of his knives for one made of obsidian, and James was able to get some Indian jewelry for his wife in trade for a silver coin.

Early one morning, all 1,500 men were mustered and standing in rows and columns.

General Jesup stood in front of them on a stage and addressed them. "You may have heard about the proposed treaty we have made with the Indians. Late last night I received word that Washington has rejected the treaty, and we are to resume our efforts to extract the Indians from the state and get them moved to Indian Territory in the west."

General Jesup paused briefly as sighs and moans emanated from the soldiers. He then continued.

"We now have five hundred Indians camped outside this fort. You are to go out and surround the Indians, disarm them, and take them captive for transport to the western Indian territories. Your officers have more specific orders for each platoon. Be prepared to move out in ten minutes."

William shook his head. It made sense why they had to do it, but it just didn't feel right. Seeing as how they were just starting to be friendly with them.

Captain Gilliam led the Missouri men in the company of the Tennessee soldiers. They left with their muskets loaded and surrounded the Indian camps. The chiefs were angry, but seeing they were vastly outnumbered, they surrendered.

~ * * * ~

When April rolled into May, General Jesup promoted Colonel Zachary Taylor to brigadier general and asked to be relieved of command.

General Zachary Taylor established a series of small posts every twenty miles connected by new roads across the peninsula. This served to help keep the Seminoles out of northern Florida. Popular opinion was in favor of ending the war, so President Martin Van Buren sent a delegation to form a treaty with the Seminoles. By May

19, 1839, the treaty was signed: a portion of southern Florida was given to the Seminoles, and in return they agreed to stop fighting.

~ * * * ~

July 24, 1839

At the morning muster, General Taylor provided an update for his troops. "A few days ago, the Seminoles broke the treaty they made with us and attacked a trading post on the Caloosahatchee River. The garrison commander and a few of his soldiers barely escaped and made it here, but the rest were massacred, including several civilians who were visiting the post. I need two messengers to visit the Indian campsite and find out the reason for the attack. They will take with them a written message that they have thirty-three days to turn over those responsible for the attack."

William, Joe, and James volunteered.

"I only need two—you and you," the general said, pointing at James and Joe. William backed away, head bowed.

Joe and James were given the message and sent on their way. They returned a few days later with a message that the Indians were not harboring the offending party and did not know of their whereabouts. Ultimately, nothing was done to resolve the issue.

Two weeks later, William, Joe, and James sat around the fire talking while waiting for some Johnny cakes to finish cooking.

Gilliam approached the fire. "How are things going over here?"

"About the same as usual. Just the same old boring routine," Joe said.

Captain Gilliam smiled. "Well, I've got an assignment for you that will liven things up. Interested?"

"You bet!" James said.

Joe leaned back. "I'm listening."

William wrinkled his brow. "Depends on what it is."

"News just came that the Mikasuki invited a few of our officers to a dancing and drinking party," Captain Gilliam said. "They can't go but wanted to send a delegation of three men with a keg of whiskey to show they appreciate the offer. Since you boys volunteered before, the general wanted to give you boys first chance at the assignment."

Joe slapped his knee. "Dancing and drinking? That's an assignment I can handle."

William nodded. "I'm in."

"Sounds like fun," James said.

Captain Gilliam said, "I'll take Joe and James. Sorry, William. They get first choice since they volunteered before."

"I thought you said you needed three!" William exclaimed.

"I do!" Captain Gilliam replied. "But do you speak the Indian language? Didn't think so. We'll need someone who can deliver the message. We've got a Seminole working for us as a scout who will accompany you."

"Sorry, William," Joe said.

"Bring me back something nice," William said.

The next morning news spread around the camp that the party sent out the previous night had been attacked. The Seminole Indian escaped, but the two soldiers who went with him were murdered by the Mikasuki Indians.

Captain Gilliam delivered the news to William. When William heard it, his breath went out of him and he fell to his knees. He felt like he had been punched in the gut. He had spent every moment of his Military career with those two. He couldn't imagine what it would be like going on without them. He buried his face in his hands and his whole body shook.

Captain Gilliam tried to comfort him. William ignored him. He didn't want to be comforted. His depression began transforming to anger. His nostrils flared and his face reddened. He stood and silently cursed the Indians. He knew his purpose now was to avenge his friends. *I'll see them all rot back into the pit where they came from!* He grabbed his gun and walked passed Captain Gilliam.

"Where do you think you're going?"

"I going to get those dirty rotten no good . . ."

"Oh no, you're not."

William ignored him and kept walking.

Captain Gilliam called on soldiers that were passing by to restrain William. They caught hold of him. He struggled briefly then realized he wasn't going to be allowed to go anywhere.

William relaxed his muscles. "All right, All right!"

The captain was satisfied that William had given up on trying to leave camp. "Let him go."

William marched back to his tent and threw the flap shut. He vowed to unleash his anger against the next enemy Indians who crossed his path.

~ * * * ~

The next day Captain Gilliam approached William. "Get ready—General Taylor is sending us out with the garrison to attack the Indians."

William shoved the hair from his face, and grabbed his gun. "I'm all in for that."

They crept up to the Indian encampment, only to find that the Indians had disappeared. As they searched the encampment, William spotted the bodies of Joe and James on the ground, scalped and stripped. William threw up. His heart sank, and tears filled his eyes.

He could scarcely see through his tears when he heard Captain Gilliam say, "Why don't you head back? We'll take care of their bodies and give them a proper burial."

"No. I want to bury them."

~ * * * ~

Five months passed, and little had happened other than regular drills and monotony. William found Captain Gilliam outside his tent. "When are we going to mete out justice on those Indian scum? We've been wasting our time in this fort and have accomplished nothing since they killed my friends."

"When we can find them, I reckon," Captain Gilliam said. "The Seminoles have become very difficult to track or find. They've reverted to hit-and-run tactics. They send raiding parties that slaughter residents in their homes and on their farms, then steal all the food and any other valuables they can find, and disappear into the night."

"General Taylor should have been able to find them by now if he was trying."

"He *is* trying, but nothing he has done has worked. The scouts he sends out don't return. He even sent out bloodhounds to sniff them out, but the dogs lose the trail every time they get to the swampy water."

William hammered his fist into a nearby tree. "I'm tired of sitting here and waiting."

"Why *are* you here, William?"

"Honestly, I was court-ordered out of Missouri for losing my temper one too many times. I went to Illinois and started a store and found a girl. Then I lost my store and my girl. I had nowhere else to go. A little patriotism crept into me, and I joined the army, brought my horse, and made some friends. Now I've lost my horse and my friends, too."

"When does the court order end?" Captain Gilliam asked.

"It ended last year."

"Your enlistment ended last year as well. Why didn't you go home? You reenlisted for four more years. Why?"

William stared into the distance. "My enlistment ended just after Joe and James died. I wanted to kill some Indians and avenge my friends, but instead I'm rotting away in this fort."

"So, you let your anger over your friends' deaths tie you up into the army for four more years?"

"Yes. But I thought I'd spend that time fighting. Not caught up in endless drills and cleaning details. It's all a big waste of time. I'd rather be home trying to figure out how I'm going to get on with my life. You can issue my discharge papers, can't you?"

"I certainly could under Colonel Gentry," Captain Gilliam said. "He didn't want to fight with anyone who didn't want to be here. But I'm afraid it's a different matter entirely with General Taylor. He doesn't see things the same way. To him, you signed a binding contract and it's your duty to serve it out. I'm sorry, William—you're here until either the war or your contract ends."

William rolled his eyes. "Wonderful."

"Don't worry too much. The Seminoles haven't stopped their mischief. They continue to attack and kill travelers and mail couriers, and they even ambushed a theatrical group that was passing through. We're bound to see some action if that continues, and it most undoubtedly will. For now, though, we'll be able to fight in only small skirmishes. It's impossible to track them in large groups. Though I did hear of a larger battle on the Indian Key recently."

"How did it turn out?" William asked.

The captain picked up some papers that sat on a table just outside his tent. "Pretty good. I believe it was a Colonel Harney who got a lead on where the biggest force of Seminole Indians were located. They were operating under the command of a Chief Chakaika, deep in the everglades. Colonel Harney took ninety of his best men, attacked Chakaika's settlement, then captured and hanged the chief along with a few of his men."

William gazed into the distance. "Wish I could have been there."

"Listen, William, perhaps you would do better as a scout. You could be at the forefront of the action, and you would be the first to spot when there is trouble."

William's eyebrows rose. "How do I become a scout?"

"I'll put you in for a transfer," Captain Gilliam said. "They're not likely to turn it down, as scouts are currently in short supply."

~ * * * ~

The end of the year had come and gone. William's transfer went through just as news came that General Taylor had moved on and turned command over to General Armistead, who was now in command of the army in Florida.

General Armistead gave regular updates to his troops in an effort to bolster morale. After six months, he reported that most of the Indians had been forced to relocate, were killed in battle, or had been decimated by disease and starvation. There were only a few rogue groups left; they seemed untouchable and were unwilling to negotiate.

The army didn't do much in the following months to fight the remaining Indians. They were content to let them occupy the southwest reservation while they tried to protect the settlers in the other parts of the state.

Armistead secured $55,000 to bribe the Indian chiefs to relocate, and by April 1841, he had successfully relocated more than 670 Seminole Indians.

Chapter 22
The Brave, and the Free

April 10, 1841

An estimated three hundred Seminole Indian warriors still resisted relocation and continued to attack Florida settlers. As a scout, William was assigned to keep watch around certain high-population settlements. He was instructed to watch for Indian scouts or raiding parties and to report any activity immediately to headquarters. Most of the time, William sat camouflaged in the brush waiting for any sign of Seminole raiders.

Most of his days staking out this area were quiet. When he did hear anything, it usually turned out to be a forest animal or settlers passing by. The only interesting news that William heard about up to that point was the death of United States President William Henry Harrison after only one month in office.

One afternoon, as he was chewing on some beef jerky, William saw movement twenty-five yards away. It appeared to be an enemy Indian. He was older and traveling alone, and he carried a rifle and a machete. William figured he must be a scout sent to gather information and return to provide a report that would aid in the attack of the settlement William was helping to protect.

William sat silently, beef jerky hanging from his mouth. He didn't dare chew, spit it out, or move in any other way except tapping his thumb lightly against the stock of the gun. The memory of his murdered friends surged into his mind. *This is for Joe and James!*

The Indian crept by William, coming within twenty feet of him. After he passed and walked a small distance, William stood and pulled up his rifle, making enough noise that the Indian spun around. William got off a shot before the Indian could respond, hitting him in the chest. The Indian dropped his rifle and fell backward.

Letting the jerky fall from his mouth, William ran and aimed his rifle at the Indian's head. He looked into the Indian's eyes; the Indian stared back at him. "What is your name, young man?"

William stared at him over the muzzle of his gun. He hesitated. "You speak English?"

"Your name," the man demanded.

"My name is William." He hadn't expected the Indian to talk to him. "I'm going to kill you now."

The Indian nodded. "I forgive you."

"What?" William asked, his confusion deepening.

"I said, I forgive you . . . William."

"I didn't ask for your forgiveness! Anyway, I'm about to kill you. Why would you forgive me?"

"Because we are both brothers from the same Heavenly Father, and because I know the Lord loves you, so I extend to you that love. I forgive you."

"You're lying so I won't shoot you! What makes you think the Lord loves me? I've lost everything I've ever cared about. The Lord has done nothing to help me."

"I do not lie. I know," the Indian said. "His Spirit speaks to me. You're worth more to Him than all the pearls in the sea." His eyes tightened shut, then opened. "Don't let your losses or your mistakes define you, William. Turn to the Lord. He can erase your shame and your guilt. He can restore all that you've lost." He wheezed, then coughed up some blood. "He will help you find happiness and joy in life. Stand up, and let His light shine through you."

William lowered his gun. "I wouldn't even know how to start."

"Start with prayer," the man said, flinching in pain. "I do forgive you. I meant it. I do."

William knelt, resting his gun on his knee. "Why would you be like this to me, a white man? I've come to kick you out of your land, and I just shot you, and I gave you a wound you might die from."

"Love is mightier than hate, William. It can change what hate cannot."

"Your love hasn't changed a thing. I still shot you, and you're still bleeding."

"You did not take the second shot," the man said.

"No, I didn't," William said, then looked at his gun. "How did you learn to speak English?"

"Missionaries came and taught us many things. Then I moved here from the north with my family when the people there drove us out."

William leaned forward. "What is your name?"

“Okara,” he said, then coughed up blood.

William’s eyes widened. He had heard that name before.

“Farewell, William. I go to meet our God. I will await you with open arms when it is your turn to come.” Okara coughed, wheezed, and then was silent.

“Wait!” William cried. “Okara!” William looked into the man’s lifeless eyes, then pushed his eyelids down.

William stared at the lifeless body. What did he feel? Guilt? Impossible. Okara was an Indian, and Indians killed his friends. They deserved to die. Didn't they? Would someone mourn Okara as he had mourned Joe and James? William breathed out. He had robbed the world of a good man. He now understood what his father told him so long ago. His grudge against the Indians hurt no one but himself, and now he had to live with the knowledge that he had killed a good person—not in self-defense, but in anger. He had let the actions of a few bad Indians poison his view of the entire race.

Okara had forgiven him for doing the worst thing one human could do to another, something that could never be undone. In that instant, William saw the world in a different light. He knew that, just as he was forgiven, he needed to forgive. He rested a hand on Okara’s arm. “I’m sorry, my friend. I hope wherever you are now, that it’s a place of happiness.”

A shot rang out and a bullet whizzed by his head. William ducked.

“If your body is still here when I come back, I’ll give you a proper burial,” William promised, then ran back toward his camp dodging in and out of the trees.

Chapter 23
The Last Stand

When he went back with a company of men the next day, there was no sign of Okara's body. William figured Okara's kinsmen must have found him.

William looked down where Okara's blood stained the ground.

A shot pierced the silence.

One of the men behind him fell to the ground. More shots penetrated the air. William ran behind a tree for cover, his gun ready, as did a few other men. Five others turned around and ran back the way they had come.

Two of the men didn't get very far before they were shot and fell dead. William, and the two men who hid behind trees near him, returned fire.

Shots continued all around. One of the soldiers fell dead.

Only William and one other soldier remained. The other soldier took shots as he could. William saw there were three guns shooting at them. He couldn't see the Indians, just the smoke that lingered from their guns after they fired. William took a shot toward one of the trees. He reloaded his gun as the other soldier aimed and shot. An Indian cried out and fell.

All fell quiet. William peered out from behind the tree. He saw movement and took another shot. As he reloaded, the other soldier lay quietly behind the tree, his gun aimed out at the quiet forest. An Indian moved out from behind a tree to shoot, but the soldier got his shot off first. The Indian fell.

The last Indian shot at the soldier before he had time to move. The shot killed him.

The Indian ran from behind his tree. The Indian needed to reload and would be defenseless until he could. William chased after him. The Indian tripped. William caught up to him and aimed at him. The Indian rolled over, staring at William, eyes full of fear. William thought of Okara and lowered his gun. "Go."

The Indian furrowed his brow and shook his head.

"Go!" William said, louder.

The Indian crawled backward then flipped around, jumped to his feet, and ran. William rested the butt of his gun on the ground, as he watched the Indian disappear into the forest.

A single shot split the air. William felt a sharp pain in his side and saw a red stain spread over his shirt. He held his hand over the wound as he turned and saw an Indian staring at him, eyes full of hate, his gun aimed at William. Smoke floated up from the barrel. *Where did he come from?* William fell.

Horses' hooves rumbled on the ground. Soldiers on horses started passing him. William heard more shots fired. One soldier saw him move and yelled, "This one is still alive. Bring the medic!"

As a man came to him and started working to stop his bleeding, William's thoughts turned to Johanna. *If I die, I'll never see her again.* He shook the thought out of his mind. If he *did* see her again, she would be married to someone else. The anguish of that thought was too much.

All went black.

~ * * * ~

William awoke on a bed inside a tent. His body ached with pain. His torso was wrapped in bandages. He surveyed his surroundings. His was the third in the second row of beds; only a few other beds were occupied. All was quiet.

"Where am I?" William called out.

A man entered the tent. "Oh, you're finally awake."

William tried to sit up. "Who are you?" William asked, closing his eyes tightly as pain shot up his back.

"Don't try to move—you'll start bleeding again. You're in the medical tent at Fort King, and I'm Doctor Weeks."

"What happened?"

Dr. Weeks looked at him and smiled. "You were shot by an Indian from behind. The bullet hit your side. Went in one end and out the other."

William winced.

Dr. Weeks continued. "The men that escaped the ambush rode back here and raised the alarm. The cavalry was deployed and found you just in time to get you the medical help you needed before you lost too much blood."

"When can I go?" William asked.

"When you're good and healed."

"How long will that take?"

"Considering the wound, it will take months. It tore through some muscles but missed your vital organs and bones," Dr. Weeks explained.

William frowned. "Great."

The doctor moved toward one of the other men. "Just lay down; you'll be needing your rest."

~ * * * ~

By May 1841, William was not yet able to stand but could be wheeled around in a wheelchair. The doctor took him to a change of command ceremony. He watched as General Worth took command from General Armistead. The change of command ceremony was simple and quick: General Armistead handed the Florida Army flag to General Worth, saying, "I relinquish command."

General Worth took the flag and stated simply, "I assume command."

On their way back to the infirmary William was pensive. As they reached the front of the infirmary William said, "You know doc I've been thinking."

"What about?"

"Well, back when I got shot. I could have died if the bullet had a slightly higher trajectory, or if I didn't get noticed in time. I almost didn't make it."

The doctor half smiled. "But you did."

"I think I know why."

"Oh?"

"Just before I got shot I did something I never thought I would do. I showed a man mercy, the week before that if I were in the same situation I probably wouldn't have. That's why God showed his mercy in saving me."

The doctor nodded. "You certainly did have a miraculous recovery. Many have died from a similar type of wound."

As the doctor wheeled him to his bed, William said, "I'm ready to go home, Doc."

"Your mind maybe ready but your body is not. Though it's too bad it's not. General Worth said his first act as commander will be to release almost a thousand of the troops and civilian employees, since most of the Indians have been removed from Florida."

"How do I get in on that?"

"Relax. You're not going anywhere until you're back to full strength."

~ * * * ~

By spring of 1842, William was able to walk around, but only for a limited time before he started feeling pain.

When a nurse entered the tent, William asked, "Any news?"

The nurse brought him a tray of food. "They just announced a search-and-destroy mission. They're going to scour the peninsula and kill or drive out all the Indians who are left."

~ * * * ~

By the end of summer, William was feeling much better and was finally released from the hospital. He was told to report to General Worth.

As he approached the general's tent, he overheard a meeting that was in progress.

"General Bailey, how did it go with the search-and-destroy mission?"

"As you know, sir, the mission lasted through the summer. The last of the raiding Seminoles were commanded by Chief Tiger Tail. When our scouts located them, I took fifty-two of our best men to chase down Tiger Tail and his braves. We overtook them by surprise, and we were able to kill all twenty-four of his warriors."

"Well done, General Bailey. That was the last of them. This war is over. The remaining Seminoles can stay in the southwest part of Florida, as long as they stay on the reservation set aside for them. I'm going to recommend to Congress that all remaining Seminoles be left to themselves and that we end the war. That will be all. Thank you, General."

As General Bailey left the tent, William entered. "I was told to report to you, sir. I was just released from the infirmary."

The general sat behind his desk and looked up at William. "What's your name, soldier?"

"William Chestnut, sir."

"When does your enlistment end?"

"October, sir."

"I see. And how long have you been here in Florida with the army?"

"Six years now, sir."

"William, this war is coming to a close, and we are going to need some help closing some of the camps and forts. I'm going to assign you to the 5th Battalion, which has been tasked with that effort. You're free to go when your enlistment ends in October."

William was disappointed; he had hoped he could return home sooner. "Yes, sir."

"Dismissed."

On August 14, 1842, the Second Seminole Indian War was declared over. Congress passed the Armed Occupation Act later that month to warn settlers to be well armed when settling in Florida. William stayed long enough to tear down a few camps, then was discharged with his company in October.

Chapter 24
Not Convincing

Rupert sweetened up to his parents and started hinting to them that he was ready to become serious in his life—to take on more responsibility, maybe start a business. His parents were encouraged by his improved behavior and started discussing different ideas with him about what he might do for the rest of his life as a career. When he mentioned he wanted to be a steamboat captain, his parents stood in shocked silence.

"Being a captain is a respectable position in society," Rupert said.

"To become a captain, one must first become a sailor, which is *not* a respectable position. Sailors are crude, dirty, nasty people. Captains are not often much different," his mother said.

"I don't need to become a sailor, Mom; I need only to learn their art. Just enough so that I could run a ship of my own. Besides, I can choose to be more civilized than the traditional sailor."

"To be a captain, one also must own a ship. How exactly do you expect to accomplish that?" his father asked.

"You know that Otto and I have been working hard over the last two summers, and we've saved all of our money together. We have half of what we need to get a ship at today's going rates."

His parents both raised their eyebrows at that revelation. "You and Otto, a sixteen- and an eighteen-year-old, made half the money you need to buy a steamboat working as hired hands on . . . farms?" his father asked, staring.

Rupert's mind started working quickly to think of an explanation. "We took the money we earned from the farms and bought retail items at the lowest cost we could find, then we resold those items at a higher price to other stores, and sometimes to people in the streets. Many folks were so impressed with our initiative that they gave us more than we asked."

"Well, that is impressive," his father said. Rupert let out a silent sigh of relief that his father bought the story.

"And you will continue that activity until you raise the money you need?" his father asked.

"It has taken so long to get this much, I was hoping I could get the rest from a loan."

"A loan?" his father asked. "You realize loans are meant to be repaid, with interest, within a set amount of time?"

Rupert fidgeted. "The money I make from the steamboat will help me pay that."

"And while you are repaying this loan, would you be expecting to eat or drink anything?" his father asked. "Rupert, I'm starting to wonder if you have any idea as to how much a steamboat actually costs."

"I saw one for sale last summer for $15,000," Rupert said.

"You were lucky to find one that low. I wonder what was wrong with it," his father said.

"What do you mean?"

"Rupert, a steamboat generally costs anywhere from $20,000 to $50,000," his father explained. "Even if you did have half of that amount, you would spend the rest of your life paying back the loan, if a loan would even be granted for that long. They aren't. You would find yourself in default. The bank would get both the steamboat to resell, and it would keep whatever money you already paid. And you would be put in debtors' prison."

Anger rose within Rupert's chest. *How dare he tell me that I can't do this?* He raised his voice. "You're wrong. I *can* do this, and I *will* do it—with or without your help."

Rupert turned away from his parents and started to run. His dad was yelling after him to watch his language. Rupert knew if his father caught hold of him after he raised his voice, he would get a sound beating—so he made sure he was far away before he stopped running.

Rupert found Otto sitting on his porch. "My parents do not believe in us. But we can still be successful without them."

Rupert and Otto went to the docks and found a posting for a 179-foot steamboat named the *Saluda*. The owners were selling it for $10,000. The old Mexican captain had decided that he had made enough money and was ready to move into retirement.

Having nearly half of the cost of what they needed to buy the ship, Rupert and Otto found the owner and told him they were interested. The owner informed them that the steamer's engine would need repair, which was why he was selling for such a low price. Rupert knew that would be a setback, but he would figure that part out later. This opportunity would at least give him a ship, and he'd work the rest out later. He gave the money he had as a down payment, then he and Otto went straight to the bank.

When Rupert applied for a loan, the banker told him he would need a second signature from someone who could guarantee the loan should he be unable to pay.

"You know my father, I'm sure," Rupert said.

"I do. Mr. Howard is a good man and a well-respected member of our community."

"He said he would sign as a second. Can I take these papers to him and bring them back tomorrow?"

"You'll need a witness to sign as well," the banker commented.

"That will be no problem."

"Very well," the banker replied, handing him the papers.

Rupert took the papers, then he and Otto headed home.

As they walked, Otto asked, "How are you going to get your father to sign the loan documents? I thought you said he didn't believe you should do this."

"He doesn't. But I know where we can get to some of his business papers; we can use them to see what his signature looks like, and we can make a convincing copy of it. You can sign the witness block—just make up a name."

"He'll murder you if he finds out about this," Otto warned.

"He won't. I've got a plan to ensure that no one will ever find out—unless you tell him."

"You know that I'd never," Otto said.

"I know, Otto. You're the best friend a guy could ask for," Rupert replied, patting him on the shoulder. "Now come on; we've got work to do."

Chapter 25
A New Chapter

January 1843

William found a wagon headed for Missouri and hitched a ride. His thoughts turned to Johanna, he missed her smile and her touch. His chest still felt hollow to know that he had lost her and would likely never see her again.

After a month and a half of traveling, William walked into the city he knew so well. The rising sun glistened off the morning frost in St. Louis. Spring was just around the corner, and the city was teeming with activity. William welcomed the familiar sight.

As he approached his parents' property, the large frame home he grew up in stood before him. The farm his parents raised him on hadn't changed much. He was about to knock on the door, then shook his head and walked in. His parents were at the dining room table.

"William!" they both exclaimed as they rose from the table and welcomed him home, embracing him.

His father held him at arm's length. "After you left for the war, we hired on a maid to replace Marybeth."

"I figured you would, Father. But I've been gone six years, and the first thing you want to talk to me about is a maid you hired after I left?"

"She is a very special person, William," his mother said.

"Well . . . that's nice, but don't you want to know how I'm doing?"

"We think you ought to talk to her first. She is right behind you. We'll leave you two alone," his father replied.

William stood dumbfounded as his parents left the room. He spun around and saw Johanna standing there, a rag in her hand, as beautiful as he remembered her. She stared at him, waiting for his reaction.

"Johanna!" On impulse he took a step forward but then stopped and frowned as he remembered she was married to someone else.

"What . . ." a lump caught in William's throat. A tear ran down his cheek as he remembered their last conversation. He wasn't sure which of the myriad of questions he had racing through his mind he should ask first, or even why she was here.

Johanna started before he could speak. "William, I never married. I came looking for you, but you had already left. I got your parents' address in New Salem and caught the first coach I could find to St. Louis. By the time I got here, you had left for the war. After I told your parents my story, they offered to hire me, and I've been working for them and waiting for you to come back ever since."

William swept her up in his arms and kissed her.

“I’ve spent the last six years thinking about you and lamenting that I’d never see you again. I can’t describe how happy I am right now.”

“I regretted not going with you from the minute you turned and walked away,” Johanna said. “When your parents told me you went to fight the Indians, I prayed every day that you would return home safe. I was afraid I might never see you again.”

William dropped to the ground on one knee.

“I don’t want to spend one more day without you by my side. Marry me, Johanna. Please.”

Tears streaming down her cheeks, Johanna threw her arms around his neck and said, “All right,” then kissed him.

William heard his mother from the other room, saying, “Ohhhh.”

“Momma, we can hear you,” William called out.

William’s mother and father walked into the room smiling.

His father said, “We said we’d leave you alone. We never said we wouldn’t listen in.”

“Congratulations, you two,” William’s mother said as she walked over and hugged both of them together.

~ * * * ~

Over the next week, Johanna and William had plenty of time to get reacquainted and court. One evening as they sat together on the porch watching the sun set, Johanna asked, “William, do you think I need to lose weight?”

“No. I think you’re beautiful just the way you are. I wouldn’t change any part of you for anything.”

Johanna folded her hand in her lap. "What would you say is the nicest thing about me?"

"You're so nice in every way I can think of, it's hard to pick just one thing."

Johanna persisted. "Yes, but if you had to, if you could pick only one thing, what would you say is the nicest thing about me?"

"I guess I'd say the nicest thing about you is that you're sweet, kind, and loving. You make me want to be a better man every day. You make my life complete."

Johanna smiled. "That's three things . . . but it's very sweet of you to say."

A moment of silence passed, and Johanna met William's eyes. "You can keep going if you want."

William smiled. "Your smile warms my soul like the morning sun warms my day. I find this world to be a beautiful place because you are in it. You're the only thing that's been on my mind for years. When I'm with you, I feel whole. Your smile is the key that unlocks mine."

A tear escaped Johanna's eye. William asked, "Did I say something wrong?"

"No, it's just . . . that's the nicest thing anyone has ever said to me."

"It's all true. If it were possible, I wouldn't let even death separate us."

They sat together in each other's arms late into the night.

~ * * * ~

In the following weeks, His father took him all over town to help him buy things he would need after he was married. William kept noticing wanted posters of the same man. They had been posted all over town, and in the newspapers. Someone had attempted to murder former Missouri Governor Lilburn Boggs. He had never really paid much attention to wanted posters since he figured his chances of running into a wanted outlaw were slim to none. But it was hard to ignore this one.

The man on the poster had a receding hairline, hair past his shoulders, and a full beard. His eyes looked dark and menacing. The poster read, *$500 cash or gold reward. Orrin Porter Rockwell.*

William's father noticed William staring one of them. "Don't think they've caught that one yet. Come on, let's get to home."

As they walked William's Father said, "William, I know you don't like farming. Since you have so much experience in store clerking I figured that perhaps it wouldn't be a bad idea to help you get another store going."

"Really? Thank you, Pa!" William embraced his father.

As they approached the house William's father put an arm around him. "Along with the store, I want to give you another early wedding present. Follow me."

They walked into the stable that housed his father's horses.

"Go check out the last stall."

William walked to the end of the stable and noticed the last stall was occupied by a dappled gray horse.

"She looks just like Lucky! Thank you. Where did you find her?"

"I went to the stables in town and found her for sale. What are you going to call this one?"

William patted the horse's neck. "I think I'll call her Destiny."

~ * * * ~

William's mother wanted to help in all planning aspects of the wedding.

Johanna had been writing to her father regularly and now had some exciting news to share about William's return and her engagement. The wedding would take place as soon as Mr. Nancy arrived in St. Louis.

After lunch one day, William's father said, "We heard of a baker who has a reputation for making the most magnificent cakes. He lives across the river. Your mom wants to go and commission him for your wedding. We should be back by supper time."

"Why not just let Bessie bake one? She makes wonderful pastries," William suggested.

"I agree that she is an excellent cook, but I don't think she has ever attempted a wedding cake," his father replied.

~ * * * ~

Supper time came and went, the sun was starting to set over the western horizon, and William's parents had not returned. He was starting to worry.

"Why don't you go see if you can find them," Johanna suggested.

"Good idea."

William got Destiny saddled up and rode her to the river. The ferry was nowhere to be seen. William saw a dock worker and asked him where it was.

The man looked up at him. "There has been a tragic accident. The ferryman was taking a wagon and team across with a group of people this afternoon. Something spooked the horses, and they ran off the edge of the ferry, tipping everything on it into the river. No one on the ferry survived. We sent some men to see if they could recover the raft down river. Not sure when they'll be back."

William spurred Destiny forward, racing down the bank of the river to see if he could find any sign of his parents or the raft. He rode for thirty minutes until he finally saw some men pulling a raft out of the water.

"Is that the St. Louis Ferry?" William asked.

"Sure is. Some horses flipped it right over. We've been chasing it and trying to get it out."

"Did anyone aboard it survive?" William asked, more forcefully than he intended.

The man spoke softly. "Afraid not; we lost the ferryman, the owner of the horses, and an older married couple. All of them perished in the river after it tipped."

William turned his horse around, tears forming in his eyes. He rode Destiny at a slow gait. William thought that maybe the older married couple on the raft weren't his parents. Then cast that thought aside as he knew they would never stay out so late. By the time he got back to his parents' home it was dark. He took Destiny to the stables and unsaddled her then fell to the ground in grief. He had no idea what he would do without his parents. He already missed them. Just knowing he would never see them again left a heavy pit in his stomach.

Eventually he got up and went into the house. Johanna sat waiting for him at the table, knitting some socks. When she saw him come in, she knew something was wrong. She ran to him. "What happened?"

"They're gone, Johanna. The ferry tipped in the river, and they're gone."

Johanna's hand flew to her mouth. "Oh, William." She embraced her fiancée, sobbing deeply as she stood in his arms. The news was devastating to them both.

News of the accident spread across the city quickly. A large memorial was organized by the city and held for those who were on the raft when it overturned.

William's father was a man of means and had left everything to William in his will. He inherited a small fortune and his parents' property. None of it brought him any peace or comfort. He was now wealthy, but he would give it all up if it could bring back his parents.

He now had his new store to manage along with his father's farm. He figured he would have to give up one of them, or hire someone to run one of the businesses. Deciding to hire someone, he went to the local newspaper office and ran an ad to see if he could get someone with experience to run the farm.

Chapter 26
Rockwell

It was almost sunset on Saturday, March 4, 1843. Few people walked the streets. William was headed toward the wharfs and stopped at the boutique where he had ordered his wedding flowers and a few other wedding accoutrements; he was excited that he would finally be married to the woman he loved.

He wanted to get some flowers to throw into the river in memory of his parents, and this shop had the nicest flowers in town. As he approached the shop, he noticed another large Porter Rockwell wanted poster on the door; he shook his head, *I would hate to run into him in a dark alley.*

William entered the shop and picked up a bundle of flowers. It included three white daylilies, his mother's favorites. They were surrounded by blue hydrangea and light-blue delphinium; blue was his father's favorite color. His money purse was half full. He kept it on the inside of his pants, so he had to loosen his belt to get to it.

That was the safest way to travel with large sums of money around town, especially where he was going. He paid the shopkeeper and went on his way.

The docks were only four blocks away. He picked up his pace but saw a boot suddenly come from behind him and wrap around his foot. William fell forward. The flowers flew from his hands as he tried to prevent his face from hitting the ground. He was stunned for a second then heard men running up to him. William thought they were going to help him, but instead they started to kick him; grabbing his legs and arms, they carried him into a nearby alley.

He couldn't tell exactly how many men were carrying him; there seemed to be four or five. He was still disoriented. Pain shot through his body. William struggled to free himself of their grip. He shook one leg free and kicked a man in the face. They threw him hard onto the ground against a building. William felt the air go out of him and momentarily lost consciousness.

By the time he came to, he sat up, his back against the building. He opened his eyes to four men surrounding him, pistols pointed at him. They all had beards, and their faces were covered with handkerchiefs wrapped around their heads. One of them said, "Listen up, Yank. Produce your pouch of money, or we're killing you here and now."

William felt for his money purse then heard a gun's click from the end of the alley. A man's voice boomed through the air. "I've got enough bullets in this gun to empty the brains of each one of you onto the ground. If you don't want that, then I suggest you drop your weapons and back away."

One of the bandits wheeled around and took a shot at the figure at the end of the alleyway, who shot his pistol at the same time. Three of the bandits ducked. The one who shot at the figure cried out in pain, dropped his gun, and clutched his bloodied hand. The dark figure still stood there, unmoving. He spoke again. "That was a warning. Next one who tries that will get one through the brain."

William was amazed at the accuracy of the man with the pistol. Apparently, the bandits were too. They took off running in the opposite direction, forgetting to leave their guns as instructed.

The man walked up to William and offered his hand to pull him up. William stared at him in disbelief. The man had hair past his shoulders, a full beard, and a receding hairline.

"Are you that Rockwell fellow? The one on the posters around town?" William asked.

"I am, but I'm no criminal," Rockwell said, his hand still outstretched.

I guess, turns out, I would like to meet you in a dark alley. William thought as he grabbed Porter's hand and was pulled to his feet. "Thank you, Mr. Rockwell; looks like I owe you my life."

"You can call me Porter. I'm happy to help. I was a way off when I saw them vermin rough you up and pull you into this alley. Came as quick as I could."

"What can I do to show my thanks?"

"You don't need to do nothing. We're all brothers in God's eye. I was just helping one of my brothers," Porter said.

"You're religious too? You're a very interesting man, Porter."

Porter nodded once. "I best be on my way. I've got to go see if I can catch a ship heading north."

"I'll walk with you. I am headed that way myself. My name's William Chestnut."

"Nice to meet you, William," Porter said, shaking his hand.

William recovered the flowers he had dropped in the street. As they walked along the street, Porter asked, "Those for a lady friend?"

"No, my parents died on the river. I'm going to pay my respects."

"Sorry to hear that."

A thought occurred to William, and he spoke it out loud. "Say, Porter?"

"Yes?"

"If you can shoot as well as you did back there, how is it you didn't kill Governor Boggs?"

"That's what I've been saying! If it were me that had shot at him, he wouldn't still be alive—not that he didn't deserve a good shootin' at, mind you, for all the bad he's done."

"What did he do that was so bad?" William asked.

"Don't tell me you haven't heard about the extermination order he signed to have all Mormons killed or driven from the state?"

"Oh, I did hear about that; I had forgotten," William said.

"I'll never forget it. Militia came in and robbed us, forced us out of our homes, and made our women folk suffer all manner of depredations that a woman should never have to experience."

"You're a Mormon?"

"I am. Best bunch of people you'll ever meet. I'm headed to Nauvoo now to join back up with them and my family."

They arrived at the piers. "Well, Porter, it's been a pleasure. Good luck on your journey."

"Take care of yourself, William."

~ * * * ~

Porter watched as William walked to the end of the pier and started dropping flowers one by one into the river, speaking as he dropped each one. Porter smiled slightly. *I'm glad I helped him so he could have this moment.*

Porter heard a voice behind him. "You sure that's him?"

Porter closed his eyes, inwardly kicking himself for not being more careful. He turned around to see a deputy sheriff, a star badge on his vest, rifle in hand, standing next to the bounty hunter Porter had evaded earlier that day.

"That's definitely him," the bounty hunter said.

"Tie him up," the deputy said, pointing a rifle at Porter's chest. "Make sure it's good and tight."

~ * * * ~

When William finished with the flowers, he turned to go home, then noticed in the distance Porter with his hands tied behind his back, being led by a lawman and another man.

"I've got to help him," William whispered to himself.

William followed the three men to the southeast corner of Chestnut and Sixth Street, where the jail stood. There was a tavern nearby, and William went there to wait until it got darker. He sat down at one of the tables and ordered two meals of fried chicken and mashed potatoes, asking to substitute one of the orders' potatoes with more chicken. He took his time eating. When he was finished, he stayed sipping his beer. He sat thinking of all the ways he could help Porter escape. He had mentally narrowed his list down to three possibilities.

The tavern keeper interrupted his thoughts. "I'm sorry, but I've got to close up. I'm going to have to ask you to leave, even if you haven't finished your meal."

"Oh, that's all right. I was saving this for later."

William wrapped the remaining chicken in a handkerchief and left. Not a glimmer of light shone through the jailhouse windows. It was a late hour, and William was hoping that the jailer either wasn't there or was sleeping.

William walked around to the back of the jailhouse where he could see the barred windows. They were high and small, but he could reach them.

He went to the first one and in a loud whisper asked, "Hey, Porter, you in there?"

A few seconds later, he heard a reply from the next window.

"Over here. Is that you, William?" Porter asked in a loud whisper.

William crept over to the next window. "It's me. I brought you some chicken."

"Well, hand it over then," Porter replied.

William stood on tip toes and forced his bundle through the bars.

"Thank you very much indeed, William," Porter said, taking the bundle.

"It's the least I could do after what you did for me. Listen, Porter, I'm going to get you out of there. From what I've seen today, the way you shot so accurately under duress, I know there is no way you shot Boggs."

"I'm very grateful you want to help me, and this chicken is a heaven send. But I didn't save your life so you could throw it away by becoming an outlaw trying save me."

"But I have a foolproof plan!" William replied.

"Ain't no way you came up with a foolproof plan in the few hours I've been in here. Now listen, I am innocent. They won't convict me of anything. All they have is theory to go on. I'll be out in a few days anyway. But I do appreciate the gesture. Now you get on home before someone sees you. And thanks again for the chicken."

William rubbed his chin. "Have it your way. But I'll be back tomorrow to bring you some more."

"I can agree to that plan," Porter replied.

After a long day of wedding planning with Johanna, William remained true to his promise and brought Porter more fried chicken the next night.

"Porter, I'm going to sneak you a gun tomorrow night; then you can get out," William said.

"I can think of something that would be more useful than a gun," Porter replied.

"What could be more useful than a gun?" William asked.

"A Book of Mormon," Porter replied.

"How is that going to be more useful than a gun?"

"You'd be surprised. Can you get me one?"

"Where do I find one?"

William heard someone from inside yelling at Porter, demanding to know who he was talking to. William figured he'd better leave while he still could.

Unsure where to start looking for a Book of Mormon, William headed for home wondering along the way how Porter planned to use the book.

~ * * * ~

In the morning, William heard a knock at his door. He opened it to see a tall, burly man with a long beard and overalls.

"Howdy, I'm Jim Beaman. I saw you were advertising for someone to run your farm."

"Yes, come in," William said, leading him to the table. "Please have a seat. Can I get you anything?"

They sat down. "No, I'm fine, thank you,"

"What experience do you have running a farm?" William asked.

"Oh, I was born and raised on a farm. I've run my own since I was old enough to own my own property."

"Would you be able to run both your farm and mine at the same time?"

"I don't have one anymore. All my land was taken in a lawsuit. I just moved here from Pennsylvania and bought twenty acres on the west end. But apparently, the man who sold it to me had no rights to the land. The man who did have the rights took it back through the courts after I had improved it." Jim lifted his shoulders. "Now I'm left with nothing, and the man who sold me the land is long gone."

"I'll give you two dollars a week, and you can keep 5 percent of what the farm produces," William said.

"That's very generous of you. Thank you."

"You can start soon as you're ready. I'll write up a contract for you to sign later."

"Thank you; I'll be back tomorrow to start."

~ * * * ~

"Where're we going today?" Johanna asked.

"I thought we might do some window shopping," William replied.

"Window shopping sounds fun. What are we looking for?"

"Just some small things for our wedding."

In shop after shop, Johanna found many things she thought would be good to get for the wedding, but William was unsuccessful in locating a Book of Mormon in any one of them. He resolved to visit Porter again that night and get a better idea of where to locate one—and perhaps gain some insight on how he intended to use the book to get out.

That night, William went to visit Porter at the jail. He went to the same window and called for Porter. Not getting a response, he raised his voice a little louder. Then he saw a light come on, and someone from inside shouted, "Who is that?" William got nervous and ran off.

The next day William found out Porter had been moved, but the jailer was unwilling to share any other details. Disappointed, William headed back home. It was time to focus on his upcoming wedding.

~ * * * ~

Johanna, dressed in a white lace wedding gown, stepped in unison with her father to the slow rhythm of the music down the chapel isle. Her hand shook as they walked. Her father gave her hand a reassuring squeeze. William was dressed in his blue frock coat, a flower in his lapel, a white waistcoat underneath, with doeskin lavender trousers. He waited in anticipation as Johanna and her father drew closer.

Johanna looked like an angel gliding toward him. Her smile lit up her countenance. Her auburn hair flowed down the sides of her face as the curls at the ends bobbed gently against her cheeks. As they got to where William and the pastor were standing, Mr. Nancy took Johanna's hand and gave it to William, then went and stood to the side.

As the pastor said the words of the ceremony and finished with until death do you part, William had a fleeting thought, that if it were possible they would never part, not even in death.

Chapter 27
First Bundle

August 1843

Johanna put her book down and went to look for William. She found him in the stables, tending to Destiny.

"Hey, handsome," Johanna said.

"Hey, darling, what are you doing out here?" William asked.

"I just wanted to talk."

"All right. I'll be in in a bit."

"Can't you talk while you work?"

"I suppose I can, but in my experience, talking while you work makes the work go slower."

Johanna tilted her head, raised her eyebrows, and slightly frowned.

Not hearing a response, William eyed her. "Come on, don't look at me like that."

Her expression remained unchanged.

"What's on your mind, then?" William asked as he continued brushing the horse.

"I think I'm getting fat," Johanna said.

"Nonsense, sweetheart; you're as beautiful as ever. Besides, you hardly eat anything. I don't think you're putting on weight."

"There are other ways for a woman to put on weight besides eating."

"I didn't think you liked beer," William said, smiling slightly, still brushing the horse.

"I don't," Johanna said, a little sternly.

"Don't worry about your weight, sweetheart. You're as pretty as a daisy blooming in the spring."

"Well, that's nice of you to say. But maybe I *want* to get a little bigger," Johanna said, putting her hand on her stomach.

"Now why would you—" William stopped brushing the horse. "Johanna, are you saying . . ."

Johanna smiled and nodded her head.

William dropped the brush and came out of the horse stall, grinning from ear to ear. "That's wonderful!" he said, embracing and kissing her.

"William?" Johanna said, pulling away.

"Yes?"

"Don't you think we ought to start attending a church?"

"I guess we should. It's just that . . . well, I'm not sure which is the right one."

"I want our children to grow up to be God-fearing Christians. They're not likely to do that if we don't take them to church every Sunday."

“I can see the wisdom in that. My parents always made sure I went to church, and I guess it helped me a little bit. We can start attending different congregations every Sunday until we find one that suits us.”

“Thank you, William,” Johanna said as she pulled him into another kiss.

Chapter 28
Realization of Truth

October 1843

William always took the weekends off from work to run errands, pick up supplies, and spend time with his wife. He and Johanna had also been attending different congregations on Sundays, but most of them made God sound angry and mean, which was not William's view of God.

One Sunday, a preacher from one of the congregations they had attended came by the house.

"Hello, William. What did you think of our service?"

"It was all right. My wife and I are trying to find a congregation to belong to; we're trying out as many as we can to see which one suits us best. So, if you don't see us again for a while, that's why."

"That's an important decision—one that has the welfare of your soul at stake. Just as I taught, the Lord will punish those who don't follow in His paths, and we teach how to do just that."

"Seems like most of the preaching I've heard talks about fearing God too much and trusting in him too little."

~ * * * ~

It had been many months since William met Porter, but as he sat tending his store, his thoughts returned to what Porter had said. He still wondered why Porter would rather have a Book of Mormon than a gun. Try as he might, he had not been able to find the book, though he searched for one every time he entered a store that sold books. He thought that for a group that made the news so much, the Mormons sure kept their book well hidden.

Just then, two well-dressed men walked in—and that was interesting, because most folks didn't walk into William's store well dressed. One of the men was clean shaven and had long sideburns and short hair. The other man had longer hair and a mustache.

William noticed they were each holding the same book. "Welcome, gentleman," William said.

"Good afternoon," the man with the mustache replied.

"What's the big occasion? Why are you so dressed up?" William asked.

"We're missionaries on the Lord's errand. I'm Elder Robert Reid, and this is Elder James Palmer," the man with the mustache replied.

"I'm William Chestnut. My wife and I have attended quite a few churches. Which congregation are you fellows with?"

"We are with The Church of Jesus Christ of Latter-day Saints," Elder Palmer replied. "We were impressed by the Spirit that we should come into your shop."

"Is that so? Well, as long as you are here, and there are no customers, why don't you go ahead and tell me a little bit about your religion. For instance, what makes it better than any other?"

Both men smiled and looked at each other. One nodded to the other, and Elder Reid answered. "One big difference between us and other religions is that we believe the Lord has restored the organization of His church to the earth, with prophets and apostles. The Lord has called a man to be his prophet in our time. He has given that prophet His priesthood authority, through the ministration of angels. That same priesthood has been given to us so that we have the authority to act in God's name, to baptize, and to teach His gospel."

"Wow. I wasn't expecting that. Prophets and angels?"

"Yes," Elder Palmer said. "The Lord Himself appeared to a man named Joseph Smith and taught him. Later, the Lord sent an angel to tell Joseph where he could find some gold plates buried in a hill. He got the plates and translated them from an ancient language into English through the gift and power of God. Now we have the words of the ancient prophets of this continent in this book." Elder Palmer set his book on the counter in front of William.

William touched it. *It's the elusive Book of Mormon.* His mind flashed back to seeing his aunt and uncle dead in their house, a book just like this one lying next to her, in her blood. He then thought of the preacher in the street in Illinois and what he had said about this book. Finally, his thoughts turned to how Porter wanted one of these books more than he wanted a gun.

"You're Mormons? I thought you said you were from The Church of Jesus Christ of . . . somethin' or other."

"Latter-day Saints. Yes, that is the name of our church, but people have taken to calling us Mormons because we have this new book of scripture," Elder Reid said, gesturing toward the Book of Mormon. "In its pages you can find answers to many hard questions. For example, did you ever wonder what the purpose of this life is, or where we go after death?"

"As a matter of fact, yes. My parents died not too long ago. I have often wondered about where they are now." William considered the two men for a moment. "What makes you two believe all this talk of angels and prophets and new scripture?"

Elder Reid answered, "There is a promise recorded in the Book of Mormon that anyone who wants to know the truth of these things need only ask God, and He will make it known to you through the power of the Holy Ghost."

"And you've tried this promise?" William asked.

"Yes. And I know this book is the word of God," Elder Reid replied.

William started to feel a warm feeling in his chest as Elder Reid spoke.

"James, from the New Testament, also said that if you lack wisdom, then you just need to ask God in faith, and it will be given to you," Elder Palmer added.

"How much for one of those books?" William asked.

"Just $1.25. We would also like to invite you to our worship service this Sunday," Elder Reid said.

William grabbed the book and handed them the money, "Well, I'll take the book and get back to you on attendin' worship service."

"All right. We'll be around town. We hold meetings on Sundays and Wednesdays in the building next to the Liberty Engine House," Elder Reid said.

This must be some book if they're selling it for what most people earn in an entire day.

William remembered something that had come up in his conversation with Porter. "Why are you folks still around preaching? Isn't there an extermination order in place for Mormons in this state?"

"Yes, but we have found that the vast majority of people in St. Louis disagree with it," Elder Palmer said. "This city has more religious toleration than we've seen in most other places in this nation. We've had a congregation here since before that order was issued, and it continues to thrive today."

"I guess I can see that," William replied. "Thanks for stopping by."

As the men left, William stuffed the book in his satchel.

His mind kept drifting to the book as he worked through the day. He was interested in how this book captured the passion of so many people. He wondered if it could really tell him about where his parents went after they died. His aunt and uncle had died because of this book, and it was heralded to him as another testament of Jesus Christ. Porter valued it over a gun. Now he was told God would communicate with him through the Holy Ghost to prove its truth.

William looked at the clock. It was finally time to go home. He grabbed the satchel, locked up the store, and got Destiny out of the stable.

As he approached his home, he went straight to the stables and did a rush job of taking care of Destiny then went straight to his tool shed. He opened the book and started to read. He read until the sun didn't provide enough light to see the words. He hid the book behind his tools, then went in the house.

"How was work?" Johanna asked.

"Sorry I'm late. I had some things to take care of before I closed up. How are you feeling?" William asked.

Johanna's belly was starting to show. "I think I've gotten over the morning sickness. I've been feeling pretty full of energy today."

"That's good," William said.

"I was reading the newspapers you brought in from town."

William looked at her. "Anything interesting?"

"There was an article that said hundreds of those strange Mormons have come from England to live in St. Louis."

"It called them *strange Mormons*?"

"No, I called them that. They believe all sorts of strange things about angels and prophets," Johanna said.

William nodded. "Yeah, a couple of them came into my store today. They said all sorts of stuff like that."

"I don't know how they can believe all that crazy talk. Though it's too bad they're being treated so poorly in the western end of the state. No one deserves the treatment they get, even if they do have some bizarre beliefs," Johanna said.

"I feel the same way," William replied.

He did think that some of what the elders said was unusual, but he wanted to know more about them. Much of what they said piqued his interest. He didn't want Johanna thinking he was strange for looking further into the religion. He thought it best if Johanna didn't know he had decided to read their book.

~ * * * ~

Because the next day was Saturday, William didn't have to work, so he told Johanna he was going to work in the barn and straighten up the tool shed. He went there, pulled out the Book of Mormon, and continued reading. He was so engrossed in the book that he almost didn't hear Johanna calling him in for supper.

As the week continued, he spent every spare moment reading the book in his tool shed. As he read, he felt he needed to turn to the Savior and repent of his sins.

The following Saturday he awoke early, got a lantern, and went back to the tool shed. He got the book from its hiding place and took it to the barn, where he could be more comfortable.

William read through the morning. When he was finally done, he shut the book and stared at the hay. He thought about the description of the Savior visiting the people on the American continent. He pondered what he read about the Savior's teachings on faith and baptism. He realized that he had never been baptized, but according to this book it was crucial to his salvation. He needed to know if this book was really God's word, or if it was just the imagination of this Joseph Smith fellow.

He remembered reading the verse in the book that exhorted the reader to ask God if it was true. William was determined to find out. Accordingly, he returned to the nearby shed, where he knew he would not be disturbed.

He started praying silently. He was grateful for the knowledge he had received and wanted to get baptized but wasn't certain who should baptize him. He thought that if he knew this book was true, then he would know where to go to get baptized.

He prayerfully pleaded, "Please help me to know with a certainty if this book is true."

A strange feeling entered his bosom, a feeling of immense peace and love. The feeling started to intensify and grew until it enveloped his entire being. He couldn't ever remember feeling like this before. Tears rolled down his cheeks, but he wasn't sure why he was crying. He felt an extreme happiness and gratitude wash over him as he realized that God heard his prayer—and he knew this was God's answer. He rose, all doubt erased from his mind. He needed to join this church, and the Book of Mormon was indeed from God.

Chapter 29
Spring Surprise

William left the shed and immediately ran into the house with the Book of Mormon in his hand, happier than he could remember ever being. Johanna was sewing at the dining table. When she looked up at him, she noticed the book in his hand.

"What you got there?" she asked.

William realized that he still had the Book of Mormon in his hand. In his excitement, he had forgotten to stash it in its hiding place.

"Oh . . . yeah, I was in town this morning, and some of those crazy Mormons insisted I read their book. I was trying to walk away but they were so persistent, I just took it so they'd leave me alone." He threw the book on the table. "Here, you can get rid of it for me."

As he walked up the stairs, an idea came to him. "Don't even think about reading it!" he called down to his wife as he disappeared from view.

~ * * * ~

Johanna eyed the book carefully and picked it up, thinking, *He can't tell me what I can't read.* Still wondering why those Mormons always seemed so happy and why everyone else was so against them, she stashed the book away in her bag, determined to get some answers.

The next morning after breakfast, William told Johanna, "I'm headed out to the market to get some tools."

Johanna gave him a kiss and a hug.

"When will you be back?"

"I've got a lot of business to attend to so probably not until supper."

"All right; be safe," Johanna said as she watched him get on his horse. "And try to steer clear of those Mormons. We don't want any more of those poisonous books!"

"Yes, dear," William called back as he rode away.

Johanna watched as he turned the corner and was out of sight, then went straight to her bag, pulled out the Book of Mormon, and started reading.

~ * * * ~

William found the Mormon missionaries preaching on the town's main street.

"Greetings, Mr. Reid."

"Hey, William!" Elder Reid said as he waved goodbye to one of his listeners.

"I've read that book I bought from you," William said.

"And?"

"And I want to be baptized," William replied.

Elder Palmer smiled. "That's wonderful news! We are having a baptismal service on the last day of the month about a mile south of the ferry."

William shook his hand. "I'll be there."

~ * * * ~

By the week's end, Johanna had read most of the Book of Mormon. She read it every time William went to work or had to pick up something in town. She hid it behind her other books when she had to put it away.

She nearly got caught reading it once when William came home unexpectedly to pick up some supplies he had forgotten to take with him, but Johanna was successful in hiding the book under the table, obscured by the dangling tablecloth, before William saw it.

She wanted to know more about the man who wrote the book. It read like it was scripture, and Johanna felt like the things she was reading were exactly what she needed to know at that time in her life to help her grow closer to God.

Johanna went out, leaving a note for William that she was on a social visit to see her friends. She needed to find the Mormon missionaries. She had so many questions. As she walked toward the barbershop, she noticed two men. Both were carrying a book that looked similar to the one she was reading. Johanna ran up to them and introduced herself. Her belly was big and round, and she held one hand to her stomach, feeling the baby kick.

"Excuse me, I am Johanna Chestnut; are you two Mormon missionaries?"

"Yes, we are. Telemachus Rogers is my name. Nice to meet you," he said, shaking her hand. "And this is my friend Benjamin Morgan."

"I've been reading the Book of Mormon. Do you have time to answer my questions?"

"Yes, of course. What questions did you have?"

Johanna walked with the missionaries and started throwing all sorts of questions at them. Did they know who wrote the book? What kind of person was he? Why would the Lord be talking to people today? What happens to us after we die? What is the purpose of this life? What did they believe about the Bible?

After talking for about an hour, Brother Rogers said, "We've got to go. We have another engagement we need to get to. Can we meet tomorrow? We could answer the rest of your questions and share what the Lord has restored through a living prophet."

"I'd like that," Johanna said.

Over the next week, Johanna kept finding times to sneak away to be taught by the missionaries. Finally, she told the missionaries, "I would like to be baptized."

"We have a baptismal service at the end of the month a mile south of the ferry. It's early in the morning, so if you can get away, we can do it then," Brother Rodgers told her.

~ * * * ~

As the day for his baptism neared, William wasn't sure what Johanna had done with the book he left her. He figured he would let her know about all this gradually—drop a few hints here and there, maybe arrange an "accidental" meeting with the missionaries.

Finally, William thought he would test the waters to see if she might be open to talking about the Mormons. "I ran into some of those Mormons again in town yesterday."

Johanna sat up straight and wrung her hands.

"Oh. I'm sorry you had to endure them again," Johanna said, eyes wide, looking away.

"They tried to talk to me, but I told them off," William lied.

They both got silent, then Johanna said, "So, since tomorrow is the last day of the month in the morning, I have an important meeting with some of the prominent women in the city and a few of my friends. It's across town, so I'll be gone most of the morning."

"Prominent women? What kind of meeting is it?" William asked.

"Well . . ." Johanna hesitated. "We're going to talk about what the women of this city can do to help the poor."

"That's nice."

"I hope you won't miss me too much."

"Actually, I'll be gone in the morning too," William said.

"Where are you going?"

William paused, frantically thinking of something to say. "Well, as you said, tomorrow is the last day of the month. I've got to leave early to get the books balanced and next month's inventory started."

"It sounds like you've got your work cut out for you. I'm going to turn in," Johanna said.

"Good idea. I think I will too."

~ * * * ~

The next morning, both William and Johanna got up early and got ready. William waited until Johanna had left the room, then went to his dresser and grabbed an extra pair of clothes. As he shoved them in a bag, Johanna walked in the room.

When she saw what he was doing, she asked, "What are the extra clothes for?"

"After I've done inventory I was going to visit the bank, and I wanted to change into some fresh clothes."

"Oh," Johanna said, giving him a queer look. "All right."

Johanna had planned to dress in a gown and would be carrying an extra set of clothes to change into after she was baptized. She didn't want William to see her leaving in a gown. The less he had to question the better—but William took his time getting out the door.

Johanna had Bessie pack William's breakfast, and she gave it to William as he came down the stairs.

"Here's your breakfast. You'd best get going," she said. "That inventory won't do itself."

"What's the hurry?" William asked.

"Well . . . I want to spend some time with you after lunch. Hurry so you can be back sooner."

"I'm going," William said, smiling as he walked toward the door. "Have fun at your meeting."

"I will. Love you, dear," Johanna said, waving goodbye.

William made his way to the river side and worked his way to the baptism location. Since Johanna was so effective at getting him out the door, he was there early.

~ * * * ~

Johanna waited about ten minutes after William left to dress in her gown, pack an extra set of clothes, and head off toward the river. By the time she got there, a large crowd of people had already gathered. They appeared to be in the middle of receiving instructions from a group of missionaries.

Johanna went to join the group, who were all standing, listening intently to one of the missionaries describe the process. She tapped a man on the back of the shoulder. "What did I miss?"

~ * * * ~

William felt someone tapping him on the back of his shoulder then was horrified when he heard his wife's voice. He slowly turned around, fully expecting a sound chastisement. He was afraid she might leave him over this. When he turned and saw Johanna standing there in a gown with a change of clothes in her hand, his jaw dropped.

~ * * * ~

As full recognition dawned on her, Johanna took a step back, and they both just stood there staring at each other.

"What are you doing here?" Johanna finally asked.

"Getting baptized," William responded, starting to smile. "What are you doing here?"

"Getting baptized," Johanna replied.

They both laughed and then embraced.

"You mean to tell me I've been spending all this time sneaking around with the missionaries for nothing?" William asked.

"Well, I wouldn't say it was for nothing. At least you came around about the Mormons," Johanna replied, smiling.

"When did you come around?" William asked.

"When you told me to throw that Book of Mormon away. I couldn't help but read it," Johanna said.

"Come here," William said as he pulled her close and kissed her. "I guess I shouldn't have been so secretive. I'm sorry."

"I was just as bad," Johanna said. "From here on out, no more secrets from each other."

William nodded. "I promise."

"Me too," Johanna said and kissed William again.

Chapter 30
Take What's Owed

September 1, 1844

Rupert handed the documents with forged signatures to the banker, who accepted them. Rupert and Otto now had the money they needed to buy their first steamboat.

Their next order of business was to get the steamboat operational. They hired a mechanic, knowing full well they did not have any funds with which to pay him for his work. The mechanic worked on the engine for several weeks, then came back to them.

"I've got it so that it's working, but you'll need a new part to equip it to take heavy stress. It's a $100 part. The engines could blow if you put it under a lot of stress before getting it replaced. For example, you wouldn't want to take it upriver in icy water."

"Until we can afford to get the part, we'll make sure we don't put too much stress on the boilers," Rupert said. He leaned forward.

"Could you show us how to operate the ship and what to watch for? We'll give you a 10 percent bonus for your trouble."

"I guess I could do that. When do you want to go?"

"We'd need that instruction right now so we can take it for a test drive and make sure everything you did to fix it works."

"Well, I suppose it's all right. Let's take her out," the mechanic said.

The *Saluda* wasn't the nicest-looking steamboat, but it had everything it needed. The mechanic gave them a tour of their ship, telling them what every part was and what everything did. Rupert paid attention only to the parts he needed to know to make the ship run. A competent crew could handle the rest.

He started the boilers, and they were underway. They went out on the river and each got a chance to stop and start the boat, put it in reverse, and pull it forward. The mechanic was also very explicit in telling them the conditions under which too much pressure could cause the boilers to blow.

"Well, you've been very helpful, but I'm afraid we can't pay you," Rupert said.

"Why not? I kept my part of the bargain. I had other things to do today and wouldn't have even come if you hadn't mentioned the bonus," the mechanic said, gruffly.

"You did a great job; we just don't have the money. Perhaps we can make payments over time until we've paid you in full," Rupert said, fully expecting the man to reject his offer.

The mechanic's face reddened. "I'll see you two in prison for this."

"You would throw us in prison, even though we're willing to pay you?" Rupert asked.

"You bet I would. I'll also take claim to your ship to pay your debt. I don't work for free, and we agreed to payment upon completion, not over a few years. I might never see you again once you leave port."

"You'd take this ship from us? You hear that, Otto? Just like I told you. I wanted to work out a deal, but he wants to take everything we've worked so hard for and throw us in prison."

"You should make a deal with us. It's not right to just take everything from us," Otto said.

The mechanic balled up his fists. "It's not right that you're not keeping your end of the deal. I'll have you arrested as soon as we reach shore."

Rupert held up his hands. "Wait, wait. Hold on. There is no need to involve the law. I have an idea, and I think we might be able to work out payment in full. Just let me talk to my friend for a second."

They left the bridge area of the steamboat. Otto looked nervous. "What we gonna do, Rupert? I don't want to go to jail."

Rupert lowered his voice. "I don't either. But I don't think we have to. Listen, nobody knows that he got on this ship with us. If we take him out permanently, he can't do anything to us, and he can't take our ship."

Otto was shocked as Rupert pulled out a long knife. "You mean . . . murder him?"

"It's more like self-defense. If we don't take *him* out, he'll take *us* out. We might as well be dead if we're in prison, right?"

Otto scratched his chin. "I guess so."

Rupert gave him the knife. "I'll talk to him and make him believe we worked it out. You take that knife and hide it behind your vest and move like you're going to inspect the controls on the ship.

Then stab him in the back, right to the heart. We'll dump him in the river, and no one will be the wiser."

"Why do *I* have to do it?" Otto asked.

"He's expecting to negotiate with me, and if I do it while talking to him, he'll see it coming a mile away," Rupert said.

"All right," Otto said. It took him a minute to mentally process what he was about to do. Finally, he nodded his head.

They carried out their design, and everything went as planned. It was over in an instant. Otto threw up the first time he tried to pick up the lifeless body. Rupert just stared, stunned. He didn't think killing someone would make him feel so different inside. They dumped the body overboard and went back to port at New Orleans.

As they sailed back, Rupert said, "We need to do the same to the banker, then break into the bank and get the records he made of our transaction. Then we will be debt free, and we'll be able to live our dream on the river."

When they got back, they offered the banker a personal ride on what they called their "first test run" of their new steamboat. He agreed, and they did the same to him as they did the mechanic. They got the bank keys from the dead banker before dumping his body into the river. That night, they broke into the bank and took their bank records.

Rupert left the keys and a note on the banker's desk that read:

Dear Boss,

I quit. This place is ridiculous. I've worked hard here and should have been promoted by now. Because of your lack of appreciation for my work, I am off to

> the eastern states to get a real job from an institution
> that will appreciate my talents.

Rupert then signed the banker's name, using his loan documents to copy the signature. Then he and Otto fled into the night.

Chapter 31
Mourning a Prophet

April 11, 1844

Johanna sat in bed holding her newborn girl in her arms. William walked into the room and sat down on the bed next to her. "She's a beauty."

Johanna handed him the baby. William gazed into his little girl's face, smiling and marveling that he had helped create something so beautiful and fragile.

"I think we should name her after you. We'll call her little Jojo," William said.

Johanna furrowed her brow. "Not Jojo."

William shrugged. "Well, then, Hanna."

"That's my grandmother's name. It's taken," Johanna said. "How about Anna?"

"I don't like the *a* sound at the end. I say it's Ann," William said.

"Ann," Johanna repeated. "Our baby, Ann Catherine Chestnut."

~ * * * ~

The Sunday after their baptism, Johanna and William attended church. President Small, the branch president, personally welcomed them. James Riley invited them to sit by his family. As they attended their church meetings, they felt like the Church had everything they had been looking for.

The month after Ann was born, they were surprised when they got to their meeting to see two of the Twelve Apostles sitting in the front. The meetinghouse held about three hundred people, and it was filled to capacity.

The Apostles gave wonderful messages, focusing on the Savior and His Atonement. They also talked about the Prophet Joseph Smith, who was running for president, and how this nation needed leadership that trusted in God and could guide the nation in righteousness, ensuring equal treatment for all.

That night, as Johanna sat in her rocking chair feeding the baby, William sat nearby cleaning his guns.

"William, don't you think it would be nice to live in Nauvoo, to hear things straight from the Prophet, instead of always hearing what he has to tell us from someone else?"

"I suppose so," William replied. "Nauvoo would be teaming with folks who think like us. Not that the people of St. Louis aren't good people. The honorable people here have more common sense and toleration for religious differences than the whole rest of the state combined. You've seen how the papers here regularly cry out at the injustices that the governor and the western part of this state have heaped on the Saints who used to be in that area."

Johanna nodded. "I agree. Our neighbors have been wonderful, even if they are not of our faith. But we could be in the heart of the Church, with the main body of the Saints, and be taught directly from a living prophet's mouth."

William touched his chin. "To actually see and hear a living prophet of God would be a wonderful experience. I'll make arrangements for someone to watch my store, and then I'll catch the next steamboat up the Mississippi to Nauvoo to see if I can find any good prospects for us there."

"Thank you, William," Johanna said, smiling.

"I love that smile," William said as he walked across the room and kissed her.

~ * * * ~

It took William about four weeks to make all the arrangements necessary for his trip to Nauvoo while leaving his wife in good hands while she took care of the baby. He ended up hiring some additional staff to take care of the things he regularly did around the home.

Since Brother Palmer had a tailor shop, William told him he could sell his clothes with William's goods if he would tend the shop while he was away. Brother Palmer agreed, since William had an existing customer base to whom he could introduce his product and increase his own sales.

William boarded a steamboat headed for Nauvoo on June 26. It would be a two-day journey. William's excitement and anticipation grew, as he would finally get to meet the Prophet Joseph. Other Saints on the steamboat were also headed to Nauvoo. One man he met, told him that the Prophet could usually be found at the Mansion House, which he and his wife ran as a hotel.

The next day the steamboat pulled into the docks at Nauvoo a little after five in the evening. As William picked up his things and said his goodbyes to his traveling companions, an intense sadness came over him. He wasn't sure of the cause of his down feeling, so he tried to shake it off as best he could and headed into town.

The beautiful limestone temple stood on the hill, towering over the city and still under construction. At the river's edge, a four-story hotel stood, welcoming visitors as they came into the city from the river. People were walking about the streets, busy with their individual priorities.

There were blacksmiths, gunsmiths, a university, rope makers, lumberyards, brick makers, and shopkeepers. It was a beautiful city, teeming with life and industry. William could see himself being successful here. Buildings were being constructed all around the edges of the city, and there was plenty of room for more growth.

William located the Mansion House. It was a large, square, two-story building with four chimneys. The front of the building had a large door with a window directly over it and four more windows on each side of the door.

Great drops of rain started to fall. He hurried in and saw an elderly man with white hair standing behind a desk.

"Hello; welcome to the Mansion House. Come in out of the rain," the man said.

"I got here just in time. I would hate to be out there caught in that storm," William said.

"Yes, you're a lucky one indeed. I'm Ebenezer Robbinson. You can see some mummies on display for twenty-five cents. Or you're welcome to rent one of the rooms."

"Thank you; I've seen mummies before, and once is enough for me. I'll be here for about two weeks," William replied.

"Very well; that'll be $1.50 per week," Ebenezer said.

"I heard the Prophet ran this place. Is he out today?" William asked.

"Oh, no, he turned this place over to me back in January. But if you're looking for him, your chances aren't very good. He went up to Carthage a few days ago. Turned himself in on some trumped-up charges."

Williams eyebrows shot up. "Turned himself in! What will happen to him now?"

"Some think he'll get free. He always has before. Although he was convinced that he was seeing Nauvoo for the last time. He said he was going like a lamb to the slaughter," Ebenezer said.

William's eyes widened. "I hope that's not true."

"Guess he just had a feeling," Ebenezer replied.

~ * * * ~

June 27, 1844

The next morning, William got up and headed over to the city offices to see about a plot of land. Just before he reached the door, he heard a faint yelling and galloping hooves in the distance. He stopped to see if he could make out what was being shouted. As he listened, the voice and the horse hooves were getting louder.

He saw a person on horseback riding through the streets. William couldn't believe his eyes as he recognized Porter Rockwell. His hair and beard were much longer than William remembered, but it was definitely him. As Porter got closer, William could see tears in his eyes. Porter kept his head straight forward, intent on his destination, and William now understood what he was saying.

"Joseph is killed. They have killed him! Damn them! They have killed him."

As Porter rode by, William stood there in shock. *How could he be dead?* An emptiness sank through his heart. He mourned that he would never see him or hear him preach. He wondered what would become of the Church without its leader and founder. A deep depression and sadness sank in. William was at a loss as to what he should do next. It didn't make much sense to keep looking to purchase or build a new home now.

Everywhere William went, the Prophet's death was all people were talking about. Melancholy rested on the city like a heavy blanket.

~ * * * ~

Later that day, a message came in from Willard Richards that was repeated to the Saints verbally. "Joseph and Hyrum are dead. Taylor is wounded, not very badly. I am well. . . . The job was done in an instant."

The next day, the whole city was in mourning. Glum expressions met William everywhere he went. As William had lunch at a local tavern, he overheard the news spreading of another message that had come in that morning from Willard, which had simply stated, "Be still, be patient." Governor Ford wrote a postscript advising the Saints to defend themselves if necessary until protection could be furnished.

Word had spread that the bodies of the Prophet and patriarch were approaching the city. By 2:30 p.m., the streets were lined with thousands of people who were waiting for the two bodies to come by. By 3:00 p.m., the wagons pulling the coffins rolled into town. They sat atop two separate wagons in rough oak boxes. The wagons were driven by Artois Hamilton, who kept the inn that housed the bodies the previous night, and Samuel Smith, the Prophet's brother; both looked forlorn and solemn. Eight members of the state militia escorted the wagons. As they drove the wagons down Mulholland Street, the thousands of people who lined the road followed them.

William didn't think he had ever felt so sad in his life or seen such a large group in such a state as these people were. Silent tears flowed freely down the cheeks of those looking on. The Saints watched in reverence as the coffins that held the dead bodies of their cherished patriarch and prophet, covered in brush, were driven through the street. The sound of the horses' hooves intensified with William's feelings of sorrow as he watched them approach and pass him.

The atmosphere in Nauvoo was permeated with mourning and sorrow, which only served to deepen William's own melancholy mood. The whole reason he was here had just been carted through the street in a coffin. He thought about how neither he, nor Johanna would ever hear Joseph Smith speak, shake his hand, or be able to look in his eyes. These thoughts only served to escalate his dreary state.

The bodies were taken to the Mansion House, where the doors remained closed to all but immediate family. William figured he would have to find alternate lodgings that night.

That evening the Apostle Willard Richards gathered the people of the city and earnestly implored the Saints to keep the peace and not retaliate. He asked for a sustaining vote in keeping the peace. It would be up to the laws of the land and God to bring the perpetrators of this awful crime to justice. William and thousands of other Saints, standing all around, raised their hands agreeing to sustain the decision of this Apostle.

The next day, a Saturday, the Saints were finally allowed to view the bodies. William got in the line of about twenty thousand people waiting to see the Prophet. The line moved for nine hours. William entered the Mansion House in half that time. William didn't mind the wait; this would be the only time he could ever see the Prophet and patriarch. It was not how he envisioned first seeing them, but he was grateful he got to see them at all.

When William finally got inside the Mansion House, he got his first glimpse of the Prophet and his brother Hyrum, the patriarch, through the glass that lay over the coffins. Both their eyes were closed. They looked peaceful and reposed. As he gazed on Joseph, William was filled with the Spirit that affirmed to him that Joseph truly was God's prophet.

Later that night, William listened as a man by the name of William W. Phelps gave a funeral sermon for the Prophet. He shared a moving poem he had written that started, "Praise to the man who communed with Jehovah, Jesus anointed that prophet and seer.

Blessed to open the last dispensation, Kings shall extol him and nations revere."

Chapter 32
Defending the Saints

June 29, 1844

William woke up the next day reflecting on his experiences of the last few days, then his thoughts turned to Johanna. He wondered what she was doing at that moment.

He left the Mansion House, remembering the governor's warning. William thought it wise to purchase a revolver. He did so and wore it in a holster around his waist in case he needed it for defense.

As he headed back to the hotel, William saw Porter walking down the street talking to another man. William approached him. "Porter! How have you been?"

Porter smiled. "Well, I'll be. William, isn't it? What are you doing in Nauvoo?"

"I came to see about potentially buying property to build a house on, but now with the death of the Prophet, I reckon maybe St. Louis is as good a place as any to stay."

"Wait—you've joined the Church since last I saw you?"

"I have. I went looking for that Book of Mormon you asked for, though by the time I found one, you were long gone. How were you going to use the book to escape jail?" William asked.

Porter smiled. "I wasn't. But since you were so eager to get me something, I thought I'd send you off to get something that would get you into less trouble, something that would be more beneficial to you in the long term. Looks like it was."

"It was," William replied.

Porter jerked his chin toward the man next to him. "William Chestnut, this is William Clayton."

Clayton shook William's hand before glancing down at his firearm and asking, "You any good with that thing?"

"Nowhere near as good as Porter, but I had some practice with one of these growing up. I also used them quite a bit when I fought in the Second Seminole Indian War."

"Porter and I were just talking about the need to keep watch for mobs around the perimeter of the city," Clayton explained. "The mob has been raiding homes and robbing and whipping the husbands. A few homes have been burned. If you're available, we could use help protecting the city."

William thought about Johanna and his need to go back to her and Ann. But it also made his blood boil knowing that the mob would be so blindly brutal to such good people. "I will for a few weeks; I need to write to my wife and see how she is doing. If she is all right with it, I'll stay a bit longer."

Porter smiled and shook William's hand. "Thanks for the help."

William went to his hotel and wrote to Johanna.

Dear Johanna,

I've arrived safely at Nauvoo. The day after I got here, we got word that the Prophet and his brother, Hyrum, had been assassinated. They are requesting help to patrol the city and keep the Saints safe. I've considered staying until the end of next month to help but won't if it will be too much of a burden on you to have me gone. Let me know your opinion on the matter as soon as possible.

All my love,

William

From that day he went on regular patrols with the city guard. Sixteen days later, he received Johanna's response.

Dear William,

It deeply saddens me to hear that awful news. Brothers Palmer and Riley are checking in on me regularly, and the Relief Society sisters have also been visiting me regularly and helping me as well. President Small also stops by on occasion. Our branch has been so supportive while you have been away. If they need your help there to keep the city safe, I think it would be all right if you stayed there awhile longer. There was a big rainstorm about a week ago that flooded the river, though the flood didn't get to our farm. Stay safe and don't do anything that would put yourself in danger. I will be praying for you.

Love,

Johanna

William went to the regular meeting of the volunteer city guard that had gathered by the temple. Porter and William Clayton were organizing and leading the group.

"This week's assignments are as follows: Brother Able, you and Brother Chestnut can take the southeast end of the city. Brother Clayton and I will cover the northeast end. We'll have Brother Picket and Brother Roberts cover the central area, and the rest of you can patrol the river side."

Elijah Able was the only black man at the gathering. William hadn't ever really talked to a black man before and was unsure what to say to him as they started off on their assignment.

William and Elijah rode alongside each other toward the edge of the city in awkward silence. William finally asked, "You're a free black man?"

Elijah seemed to contemplate him for a minute. "What do you think?"

"Sorry, I guess that's obvious." William tried to break the silence changing topics. "How long have you been a member of the Church?"

"Fourteen years."

"What do you do when you're not patrolling the city?"

"I'm a carpenter by trade, though lately I've been working as the undertaker. How about you?"

"I own a general store in St. Louis."

"You have a family?" Elijah asked.

A shot pierced the air. He felt a sudden pain in his shoulder as an invisible force pushed him off his horse. William fell to the ground and grabbed at the searing pain.

Elijah took two shots aimed at a spot in the brush where gun smoke hung in the air. William heard a shout. A rifle aimed at Elijah fell to the ground.

Two men came out of hiding. One of them turned and ran while the other exclaimed, aiming his rifle at Elijah, "You killed my brother! You ni—"

Elijah shot once. Before the man could finish his sentence, he fell to the ground dead.

Elijah quickly dismounted and ran to William, who was bleeding from the shoulder.

"You all right?" Elijah asked.

"I don't know. I'm losing a lot of blood. It hurts something awful."

Elijah examined William's wound. "Looks like it's in your shoulder." He used a knife to tear off pieces of his shirt, which he tied around William's shoulder to stop the bleeding. "I'm going to give you a blessing of healing, Brother Chestnut."

William squinted his eyes. "How does that work?"

"Joseph Smith gave me the same priesthood that Jesus had. Every elder in our Church holds this priesthood. I'll lay my hands on your head and pronounce the blessing."

William nodded his agreement.

Elijah anointed him with oil, laid his hands on William's head, and said a short prayer. He then gave him a blessing, promising he would have a quick, full recovery.

"Let's get you to a doctor," Elijah said, helping William to his feet.

~ * * * ~

The next day, William sat up in bed and was given a bowl of soup. His shoulder and arm were wrapped in bandages.

Porter and Elijah entered the room.

"How you doing, William?" Elijah asked.

William turned his head toward his friends. "I can't believe that people so ignorant and bigoted exist in this day and age!"

Elijah furrowed his brow. "I thought you were from Missouri."

"I am. I know they expelled our people from the western part of the state. But St. Louis is a place of religious toleration."

"In the rest of the nation, religious bigotry is the norm," Porter said.

William started rapidly tapping his thumb against his thigh. "The fact that we even need to protect ourselves from people like that is a sad statement on the state of humanity!"

"Don't I know it," Porter said.

William gritted his teeth. "How in this civilized nation could there be so many people full of ignorant, blind hate still out there seeking to kill people who are doing their best to follow the Savior? If I could, I would eradicate those vermin who hunt and prey on the innocent!"

Elijah and Porter were taken aback by the passion with which William spoke against those from whom they were protecting the city.

~ * * * ~

After Porter bid William farewell, he went to see Willard Richards.

"Willard, it's good to see you again."

"How's Brother Chestnut doing?" Willard asked.

"He is healing much quicker than the doctor expected. Must be because of the blessing Elijah gave him. Though his head is not in the right place. I fear his heart is growing hard because of those who would do us harm. I was wondering if you could talk to him. Maybe say something to him that would strip the hate out of him."

"I'll see what I can do, Porter. Though I can't promise you anything I say will change his heart."

"You are an Apostle of the Redeemer of this world. I have no doubt that whatever you tell him will be exactly what he needs to hear," Porter said.

Willard considered Porter for a moment. "Thank you for your faith, Porter. I'll go and tell him what comes to my heart."

"I ask nothing more," Porter said.

~ * * * ~

Willard went to see William at the hospital. William turn his head toward him as he entered the room. “You’re the Apostle, Elder Willard Richards.”

“I am, and you are Brother William Chestnut, who so bravely took a bullet for the Lord, protecting His people.”

“I’m not sure bravery had much to do with it. But I did take what was given,” William said.

Willard put his hand on William’s good shoulder. “How do you feel?”

“I’m healing quickly, feeling better every day,” William said.

“That’s good. How do you feel about those who put you in this condition?”

“I want to get ’em—each and every one—and make them sorry for what they’ve done to make me and our people suffer,” William said.

~ * * * ~

Jefferson sat up at this part of the story. “I don’t blame him. They shot him for no reason! Does he get his revenge?”

Sarah blinked, then looked at Jefferson. “No, and that kind of thinking is what got a group of Saints in Southern Utah in trouble about eleven years ago in the Mountain Meadows. Truth is, we reap what we sow. Revenge does not bring happiness. If we sow hate, then hate is what we will get.”

“But . . . they shot him,” Jefferson said, “and they hurt all those other people. How could he forgive that?”

“The Apostle that came to him had a good answer,” Sarah said.

~ * * * ~

Willard looked into Williams eyes. "William, can I share a scripture with you?"

"Sure, go ahead."

"It's in 2 Nephi 4:27–29. It reads:

> And why should I yield to sin, because of my flesh? Yea, why should I give way to temptations, that the evil one have place in my heart to destroy my peace and afflict my soul? Why am I angry because of mine enemy?
>
> Awake, my soul! No longer droop in sin. Rejoice, O my heart, and give place no more for the enemy of my soul.
>
> Do not anger again because of mine enemies. Do not slacken my strength because of mine afflictions.

Willard closed the book. "William, it is the evil one who wants to destroy your soul and wants you to have hard feelings against those who have hurt you—who have hurt us. But we are disciples of the Holy One of Israel. We follow Him, not the one who would destroy our souls. Jesus has taught that we should love our enemies and pray for them."

"How? It's so hard to do that. How do you just let it all go?" William asked.

"You're right. It is not easy, but it is what the Lord asks of us. If we start to hate our enemy, then we let Satan win and take hold of our souls."

"I never thought of it like that," William said.

"We can't let that happen, William. We are commanded to forgive. It's not easy, but it is possible. We are told in scripture that He gives no commandment save He shall prepare the way. But He will make it possible. He is the only one who can, but you have to be humble and ask for His divine help and guidance, His grace, which He is more than willing to give when we ask for it."

"Thank you, Willard. I see that my heart is not in the right place. And it may take me a while to get it to where it should be."

"That is all the Lord asks—that we try and never stop trying. That is the secret to enduring to the end. We will not lose the battle if we never give up."

"I won't give up, Willard. Thank you."

"I'll leave so you can get your rest. Just remember, the Lord loves you more than you can possibly know, and He is on your side. Stay close to Him, and He will stay close to you. Good night, William."

"Good night, Willard." William thought deeply on what Willard told him.

William was visited throughout the rest of the week at different times by William Clayton, Porter Rockwell, and Elijah Abel, each checking up on him. By the end of the week, William's arm had regained full function, and he could barely feel the pain. After another few days, he was ready to go back out on patrol.

The patrols in the following weeks were mostly uneventful. Every so often they would come upon someone harassing someone else, but never in large groups. They generally dispersed when they saw William riding up to them. He had a system where he would check in with Porter and give status updates every fourth hour.

On one occasion, William was riding with Porter, William Clayton, and Elijah Abel down the main street when Porter spotted someone he recognized. "Foster! That no-good, murdering . . ." Porter swore and picked up his pace. He pointed his gun right at Foster's chest. "Foster, I'll see you six feet under if you don't turn around and crawl back into the hole you came from!"

"This ought to be good," Elijah whispered to William.

William Clayton rode forward. "Porter, stand down, please!"

Porter stared into the frightened man's eyes.

Foster stuttered, "N–N–Now wait a minute. I–I'm just here on business. I'm not here to do harm to anyone."

"Harm has already been done. Joseph and Hyrum are dead, and you were a party to it," Porter almost growled.

Foster smiled slightly. Porter cocked his gun, and Foster stumbled backward, losing his grin.

William Clayton spoke up again. "Porter, I detest him as much as you, but if he or anyone else gets assassinated, the governor will hold the entire city accountable. We cannot afford that!"

Porter lowered his gun. "You'd better hope we don't cross paths again." They all turned their horses around and rode off.

Brother Clayton explained to William as they rode away, "That was Robert Foster. He is an apostate and likely had a lot to do with the murder of the Prophet."

Porter and Elijah rode ahead of them. Noting how much longer Porter's hair was now, William turned to Brother Clayton. "I know it's really none of my business, but I'm just curious. Why does Porter let his hair grow so long?"

"He used to cut his hair until last year when he was blamed and arrested for shooting Lilburn Boggs."

"That's when I first met him," William said. "He saved me from being robbed. I tried to spring him from jail, but he talked me out of it. Said he didn't think he would be in that long since he was innocent."

"He was imprisoned for around ten months," Brother Clayton said. "Couldn't cut his hair in jail because they'd never give him anything sharp enough. They finally let him go in December since they couldn't convict him. Christmas day he walked right into Joseph Smith's Christmas party straight from the prison, dirty and tired.

"Many at the party thought he was a Missourian who had come to attack the Prophet or take him away again. It was Joseph who first recognized him and embraced him. They had been friends since they were little. Brother Joseph gave him a blessing; in it he told Porter that, like Samson of old, if he never cut his hair, he could never be hurt by bullet or blade. He never did cut his hair after that, and he has had more than a few scrapes with criminals since then—has been shot at many times, and the promise has held true."

"He's quite a man. I'm glad he's on our side," William said.

"Me too," Brother Clayton agreed.

~ * * * ~

On July 10, Samuel Smith noted in a meeting that he was designated by his brother to be president of the Church should both Hyrum and Joseph die. Willard Richards was adamant that they should wait to make that decision until a majority of the Church leadership was present. No one objected to that, so the matter was put on hold.

By the end of the month, news spread around the city that Samuel Smith had died on July 30 of bilious fever. Samuel was known to have been sick and was taking medicine, but few knew it was so serious. William had thought Samuel would definitely lead the Church, but now he wondered who would fill that gap.

Samuel was the third member of the Smith family to die within two months, which did not help the mood of the city. Four days later, Sidney Rigdon came to Nauvoo and told all congregated that he had been given a vision in which he was to act as guardian of the Church. The local stake president, William Marks, supported his claim, as he was the last remaining member of the First Presidency, which was the governing body of the Church.

That made sense to William. But Willard Richards thought differently. He was still adamant that they should wait for Brigham Young and other members of the Twelve to arrive before a decision was made. William Marks called a conference to settle the matter to be held in five days. After three days, most of the Twelve had arrived in Nauvoo. The next two days were spent anxiously awaiting the coming meeting.

When the day finally arrived, Sidney Rigdon got up first to speak to the large congregation. While many people were seated, many others were standing around the edges of the clearing.

Rigdon talked about his vision and said that while he could not replace Joseph, he would be the "guardian of the Church." He also claimed that he, as a member of the First Presidency, had the right to lead the Church. Rigdon kept talking for ninety minutes before finally sitting down. An older couple near William had fallen asleep, and they didn't appear to be the only ones.

Brigham Young stood up and suggested a two-and-a-half-hour break. During the break, William overheard two of the Apostles criticizing Rigdon's claims. Though, from what William had heard so far, Sidney Rigdon appeared to be the obvious choice. Stake President William Marks had even affirmed that.

The hour for Brigham to speak had finally come. William was hoping that they weren't in for another long speech. Brigham didn't quite have the polish that Sidney did as he spoke. He talked about following by faith instead of sight and how Sidney needed to go where the Prophet was beyond the veil to continue as counselor to him.

William could feel power in Brigham's words when he said, "I know where the keys of the kingdom are, and where they will eternally be. You cannot call a man to be a prophet; only God can do that. You cannot take Elder Rigdon and place him above the Twelve; if so, he must be ordained by them."

After that, William found it hard to concentrate on what Brigham was saying because his voice and appearance had changed. The Prophet Joseph who William saw laying in a coffin in the Mansion House appeared to now be speaking to the congregation instead of Brigham. William heard gasps throughout the crowd. Some people whispered, "It's Joseph," confirming to William that he was not the only one seeing and hearing this. Others in the crowd replied incredulously to the awe that overtook their neighbors.

When Brigham sat down, William Marks gave Elder Rigdon a chance to respond. Elder Rigdon deferred his comments to W.W. Phelps, who stood and encouraged the congregation to support the Twelve.

When the question was put to a vote, William knew he had seen the mantle of Joseph settle on Brigham, so he voted for the Twelve. As he looked around, nearly the entire congregation also voted to sustain the Quorum of the Twelve Apostles.

Fully satisfied that the question of Church leadership was settled, William prepared to get on the next steamboat and head back to St. Louis. He had told Porter and William Clayton that he could help until the end of the month. The end of the month had come and gone, and it was time for him to return to his wife and baby. The Church was in good hands under the direction of the Twelve, but he no longer felt compelled to relocate to Nauvoo.

Chapter 33
Back in St. Louis

August 10, 1844

William chartered a steamboat to St. Louis and made his way back home. The two-day journey was long and uneventful.

When William walked into his house, it appeared empty. "Hey, is anyone home? I'm back," but his call was met with silence.

William shut the door behind him and went into the kitchen, which was empty. When he turned around, he saw Johanna running toward him, smiling from ear to ear.

She embraced him. "I was putting the baby down to sleep, or I would have come sooner. I'm so happy you're home. I missed you."

"I missed you too. How have you and the baby been holding up?"

"We're fine. Ann is healthy; she is a happy little baby," Johanna said. "How was your trip? News from Nauvoo has been in all the papers. What will the Church do now that the Prophet Joseph is gone?"

William described the experience he had in Nauvoo with the debates about who should lead the Church and told her the Church in Nauvoo voted to sustain Brigham Young and the Twelve Apostles.

"Is that really the best thing? I mean, Sidney could be ordained to be the prophet by the Twelve, couldn't he?" Johanna asked.

"I guess, if the Church voted that way. But it was obvious that Joseph's mantle had fallen on Brigham; it was like he was Joseph at one point. The Church in Nauvoo voted to sustain the Quorum of the Twelve as the leaders of the Church."

"Do President Small and Elder Riley know about any of this yet? I'd be interested to know what they think," Johanna said.

"I'm not sure; I'll go talk to them after I get all our affairs in order here. I've got to take my store back and make sure everything is going well on the farm. With the Prophet's death and the threat of mob violence constantly over the city, I don't see any need for us to relocate to Nauvoo," William said.

"No, I suppose there isn't," Johanna replied.

~ * * * ~

Johanna sat in the front room reading a letter from her father, tears running down her cheeks. William came in holding Ann and saw Johanna crying.

"What's the matter, Johanna?" William asked.

"My father wrote to me and said he wants to visit," Johanna replied.

"Why are you sad about that? I thought things were going well between you and your father," William said.

"Things are good between me and my father," Johanna sobbed.

"Then what's the matter?" William asked, bewildered.

"He's bringing my grandma!" Johanna said, crying harder.

"I thought you loved your grandma," William said.

"I do!" Johanna said, still crying.

"Then what's all the fuss about?"

"They don't know we're Mormons. They hate Mormons," Johanna sobbed.

William blinked. "Oh. You never told them we got baptized?"

Johanna shook her head. "No! I don't want my family to hate me."

"When were you planning on letting them know?" William asked.

"I hadn't thought that far yet."

"Johanna, being Mormon is part of who we are. You can't take such a significant part of your life and just tuck it away from your family."

"You don't understand, William. When I went to live with my grandma in Ohio for three months, we were visited by some Mormon missionaries. They were so persistent, and my grandma treated them like they were trying to convince her to drink poison. At the time, they were everywhere in Kirtland."

"That makes sense—that's where the first temple was built," William said.

"And in the letters my father sends to me every month, he doesn't talk about Mormons much, but he has mentioned them a few times—and it has always been in a negative light."

"Don't you think they might be softened to our religion if they knew we were a part of it?" William asked.

"I'm scared of what they'll think. That's why I haven't told them. What if they disown me and never want to see or talk to me again?"

"Johanna, we kept it from each other because of the same fear, and look how that turned out."

"That was different; we both were investigating and interested."

"Think of little Ann. Could you ever stop loving her even if she grew up and joined some strange religious group we've never heard of, or if she decided to become a Quaker? Would you hate her for it?"

"I suppose not. I would be sad and disappointed that she didn't stay in our faith, but I wouldn't hate her or stop talking to her. I would probably try to convince her to come back, if anything."

"That is likely how your father and grandma will react. Why don't you write them about it before they come? Then they will have some time to digest the idea and may even look a little more into it so they can understand it better. If you wait until they get here to tell them or if they find out by accident, it will be much worse."

"You're right. I need to let them know," Johanna said.

"Tell them how happy we've been since we joined, and how we are closer to God now than we ever have been. They can't begrudge us our happiness," William said.

"I'll write them today and pray they'll understand," Johanna replied.

~ * * * ~

Johanna took out an ink bottle and pen and wrote:

Dearest Father,

William and I have been searching for a religion to belong to, and I believe we have found one that has helped us draw closer to God than we ever have before.

We were both baptized after carefully investigating their doctrines and practices. They teach that family relationships can last into the next life and that we should each have a personal relationship with our Lord and Savior.

We have never been as happy as we are now, nor have we ever been closer to God. The name of the Church is The Church of Jesus Christ of Latter-day Saints. The Church is organized just like it was when Jesus walked the earth, with teachers, deacons, priests, elders, and twelve Apostles.

They teach that each person can know the truth of the Lord's gospel through prayer and the Spirit of the Holy Ghost. I have felt the Holy Ghost in my heart, and I feel this is the church that the Lord wants me to be in. William has felt that as well.

The members of this Church are also known as Mormons. They are a good people and have taught us how to be the best Christians we can be.

I love you with all my heart. You are continually in our prayers, and I hope you will support us in our decision to be members of this church.

All my love,
Johanna

~ * * * ~

The following week, William found President Small at home. He had already heard a lot about the Prophet's death and was fixed on the issue of who should run the Church. President Small argued that Sidney Rigdon was the higher authority and that since he was in the First Presidency, he should lead the Church. William thanked him for his time and went to see his friend James Riley.

When William got to the Riley home, he wondered if James would be on the same page as President Small. Those two were such good friends, he worried that they might be thinking the same way. William knocked on the door and waited.

Eventually the door opened. Sister Riley took one look at him and smiled. "William, you're back from Nauvoo! Please come in. My husband and I want to hear all about your experiences there."

William walked in and found James coming to greet him from the kitchen.

"William, welcome back! I'm glad you came by to visit. Are you still planning on moving to Nauvoo?"

"No. We figured with the Prophet's death it would be best to stay here. Besides, Nauvoo is under constant threat of being attacked by mobs. I helped keep the safety of the city there for several weeks, which is why I'm so late in returning."

"Well, we're glad of that decision. Our St. Louis branch needs good, strong Saints like you and your wife in our midst. We'd miss you too much if you moved on," James said.

"Thank you," William replied.

"Come and sit. Tell us all about your experience in Nauvoo," Sister Riley said.

When they were all seated, William said, "I got there the day the Prophet was assassinated, but no one in the city knew about it until the next day. When the news came, a blanket of sadness overtook the city."

"It was quite the shock to us too, when we heard about it. We held our own memorial services for him here the week we got the news," James said.

William told them of his experience in Nauvoo and how they thought Samuel would lead the Church and then died. He told them about Sidney and Brigham and the transformation that happened and how the Church voted to sustain the Twelve.

"As well they should," James said. "The Twelve as a body hold all the same keys and authority as the First Presidency. They are the only ones who have a right to lead the Church. Sidney's position in the First Presidency dissolved with the death of the Prophet, who was president. Sidney was never ordained an Apostle, and therefore he has no legitimate claim to leadership or authority."

"I'm happy to hear you say that. I agree, though I just came from President Small's home. He is already convinced that Rigdon should be leading the Church," William said.

"Rigdon has been in St. Louis spreading his message and claiming the Twelve have been doing all sorts of wrong," James said.

"The Apostle Orson Hyde is here also and is setting the record straight. If President Small wants to follow after Rigdon, let him go. We'll be better off without him if he is headed down that path."

"I can see how Rigdon's argument would hold sway on some people, but when Brigham speaks you can feel the power of his words," William said.

"You know, it was just last October that Joseph tried to remove Sidney from the First Presidency for secretly working with enemies of the Church. But after Sidney appealed to the congregation, a vote ended in Sidney's favor. Joseph stood up after that and rebuked the congregation; he said he had thrown Sidney off his shoulders, but they had put him back on. He told them they would have to carry him because he wouldn't."

"I hadn't heard about that. Why did Joseph choose him as his vice president in his run for president if he was so against him?" William asked.

"Maybe they put aside their differences for the greater good after that. Not sure. But I do know that Rigdon is actively speaking out against the Twelve when he should be sustaining them. If President Small has been convinced about him, he is sure to be helping Rigdon draw others away."

"You said that the Apostle Orson Hyde is in town. Maybe he should call a meeting of the Saints and have it all straightened out," William said.

"If I'm not mistaken, I do believe that is his plan," James replied.

Chapter 34
Sidney or Brigham

After his conversation with the Rileys, William's thoughts turned to his parents and how much he missed them. He walked toward the river and thought about how happy his parents would have been if they could have embraced the gospel. As he passed Front Street, he noticed a monument that had recently been placed there. He read it and marveled at what he saw.

He went home and saw his wife reading the paper at the table. Ann was on her lap, trying to grab at the papers.

William kissed his wife and picked up Ann.

"Thank you," Johanna said.

"My pleasure," William said as he whispered to Ann and tickled her.

"How were your visits with the brethren?" Johanna asked.

"President Small was convinced that Rigdon should lead the Church, but James thinks the Twelve have more claim to lead based on their authority being equal to that of the First Presidency. I reckon the Twelve are better fit to lead anyway."

"James Riley is a good man, and he has a good head concerning spiritual matters. I trust his judgment in this case," Johanna said.

William threw Ann in the air and caught her. Ann squealed with delight.

"You be careful with her," Johanna said.

William smiled. "I am being careful," then threw her in the air again.

Johanna eyed him seriously. William stopped and started rocking Ann.

"I went down to the docks this morning to remember my parents. You'll never guess what I saw there," William said.

"What?"

"A monument I hadn't seen before read, 'High waters, June 27, 1844.' That was the day the Prophet was assassinated."

"Oh, yes—I remember there was an awful rainstorm that day. The water overflowed from the Mississippi. Covered Front Street in as much as eight feet of water, they say."

"Even the heavens wept at his passing," William reflected.

"Speaking of that, I was reading the paper you brought in yesterday. It talked about the murder of the Prophet Joseph and his brother," Johanna said.

"What did it say?" William asked.

"It said that the homicides were nothing more than murder in cold blood. Called it atrocious and unjustifiable and said it left the blackest stain on those who perpetrated the murders."

"It's nice to see that those who write the newspaper articles see Joseph's murder for what it is. Is that from the *St. Louis Evening Gazette*?" William asked.

"That's the one," Johanna replied. "There is another article in *The People's Organ* published four days ago that said Samuel Smith died, and Sidney Rigdon will be the chosen patriarch."

William shook his head. "The Smith family has lost a lot. But they're wrong about Sidney. He has turned against the Church, so he won't be the next patriarch. There was an article in the *Daily Missouri Republican* today that said he had been unchurched by the Twelve. The office of patriarch will probably fall to the only surviving brother, William Smith. I heard talk of that before I left."

"Have you heard back from your father since you wrote to him?" William asked.

"I got a letter from him a few days ago."

"What did it say?"

"I've been too afraid of what it might say to open it," Johanna said.

"Aren't you even curious?"

"I don't think I could take it if he is harsh with me. I'm afraid that's what I'll find," Johanna said, her eyes starting to tear up.

"I hope he would be more civilized than that to his only daughter. But even if he's not, then it's likely just an automatic response to unexpected news. If he is harsh with you, you just need to remember that. He'll come around with time. Even if he never comes around to our faith, I don't think he would ever stop loving you, though if he gets upset for a while about our religion."

Johanna set the baby in her bassinet and slowly opened the envelope. She took out the faded yellow paper, unfolded it, and started reading. Her eyes teared up and she dropped the letter. She hid her face in her hands and started to sob. William rushed over to her and held her, understanding what her father must have written. They sat together for what seemed to William an eternity until the baby started to cry. Johanna got up, picked up the baby, and rocked her in her rocking chair. Unable to console her, they cried together.

~ * * * ~

The following week at Sunday dinner, Bessie had just left the room and William blessed the food. After the prayer was over, Johanna said, "I'd like to go for a walk after dinner. I'm tired of being cooped up."

"Sounds good to me," William said. "I ran into Brother Reid today. He was going around and talking to each of the members of our branch about the importance of following the Twelve. He said that he once heard Joseph Smith say that he would give them a key that would never rust. The key was to stay with the majority of the Twelve Apostles and the records of the Church, and you will never be led astray. From what he told me, his message is getting through to most of the members and convincing them to follow the Twelve."

"That's good," Johanna said, as she started feeding Ann the mashed carrots that Bessie had prepared. "*The People's Organ* published a letter from Sidney Rigdon yesterday. President Small brought it by and said that according to the Doctrine and Covenants, Brother Rigdon was the rightful successor of Joseph Smith and that the Twelve are going out of their way to blacken his character."

"It's too bad President Small has bought into Rigdon. He's wrong about the Twelve. They are being guided by the Lord. Brigham had kind words to say about Sidney when he spoke to us. The only point they called him out on was his claim to lead the Church. Elder Orson Hyde published a letter in that same paper today that said Rigdon had misrepresented him and the Twelve, and most of Rigdon's statements were untrue."

"Too bad Brother Reid's message will likely never sound in the ears of Sidney or President Small," Johanna said. "I think I'm ready for that walk."

~ * * * ~

As William and Johanna walked down the street, Brother and Sister Riley were coming from the other direction. As they approached, Sister Riley said, "How are our friends, the Chestnuts, doing on this beautiful day?"

"I was going stir crazy," Johanna replied.

William smiled. "James, how have you been?"

"Good as can be expected. How's your store doing lately?"

"Business is steady. I thought I might start selling more candy to appeal to the younger crowd."

James nodded. "By the way, this Sunday Elder Hyde from the Quorum of the Twelve will preside. Brother Small has left the Church to follow after Rigdon. They've made me branch president."

"Congratulations. They couldn't have chosen a better man," William said.

"Oh yes, they could have. I know a lot of men better than me," James said. "At the meeting, we will be discussing that and sustaining the Twelve, with President Brigham Young at their head."

"Sounds like it will be a good meeting," William said. "We'll look forward to seeing you then."

~ * * * ~

September 29, 1844

The meetinghouse was nearly full. William estimated that close to three hundred people were in attendance. Orson Hyde sat on the stand next to President James Riley, who stood up and opened the meeting. He read a letter from Brother Small declaring that Sidney Rigdon was the only man to lead the Church after the death of Joseph Smith. Afterward he read the transcript of the trial of Sidney Rigdon. He addressed the Saints and talked for more than thirty minutes about the authority and role of the Quorum of the Twelve Apostles in the Church. He asked for a vote to see who sustained the Twelve. All but four voted in favor of the Twelve.

~ * * * ~

William saw an increase in business at his store, and he used a portion of the extra income to contribute to the building of the temple in Nauvoo.

Orson Hyde came to St. Louis at the beginning of November and called for a conference of the Saints to be held on November 10. William and Johanna attended with Ann and listened as Orson Hyde and James Riley encouraged Saints to contribute money to help build the temple, to subscribe to *Times and Seasons* (the official Mormon newspaper), and to subscribe to *The Neighbor*. They also asked that all Mormons in the area join the branch and that the Saints continue to adhere to the principles taught by the Prophet and Patriarch and sustain the Quorum of the Twelve Apostles.

After the meeting William and Johanna, holding baby Ann, walked home.

"That was a nice conference. I'm glad they're still moving forward with building the temple in Nauvoo," Johanna said.

"Me too. President Riley showed me a handout he prepared addressed to all the people of St. Louis inviting them to make a contribution to go toward to the building costs. I thought that was quite bold, but with all the German and Irish immigrants coming to St. Louis, he just might get some donations from non-members."

"There seems to be a lot of sentiment against the newer immigrants. Maybe they will be sympathetic to another oppressed group and contribute to the building of the temple," Johanna said then paused for a moment, twirling her hair. "William? I was thinking we are so well off we should be contributing to the building of the temple too?"

William nodded. "I already am. I've been sending 10 percent of our income to help pay for it."

"Good. It will be nice when it's finished. Then we can go and get our ordinances done," Johanna said.

"That will be nice," William agreed.

~ * * * ~

March 1845

A cool breeze followed William into the house. As he stepped inside, he felt the warmth emanating from the fireplace. He heard Ann giggling and Johanna talking to the baby in a high-pitched voice. In the nursery Johanna held Ann in her lap, cooing at her and tickling her.

"Looks like you two are enjoying yourselves," William said with a grin.

"William, don't you think Ann should have a little brother or sister?"

"Yeah, I think she would enjoy that," William replied.

Johanna put a finger to her lips and shifted her eyes upward. "Well, I reckon she'll have to wait until about September."

William briefly lost his balance. "Wait—are you pregnant?"

"I reckon so," Johanna said, smiling.

"That's great!" William said, giving her a hug and a kiss. Then he turned to Ann. "Did you hear that? You're going to be a sister."

Chapter 35
Kids!

May 1845

William came home from work and saw his wife rocking the sleeping baby in the rocking chair, resting Ann on her rounded belly. He put both hands on the arm of the rocking chair to support his weight and leaned in to give Johanna a kiss. Suddenly one of the rocking chair arms made a loud cracking noise and gave way.

William fell on top of Johanna and the baby as they sat in the chair, then continued falling to the ground. The chair tipped, spilling Johanna and the baby. William cushioned the fall of his wife and child as they landed on top of him, with the rocking chair on top of them all.

Bessie started to call, "Dinner is rea—" but stopped as she walked in the room and saw the scene of the family all on the floor.

Her hand flew to her mouth. "Oh, my."

She rushed over and grabbed the rocking chair and set it to the side. She helped Johanna, who was clutching her crying baby tightly to her chest.

"Are you all right?" Bessie asked Johanna.

"The baby and I are just a little shaken and scared," Johanna said. "Luckily, William broke our fall."

"You all right, Mr. Chestnut?" Bessie asked.

William got up and looked over at the broken rocking chair. "I'm a little bruised, but I'm fine. Sorry about the rocking chair, Johanna. It was passed down from my grandparents; I guess it's time to replace it."

As they sat down at the table to eat, William blessed the food, then picked up his fork. "Brother Reid stopped in to see me at the store today."

"Did he have anything interesting to say?" Johanna asked.

"Turns out William Smith was ordained patriarch," William said. "I invited the Reids over for dinner Saturday night."

"We need to replace that rocking chair before they come. I will not be entertaining guests without a proper rocking chair," Johanna said.

"All right, dear," William said, taking a bite out of his roll.

~ * * * ~

Saturday morning Johanna and William rode in their buggy down the St. Louis main street heading toward Joe's Furniture Shop. Arriving at the furniture shop, they noticed all sorts of furniture throughout the large, open space. "You go ahead and pick out a rocking chair that you like, and I'll watch Ann," William told Johanna.

William sat down on one of the wooden benches, set Ann down, and watched as she ran from one piece of furniture to another. After talking briefly to a Mr. Nichols, who offered to help Johanna pick out a chair, William scanned the room for Ann. Panic started to take hold when he saw no sign of her. He started calling her name, looking under the furniture. He searched for her behind the counter and didn't see any sign of her. Johanna noticed him searching and calling Ann's name then stood up from a rocking chair.

"Do you like that one?" Mr. Nichols asked.

"Excuse me, Mr. Nichols. I need to talk to my husband," Johanna replied. Approaching William, she said rather sternly, "William, where is Ann?"

"I took my eyes off her for only a second to talk to Mr. Nichols, and she disappeared."

"She has been missing that long and you didn't say anything?" Johanna asked, now frantically looking around the store.

"I thought she was just hiding, but I can't find her," William said.

Mr. Nichols approached them. "Is anything wrong?"

"Our daughter is missing," Johanna said.

"Well, she can't have gone far," he replied, starting to help with the search.

"The door is open!" Johanna yelled. She might be outside!" She rushed outside looking in all directions. She started running down the street, with William right behind her. As they ran, someone behind them started calling out to them.

They whipped around and saw James Riley holding Ann and walking next to a couple coming toward them. They rushed up to him.

"I was just welcoming Thomas and his wife, Grace, to St. Louis. They came with a ship of Saints from England. I was showing them the city when I spotted this little bundle of joy toddling her way down the street, happy as a jaybird," James said, smiling. "I didn't see either of you in sight, so I scooped her up."

"Thank you so much," Johanna said as she took Ann in her arms, tears running down her cheeks.

"Thank you, James. We were looking at furniture, and she snuck away," William said.

"Well, I'm glad I spotted her before she got too far," James said.

"We're William and Johanna Chestnut, by the way," Johanna said.

"Pleased to meet you, William and Johanna, we are the Wrigleys," Thomas said, shaking William's hand.

~ * * * ~

September 4, 1845

Johanna was upstairs in labor. Sister Reid, Sister Riley, and Sister Wrigley were in the bedroom taking care of her. William was downstairs in the kitchen tending Ann and talking to James Riley.

"Stop pacing and sit down. Johanna is in good hands. Sally has helped deliver hundreds of babies and has had complications very few times. She knows what she's doing," James said.

"All right, all right," William replied.

"How are Johanna's parents doing? Are they planning on coming after the baby is born?" James asked.

"Ever since Johanna told them about our baptism, her father has cut off all communication. Her grandma still writes, but only to tell us how wrong she thinks Mormonism is."

"What about her mother?"

"She died after giving birth to Johanna. Her father never remarried."

"Oh, I didn't know about that. Well, don't worry—our wives are as close as friends can be. We'll make sure Johanna is taken care of while she recovers," James said.

"I really appreciate that, James."

"You're the closest thing I ever had to a brother, William, and you've done plenty to help me too. This is the least I could do."

A knock sounded at the door. William went to get it and saw Robert Reid with a gift in his hand.

"Come in. What's this?" William asked, taking the gift.

Robert glanced at the items. "Baby things."

William took the items, "Thank you."

The next few hours the three men talked and waited to hear word from the women. Sister Reid periodically came down for supplies, rags, or water, hurrying past the men without giving much information about how things were going.

Finally, they heard a baby cry. Sister Riley came down the stairs and told William, "Congratulations! You have a beautiful baby girl."

"How's Johanna?" William asked.

"We've cleaned her and the baby up. You're welcome to go up and see them. They're both doing just fine," Sister Riley said.

"Thank you, Sally," William said as he bounded up the stairs. He went in and saw Johanna smiling, feeding her newborn. William kissed Johanna and caressed the baby's hand as she fed.

"Let's name this one after your mother," Johanna said.

"All right, and my grandmother," William said.

"Sarah Mary Chestnut it is," Johanna said, smiling at her new daughter.

Chapter 36
Follow the Twelve

As William rode Destiny home from work in the cool November air, his thoughts turned to his parents and how much he missed them. He yearned for his dad to be able to see the achievements he had both in starting a successful business and a successful family. The sun was about to set on the horizon as he arrived home.

As he walked through the front door, the smell of roast beef invited him in. Johanna was at her loom busy making cloth. Sarah lay in a bassinet near the loom, and Ann was playing with her ragdoll in the corner on a blanket.

"President Riley came to see me at the store. William Smith, the patriarch, is in town and is calling a meeting," William said.

"Wasn't it only six months ago that he was set apart as the patriarch to the Church?"

"Yes, and it sounds like he has had some clashes with Brigham Young and has come to tell us his side," William said.

~ * * * ~

November 10, 1845

After William closed his shop he went over to the meetinghouse, which was full by the time he got there. President Riley and Robert Reid sat next to William Smith, deep in discussion as they waited for people to come in and take their seats.

Following a prayer, James said, "Thank you, brethren, for coming to listen to our beloved patriarch speak to us. His message is of grave importance to us all. I have been to Nauvoo and verified that what he is about to tell you is true. Please listen with an open heart. I will now turn the time over to Patriarch Smith."

"Thank you, President Riley, and thank you all for being here. As you know, my brother Hyrum was the patriarch before me and was instrumental in the hands of the Lord in leading the Church side by side with my brother Joseph."

"As you also know, the Lord has established a patriarchal order in the Church. In that patriarchal order, the right of leadership is passed down to a patriarch's kin.

"The mantle of leadership should go to me, then to Joseph the third as soon as he is at an age to lead. We are the only ones with legal right as the brother and son of the Prophet. As the patriarch of the church, and as brother of the prophet, I will lead the Church and the Saints in these latter days.

"I know the Twelve have a part to play in the leadership of the Church as long as they do not fall into the pathways of sin, as many of them have. The Church has, in essence, two heads. One with blood line patriarchal authority to manage the organizational needs of the Church, and the other is to minister to the spiritual needs of the Church. The second is the proper role of the Twelve.

"I was compelled to flee Nauvoo because the Twelve sought to take my life. Now because the current body of the Twelve has fallen into treasonous, wicked paths, a new quorum will need to be formed. The Church in Nauvoo currently has no head to lead them, as many of the Twelve are guilty of adultery and apostasy. The Twelve never were ordained to lead the Church. I should know, having been one of them for many years."

William wondered how much of this was true—and with this kind of talk, whether Will Smith was even still a member of the Church. He continued to listen as the patriarch railed against the Twelve and accused them of all manner of wrongdoings. Even more surprising to William was that President James Riley had started the meeting by encouraging everyone to listen to this—he was such an ardent supporter of the Twelve after the death of Joseph Smith.

William's thoughts went back to when he heard and saw Brigham Young transform before his eyes into Joseph Smith. It was as though the mantle of the Prophet was on Brigham.

The patriarch continued speaking, but William had heard enough. He wasn't sure what to think about the accusations William Smith laid out against the Twelve. He had met several of them, and it just didn't seem like they would do those kinds of things. William was determined to talk to President Riley about it later.

William headed home still somewhat confused. Thomas Wrigley caught up to him. "William, I noticed you left the meeting early."

"I don't know where you stand on this, Thomas, but I just can't wrap my head around why James of all people would be taken in by an apostate. Brigham was chosen by the Lord to lead the Saints. Of that I am certain."

"I couldn't agree more. I think the fact that he is connected by blood to the Prophet makes his argument more persuasive than those of other apostates. But I don't think for a minute that the entire body of the Twelve has fallen away. I've met most of them; they're all good men doing their best to serve the Lord."

"It's good to hear someone talk sense. I'd better get on home." They bid each other farewell, and each went on his way.

As William sat thinking over what he heard in the meeting, some of the things he heard still bothered him. The Riley and the Reid families were good friends of his. He knew if he chose to stick with the main body of the Church, he would be turning his back on them. He didn't want to lose his friends. He also knew that James Riley and Robert Reid were reasonable men, and he trusted them. But he didn't want to turn his back on God if they were wrong about William Smith.

He decided to take the matter to the Lord. Either the Twelve were called and leading His Church in the right direction, or William Smith was.

As he knelt to pray, he thought about Brigham Young and the Quorum of the Twelve, and his heart filled with a feeling of peace and warmth. That feeling instantly left him as he thought about William Smith and the things he had said that night. He closed his prayer and stood up. "Will Smith is wrong," William whispered. The Lord had just confirmed that to him.

As the week passed, William ran into James Riley twice. Both times James tried to convince William that the Twelve had fallen into apostasy and thus lost their right to lead the Church. William was distressed to find that many of the members of the branch were following after William Smith and James Riley.

Thomas Wrigley, a high priest in the congregation, came to visit William and informed him of William Smith's excommunication the previous month. He reaffirmed that the Twelve were still leading the Church with full power and authority from God.

~ * * * ~

Johanna walked into a room full of sisters. Looking for her friends, she noticed them across the room. President James Riley sat next to the Relief Society president. As the meeting started, the Relief Society president stood up and started speaking.

"Sisters, there has been a great division in this branch over the question of who should lead the Church. I have asked our leader, President Riley, to talk to us today and help us understand the issue at hand. I now turn the time over to President Riley."

President Riley stood. "The Twelve have fallen into adultery and many other ungodly practices. They have mistreated William Smith and threatened his life. I did not believe any of this until I saw it for myself, when I went to Nauvoo to investigate, and I found that matters were exactly as he described them.

"The proper order of the church is that the prophet be succeeded by a member of his family. Since all other brothers have passed away the right belongs to his last living brother William Smith, and then to the prophet's son."

He continued speaking until an hour had passed and then asked for questions.

It quickly became clear that the room was divided on the issue. No resolution could be agreed upon by the sisters. However, Johanna knew President Riley was a good man, and she trusted his judgment.

Johanna spent a long time discussing it with her friends after the meeting, and they all agreed with President Riley. She went home and found William alone at the table, reading the paper.

"Oh, welcome home," William said. "How was your meeting?"

"It was very enlightening," Johanna said. "President Riley spoke to us about all the bad things the Twelve have been doing. Not everyone agreed with him, and there were a lot of questions he didn't have answers to. You've been keeping up on the issue; what do you think?"

"I think we should trust in the Twelve Apostles. William Smith was excommunicated. I don't think we can believe most of what he has been saying about them."

"But William Smith is the brother to Joseph the Prophet and Hyrum the patriarch," Johanna said, folding her arms. "Now that they are gone, William is the only surviving brother. Of a right, leading the Church should go to the Prophet's family. Plus, William was a member of the Twelve and was ordained the patriarch to the Church, a position that has been kept in the Smith family. President Riley trusts him, and I think we should too."

"Johanna, God's house is a house of order," William said. "God is the one who chooses His prophets. How can he do that if the position of president and prophet is tied to one patriarchal line? Just like with the kings of Europe and like King Noah from the Book of

Mormon, there are bound to be descendants in any line who turn wicked. How is the Lord to lead such a church?"

William continued, "The Lord leads His church through revelation. He can't do that if He is not allowed to pick the righteous out of His people to lead His people, because His hands are tied to a patriarchal line that may or may not be inclined to follow Him. In a patriarchal succession line, it's not possible to remove the wicked."

Johanna reflected on her experiences of the past week forming her thoughts. "President Riley has brought many of the Saints in this area into the Church and is driven to always choose the right. He and his wife have helped us so many times. You can't just turn your back on him after all he has done for us. He has always been guided by the hand of the Lord."

"You are right. He has done a great deal of good for us and for the Church in St. Louis. President Riley is a good man, but in this case, I think he is wrong to follow William Smith."

"The Lord would not let a good man like President Riley be led astray," Johanna replied. "He cares about the salvation of this people more than anyone. As president, he has the right to revelation for this branch. He has studied this issue in his mind and in his heart. He has been to Nauvoo and knows the right way. We need to follow him. It's not just the Rileys who believe in William Smith; the Reids also know that we need to follow him. These are both good, strong families, and they are our friends."

"You're right," William said. "Both the Reids and the Rileys have been good friends, and they have done a lot of good for us and for the Church. I will always consider them my friends, even if they leave it. But even if half our friends go one way and half go another, the most important thing for us to do, regardless of what anyone else is doing, is to follow what the Lord wants us to do.

"You love your family, but even though they disapprove of the Church, we have stuck with it because we know it is what the Lord wants us to do. We need to find out what the Lord wants us to do in this case and stick with it, even if our friends have chosen a different direction.

"The Prophet Joseph taught that we are entitled to personal revelation from God. Let's use that now to make this decision. The Lord will tell us—you and me—who He wants to lead His Church. We don't need other men to convince us. We just need the Lord to tell us.

"We have His promise that if we lack wisdom, we only need to ask in faith. He will give us the wisdom we lack, then we need to follow His guidance and direction, because if we turn to Him, He won't let us be led astray."

"You're right. Let's pray about it," Johanna agreed.

"Thank you for being willing to pray about it."

"You're going to pray about it too, aren't you?" Johanna asked.

"Johanna, I have already received an answer on the subject, and I know I'm right."

"Well, I already know that *I'm* right. I feel good about following what President Riley has told us. I was hoping you would pray about it and come around to the right decision."

William responded in frustration. "Fine. I promise I will go to the Lord with an open heart and ask Him if we should follow William Smith or the Quorum of the Twelve Apostles—if you will do the same."

"Will you pray out loud so I can hear you?"

William's jaw dropped. "Don't you trust me?"

"I want to make sure you're not just giving me lip service and that you will actually ask. I'll do the same," Johanna said.

"Fine. Let's do it after dinner."

"Why wait?" Johanna asked.

"Because I need some time to prepare myself."

Johanna gave a short nod. "Fine. After dinner, then."

William sat down. "I will bless the food."

Johanna bowed her head, closed her eyes, and listened, as William began, "Dear Lord, we thank thee for our bounty. We ask thee to bless this delicious meal before us. We thank thee for personal revelation and pray that Thou will make Thy will known to us, as we pray this evening regarding who we should follow to lead Thy Church. We ask in Jesus's name. Amen."

As they started to dish up the food, Johanna said, "I saw President Riley's wife at the store yesterday. You wouldn't believe some of the things she has heard about the Twelve—"

William interrupted. "You're right. I probably won't believe it. I've heard what William Smith is spreading around about them, and know they wouldn't do half the things he's claiming."

Johanna replied forcefully, "William, President Riley has been to Nauvoo since meeting with William Smith and is convinced he is right."

"Johanna, please," William said, slamming his fork to the table. "I don't want to hear another word on this until both of us have taken the matter to the Lord. We both have to be open to either one of us being right so we can accept the Lord's will in the matter.

"I know that because of our own personal experiences, I'm being pulled in one direction, and you are being pulled in the other. But unless we are both willing to give up our own personal biases and submit to the Lord's will, whichever way that takes us, then we might as well forget about praying altogether. I am willing to do that even if it goes against what I previously thought. Are you?"

Johanna stared at her plate and let her gaze linger, then finally looked back at William. “I am,” she said softly, her eyes moist.

“Then let’s pray.”

Johanna’s eyebrows shot up. “Right now?”

“Right now,” William responded, his determination firm. He walked over to her and took her hands in his. “Let’s kneel. I’ll go first,” William said.

Johanna met his eyes. “William.”

“Yes?”

“I love you.”

“I love you too,” William responded, then closed his eyes. “Dear Lord, we come to Thee in the humility of our hearts willing to accept Thy will, whatever it may be. Please answer our prayer and give us the revelation we desire right now concerning who we should follow as the leaders of Thy Church. Is it right for us to follow the Quorum of the Twelve Apostles or—”

William’s throat suddenly caught, and he opened his eyes. A sensation, that enveloped his soul, overcame him. Feelings of love and happiness filled his being.

William looked at Johanna. Tears puddled in her closed eyes and slipped down her cheeks. Overcome with emotion, she looked at William and smiled then wrapped her arms around him.

“William, it’s the Twelve,” Johanna said.

“I feel the same,” William said, marveling that the Lord would answer their prayer so quickly and directly.

Chapter 37
The Steamboat

February 16, 1846

William walked in the door and saw Johanna reading to the girls. Ann jumped off her lap and ran to him, exclaiming, "Daddy!" He crouched down to pick her up as she flung her arms around his neck.

William smiled, "Hey there, sweetie."

"How was work today?" Johanna asked.

"It was good. A man, who moved here from Nauvoo last month, came in today. Said his name was Joseph Stratton. He was telling me about how the Nauvoo Temple is being used now to perform ordinances for the Saints. Says they are doing one hundred or more every day in preparation for moving the Saints west. He thinks we could go and get our ordinances done if we hurry. He thinks they were planning to leave this month."

"That would be wonderful!"

"I'll see about chartering a steamboat to Nauvoo. Though, with the threat of the mob hanging over that city all the time, I'd feel better if we could find someone to take care of the girls while we're gone."

"Sarah still isn't weaned. She'll have to come with us."

"I guess that will be all right, especially if we don't linger. I don't think it would take longer than a week. Two days to get there, one or two days in town, then about two days to travel back. We'd only be gone for four to six days."

"I'll talk to the Wrights, and see if they can watch Ann for that long," Johanna said.

"Good idea, Phineas and Alta are about as good as people come."

Over the next few days, Johanna and William made all the necessary arrangements and chartered a steamboat that was headed up the Mississippi River.

This was Johanna's first time on a steamboat. William wanted her to have a good experience, so he booked the first-class section on the upper deck. That way they could have their own room, regular meals, and professional entertainment. He knew the cost was much higher to travel first class, but the lower deck experience was very different. One would sleep wherever they could find a spot, sometimes next to the livestock. He didn't want Johanna to have to endure the lower deck on her first trip.

They boarded a large steamboat named the *Saluda.* It had three main decks, with a smaller room centered on the third deck, and an even smaller room on top of that, from which the ship was navigated. Two giant pipes jutted into the air on each side of the front end of the ship. Toward the back end was a great, wide, circular, paddled wheel protruding from the starboard side of the ship.

Johanna held tightly to Sarah, as she and William made their way through the crowded lower deck to the stairs. When they got there, a large, muscle-bound sailor blocked their way.

"Do you have first-class tickets?"

"One sec," William said, searching his pockets, but was unable to find them.

The man waited while William searched. "If you haven't got tickets, then you stay down here."

William remembered he had put the tickets in his bag. "Wait! I remember where they are," he said, pulling them out of his bag and handing them to the annoyed sailor.

"Fine, up you go then." The sailor moved and let them pass.

The first thing they saw as they reached the upper deck of the ship was a large grand saloon area. Twelve feet wide and two hundred feet long, it was ornately decorated with flowers and wall hangings. Persian carpets decorated the floor. Fine chairs and tables were neatly placed throughout the deck. There was an area at the opposite end with a piano and chairs. Doors lined the walls leading to the passenger cabins.

William and Johanna found their cabin. The room was nine feet square and had a large bed in the corner and a door at the other end leading out to the promenade, where they could look over the rail of the ship and enjoy the passing scenery. A dresser, an end table, a bassinet that William had ordered for the baby, and two chairs also adorned the room. There were windows in each of the doors that were covered with curtains for privacy.

William put down the luggage and sat in one of the chairs. "Here we are."

Johanna sat on the bed. "This is nice. I'm glad we don't have to travel on the lower deck."

William smiled. "Only the best for you."

Johanna laid her sleeping baby in the bassinet. "I've heard they have gambling on these ships. Let's make sure we steer clear of that on this trip. There is no use in throwing our money away."

"I guess I can live with that," William said, then stood up and laid down on the bed. "We've got a long trip ahead of us. How about we take a nap?"

"I guess I can live with that," Johanna said, smiling as she joined him on the bed.

~ * * * ~

Around noon, Johanna and William emerged from the cabin and enjoyed a fine lunch served restaurant-style by the ship's waitresses.

Johanna took a sip from her cup. "I could get used to trips like this."

As the evening wore on, a pianist came out and played several classical pieces that Johanna absolutely enjoyed. About that time, many of the tables turned into gambling tables. Songs on the piano and the clicking chips almost drowned out the sound of the steady swoosh of the paddle wheels and the ever-consistent purring engines.

William and Johanna sat listening to the pleasant music, then went for a walk with Sarah around the upper deck of the ship.

They felt the boat come to a stop. William peered over the side. They were near the bank of the river, and the lower-level passengers were being offloaded onto the bank. William stopped one of the sailors. "Why are they unloading passengers in the middle of nowhere?"

"There's a sandbar up ahead that we can't get over it with all the cargo we've taken on. Some of the people will have to get out to lighten the load so we can make it over. They'll be picked up once we're clear."

The people who had gotten off walked along the bank of the river as the steamboat started pulling forward. The steamboat kept picking up speed, and soon those on the bank started screaming and waving their arms as they were left behind.

William and Johanna watched as the people on the bank disappeared from sight. Johanna said, "That's awful. The captain just left those poor people stranded on the side of the river!"

"I know; I can't believe it either." William stopped another passing sailor. "Why were those people left stranded on the side of the river? The captain needs to go back and get them."

"He ain't got to do nuthin of the sort. Says it would put too much stress on the engines if he did. You want us all blown sky high?"

"Well, no," William replied.

"Then shut yer trap, and mind yer own," the sailor said as he walked away.

As darkness started to fall, the ship pulled off to the side of the river and was tied to the bank. It wasn't safe to try to navigate the river in the dark, so the steamboat would stop here for the night.

As Johanna and William walked back to their cabin, two men approached them. They were both clean shaven and wore fancy outfits.

"Howdy, friend," one of the men said, addressing William and stopping in front of them.

"I don't believe we've met," William responded.

"No, I don't think we've had the pleasure yet," the other man responded.

"I'm William Chestnut, and this is my wife, Johanna," William said.

"Pleased to make your acquaintance. I'm Ted O'Riley, and this is Preston Banks."

"We noticed you haven't joined our gentlemen's game and wanted to make sure you knew that you're welcome to join our table if you'd like," Preston said.

Johanna's face went stern. William glanced at Johanna. "No, thank you. We were just about to turn in for the night."

"Surely you wouldn't mind one quick, friendly game before you turn in," Ted said, smiling.

Johanna interrupted. "I would mind. We don't want anything to do with that horrid game. Now if you'll excuse us."

Dropping their smiles, the two exchanged a glance as if a silent conversation passed between them. Then Preston said, "Beggin' your pardon, ma'am, we were just being neighborly."

"Thanks for the invite, but we'll pass. Nice to meet you," William said as he walked with Johanna back to their cabin.

The next morning, the steamboat continued on its way up the river. The morning passed pleasantly with a hearty breakfast and more music and gambling in the Grand Saloon. Leaving Sarah with William Johanna went to the ladies' room. After she had disappeared from sight other men approached William. They encouraged him to join in the games. "No, thank you, boys, I'd much rather keep my money in my own pockets. Besides, I need to look after this little one. But thank you for the invitation."

They didn't know how to take no for an answer and kept after him to join in their games. Johanna returned, overhearing their conversation as she approached.

"If you gentlemen don't mind, I'd like to have my husband back," Johanna said, taking William's hand and leading him back to their cabin.

"I can't believe those hustlers won't leave us alone," Johanna said as they entered the room.

William shut the door behind him. "Don't worry. We'll be off this boat within the next hour or so. Nauvoo is the next stop."

Johanna took the baby. "Oh, William, it will be so nice to see Nauvoo and the temple, and then have the chance to get our ordinances done."

"I'm looking forward to it too," William said. "We'd better start packing so we can be ready to disembark."

~ * * * ~

Ted knocked on the captain's cabin door and was invited in. "Sorry to bother you, Captain, but we have a couple who don't want to partake in the gambling."

Rupert was counting his money. "Do they look like they're well-to-do?"

"Yes."

Rupert looked up and smiled. "Then bolt their door shut until they miss their stop. We'll charge them extra for the longer ride."

Ted smiled. "Yes, sir," he said, leaving the room.

~ * * * ~

As William and Johanna packed their things, they heard clinking noises coming from each of the doors on either end of the room.

"What was that?" William and Johanna said together.

William tried to open one of the doors. It wouldn't budge. He went to the other door, and it was just as immovable.

"We've been locked in!" William exclaimed.

William and Johanna each pounded a door, both hollering for someone to let them out. Sarah started crying, Johana picked her up. They felt the ship stop. They had reached Nauvoo, but had no way of getting out of the room.

William continued pounding on the doors and yelling for help. They felt the boat start moving again. Finally, someone came to the door but was unable to open it.

Several hours passed, and they were still trapped in the room, though it was obvious a crowd of men were trying different methods of getting the door to open.

"It was probably those gamblers who wouldn't leave us alone who did this," Johanna said, as she fed the baby.

"Well, at least we have help now," William said.

It was getting dark, and the boat had stopped for the night when the door was finally removed from its place. They had dislodged the pins from the hinges and taken the door right off the wall.

It seemed as if the entire boat erupted in applause as Johanna and William stepped out of the room.

"Thank you. Where are we?" William asked a man who had helped with the door.

"We're in Le Claire, Iowa," the man said.

"What? Where is Le Claire?"

"It's right here," the man responded.

"We're about half a day up river from Nauvoo. We've got to get off and make our way back," William said.

"Hold on just a minute," a bearded man with a long fancy jacket said. "You paid only enough to get to Nauvoo. You're going to have to pay the extra fare before we allow you to disembark."

"What? You can't be serious!" Johanna exclaimed in disbelief.

"You're the captain?" William asked.

"No, I'm the ticket master, and I have full authority from the captain on these matters," the man replied.

"We didn't have any choice about staying on. As you well know, we were locked in our cabin when it was time for us to disembark."

"Unfortunate as that is, you still have to pay the extra fare before you can go ashore," the ticket master replied.

"It's highway robbery!" Johanna exclaimed.

William argued with the ticket master for a few more minutes, to no avail. In frustration, he paid the ticket master the extra fare, and they were allowed to leave the steamboat.

Chapter 38
The Codys

Le Claire was a small town that reminded William of New Salem. They quickly found lodging at the local inn, then went to the tavern to get some food. As they sat waiting, Johanna asked, "How are we going to get back to Nauvoo?"

"We'll have to see if we can find a boat headed south in the morning," William replied, staring at a man at the table behind Johanna.

"What if we can't find one?" Johanna asked, then noticed that he was staring past her. "What are you looking at?"

"That man at the table behind you looks so familiar."

Johanna turned to look and saw multiple couples enjoying their meals.

"Who are you talking about?"

"That man with the long beard and mustache with a woman and three children next to him. I feel like I've met him before," William said.

The man lifted his head and noticed William and Johanna staring at him. He first seemed annoyed, but then did a double-take. "William Chestnut, is that you?" the man called out.

William stood up and walked over to the man. "In the flesh. You'll have to forgive me—I know I've met you, but I can't place your name."

The man smiled. "That's probably because the last time we were together, I didn't have all this hair on my face. It's me—Isaac."

It was William's turn to look surprised. "Isaac Cody?"

"In the flesh," Isaac responded.

William grabbed his hand and started shaking it. "This is amazing; what are you doing here?"

"I live here. This is my wife, MaryAnn." Turning to MaryAnn, he said, "This is William Chestnut; he's an old friend who saved my life on more than one occasion."

MaryAnn waved her hand. "Pleased to meet you, William."

William put his arm around his wife. "This is my wife, Johanna, and this cute little baby is our daughter Sarah."

Johanna waved at them. "Pleased to meet you."

"What happened to Rebecca?" William asked.

Isaac looked down. "She died in bearing the child she was carrying when you last saw us."

"I'm sorry to hear that," William said.

"Yes, well," Isaac said, putting his hand on the shoulder of the little girl next to him, "this is Martha. She's eight. Next to her is Samuel; he is five. And the little one is Julia; she is three. And as you can see, we have another one due to come any time now."

"Have a name already picked out?" William asked

MaryAnn spoke as Isaac started to open his mouth. "If it's a boy, we'll name him Fredrick. If a girl, Lucy."

"That's right," Isaac said.

"We hope everything goes well for you in delivery," Johanna said.

"Thank you," MaryAnn replied.

Isaac asked, "What brings you and your wife to Le Claire?"

William related the story of their journey.

After hearing all they went through, Isaac nodded. "Those steamboat captains can be the worst. I had a friend who took passage on the lower deck of a steamboat. He had a similar experience as the people you just mentioned from the *Saluda* that got left behind."

"What did they do?" Johanna asked.

"They had to walk to the nearest town and catch stagecoaches to finish their trip," Isaac replied.

Johanna responded, "That's awful! Maybe it was the same one."

"I'm afraid that practice is way too common," Isaac said.

William scratched his cheek. "I think they jammed our door because I refused to gamble. The only way they could get more money out of me was to make me stay on the boat longer than I had intended to so they could charge me an extra fare."

"Some riverboat captains have really taken to creative pirating. They find ways to steal your money and pretend its legal," Isaac said.

MaryAnn cut in. "We'll let you two get back to your dinner. We've got to get these children home and put them to bed."

William shook Isaac's hand. "It's good to see you again, Isaac. Nice to meet you, MaryAnn."

After they had eaten, William and Johanna got up to leave when Isaac came into the room and approached them. "My wife and I were talking on the way home, and we have some extra space where you could stay. Even have a basinet we're not using yet. You've already had some unplanned expenses on your trip. We would consider it an honor if you stayed with us while you're in town."

Johanna smiled. "Oh, that's very kind of you."

"We'd be honored to stay with you. Thank you," William said.

As they walked toward the Cody home, Isaac said, "I'll take you in the morning to see when the next southbound boat is expected."

"We really appreciate you helping us like this," William said.

"What are friends for if they can't help each other?" Isaac responded.

When morning came, Johanna helped MaryAnn prepare breakfast while William and Isaac entertained the children.

When breakfast was served, Isaac blessed the food, and they all dug into a hearty meal of flapjacks and bacon.

"MaryAnn has been having regular contractions, so if Johanna could watch over her while we're gone, that would be appreciated," Isaac said.

William looked at Johanna, who held Sarah; she nodded. He turned back to Isaac. "I think she'd enjoy helping your wife. Let's go."

William and Isaac went to the docks to check the boat schedule. They found that the next steamer wasn't scheduled to arrive until the following morning.

"Looks like you'll be with us another night," Isaac said.

William shrugged. "At least I'll be in good company."

"Mind if we stop by the printing shop on the way home? I've got a small bit of business to take care of," Isaac said.

As they walked toward the printing shop, Isaac asked, "How's your shop doing? Did you get all those specialty items from Ohio sold?"

"No. New Salem fast became a ghost town, so I had to close up shop. I've got a new one now in St. Louis that's really doing well."

"Glad to hear it," Isaac said.

They approached a two-story brick building with large windows and a sign that read, *The Evening Herald.*

"I've got some business with the owner. I'll be back soon," Isaac said as he headed for the front door.

"I'll wait out here," William said as he walked to the corner of the building, leaned his back against the wall, and studied the layout of the town.

After about five minutes, William thought he heard raised voices. The door burst open. A large man came stumbling out and fell down by a water trough. Isaac followed, but before he could get to him, the man was on his feet ready to go again.

William straightened up, unsure whether he should try to help, since it seemed Isaac was winning. Isaac threw another punch; the big man dodged it and grabbed hold of Isaac, positioning himself behind him and forcing Isaac's head into the water trough.

William had seen enough. He ran full speed into the man, striking the back of his neck with his might, and bowling into him. William fell forward, landing in the water trough. Isaac extracted himself and saw the big man sprawled on the ground, and William laying in the water.

Isaac smiled at the sight and helped William up. "Looks like I owe you again, William. Crazy bastard would have drowned me in the trough if you hadn't stepped in—or should I say fell in?" Isaac chuckled.

"Very funny. What were you two going on about?" William asked.

"The paper was recently bought out by this pro-slavery ratbag," Isaac explained as he gave the unconscious man a kick. "I paid the previous owner for an article to run in Sunday's edition last week. The new owner refused to honor that agreement or give me a refund. When I persisted, he started cussing and throwing punches. I bested him, and he fell backward out the door. You saw the rest."

"What was the article about?" William asked.

"It was an abolitionist piece, but still, a deal is a deal—plus, I paid for it!"

"No wonder he wasn't excited about it. We better be getting on before he comes to," William said.

"I suppose you're right."

~ * * * ~

Johanna and MaryAnn got along like long-lost sisters. Johanna helped her clean up breakfast, then tended the children. Then they sat together in the parlor, while Martha and the other children played with baby Sarah. MaryAnn' contractions were growing stronger, but she got through them and continued the conversation.

"How did you and Isaac meet?" Johanna asked.

"I was a schoolteacher in Cincinnati, where I was living with my stepmother. My real mother died when I was fourteen, and my father disappeared when I was seventeen. He was a sea captain; he went out to sea one day, and his ship never returned. I stayed with my stepmother and taught school until I met Isaac."

"It must have been hard to lose your parents at such a tender age."

"It was, but I got by—whoa," MaryAnn said, grabbing her belly.

Johanna stood up. "Should I send for help?"

"I think the baby is coming," MaryAnn said. "I might need your help. Send Samuel; he'll know who to bring. Martha can tend Sarah."

"Come on," Johanna said, taking her arm. "We need to get you to the couch. Samuel, go for help!" Johanna exclaimed.

Samuel was on his way out the front door as Johanna helped MaryAnn up the stairs, which was a difficult task. The contractions continued as they climbed. The other children were unsure what was going on, and Julia started crying.

"Martha, help your sister!" MaryAnn called out.

"All right, Mama," Martha said.

By the time Samuel came back with the midwife, the baby was already in its mother's arms. Johanna had helped in a few deliveries in St. Louis. The midwife took over for Johanna while she went to clean up.

William and Isaac returned in soaking-wet clothes. Johanna saw them come in. "What happened to you two?"

"Just had a run-in with a water trough," Isaac said.

"Well, while you two were swimming, your wife had the baby, and they're both doing fine. Congratulations!"

Isaac froze. "The baby! It came? Is it a boy or a girl?"

"It's a beautiful baby boy."

"Excuse me," Isaac said as he ran up the stairs.

~ * * * ~

William changed, then Johanna and William swapped stories as Isaac and MaryAnn spent time together with their newborn and the children played games in the dining room.

Isaac called the children up to see their baby brother, then invited William and Johanna to come up as well. They all went upstairs, and the children crowded around the bed to get a better look at the baby.

"So cute," Johanna said.

MaryAnn smiled at William. "Isaac told me how you saved him. Thank you for making sure he got home safely."

"It was nothin'—I was just helping where I saw a need."

"William, you've saved my life so many times. I talked it over with MaryAnn, and we've decided to name our baby after you. We'll move the name we selected to his middle name and call him William Fredrick Cody," Isaac said.

William put his hand on his chest, and briefly closed his eyes. "I'm honored."

Everyone took turns holding and cuddling the baby. Then Isaac said, "Let's go downstairs and let MaryAnn get her rest."

That night, Johanna took care of dinner and tended the children so MaryAnn could recuperate.

The next morning, they said their goodbyes and caught their steamboat to Nauvoo. This time they opted for the lower deck, as the trip was only four hours.

Chapter 39
Nauvoo

February 21, 1846

Johanna and William stepped off the bobbing steamboat with Sarah, happy to have their feet on solid ground again. They finally made it to Nauvoo. Johanna was excited to finally be in the main city of the Saints.

Beautiful buildings dotted the landscape, but the streets were empty. It was not the same bustling town that William remembered. The temple was easy to find, as its beautiful walls towered above the city. When they got to it, though, they found it was closed. As they stood there wondering what to do next, they noticed a lone man crossed the street toward them.

"Excuse me, sir," William called out.

The man asked, "Yes, how can I help you?"

"Who can we talk to about getting our ordinances done in the temple?"

The man considered William. "Everyone who might have been able to help you has left, I'm afraid. All but the few Saints who are still here have crossed the river and are headed west."

"Oh, no!" Both William and Johanna exclaimed.

"Where you folks from?" the man asked.

"St. Louis. I'm William Chestnut. This is my wife, Johanna."

"I'm David LeBaron. Pleased to meet you," David said as they shook hands. "I recently moved my family here from Hancock County. We were in the village of Macedonia. The last day any ordinances were done here was February 8, a few weeks ago."

William slowly nodded. "I had heard they were planning on going west, I just didn't expect it to be so soon. Do you have any recommendations where we might stay until we can book a steamer home?"

"There's plenty of room in the hotel wing of the Mansion House. That's where my family and I are staying. Emma Smith is living there as well."

"Do you mean Joseph Smith's widow?" Johanna asked

"Yes. Brother Brigham asked us to stay back and look after her when he left. I'll walk you over there. I'm headed that way now," David said. They walked down Durphy Street toward the Mansion House.

"What do you do now that most people are gone?" Johanna asked.

"Besides looking after Emma, Brother Brigham asked that I help my brother-in-law try to get the temple and some of the homes here sold. You wouldn't happen to be in the market, would you?" David asked.

"No, we're happy in St. Louis. Why are they trying to sell the temple?" William asked.

"We won't be able to control or protect it once we've all moved west, and the money from the sale will be used to help Saints make the move. We're hoping to get $200,000 out of it," David replied.

William whistled. "That's quite a sum."

"We're hoping that whoever buys it will value it enough to protect it and keep it in good condition. They won't be motivated to do that if they pay a low price," David said.

"I can see the wisdom in that," William replied.

As they approached the Mansion House, William remembered the last time he had come here. It was a solemn occasion when he briefly saw the bodies of the Prophet and his brother in caskets covered with glass.

After checking into their room, William turned to Johanna. "I'd better go see if I can find us passage back to St. Louis. You stay here with Sarah and get comfortable."

~ * * * ~

William left, and Johanna was instantly bored, so she decided to explore a little. She took Sarah and wandered the Mansion House until she found the dining area. Two women sat sewing at the table. The one on the right had curly black hair. The one on the left was shorter and had long straight brown hair. They stopped sewing and looked up as Johanna walked into the room.

"Sorry. I didn't mean to intrude."

"Oh, you're fine. What a cute baby! Come over and have a seat. We could use some more company. Ester was just helping me make a dress for my daughter. Are you renting a room here?"

Johanna smiled. "Yes, my husband and I are."

"Welcome to the Mansion House. I'm Emma Smith, and this is my good friend Ester LeBaron."

Looking at Ester, Johanna said, "My husband and I met your husband David on the way here. He is a nice man. It's an honor to meet you both. I'm Johanna Chestnut."

"Pleased to make your acquaintance. I'm glad you're here. How long will you be staying in Nauvoo?" Emma asked.

"I'm not exactly sure. We came to attend the temple, but we learned that the temple is closed, and there is no one left here to perform the ordinances. My husband is out looking to find passage on a steamboat back home."

"It's a shame you traveled to Nauvoo just to find your whole reason for coming frustrated," Ester said as she got up and put her sewing aside. "I left soup on the stove. I'd better go tend to it. I'll leave you two to talk," Ester said, smiling and nodding a goodbye as she left the room.

"I'm sorry to hear that you weren't able to attend the Temple. Where did you travel from?" Emma asked.

Johanna opened up to Emma and spent the next twenty minutes relating everything that had happened to her and William since leaving St. Louis. Emma listened with interest. When Johanna was done, Emma said, "I'm sorry about all the troubles you've had. Sometimes God brings us low so He can lift us higher. The best we can do is to keep praying. God hears every prayer of our heart, even those that go unspoken."

"I'm sorry for going on like that. You've been through much more than I could ever imagine. I was devastated to hear the news of your husband's death. I cried when I heard about it," Johanna said.

Emma looked at the wall, her eyes starting to moisten. "It is hard. It's very hard. I miss Joseph with my whole soul. But I know we'll be together again in the eternities, and that is what keeps me going." Emma turned back to Johanna. "You must have a good husband to bring you all this way to get you to the temple."

"I do. He is a wonderful man," Johanna responded.

"Hold on to him, dear, and don't ever doubt him. As long as he follows the Lord, you hold on to him," Emma said.

"How is it that you're still so strong after the tragedy you've been through?"

"I find strength one day at a time. I won't let sorrow rob me of my faith. Sorrow can hollow you out inside—leave you empty if you let it. Joseph always said that sometimes the Lord tries our faith but will never give us more than we can handle. Truth is, sometimes I gain more strength from having faith and trusting in the Lord than I could ever find on my own."

"Do you ever wonder when the persecution and trials will stop?"

"I've found, and I guess this applies to most of us, that we seem to have to learn the same lesson over and over before it finally sticks. Trials are just the Lord's way of helping us become more like Him, if we endure them well—and that's the hard part."

Johanna sat silent, pondering what Emma had said. Then Emma spoke again. "We've been driven from place to place, and now the mobs are trying to drive us out of Nauvoo. How have you held up through it all?"

"I guess I've been pretty sheltered from all of that living in St. Louis. The people there are very tolerant of religious differences. Our struggles have mostly been who to follow to lead the Church, and for that we have been relying on the Lord to guide us," Johanna said.

"Always rely on the Lord. He'll never lead you astray. Even if you don't like the direction He has taken you. You'll always be better for it," Emma replied.

A man came into the room. "Emma, I have a matter that needs your attention regarding the Mansion House."

The man stopped when he saw Johanna. "Oh, sorry. I didn't know you were entertaining company. But this really shouldn't wait."

"Brother Marks, this is Johanna, she's staying at the Mansion House. Johanna, this is William Marks. He's helping with the affairs of this place," Emma said, then glanced up at him. "Well, what is it?"

William started to speak, then looked at Johanna and then back to Emma.

"I should go. It's been so nice talking to you," Johanna said as she stood up to leave.

"I hope we get the chance to visit again," Emma replied.

"I'd like that," Johanna said and took Sarah back to her room.

~ * * * ~

When William Chestnut got back to the Mansion House, Johanna was reading a book in their room. Sarah lay sleeping on some blankets.

"Have you been in here the entire time?" he asked.

Johanna shook her head. "I met Emma Smith. She is so amazing. She has endured so much hardship and fatigue over the years yet is full of patience and courage."

"I'm glad you got the chance to meet her. It turns out the next steamboat arrived and is docking the night at the Nauvoo port. I got us a first-class cabin. They'll be leaving in the morning. We probably ought to go now so we don't miss it in the morning."

"What time will the ship leave?" Johanna asked.

"As soon as day breaks."

"I promise to get up early if you let me stay the night here. It's so hard to fall asleep on a ship," Johanna pleaded.

"I suppose it should be all right. But if we stay, we're sleeping on farmer's hours. We go to bed now, and get up early. Early, early!" William said, sternly.

"Fine. Now's as good a time as any," Johanna said as she stood up and pulled William onto the bed.

Chapter 40
The New Deal

March 1, 1846

Orson Hyde returned to St. Louis in May and made Joseph Stratton the branch president. Not too long after that, Saints migrating from England and Nauvoo started flooding into the city. St. Louis was quickly becoming a place of refuge for beleaguered Saints. There was plenty of work for those who wanted it. Those who were well established took in new families until they were able to make it on their own. Johanna and William had taken in three different families from England over the summer. William hired one of them to help in his store for a few months.

One day, President Stratton approached William in his store. "A man by the name of Haywood just came from a place along a horn in the Missouri River near Kanesville, Iowa. They're calling it Winter Quarters. He and Brother Camden have petitioned the people of this city for help, they even got the mayor to send a petition to the city to help the Saints."

William narrowed his eyes. "I was hoping the mob wouldn't be successful in their designs. But I'll be happy to donate some supplies to help."

"Thank you for your generosity. The Saints in Nauvoo will be very appreciative. Also, I got some correspondence from Brigham Young. As you know, last February Brigham Young took a large portion of the Saints from Nauvoo to Winter Quarters.

"He sent about five hundred men to help fight the war in Mexico, and he has asked that as many men who can, go west with him into the Rocky Mountains, with the understanding you could bring your family later. He wants to establish a colony and get shops and homes built so that when other Saints arrive, they can settle in an established community. They plan on leaving next spring when the snow melts."

"Well, I've got my wife and two girls, but I suppose if I make sure they're taken care of while I'm gone, it should be okay," William responded.

"Give it some thought. You don't have to make a decision right away," President Stratton said. "One more thing—a man by the name of Nathaniel Felt recently arrived with a group of Saints who were driven from Nauvoo. Brother Felt is a tailor by trade and doesn't have a place to sell his clothing. Would it be all right if he uses a corner of your store to get him going?"

"I would be happy to help. Just send him over to my store in the morning, and I'll get him set up."

"Thank you, William."

"I like to help wherever I can. Speaking of that, I have a friend, Berrill Covington, who is a regular at my store. He moved here with his family from England with a group of Saints not too long ago. Berrill is an older gentleman, but he has a daughter around our age. Every time she comes into the store, I think of you. She seems to talk about a lot of the same things you do, and she's as pretty as a picture. I'd like to introduce you to her."

President Stratton rubbed his chin. "I suppose that would be all right. What's her name?"

"MaryAnn Covington. I'll talk to Berrill and arrange for you to meet her."

"That will be fine. Thank you, Brother Chestnut. Have a nice day."

~ * * * ~

When William got home, he told Johanna about the conversation he had with President Stratton. "What do you think? Could you make it on your own if I left to help Brigham for seven to nine months?"

Johanna went rigid. "I don't think I could bear to be without you for that long, and the girls need their father."

"But, President Young needs our help. It's for the greater good."

Johanna's eyes went wide and her lips were tight. "Is it for the greater good that our family be torn apart?"

William raised his voice. "Our family won't be torn apart. I'll make sure you're taken care of while I'm gone."

"Oh really? Well—"

William interrupted and walked to the door. "I've got some business with the Covingtons. I'll be back for supper."

"Don't you dare leave," Johanna said.

William walked out the door.

~ * * * ~

After talking to Berrill, William arranged for Joseph to meet MaryAnn. When William returned, his home was completely dark except the faint glow from a dying fire in the fireplace.

William called out for Johanna but was met with silence.

Maybe they all went to bed early. He went to the bedrooms. The beds were made and lay empty.

"Johanna!" he called out again, grief starting to bubble in his chest. He searched the rest of the house. He found Bessie in the kitchen preparing dinner.

"Bessie, where are Johanna and the girls?"

"I couldn't say, Mr. Chestnut. She didn't say anything to me. I've been in here getting supper ready."

William left the kitchen and walked to the porch. He scanned the farm. There was no one in sight.

"Johanna!" William cried.

He fell to his knees, unsure of what to do or where to go.

~ * * * ~

When William went to work the next morning, his heart was heavy. As he opened his store, it took him twice the amount of time to get things ready for the day. His thoughts turned to his family, unsure of where they might have gone. He regretted being so abrupt with Johanna, but he was starting to get angry that she left without giving him a chance to say anything.

As he sat on his stool, his old friend Robert Reid walked in and approached the counter.

"How's it going, William?"

William hung his head staring at the counter. "She left me, Robert."

"Why?"

"I told her I was going to help Brigham Young move the Saints west."

Robert shook his head. "You haven't figured out that he is leading the Saints astray?"

"Listen, I know you and James followed William Smith—"

"He is the rightful leader of the Church. I think Johanna has finally come to that realization as well."

William's eyes left the counter and fixed on Robert's face. He squinted. "You know where my wife is."

It was more a statement than a question.

Robert closed his eyes and dipped his head. "She can't stand you following after Brigham Young anymore, William. He is a fallen Apostle. He is an adulterer. And he is leading those who will follow him to hell."

"Where are Johanna and my girls, Robert?"

"She is staying with friends, waiting for you to come to your senses about the Church."

William's nostrils flared. He closed his eyes and took a deep breath. He spoke slowly and deliberately, his eyes burning into Robert's. "How can I contact her?"

"Come by my place in about a week, and we'll talk about how you can contact her."

"You bastard!" William said as he reached over the counter and tried to grab Robert, who stepped back just out of reach and moved to the door.

"Where is my family?" William shouted.

"I'll see you in a week, William. In the meantime, you'd best be thinking long and hard about whether it's worth losing them to follow that charlatan Brigham Young, or whether you should return to the true church and have your family with you forever," Robert said as he left the store.

William rushed to the door and almost ran into a man who had his hands full of clothing.

"Are you William Chestnut?"

William stepped back to let him in. "Yes. You must be Nathaniel Felt. President Stratton said you would be by this morning."

Nathaniel strolled past him and set his things on the counter. "Yes, thank you for letting me use a corner of your store for my goods."

"You're welcome. I cleared out that corner over there for you," William said, pointing. "Listen, I've got a bit of an emergency I have to attend to. Do you mind watching the store while I take care of some personal business?"

"I don't mind."

"Thanks, Nathaniel," William said as he rushed out the door.

Robert was riding his horse down the street. William ran to the back of the shop to the stable and mounted Destiny. He rode full speed in the direction that Robert was headed. William looked for him, but he was nowhere in sight.

He rode to Robert's home and found it deserted and empty. He then went to James Riley's house and knocked. He waited, but there was no answer.

He returned home angry and overwhelmed. Why hadn't he seen this coming? He didn't ever think Johanna would leave the Church. He never thought she would leave him. He missed her, and he missed his two girls.

~ * * * ~

The next morning there was a knock at the door. Mrs. Riley stood before him, a worried look on her face.

"Sally? Come in. What brings you around?"

Sally was frowning. "James is keeping your wife at our home against her will."

William's eyes widened, "What! How did she get there?"

"She came to us, distraught that you might be leaving her for so long. She asked James if he would help by talking to you. He convinced her to stay with us one night so he would have time to persuade you. Instead, he and Brother Reid hatched a plan to get you to leave the Church. When Johanna found out about it, she got upset and tried to leave, but they wouldn't let her."

"What? Where are they now?" William demanded.

Sally moved to speak, then paused and looked down. "She and your children are on the second floor of our home."

"I came by yesterday, but there was no answer when I knocked."

Sally nodded. "James made us all be quiet and sit still so you would think we weren't home. One more thing. Whatever you do, please don't involve the authorities. We still have our two children to raise, and James is a good man. In his own mind, he believes he's helping you.

"I need to go now. Please don't let James know I told you; he'll be so angry if he finds out. He hasn't been the same since we started following William Smith. I really must go. Good luck, William."

William nodded. "Thank you, Sally."

~ * * * ~

At sunset, William hooked Destiny up to his carriage and rode to the Riley home. He stopped the carriage just far enough from the house so they wouldn't hear him coming. He took his pistol and a rifle with him as he approached the door. He was about to knock but then paused and slowly opened the door.

As he snuck in, he heard laughter. There was a staircase in front of him and an opening to his right through which light emanated. The laughter came from that room. He could hear James telling a story. William stepped quietly to the stairs and started climbing.

At the top of the stairs there was a hallway. At the end of the hallway there were two doors. William heard laughter again, coming from downstairs. William crept down the hall and opened the door to his left. It was a nicely furnished bedroom, but it was dark and empty.

He closed the door and tried to open the one on the right. It was locked. William stepped back and tried to kick in the door. It gave slightly. He heard James yell, "What was that?"

William kicked again. This time the door gave way and flung open. There was a large bed in the room. To his left was a small table where Johanna sat, holding Sarah. Ann sat next to her in a chair. Bowls of soup were on the table.

Johanna gasped. "William!"

Ann was about to cry, but as recognition set in, she smiled and cried, "Daddy!" Dropping her spoon, she ran to him.

William embraced Ann, then heard boots thumping up the stairs. He set Ann down. "I've come to take you home."

He turned around and aimed his rifle at the door. James Riley appeared in the doorway. He stopped and raised his hands when he saw William aiming his rifle at his chest.

"William!" James said.

"James—looks like following William Smith has turned you into a backstabbing, no good—"

"This isn't what it looks like."

William shook his head. "Johanna, do you want to come home with me?"

"Of course, but—"

William turned his head to Johanna. "But what?"

Johanna looked down at Sarah. "Are you still planning on leaving us?"

William's face turned red, and he narrowed his eyes. "Johanna, I'm . . ." William paused. He knew his next words mattered and might be the last thing he said to her if he spoke in anger. He took a deep breath and relaxed his muscles. He glanced at James, who still stood at the door, his hands raised, waiting to hear what William would say.

William narrowed his eyes again then turned to Johanna, "Listen, Johanna, I know you don't want me leaving you alone. I won't. I'll be by your side until we are ready to make that trip together."

Johanna smiled at William and stood up. "Let's go home."

"Brigham Young is an adulterer," James blurted out. "I saw it with my own eyes. He will lead you straight to hell if you follow him."

"I suppose you're smarter than God, then, James," William said. "Because we've already prayed about who to follow. Brigham Young is God's prophet on earth. I'm not going to listen to a confirmation from you that he is bad, because Johanna and I already got a confirmation from God that he is good. Now, if you'll be so kind as to get out of our way, I'm going to take my family home." William flicked his gun forward, urging James to move.

James narrowed his eyes but backed down the stairs. Johanna embraced William, then gave him a kiss.

William smiled. "I'm sorry I considered leaving you and the girls alone for so long. Let's go home."

Chapter 41
Number Three

January 8, 1847

The blustery January air meant that many of William's customers were staying at home. He sat on his stool behind the counter, waiting for someone to enter his store. Finally, he stood up, added more coals to the stove, then looked around. The shelves were tidy and dust free. He finally decided that the rope and chains in the corner could be better arranged. As he started rearranging the them, the shop door opened. Joseph Stratton walked in, accompanied by a chill breeze and a flurry of snow.

"Joseph, good to see you again," William said.

"It's good to be seen. I'm glad it's warm in here. The weather outside is awful."

"How are you and MaryAnn getting along?"

"She is an absolute angel. One month of being married, and she has me more organized and focused than I have ever been. She runs a tight ship."

William patted his shoulder. "That's good to hear. I knew you two were meant for each other."

"William, have you given much thought to going west with Brother Brigham?" Joseph asked.

"Yes, and I think it might be better if we waited until things are more established in the west. Because our children are still so young, I think that would be best."

Joseph looked him in the eyes. "That's fine, you need to take care of your family. I have been thinking about it as well, and talking it over with my wife. We've prayed about it and decided that the Lord needs us more with the main body of the Saints than here right now."

William raised his eyebrows. "You're kidding. If you leave, who will lead the Saints in St. Louis?"

Joseph didn't say anything but stared at William and cracked a smile.

"What? Don't look at me. I'm no leader."

"I don't know, William. I'll have to pray more about the matter. As I've thought about who to recommend to the Twelve, I've had names that keep popping into my mind again and again." He paused. "You know, you may not see your potential as a leader, but I do."

"What other names have you been thinking about?" William asked.

"Besides you, Nathanial Felt, William Picket, and Thomas Wrigley."

"They're all good men. Any of them would do a much better job at leading the Saints than I would," William suggested.

"They *are* good men. But don't underestimate your own abilities. There is a lot of good in you that you're not likely aware of. I can see it, and I know the Lord can see it too," President Stratton said.

"That's very kind. Though I am afraid I might cause the next great apostasy if I'm left in charge."

Joseph laughed. "Well, I'd better get the supplies I came for so we can start preparing for our journey."

"Fair enough," William said and started recommending items most people had purchased from him for such trips.

~ * * * ~

On February 8, President Stratton called a conference of the Saints. He announced that he had received a letter from the Twelve confirming the appointment of Nathaniel Felt to succeed him as president of the St. Louis Conference of the church. He expressed his love for the Saints, wished them well, and said that he looked forward to joining the Camp of Israel.

After the conference was over, a line formed to say farewell to President Stratton and congratulate President Felt. When it was William's turn, he told Nathaniel he should come by for dinner, and Nathaniel accepted the invitation.

Around dinner time, President Felt and his family knocked on the door of the Chestnut home. William opened the door and welcomed them in. "How does it feel to be the president of the St. Louis conference?"

"A bit terrifying, really. I reviewed the records of the Church for this area, and it turns out that there are more than eight hundred Saints in the St. Louis Conference, and convert baptisms aren't slowing down—there seems to be baptismal services every week. It might be more manageable if I broke the conference up into wards and called bishops to preside over the wards."

"That's kind of what Moses did when he was overwhelmed with Israel," Johanna said.

"Yes," Nathaniel said. "I'll call a conference at Lyceum Hall in March and see to it. I think six wards ought to do."

~ * * * ~

March 15, 1847

Johanna sat working at her loom when William passed by on his way to the kitchen.

"William? I've been feeling a little sick this morning. Will you help me get the girls to the dining table for lunch?"

As William went to get the girls where they were playing in their room, Johanna went to the dining table and waited.

William started putting the girls in their chairs and finally noticed the table was set for five. "Are we expecting anyone?" William asked.

"Yes," Johanna said.

William sat at the head of the table, "Who?"

"Well, I'm not entirely sure. It will take some time to really know," Johanna said.

"How much time will you need to figure it out?"

"About eight more months now," Johanna replied.

William's eyes got big. "You're pregnant again?"

Johanna nodded, a smile forming on her face. William gave her a hug.

~ * * * ~

October 11, 1847

Johanna lay in bed holding her newborn in her arms. William knocked on the door, then walked into the room.

"Bessie said I could come to see you. How are you feeling?"

"Much better now. It was a long labor. I'm just tired. Come and see your new baby boy."

William knelt beside the bed and gazed into the face of his newborn son, marveling at the miracle of life that lay before him.

"We finally have a baby we can name after you," Johanna said, smiling.

William smiled and picked up the baby. "Baby William. I like it. I want him to have the same middle initial too. Maybe . . . Alfred."

Johanna smiled. "That's our boy. William Alfred Chestnut. Come and sit by me, dear."

William sat on the bed next to his wife, and they both gazed into the face of their newborn son.

Chapter 42
Double Trouble

November 20, 1848

Otto and Rupert sat in the captain's lounge of the *Saluda*, drinking whiskey and chewing on a piece of beef jerky.

"Otto, I think we've made enough money that we can sell this old clunker and buy a nicer, bigger steamboat. We could fit more cargo and get more passengers. Means more money for us."

"And we won't have to be in constant worry about whether we are putting too much stress on the engines," Otto said.

They stopped in New Orleans and advertised the sale of their steamboat. It only took a week before some prospective buyers showed interest. As they stood on the docks discussing their plans, they were approached by a nicely dressed man.

"Hello, I'm Francis Belt. I've heard you have a steamboat for sale; I'm interested if the price is right."

"That's right. I'm Rupert, and this is my first mate, Otto. Pleasure to meet you. It's this one right behind us. She's in tip-top shape; let me show you around," Rupert said, leading the way to the ship.

After giving him a full tour, Rupert said, "She's a fine ship, isn't she?"

"Could use some touch-up work. How much you askin' for her?"

"For a nice steamer like this, I think $80,000 ought to be a fair price," Rupert said.

Frances grunted a half-laugh. "This is not a brand-new ship, and it needs a lot of work. You've neglected some basic upkeep on her. I'll give you $40,000. That's what she's worth in her condition."

"Be reasonable. We paid top dollar for her, and she has been a good, sturdy ship. There might be a few things here and there that need a little work. I guess we could come down to about $59,000."

"Are you trying to rob me? The repairs I need to make are going to cost me between $10,000 and $20,000, and that's just on the woodwork alone. I'll give you $45,000. I dare you to get a better offer from anyone else."

Rupert stuck out his hand. "Well, I suppose it is a reasonable offer. We'll take it."

Otto tugged on Rupert's sleeve. "Rupert? Shouldn't we—"

"Not now, Otto," Rupert interrupted.

"But—"

"We'll talk afterward, Otto. I'm sure Mr. Belt has other business he has to attend to."

They parted ways, and Rupert led Otto back onto the ship.

"Time to pack, Otto. We've got some steamboat shopping to do!"

"But Rup, don't you think we ought to tell him about the faulty part in the boilers?"

"If we do, he won't give us half the price he offered us."

"Maybe we should tell him after the sale is final, and we got our money. There could be a lot of people hurt if he doesn't know," Otto said.

"That's not our problem. If he finds out about the boiler after the sale, he'll have us arrested, then instead of spending our days in luxury on our new ship, we will be rotting in prison. Is that what you want?"

"Well, no, but—"

"Otto, have I ever let you down?"

"No, Rup, you haven't."

"We have to think about what's best for us. Besides, he seems like a pretty smart guy. After he runs the ship awhile, he'll figure out something's wrong with the boilers on his own, then he'll fix it. If he comes back to us at that point, we can claim it was in good condition when we sold it and that the problem likely occurred sometime after he bought it. It will be his problem, not ours."

"You think he will figure it out and fix it?" Otto asked.

"I'd bank on it," Rupert said.

~ * * * ~

Rupert added the money from the sale of the *Saluda* to the profits they gained from transporting cargo and passengers, and they now had enough to buy a bigger, nicer steamboat. They found what they were looking for in a large steamboat called the *Charlton*. It was definitely an upgrade from the *Saluda*. The first-class deck was fancier and had more cabins. It was twenty-five feet longer, and the captain's and first mate's quarters were bigger and more luxurious.

The only problem was that the cost was about $15,000 more than the cash they had on hand. Rupert went to a local bank to see if he could take out a loan. This time he had no issues either getting the loan or agreeing to pay it back. He thought he could have it paid off after the first six months of operation.

With this bigger boat, Rupert convinced Otto that they should be making longer trips around Florida and up to New York. Doing so would enable them to triple their income.

On their first trip around Florida, they made stops in Miami and Savannah. When they got to Charleston, they found that twice as many people wanted to go to cities in Florida, Louisiana, and Missouri. They had picked up livestock and other cargo. Their lower deck was packed with four hundred passengers, which left standing room only as they headed south. Another two hundred passengers occupied the quarters of the first-class deck.

Rupert was in his cabin counting all the money they had made from this haul. They were rounding the tip of Florida when there was a knock on the door.

"I'm busy; go away," Rupert called out.

The knock came again.

Now annoyed, Rupert called out, "Who is it, and what do you want?"

"It's me, Otto."

"Give me a minute to get decent, Otto. I'll be right there," Rupert called back. He quickly put all the money into a wooden box, put a lock on it, then threw some clothes over it to hide it. "Come on in, Otto."

As Otto walked in, Rupert asked, "What's so important that it couldn't wait?"

"Passengers are dying on both decks."

"What?" Rupert exclaimed.

"There are ten dead."

"How?"

"A doctor aboard thinks it's cholera. About thirty other passengers are showing symptoms."

Rupert felt panic starting to rise. "We can't show up to port with a bunch of dead people on board. No one will dare do business with us. Instruct the crew to dump the dead bodies overboard."

"What about their families?" Otto asked.

"What about them?"

"What if they want to give them a proper burial?"

Rupert was on the edge of losing his temper. "See if you can find a pastor on board that can say a few words for them and then dump them. If they still give you trouble, tell them they can join their dead in the ocean."

"All right, Rup," Otto said.

Otto returned two hours later. "There are more dead."

"How many?"

"About twenty or so. The doctor says we should stop and let all the sick off in Florida so the sickness doesn't spread in New Orleans."

"What? That would delay us by two to three days. Forget it. We can't afford the delay."

"But the doctor is quite adamant that—"

"Is the doctor running this ship?"

"No," Otto said.

"Move everyone who has symptoms to the end of the ship. If they die, have them cast overboard."

As they pulled into New Orleans, their five hundred remaining passengers disembarked. Those who had paid to go further were reimbursed a small portion of their fare. Otto was adamant that they should have the ship scrubbed for their own health; even though Rupert knew that would eat further into their profits, he finally agreed.

Chapter 43
Carry On

October 17, 1848

William was doing inventory at his store when two men came in.

"Good evening, gentlemen, how can I help you?"

"Are you Brother Chestnut?"

"I am."

"I'm Brother John Beach, and this is my business partner, Brother Joseph Eddy."

"Nice to meet you brethren. I don't recognize you. You fellows must not be from around here."

"We just came from Winter Quarters. We've been trading with the Saints down there for supplies they need. We were hoping to trade for supplies here they are still in need of," Joseph said as he looked around the store. "Looks like you carry a lot of what we're looking for."

"I've traded with Saints from Winter Quarters before. I got mostly willow baskets, washboards, and tables, all made at Winter Quarters. I can sell most of that kind of thing, but do you fellows have anything else?" William asked.

"We've got some of that, but we also have bandanas," Brother Beach said.

"Bandanas? How many?"

"About a thousand."

"What am I going to do with a thousand bandanas?"

"Sell them, of course."

"I'll never sell a thousand bandanas."

"Brother Chestnut, the Saints in Winter Quarters desperately need these supplies. I feel to promise you in the name of the Lord that if you trade the supplies we need for these bandanas, the Lord will provide a way for you to sell them," Brother Beach said.

William felt a tingling sensation all over his body as Brother Beach spoke.

"All right, I'll do it. If you fellows come across coal, I could use some more of that. My coal stores are running low."

"We tried mining and selling coal, but the ship we contracted to transport it sunk. We've vowed not to go back to coal since," Brother Eddy said.

"That's fair. So what news do you have from the Saints up north?" William asked.

"A company of Saints at Winter Quarters are planning to make the trek to the Salt Lake Valley in a few weeks. A number of them are staying at Winter Quarters, though. We have chartered two steamships to take all the stuff we've accumulated to them, along with a few hundred Saints here in St. Louis. We plan on leaving on the twentieth," Brother Eddy said.

"Have you heard about the Nauvoo Temple?" Brother Beach asked.

"No, what's happened?" William asked.

"About a week or so ago, the Church sold it to Brother David LeBaron for $5000," Brother Beach said.

"You don't say. I met Brother LeBaron on a visit to Nauvoo. He said he was trying to help sell the temple for a lot more than that. He and his wife were also caring for the Prophet's widow, Emma," William said.

"That's the one. He and his brother give paid tours now," Brother Beach said.

"That is interesting news. Well, let's get the supplies you need so I can start selling those bandanas," William said.

~ * * * ~

November 12, 1848

Johanna was chatting with a few of her friends after sacrament meeting about the unfortunate news from Nauvoo that the temple had been torched by arsons the previous month. William was paying little attention to the conversation, as he was keeping an eye on Ann and Sarah, who loved to run around the people and chairs after sacrament meeting every Sunday.

There were a lot of new faces on this particular Sunday, as there had been over the last few months with the flood of immigrants members coming from England. As his children ran past President Felt, William started listening to his conversation with some of the new arrivals.

"Welcome to St. Louis," President Felt said.

"Thank you, President, I'm John Sharp. This is my wife, Mary. We have just arrived from England with our children and grandchildren on the *Erin's Queen* last Monday. We're wonderin' if you know of any job opportunities nearby."

"Yes, there is a coal mining community seven miles south of St. Louis called Gravois Diggings. There is plenty of work for mining coal there."

William left Johanna, who was still talking to her friend, Grace Wrigley, and walked over to President Felt. "Excuse me, President, but I couldn't help but overhear these good people are looking for work. I just happen to need a farm hand to help my farm manager."

John turned to William. "Well, thank you, young man. My son"—he reached out and put his hand on a man that appeared to be about William's age—"enjoys that kind of work and is really good at it."

The man stuck out his hand. "Name is John." After looking at his father, he added, "Junior."

"Pleased to meet you. I'm William Chestnut. Pardon me if I don't shake your hand; there has been a recent outbreak of cholera."

"The cholera outbreak is really not that bad," President Felt said. "Papers are saying that some people are making too much of it. I've only seen a few families from our congregations that have had issues with it."

"If it's all the same, I'd rather be cautious than sorry," William said.

"Don't blame you one bit," the older John said.

John Jr. fidgeted. "I'd be happy to come and work on your farm."

William grinned. "Great! I'd be happy to have you. Come by tomorrow and I'll introduce you to my farm manager, Jim Beaman."

~ * * * ~

After a few weeks of work, John was proving to be a great employee. William ran into him and President Felt as he was on his way to the store one morning.

"Good morning, William," President Felt said.

"Morning," John said.

"Good morning, Brethren," William replied.

"How is your family?" President Felt asked.

"We're holding up. John has been a heaven send. Couldn't have asked for a better worker. Though it must be hard for you being away from your family for days at a time. How is your family doing down in Gravois Diggings, John?" William asked.

"Good. Turns out several of our friends from England are there already; they came last year. My father bought a bunch of gun barrels at an army auction held here in St. Louis, and he got some gunsmiths to make stocks for them. He is now selling them for a profit."

"Next time you see him, send him my way I could use a few more guns in my inventory at the store," William said.

"I'll do that, Brother Chestnut. Thank you."

Chapter 44
From Bad to Worse

Sales of William's bandanas soared. Everyone wanted one to cover his or her face, hoping it would protect them from catching cholera. Handshakes became taboo, and the sale of vegetables and fish went down to almost nothing, causing several businesses to shut down.

Cholera spread quickly in New Orleans. By January 1849, word had spread to St. Louis of the sickness that was running amuck in New Orleans. City officials decided to drain Chouteau's Pond, their largest body of standing water. They also banned the consumption of fish and vegetables.

By May, the papers were starting to publish the death tolls that the cholera was exacting on the local population. They labeled it an epidemic.

Many businesses complained that they were blowing the situation out of proportion. But the fear of getting sick spread faster than the disease.

It got worse as people stopped going out and preferred to stay at home, where it was presumably safe. William's store was able to stay afloat because it became well known that he had one of the only supplies of bandanas left in the city.

The way of life had changed drastically. Covering the face was encouraged, as was avoiding large groups and public places, which effectively shut down many businesses. The courts struggled as juries refused to show up, effectively shutting down the courts; schools shut down, and church congregations stopped meeting together.

Doctors were largely ineffective; they treated the symptoms as best they could but did not know how to cure the cholera—and nothing they thought of stopped the spread. Generally recommended treatments consisted of bathing weekly, avoiding public gatherings and public places as much as possible, keeping fish and vegetables out of one's diet, and staying out of cold or damp weather.

As many businesses closed or significantly reduced their workforce, the number of unemployed grew steadily. Soon wagons trolled the streets, driven by those who had overcome the sickness and were now immune, with calls of "bring out your dead." After loading bodies into the wagon, the drivers took them to the cemetery, where trenches had been prepared for the piling number of bodies that regularly came in.

President Nathanial Felt kept himself busy checking on the Saints and administering blessings where needed. Everywhere he went, either someone in the family had it or they knew someone who had it. It seemed to hit people so randomly. He decided it was time to check in on the Chestnuts, and he headed to William's store.

As President Felt entered the store, William greeted him. "How are things, President? Is your family well?"

"Yes, thank heaven. There is a lot of work for the Saints to do to help the sick. I have asked the bishops of the six wards here to report back to me on whether the Saints are administering to the sick and faithfully discharging their duties by comforting the hearts of their neighbors. We need to make sure everyone is taking the proper precautions and helping where they can."

William said, "It was quite the sight in church to see everyone sitting two seats apart and all wearing bandanas. First time I saw it, I wondered if I had come to worship or get robbed," William joked, and they both chuckled.

"How are things in your area?" President Felt asked.

"I have two neighbors who have caught it."

"Oh my. Cholera is a nasty disease. Do you know what to watch for?"

"Just that it gives you the runs and vomiting," William said.

President Felt nodded. "Some other symptoms you'll want to watch for are a deathly look with sunken eyes; cold, bluish skin; and wrinkled hands and feet."

"This disease is turning into more of a plague with the thousands it has taken. I saw just yesterday a few small children being loaded into one of those death wagons," William said.

"Yes, even in the Church it has become quite the crisis. Do you know the Westwood family who came from England two months ago?" President Felt asked.

"Yes, they've been in several times," William replied.

"They lost both parents and their newborn baby to the disease last week, leaving the other seven children orphans. It has been difficult finding them all a place. People are scared and don't even want to come to church. I was successful, however, in finding a few families who would care for the children," President Felt explained.

"That is awful. That'd be difficult to lose parents at such a tender age. When I lost my parents, I thought my whole world had crashed. If I didn't have Johanna to help me through it, I don't know what I would have done. Poor children don't have anyone familiar they can turn to."

"No, they don't. But the families who took them in are kind and caring. They'll not be left destitute."

"This epidemic has made people afraid. I've never seen anything like it in the way our lives have changed since it started. When it began, I think the city was trying to cover it up for the sake of the businesses, which is why it got so bad. Now it's worse than ever. People won't go shopping, and many won't go to church. And those who do leave their homes wear bandanas to cover their faces," William added.

"You're right—the cholera crisis is causing a financial crisis. Starting next Sunday, we are going to ask members to hold sacrament meeting in their homes. Hopefully, that will help to stop the spread of cholera to our congregation," President Felt said, then leaned on the counter, catching himself from falling.

"You all right?" William asked.

"I've been going most the day, administering to the sick, giving blessings and comfort where I can. I haven't had much time to eat."

"Take some of this beef jerky home with you," William said, handing him a package.

"Thank you, William. That's very kind of you."

"You need to stay home and rest. What if you get the disease?" William asked.

"I've given blessings to hundreds that have the wretched disease, and I've been all right. This is the Lord's work, William; I dare not stop. He has called me to watch over this part of His vineyard. I will continue to act in His name and try to do what He wants me to do. I have faith that the Lord will protect me if I stay faithful in the discharge of my duty."

"I'm glad you're leading us, President. You're a better man than I'll ever be."

"Don't sell yourself short, William; you're a good man in your own right."

"Thanks, President. I'd better close shop and get home."

"You do that. Say hello to Johanna and those cute children of yours."

"Will do," William responded.

~ * * * ~

May 16, 1849

"I just landed us a huge cargo of cattle headed for Winter Quarters, Iowa. There will be no room for passengers on the lower deck. They're paying us a small fortune for this load," Rupert told Otto.

"That's great, Rup."

Rupert grinned. "We'll have enough in our lock box after this that we won't have to worry about money for years to come."

"Perhaps we should keep some of that money in a bank, Rupert. You know, just for safekeeping."

"There ain't anything safe about banks, they get robbed all the time. Plus, you probably don't remember the banking crisis in 1837. Banks closed all over the place, taking people's fortunes with them. I remember my parents lost half their savings. Banks are not a trustworthy establishment. But I can trust this lockbox, and the place we hide it is one no one would ever find."

"I guess that makes sense," Otto replied.

"Of course, it does. You leave the thinking to me, Otto. I've got a knack for these kinds of things. I mean, just look at us, did you ever imagine we'd be this rich?"

"Never."

"Well, I knew we would come this far because I have vision. I can see us going even further after this haul. We can buy another steamer that's bigger and nicer; you can captain it yourself. In a few years, we'll own all the steamers along the Mississippi," Rupert said.

"Why don't we go out on the town and celebrate tonight—get us some women and some real whiskey," Otto suggested.

"I like your way of thinking, Otto, but let's just do the whiskey. With the cholera epidemic still raging, we're likely to catch it if we go out with women," Rupert said.

As Rupert and Otto disembarked, they ran into Nathaniel Felt. "Mr. Howard, I was just looking for you."

"Otto, this is Mr. Felt, he is the one that needs the cattle transported. Mr. Felt, this is my business partner Otto Flint."

"Pleased to meet you, Mr. Felt," Otto said.

"Pleasure is all mine. Listen, Mr. Howard, I need to cancel our arrangement."

"What! Why?" Rupert said, his eyes blinking rapidly.

"Another steamship offered to take them for a third of what you're charging me."

"You can't do that. We made a deal! You paid a retainer, and I've been refusing passengers based on our agreement," Rupert exclaimed, his eyes bulging.

"Listen, I'm sorry. You keep the retainer I paid you as compensation for your troubles. Besides the cattle, we have a lot of people we need to move down there, and with the money I'm saving with this other company, we'll be able to get a lot more people down to Winter Quarters."

"Who is it you're going through instead?" Rupert insisted.

"I'm afraid that's my business, gentlemen. Good day to you," President Felt said, tipping his hat and leaving.

"It's not right for him to back out on us like that," Otto said.

"No, it's not. I've got an idea that might get us our deal back," Rupert said with a smile.

"What is it?"

"You follow him and see where he goes and who he talks to. We'll find out who he has switched to, and we'll sink their ship. Then he'll come back to us."

"What if he goes to someone else instead of coming back to us?" Otto asked.

"We'll take care of them too, though if we position ourselves right, we can make sure he talks to us first. We might have to lower our price a little to convince him, but I think it won't be a hard sell once his other options start sinking." Rupert looked up to see that Felt was still in sight. "Hurry after him before he disappears."

Otto followed President Felt into the city. President Felt walked up to a home and knocked on the door. A few moments passed, and the door opened. They greeted each other, and President Felt went inside. After about thirty minutes, he came back out and headed in another direction.

Otto followed him at a distance for several hours, watching him enter and leave homes. Finally, President Felt headed back toward the docks. He walked toward a large steamship painted all in white.

He looked at the name, committed it to memory, and went back to see Rupert.

Otto found Rupert on board the *Charlton*. "I followed Felt most of the day."

"What did you find out?"

"He visits a lot of people," Otto replied.

"I mean about who he is having ship the livestock."

"I saw him go into the steamboat called the *White Cloud* about ten minutes ago," Otto said.

"Good. We'll wait until midnight and light up a mattress in its passenger quarters. If all goes as planned, tonight we can turn the *White Cloud* into a white cloud. Let's go and get fuel from our stores below deck and get ready for tonight."

Just after midnight, Otto and Rupert walked along the decks carrying a small keg of kerosene fuel used to light lamps. They crept along as they approached the ship.

Rupert whispered to Otto, "Looks like all is quiet."

He looked up toward the entrance and saw a sentry. Rupert tapped Otto on the shoulder and pointed.

"I see him," Otto whispered.

"Quiet. He might be asleep, but I don't want to take any chances. Here, take this." Rupert handed Otto a long bowie knife.

"What you want me to do with this?"

"Walk up there. If he is awake, cut his throat. If not, plunge it into his heart," Rupert said.

"I don't want to kill him. Let's just sneak past him."

"Better he die now than wake up while we're on board and raise the alarm," Rupert reasoned.

"It's your knife; you do it," Otto said, handing back the knife.

"Fine. We'll try to sneak past, but if he wakes up and catches us, it's on you."

"Let's go," Otto said, creeping on board the ship.

Rupert waited until Otto passed the sentry, then he followed.

They crept across the deck of the ship. Rupert noted the layout was very similar to that of his own ship. They snuck into one of the empty passengers' quarters and then poured kerosene all over the mattress in the room.

"Take that lantern off your belt and light it," Rupert said.

Otto lit the lantern. Rupert joined him. "I'll take the lantern and throw it on the bed. You take my knife and go stand by that sleeping sentry. If he wakes up, then take care of him. If you don't kill him, stay there until I reach you, just in case he hears me running toward you. If he wakes up at any time, take him out, or he'll catch us, and we'll end up in prison."

Otto handed Rupert the lantern and took the knife. He ran off and left Rupert standing at the room entrance. Rupert swung the lantern, and just at the right moment, let it fly through the air. He watched only a split second to ensure his aim was true and then took off. When he got to the place where he expected to see Otto and the sentry, he saw neither and hurried off the ship.

The fire behind him spread quickly to other parts of the ship as he continued to run down the docks. As he ran, he saw a man about fifty yards ahead of him running like a woman with her hair on fire. Rupert knew it had to be Otto, except he was running away from the shipyard into town. Rupert followed him, unsure as to why he didn't head back to the ship. Rupert yelled after him. When they had gone a fair distance away from the docks, Otto finally stopped running and heard Rupert's voice.

After he caught up to Otto, Rupert asked, wheezing and huffing, "What were you thinking, Otto? What are we doing out here instead of back at our ship?"

"The guard woke up when I came running and attacked me. I used the knife on him and pushed him into the water, then I just kept going and couldn't stop," Otto said, out of breath himself.

"It's all right, Otto; you did good. We did it. Let's go back to our ship and get some rest. In the morning, we'll find Felt and negotiate the shipment with him."

Rupert put his arm around Otto. Fire bells rang out into the night. The city's firefighters were being dispatched to put out the fire that was blazing on the river.

"What if they save the ship?" Otto asked.

"I don't think they can completely. Even if they do get the fire out before she sinks, they won't sail with a half-burnt ship. There is no way the ship could take on Felt's shipment now, even if they save the ship, which I don't think is likely."

Rupert patted him on the shoulder. "Come on. Let's go watch. You'll see."

Rupert and Otto went back and watched the firefighters fight the blazing ship. The fire had spread to a neighboring ship, the *Bates*. As fire crews shifted their attention to that ship, they heard someone yell something about a burning rope then watched in horror as the *Bates* floated away and started running into other ships. Rupert looked at its trajectory and saw that the river was taking it toward his ship.

"No!" Rupert and Otto said in unison as the *Bates* rammed into the side of the *Charlton*, setting it ablaze as well.

Rupert sprinted to the ship, hoping he could get to his cabin and extract the lock box before it was too late. But by the time he got there, he couldn't board the ship without being consumed by the flames.

At first, he thought he might try to run through the flames and see if he could make it, but Otto caught hold of him and held him tight.

"It's lost, Rup. It's gone. We'll have to start over."

Rupert was in tears. He had given up struggling against Otto and cursed first God, and then the firefighters for not doing a better job at containing the fire.

Chapter 45
Fighting Fire with Fire

Twenty-three steamboats lit up the night sky. The whole city was on alert, and the fire had spread from the ships to the shore. Freight that had been stacked on the levee helped the fire spread more rapidly until it started burning nearby buildings.

William awoke to the sound of pounding on his door. President Felt stood there, the sky irradiated orange behind him. Smoke billowed all around. "William, come quickly! A fire started on the river and has spread into town."

William nodded and ran back in to get his clothes on.

"What's going on, William?" Johanna asked as William got into his boots.

"There is a fire in the city. I'm going to go help."

By the time William found the firefighters, they were breaking into his store and the buildings all down the south side of Market Street and moving large kegs of black powder into them.

"Hey, wait! Stop! What are you doing? That's my store," William yelled as he ran up to the men moving the keg of black powder.

"We're supposed to be stopping the fire, not helping it," he yelled at the firemen.

The one closest to him looked at the other fireman helping him move the keg. "Hold on, Phil." He set the keg down and turned to William. "You're Mormon, aren't you?

"Yes."

The man smirked. "Then your store ain't worth a spit anyway."

William charged forward and tackled the man, knocking him over. Phil bowled into William, who fell to the ground. He heard Phil call for help. Before he could get up, he was surrounded by firemen who pulled him away from the building.

The fire chief approached William, who had stopped struggling. "Listen, I know you won't like this, but you see that fire over there? It's headed in this direction, and we can't stop it. These stores are going to burn down anyway and will spread the fire to the cathedral and the rest of the city. We need to blow up these buildings to create a fire barrier to save the rest of the city. The fire can't spread if we create this gap."

William didn't say anything. He stood watching, his mind going numb. The men continued their work. William had a thought to save as much of his goods as he could, and he grabbed a wheelbarrow from behind his shop.

He was stopped by a fireman, who asked, "What are you doing?"

"Trying to get my things."

The fireman shook his head. "We're out of time. You need to leave."

William emptied the cash register, took one last look around the store, and walked out. The firefighters cleared everyone away from the buildings.

There was an explosion down the street in Phillips Music Store. One of the firefighters was there spreading black powder. Several men shouted, "Thomas! Captain Targee!" The fire captain had been killed in the explosion, but the work needed to continue. The other buildings were all prepared in a similar manner and were ready to be demolished.

There was a countdown and a deafening noise as the explosion took down the row of businesses. William's heart sank, but he knew he had to keep moving. He went to work helping fight the fire.

The gap created by the explosions effectively stopped the fire from moving south. But two blocks south, another fire ignited from the blazing boats on the river. The new fire moved south of Elm Street and consumed wood homes all the way up to Third Street before the fire was finally contained.

Back in the business district, another large explosion boomed. A large copper shop had blown up in the blaze, and spread the fire down two more city blocks. Bucket brigade lines formed all over the city as people frantically fought to save their homes and businesses.

The work of fighting the fire continued for eight more hours until it was finally contained. It had reached twenty-seven blocks of the city, fifteen of which were completely destroyed. Almost everything east of Second Street had been consumed between Market Street and Locust. Nine of the blocks east of Third Street between Spruce and Walnut had also been destroyed by the fire. In all, more than four hundred buildings were destroyed, along with the twenty-three steamboats, and more than a dozen other boats on the river.

Three had died fighting the fire. The property damages were catastrophic. William stood in the street physically exhausted, surrounded in every direction by the charred remains of the business district. He wandered over to the second area that had been set ablaze by the steamboats. He was shocked at the magnitude of the destruction.

William found President Felt leaning against a half-burned building.

"Thanks for coming to help, William."

"It's not enough that the city is ravaged with cholera—it has to be burned to the ground too?" William said, bitterly.

"William, the Lord is in charge. All this is unfortunate and tragic, but the Lord will still help us if we turn to Him. He can turn our tragedies into blessings if we don't abandon Him."

William kicked the ground, spraying ash into the air, bitterness spread over his face.

"Don't harden your heart, William. The Lord needs you now more than ever. At times like these we are each faced with a crucial decision that could affect our eternal welfare. Whatever choice we make, there is one eternal truth we can rely on. The unconditional love that the Savior and our Heavenly Father have for us is constant and unchanging. We are never abandoned, we are never forgotten, we are never alone."

"It seems like every time I run into good times and things are going well, life turns me upside-down and throws me into a rut. Sometimes I feel I am being picked on, like the Lord thinks I'm getting too happy, so He knocks me down," William said.

"Sometimes on our journey to our celestial home, we allow ourselves to get snagged on the barb of a spiritual fish hook," President Felt said. "The only way for Him to help us off the hook is to push us down or bring us low enough that we can get away from the snare. Then He can lift us higher than we thought possible. Many want to hang on to that hook, not trusting that the Lord will catch us when we fall, remaining content in their stagnation. But, if we trust in Him, He will catch us and lift us to greater heights."

"Why does it have to be so hard?" William asked.

"Well, you do own a farm. Don't you use manure on your crops?"

William shoved a hand through his hair. "What does that have to do with anything?"

"Sometimes our trials and hardships are like manure."

"How do you mean?"

"Like manure, hardships stink. But just like manure, hardships spur growth. The Lord has a way of making us better, stronger, more like Him through our trials. Don't abandon Him, William. He will never abandon you."

A calm swept through William as President Felt spoke. "You're right. I wish my faith was as strong as yours."

"You show your faith through your actions regularly. You did today. After you lost your store, you forgot yourself and went to work helping others. I have no doubt your faith is as strong as any I've seen."

"Thank you, President," William said. "I noticed the fire made it to your end of town. How is your home?"

"Interestingly enough, some of the houses around mine burned down, but my home was untouched by the flames. The Lord saw fit to spare my home for some reason, for which I am very grateful."

"Wow. You must be living right, President."

"I know plenty of others who are living right that weren't so fortunate, and they will need our help. Your home wasn't near the fire, and mine was passed over. Luckily, most of the buildings burned were businesses. But I do know a few of our brethren who lost their homes. I'll be opening my home to one of those families; can the Lord count on you to open yours?"

William nodded. "He can."

~ * * * ~

That night William and Johanna sat on the porch swing discussing the terrible toll the fire took on the city.

Johanna asked, "Do you think the Saints who had their houses burn down were bad people?"

"No, Johanna, I know plenty of good people who lost their homes to the fire. The Lord says it rains on the good and the bad. When it comes to nature's forces, everyone suffers equally."

"Why would the Lord spare President Felt's home and not the rest?"

"Perhaps it is because that home being there is important to the Lord's work. How effective do you reckon President Felt would have been at organizing us all as well as he has and getting those Saints who lost their homes taken care of if he was too busy worrying about how he and his family were going to get by? I think the Lord needed President Felt to strengthen the Saints."

"Yes, and I don't know where the St. Louis Conference would be without him."

They sat silently together looking out over the smoke-filled sky. Johanna thought of all the loss and the suffering many would experience in the coming months.

"How are they going to find happiness again having gone through such tragedy? They lost everything—their homes, their paintings, their nice rugs, their fancy furniture. For some of them it was everything they owned, gone in a day," Johanna said, with a forlorn look.

That sparked a memory in William. "My mother once taught me that true riches lie not in the material things in life, but in our relationships."

Johanna looked at William. "I never thought about it like that, but it rings true. My relationship with you, with our children, with the Lord; those are the things that make me happy—truly happy."

Chapter 46
The St. Louis Plague

By mid-June 1849, President Felt held a meeting and prayed that the epidemic would be stopped among the Saints in St. Louis. He had also organized the Saints to help administer relief to those who were suffering due to the fire. Several homes were being rebuilt using donations from the members.

William was using his spare time helping to rebuild some of those homes that were taken by the fire. He was sitting on an unfinished roof attaching shingles when he heard President Felt calling up to him.

"President Felt, how are you?"

"Good; just stopped by to see how things were going. How's your family?"

"My family is well, but I lost my farmhand. You remember John Sharp?"

"Yes, if I recall correctly, his parents, John and Mary, went to work in the coal mines at Gravois Diggings. Did he fall sick too?" President Felt asked.

"No, he moved to be with his family. Near the beginning of June his mother, Mary, died within four hours of showing symptoms of cholera."

"That's terrible. I pray this epidemic will end soon. It's taken a terrible toll on this city and on our congregations as well. How are you doing financially? Now that your store is gone, are you struggling to feed your family?"

"No, I've got the income from the farm; that's where I've been spending most of my time since the fire. We're having to travel to other cities not affected by the plague to sell anything, but we're getting by. Though even if we weren't, I've got a large sum at the bank that could sustain us for several years if we didn't have any income," William said.

"It's good to hear you're not left destitute with the loss of your business, as many business owners have been. You've structured your life well with the two businesses and money in reserve."

"The reserve money and the farm came from my parents dying and leaving me what they had. I guess that was the blessing from that tragedy. I still wonder what blessings will come from the two we're faced with now—the epidemic and the fire."

"Often we have to get through it, and then look back on what has happened to see the blessings that have come. Sometimes it seems too difficult for us to recognize them as they are happening. Are you going to switch to farming, then?"

"I'm hoping I won't have to farm for too much longer. It's not the kind of work I enjoy. The city has offered to help rebuild the store, since the firefighters are the ones who destroyed it."

"Sounds to me like you're already seeing the blessings come," President Felt said.

"I reckon you're right. I'd better get back to this roof. Shingles won't attach themselves, you know."

"Thank you for your service, William," President Felt said.

"I'm glad I can help," William replied and got back to his work.

The roof finally finished, William found Destiny and headed back home.

As William walked in the door, Bessie rushed into the room. Worry lined her face. "Mr. Chestnut. Your wife. She—"

"What's wrong? Where is she?" William asked.

"In bed," Bessie said.

William rushed to the bedroom. Johanna lay on the bed; her hands looked wrinkled, and her eyes were sunken.

"Johanna!" William gasped, as he rushed to her side and felt her forehead. Her skin felt cold. "No! Why? Why is this happening?" William pressed his palm into his forehead.

"William," Johanna whispered. "I'm dying, I've got cholera."

"No!" William cried.

William knew that most people who got cholera died within a day, sometimes within hours. He didn't know how much time he had, but he knew he needed to get help quickly. Leaving the children in Bessie's care, he ran to the neighbors' house and gave them instructions on how to get to President Felt's home. "Tell him to find the fastest horse he can and to come right away."

William rushed back to Johanna and put a warm, wet washcloth on her forehead.

"Johanna, I can't lose you. Please fight this. Please stay with me," William said, sobbing desperation in his voice.

"Johanna, I can't do everything you do for our family. I don't know how. How I could go on without you? I don't know how any of us could."

~ * * * ~

Jefferson was sitting on the edge of his bed, eyes wide. "Is she going to be all right?"

Sarah met his eyes. "Sometimes the only thing you can do to get through your difficulties is take the matter to the Lord, then trust that He will help."

"Is that what Grandpa Chestnut did?" Jefferson asked.

Sarah nodded. "It is, but he needed a little help."

~ * * * ~

"Daddy?" Ann came up behind William, Sarah stood beside her. "Is mommy going to die?"

"I don't know," William replied.

"You told me God answers our prayers," Ann said.

"I know I did, sweetie," William said.

Sarah jumped into William's arms. "Let's ask God to make Mom better."

Ann nodded her agreement.

William gazed into his girls' earnest faces. Had they been the same age, he didn't think he would be able to tell them apart. Their wide, tear-filled eyes stared back at him. "All right, girls."

They folded their arms and William was about to start when he heard Sarah say, "Dear Father in Heaven, my mommy is really sick. Please make her better. I love my mommy so much, so much. I know you love us and don't want us to be sad, so please don't let her die. And bless my daddy that he can be happy. In the name of Jesus Christ, Amen."

William's heart melted as he listened to his daughter's prayer. He wrapped both of them in his arms, hugging them as if they were the last thing he had to hold on to.

A thought struck William, that he should go to the kitchen. He ignored it, and kept hugging his girls. The thought came back to him more forcefully than before. He didn't know why this thought kept coming to him, but right now he just wanted to comfort his girls.

Ann pushed him away. "Daddy?"

"Yes, Ann?"

"I think you should go to the kitchen," Ann said.

"You do?" If they both had the feeling, William decided he'd better go, even if he wasn't sure why.

"I think you're right. You girls stay here and look after your mother. I'll be back," William said.

As soon as he walked into the kitchen the thought came that he needed to boil a pot of water.

"Bessie," William called out. "Bessie! Bessie, I need your help. Please come to the kitchen."

Bessie walked into the kitchen. "Mr. Chestnut, what are you doing in the kitchen?"

"Never mind that. Where is the salt?" William asked as he filled a pot with water.

Bessie grabbed a bag of salt off a hook and handed it to William.

William put the pot on the stove and lit the fire. He grabbed a handful of salt out of the salt bag and threw it in the pot.

Thoughts kept coming to his mind. Once he had followed one direction, a new instruction came.

"Get me some lemons and limes and oranges and cut them in half," he told Bessie. She went to work, following his instructions.

"What are we making?" Bessie asked.

"I'm not really sure—just keep going, please. We have to get this done quickly. There's not much time."

William grabbed the lemon, lime, and orange halves and started squeezing the juices out of them into the pot.

"Do we have honey?" William asked.

"Yes, I'll get it." Bessie opened a cabinet and handed the honey to William.

He poured what honey was left in the bottle into his mixture. When the concoction came to a boil, he took it off the stove.

He turned to Bessie. "I need a mug."

Bessie fetched a mug and handed it to him.

William poured the liquid into the mug and took it to his wife. Bessie followed. When he entered the room, Ann asked, "What did you make, Daddy?"

"A drink. I think it could help your mother."

William knelt beside his wife. "Johanna, I made you a drink."

Johanna just laid there not wanting to move. William blew on the drink to cool it down.

"Girls, can you go and check on your brother for me?"

"All right, Daddy," they said then ran out of the room.

"Johanna please drink this." She shifted her eyes to him but continued to lay there unmoving.

William set down the mug. "Bessie, help me sit her up."

They got on either side of Johanna, grabbed her upper arms, and pulled her into a sitting position. She fought a little and tried to lay back down.

"No, Johanna. You need to drink this," William said, picking up the mug and putting it to her lips and making her drink slowly. She coughed, and he put it down. After a few moments he said, "We're going to try again."

Once he had persuaded her to drink half the mug, she threw it all up. Just then William heard a knock at the door.

"That must be President Felt. Bessie, will you please let him in?" William said as he cleaned up the mess.

"Yes, Mr. Chestnut."

Bessie went to the door and found President Nathaniel Felt standing there.

"Good evening, Bessie. William sent for me. I came as quickly as I could."

"Please come in. Mrs. Chestnut is deathly ill. They're waiting for you in the bedroom."

William turned to see President Felt enter the room.

"Nathaniel, Johanna's got cholera. Please give her a blessing?"

"Of course. I'll just go wash my hands and be right back."

When President Felt returned, he put a drop of oil on Johanna's head, laid his hands on her head, and said a short prayer. "Johanna Chestnut, by the power of the priesthood I hold and in the name of Jesus Christ, I command you to be whole. You have more yet to do on this earth before the Lord takes you to Himself. Amen."

Johanna's eyes opened and tears were flowing down her cheeks. "Thank you, Nathanial," she said.

President Felt backed away and put his hand on William's shoulder.

"Keep giving her plenty to drink, and let me know if there is anything else I can do to help."

William handed Bessie the mug, "Bessie, will you refill this mug for me?"

"Yes, Mr. Chestnut," Bessie said and left the room.

"I'd better go now. Another family requested I come to their home at the same time I got your message," President Felt said.

"Thank you for coming," William said.

Later that night. Johanna was sitting up in bed smiling. Color had returned to her skin, and she was eating a soup Bessie had prepared. She had downed the entire concoction William had made for her. That combined with the soup she was eating helped improve her condition. William sat in a chair by her side as she ate.

"I'm so grateful President Felt was able to give me that blessing. I feel almost back to normal," Johanna said.

"I'm glad, too. he made it just in time," William said, then recounted his experience praying with the girls and making the drink. "The Lord must have wanted you to get better. He was guiding me every step of the way."

~ * * * ~

August 20, 1849

Johanna sat at her loom making cloth, and Sister Felt sat by her side, helping wind the yarn. Children ran around the house playing.

"The city dedicated a large sum of money to help rebuild the business district," Johanna explained. "They told William that they would start with the businesses they had to blow up to stop the progress of the fire. They just finished the store last week. It's a much nicer building than it was before."

"That's wonderful," Eliza said.

"Yes. The building is bigger and was built to be fireproof, with brick instead of wood. I'm glad your home was spared. I was praying your home would be saved from the fire," Johanna said.

"Thank you. Johanna, and thank you for donating all this cloth we've made. It will be a blessing to the sisters who have lost their homes to be able to make clothing for their families."

"I'm glad I can help in some way," Johanna said then looked down. "So much suffering has plagued this city this year. I don't know why the Lord allows so many of His children to suffer so."

"The Lord works in mysterious ways." Eliza said. "Cholera spread throughout the city, and it seems like the fire helped cure it. The city will be rebuilt to be bigger and nicer than it was before. My husband says the Lord gives us trials to help us to grow closer to the Lord as long as we keep our faith."

"Keeping our faith doesn't change what happened," Johanna said.

"No. No, it doesn't," Eliza said, "but it can make things seem less overwhelming to us, take away our sorrow, and give us strength to move forward."

"That reminds me of something Emma Smith once said to me. I was visiting with her in Nauvoo. It was a chance meeting. But we got on to this topic and she said that God lets us fall low so we can be lifted higher. Then she said that she wouldn't let sorrow rob her of her faith, and that the Lord would never give us more than we could deal with—that trusting in the Lord is what made her stronger."

"Sounds to me like she is still wise beyond her years," Eliza said.

Chapter 47
Hired Hands

March 14, 1850

Rupert and Otto knocked on the front door of the Chestnut home. William came to the door. "How can I help you gentlemen?"

"Are you William Chestnut?" Rupert asked.

"Yes," William responded.

"I'm Rupert Howard, and this is my friend, Otto Flint. We saw the ad you put in the paper that you needed two farmhands," Rupert said.

"Yes. Do you have any experience in farming?" William asked.

"Oh, yes, Mr. Chestnut, we've been doing farmhand work for years," Rupert said.

"I see. Whose farm have you worked on?"

"We worked on a farm not too far from here about six years ago for Mr. Temblor."

"Yes, I know Frank and his wife, Rhonda."

"Them is the ones!" Otto said.

Rupert nodded. "We're hard workers and know our way around a farm. Don't we, Otto?"

"We sure do," Otto said.

"Well, come back tomorrow morning and I'll introduce you to my farm manager. If he approves of you, we'll hire you on," William said.

"Thank you, Mr. Chestnut," Rupert said. He and Otto turned to leave then stopped and turned back. "Mr. Chestnut?"

"Yes?"

"Would you mind if we stayed in your barn tonight? We don't really have anywhere to stay the night," Rupert asked.

William considered the request for a moment and started to get a bad feeling about these two.

Rupert scrunched his hat in his hands. "Please, Mr. Chestnut, we don't have anywhere else to go. Fire burned down our homes, and you can check with Mr. Temblor. He'll verify we are hard workers."

William thought about scriptures that talk about helping the poor.

"That should be all right," William said.

"Thank you, sir," Rupert said.

"I'll show you to the barn."

William walked them over to the barn and bid them good day. He returned to his home, and as he walked in the door, Johanna asked, "Who was at the door?"

"A couple of men who were looking to work as farmhands," William replied.

"Oh, did it look like they would be good?"

"They said they used to work for our neighbors, the Temblors."

"I was just going to go over and ask Frank if he remembered them and what he thought about their work," William said.

"Good idea. What did you go out for?" Johanna asked.

"They said that they didn't have a place to stay, so I offered our barn."

"What! You don't know them at all, and you invited them to stay on our property?" Johanna exclaimed.

"Well, I didn't invite them exactly; they asked if they could stay in the barn," William explained.

"And you told them to go right ahead?"

"Well, they said their homes got burned in the fire."

"What if they're thieves or killers? You don't know anything about them, and you just let them stay on our property? I want them gone," Johanna said, clearly upset.

"Wait. Listen, it's true I don't know them, but before we send them packing let me go and talk to someone who did know them. If they turn out to be terrible people, I won't hesitate to tell them to leave."

"Fine, but I don't feel right about this. What kind of men ask to stay in a stranger's barn unless they are planning on robbing him?"

"You can't just make irrational judgments about people based on knowing one or two facts that you may not even be interpreting correctly," William said.

"Fine. Go talk to the Temblors, but I still don't feel right about this."

William got his vest and hat and rode Destiny over to see his neighbor Frank.

Frank was a gruff man. Though anytime he started something, he was very good at it and had a work ethic like a horse. He was also very hospitable and friendly to all his visitors.

William knew that he would get an earful of complaints from Frank about anyone who worked for him down to the smallest detail, especially if they were not good workers. That was good, William thought. That way he would know exactly what he was getting with these two.

William knocked and Frank answered. "Well, hello, neighbor, come on in. Can I get you a beer or a whiskey?"

William shook his head. "I hope I'm not bothering you coming at this late hour."

"Nonsense, sit down. To what do I owe the pleasure of your visit?"

"Some boys who used to work for you years back are at my place wanting to do some farmhand work. I wanted to see if you happen to remember them and what you thought of their work," William explained.

"Sure, I'd be happy to help. What're the names of the lads?" Frank asked.

"Rupert Howard and Otto Flint," William said. "Those names ring a bell?"

"Actually, I do remember those boys because they did such a good job and only worked for me for three weeks. I got robbed during that time. I had to let them go. Couldn't afford their services after that," Frank said.

"Well, sounds like they are worth hiring. Thanks, Frank; I appreciate you taking the time," William said.

"No problem; that's what neighbors are for. You can stop by anytime. Sure you don't want a drink of something before you go?"

"No, but thank you. You've already given me plenty."

William went home and told his wife about his conversation with Frank Temblor and tried to ease her mind on hiring Rupert and Otto.

"What if they staged the robbery?"

"Johanna—whatever happened to not thinking the worst of people? You haven't even met them, and you've already made up your mind about them. Try extending a little bit of charity. What would the Savior do?"

"You're right, of course, William. I guess I just get nervous around people we don't know."

"Well, we do know someone we both trust and respect; he knows both of them and speaks very highly of them—and coming from Frank, that's saying something," William said.

"Yes, you're right. That *is* saying something, coming from him. He complains about most everybody," Johanna replied.

"All right, then. We'll let them stay the night in the barn away from us. Then I'll let them know once they start working that they need to find their own place," William said.

"All right. But—" Johanna said.

"But what?" William asked.

"Maybe we should pray about hiring them," Johanna suggested.

"I think we've already done our due diligence. They check out to be good men," William said.

"Well . . . all right," Johanna said.

~ * * * ~

March 15, 1850

William introduced Rupert and Otto to Jim Beaman the next morning and left them in his charge.

"Welcome to the Chestnut farm, boys. I hope you both have a hearty appetite for work, because there is plenty of it to do on this farm."

"We're no strangers to farm work, isn't that right, Otto?" Rupert said.

"That's right," Otto responded. "We've done our share of that."

"Good," Mr. Beaman said. "I've already plowed the fields. I'll need you two boys to plant and water the crops. But first you'll need to cover the field with plaster of Paris."

"We've done this kind of work before; you can count on us," Rupert said.

Later that week, after they had finished laying the plaster of Paris, Otto said, "I preferred the easy life on the river. This is hard work. At least on the ship we could tell others to do our work for us."

"I know. But we'll have to stick this out until we can build our fortune again. These folks seem pretty well off. Let's do what we've done before, and as soon as we find the right opportunity, we can relieve these good folks of their riches and put those riches to our own good use."

"Like what?" Otto asked.

"Perhaps it could be enough to get us to California; you've heard they discovered gold out there last year. They say it's in the mountains and in the streams—it's everywhere just waiting for people like us to pick it up and become rich. We could make more than we did with the steamboats."

"Now that's a plan I can support," Otto said.

"That's right. I've also got a plan to reduce the amount of work we'll have to do here."

"What's your plan, Rup?"

"We'll poison half the field when we go to plant the crop, then we won't have to do as much when it's time to pull the crop."

"I like it."

The next day Rupert and Otto planted the field. The night before, Rupert was able to convince William to give him an advance based on the good work already done. He used the money to buy the poison he needed to kill the crop, which came in a half-gallon jug.

As they started planting Otto said, "I was thinking. If we use that poison on these plants now, they won't grow. Maybe the farm manager will think we never planted them."

"You may have a point. We'll save the poison for after the crops start growing," Rupert said. "Why don't we take a break and we can hide the poison. Let's put it in the barn. There are plenty of places to hide it in there."

As Rupert and Otto got to the barn, the door opened and Jim Beaman stepped out, almost running into them. He looked at the poison that Rupert was holding then looked back at Rupert.

"What is that for?" Jim asked

"None of your business," Rupert said as he pushed Jim back into the barn. "Otto, I think we'd better take care of him."

Otto tackled Jim. Rupert put the poison down and helped Otto restrain him. Otto had him on the ground in a choke hold. Rupert sat on Jim's legs and grabbed his arm so he couldn't resist. Jim finally went still.

"Hold him, Otto, in case he comes to. We can make him drink some of this poison to finish him off." Rupert opened the jug of poison and forced it into Jim's mouth. Jim choked and convulsed, then went still.

"Hide the body in the empty horse stall and throw some hay over it," Rupert said.

"How are we going to cover up his death?"

"Hush, I'm thinking." Rupert sat silent for several minutes. "All right, I have an idea. What's the sickness that's killing most folks now that cholera is gone?"

"You mean the fever and ague?"

"Exactly. Well, guess what our friend Mr. Beaman just caught? A bad case of ague. Let's go finish our job, and I'll explain the plan to you," Rupert said.

After finishing their work, Rupert and Otto knocked on the front door of the Chestnut home.

Johanna answered. "Yes, how can I help you?"

"Beggin' you pardon ma'am. We just wanted to let you and your husband know we're done with the day's work, and we didn't know if Mr. Beaman talked to you before he left. He said he was feeling awful sick. Went home in a sweat, looked real bad. We were hoping to visit him and take him some soup from Bill's tavern. Do you happen to know his address?"

"Well, yes," Johanna said then explained how to get to Jim's home.

"Thank you, ma'am," Otto said.

"You're welcome. You tell him that if he's not feeling well he should take some time off to get better," Johanna said.

"We'll let him know, Mrs. Chestnut. Thank you."

Rupert and Otto got a wagon. They threw the body in the back and covered it with blankets. They took the body to the address described to them. They found the key to the house in Jim's pocket and let themselves in. They put Jim in his bed, then searched for any money or valuables. They found $20 in a jar in the cupboard. Then they left.

"Let's go get some soup," Rupert said.

"Why? He ain't gonna drink it," Otto said.

"I know that. But we said we were taking him some soup. If we leave a half-empty bowl in his house, it will look like we were trying to nurse him back to health," Rupert said.

"Oh, didn't think about that," Otto said.

After they took the soup to Jim's house and staged the scene, Rupert and Otto returned to the apartment they had rented. The next day when they reported for work, they met William, who asked, "I understand you boys took some soup over to Jim; how's he doing?"

"Not too well, I'm afraid, Mr. Chestnut. Looks like he caught the ague. He was fevering bad from the time we got there until the time we left. We helped him as much as we could before leaving."

"I'll go by in the morning and visit him to see how he's doing; maybe see if I can get President Felt to come and give him a blessing. Thank you two for your efforts to help him," William said.

"We do what we can. He has been real good to us since we've come here, and we're hoping he makes a full recovery. Good man like that deserves the Lord's blessing," Rupert said.

That night as William was tucking the girls into bed, they asked him to read them a story. William rubbed and tapped his chin. "Let's say our prayers first. Don't forget to mention Mr. Beaman in your prayers."

"What's wrong with Mr. Beaman?" Ann asked.

"He is sick with ague. Some people die from that, but we want him to get better. I'm going to ask President Felt to give him a blessing so he can get extra help. Let's say our prayers now," William prompted.

The girls sat up in their beds. Clasping their hands together and squeezing their eyes shut, they both said silent prayers.

~ * * * ~

The next morning instead of going to work, William went straight to President Felt's home.

Nathanial opened the door. "Brother Chestnut. To what do I owe the pleasure of your visit?"

"It's my farm manager. He has fallen sick with the ague, and I was wondering if you would give him a blessing."

"Of course, I will. Is he a member of the Church?"

"No, he is not, but he's a good man. He has been a friend to us for years," William said.

"Let me go and get ready and I'll be out in a few minutes."

"Thank you, President," William said.

As they walked to Jim's house, President Felt said, "I've been thinking about the conference we had in January. Remember when John Taylor spoke? He was quite adamant that we prepare ourselves to join the Saints in Deseret. I've made it a matter of prayer and feel that the Lord wants me to take my family to the Salt Lake Valley. I have asked around and have a group of Saints who will be coming with us."

William looked at him. "How will your children handle the trip?"

"I've hired two teamsters to help us drive the wagon and prepare the meals. That should enable us to better attend to the needs of our children as we travel. We'll be departing on a steamboat next month for Winter Quarters."

"We'll sorely miss you and your family, President."

"What about you, William? Have you given much thought to coming west?"

"I would like to, but trips like that can be very hard on infants. I thought I'd wait until William has grown a bit."

"I was hoping to have your company on this trip. But you need to do what's best for your family. I'll miss having you around to talk to."

"I'll just have to look forward to meeting back up with you when we get to Deseret. This is the house," William said as they approached Jim's home.

William knocked on the door. Not hearing a reply, William hollered, "Jim, it's me, William. You doing all right?" William's words were met with silence. William opened the door and called out, "Jim, you here?"

He walked in and went to the bedroom. William saw Jim lying in his bed, his skin discolored. Half a bowl of soup sat next to him on the nightstand. "Oh, no! We're too late," William exclaimed, grief evident in his voice.

"I'm sorry, William," President Felt said. "We'd better leave and call the undertaker. We don't want to catch what he had."

"I should have come as soon as I found out!" William said.

"It's all right, William. There is no way you could have known. He is in the arms of the Lord now. Come on. We need to be on our way."

Chapter 48
Transition

April 15, 1850

William enjoyed his new store. It was built bigger and better than he would have expected. It was now made of brick instead of wood. With the discovery of gold in California the previous year, together with St. Louis fast becoming known as the "gateway to the west," an endless stream of customers came through William's store buying supplies to take west.

One day, President Felt stopped in among the throng. William saw him waiting in line to check out. Finally, it was his turn to approach the counter. "How are things, William?"

"As you can see, business is doing great. Half of my customers are headed to Deseret to be with the main body of the Church to worship God, and the rest are heading for California to dig and worship gold."

"God worshipers and gold worshipers," President Felt said, pensively. "Most of them likely used to be God worshipers until '*L*' got in the way," President Felt quipped.

William grinned. "That will be seventy-five cents. You need to get much more for your trip?"

"No, I think this is the last of it." President Felt said. "I wanted to bring more, but the wagon holds only so much. The two teamsters I hired to drive the wagon are pretty insistent that we don't take too much. They say it will bog the wagon down into the mud if we do. We'll be taking the steamboat to Winter Quarters, then we'll walk from there to Salt Lake City."

"I hear my old farmhand Brother Sharp and his family are going with you," William said.

"Yes, they've suffered a lot of loss in that family. Their three-year-old came down with the ague and died just like your friend. It was quite tragic for them."

William blinked. "Losing one of my children at that age that would be very hard."

"A handful of other families will be joining us as well."

William nodded. "I wish you well. Johanna and I will surely miss you and Eliza."

"I'm sure I'll see you in the Salt Lake Valley before too long," President Felt said.

"You probably will," William replied. "Who will preside over the St. Louis Conference after you've left?"

"Elder Hyde has picked my first counselor, Alexander Robbins, to take my place. He will be ordained at the next conference in April."

~ * * * ~

September 20, 1850

As William started preparations to close up the store, Orson Hyde walked in. "Hope I'm not too late. We're out of sugar, and I was hoping to get some on my way home."

"Elder Hyde, welcome! I'm still open for a few minutes yet. Sugar is over there," William pointed across the store. "Help yourself to whatever you need."

"Thank you," Elder Hyde said as he walked to the back of the store. He poured sugar into a bag. "Have you heard the news about Deseret?"

William shook his head. "Last I heard, the Saints are building up the Salt Lake Valley into a fine city and doing the same in surrounding areas. In the last three months, we have had more than three thousand immigrants pass through St. Louis on their way to the Salt Lake Valley. Many of them stay to find work until they can get enough supplies to head west."

Elder Hyde stroked his short beard. "President Robbins has helped thousands who have arrived in St. Louis to start their journey to the Salt Lake Valley. It has grown so much there, that they created a proposal to form the State of Deseret. It was rejected and was replaced with a grant to become a territory of the United States. They're calling it the Utah Territory, after the Ute Indians. They will send three United States officers, two judges, and a secretary appointed by President Fillmore to serve in the new Utah Territory. They'll likely leave for Utah next spring."

"Hopefully, they won't clash too much with the Saints in Deser—uh, Utah."

"Hopefully not, but Gentiles have a way of stirring things up among the Saints, especially ones with political interests. Only time will tell. How are things going for you?"

"The store is doing really well, but I just found out yesterday that my farm is having problems. Half or more of the crop seems to be dying. I need to meet with my farmhands and find out what's going on."

"Well, you're a good man. The Lord needs Saints like you in the Salt Lake Valley. Perhaps the Lord is sending you that message through your crops."

"Maybe," William said as he handed Elder Hyde his change. "Thanks for stopping by."

"Thanks for staying open a little longer for me," Elder Hyde said as he headed out the door.

After locking up the store, William rode Destiny home and found Rupert and Otto putting their tools away.

He rode up to them. "I noticed the crop is struggling. Any idea why half the crop is dying?"

"Yes, I think we know the problem," Rupert explained. "There was a bug we discovered as the crop was growing. We went into town and bought a pesticide and applied it to the entire crop to kill the bug, but by the time we had finished our work, the bugs had already done their damage to most of the crops."

"Why didn't you tell me about any of this before? I would have paid for the pesticide."

"We knew you were busy with your store and helping your church friends getting outfitted to move west. Since you entrusted us with the responsibility of the farm, we figured it was our duty to take care of it along with any problems we found along the way."

"Well, thank you for addressing the issue. If anything major like that happens again, just be sure you let me know about it as soon as you find out there is a problem."

"We will, Mr. Chestnut. We're sorry we didn't say something sooner. We're just happy we didn't lose the entire crop."

"Yes, that would have been a hard blow. Keep up the good work."

As William rode off to the stables, Otto said, "That was a nice story you fed him."

Rupert replied, "All that matters is that he ate it. Come on, let's go get some whiskey and enjoy the rest of our evening."

~ * * * ~

July 15, 1851

William said farewell to the last customer who came after a big rush that kept him busy most of the day. While he was enjoying the respite, President Robbins came into his store with three other men William did not recognize. "Hello President, to what do I owe the pleasure?"

"Brother Chestnut, this is James McGaw, William Howell, and Orson Pratt. Brother McGaw is a missionary who has just come from Texas," President Robbins said.

"Nice to make your acquaintance," James said.

"Brother Howell has just come from New Orleans, and before that from England on the ship *Olympus*. He came to America with two hundred people, all but fifty-two of whom were Latter-day Saints. By the time they arrived at New Orleans, Brother Howell had converted all but two of the fifty-two," President Robbins said.

"It's the Lord who did the converting. I just open my mouth and speak," Brother Howell said.

"This is Orson Pratt. As I'm sure you know, he is one of the Twelve Apostles," President Robbins said.

"Hello, Brother Chestnut," Elder Pratt said. "How are things going for you and your family?"

"We're doing well, thank you. Half our crops failed this year, but we're weathering it," William said.

"William, you have been greatly blessed with riches throughout your life. But remember—to whom much is given, much is required. If you don't give what is required, the Lord will take more. Elder Pratt was just returning from his mission in Europe organizing the work and the Saints there," President Robbins explained.

"We've chartered a steamboat called the *Statesman* to take us up the Missouri River to Kanesville, Iowa, to get ready to go west. It leaves in three days. We need some supplies for our journey," President Robbins said.

"When you say 'we,' does that mean you're going with them?"

"Indeed, I am, William. I believe now is the right time for me and my family to go," President Robbins said.

"Well, what about the St. Louis Saints? You became president of the conference just last year."

"I know, William. Believe me, there are many worthy and qualified brethren still in St. Louis to lead. In fact, Thomas Wrigley will be the next conference president; he has already been set apart and will be confirmed by the members in the next conference."

"He is a good man. We'll miss you, President," William said.

President Robbins smiled. "Likewise, William—and, uh, call me *Brother*."

~ * * * ~

November 14, 1851

William was busy straightening up his store when President Wrigley walked in and greeted him. "Brigham Young has called on all Saints in the eastern states to gather to Utah. He is asking that everyone prepare so they can leave for Utah in the spring. I'm preparing to charter steamboats and import wagons and other supplies to get people ready. I'll be going in the spring, and I'd like you to come with me."

"I've thought about making the move several times," William answered. "I haven't wanted to take my kids so young. I also usually come back to how much I'd miss the life I've created for myself and my family here. We're comfortable, and we have things figured out. If we move, all that changes, and it's like starting over again."

"Well, maybe. You could sell your store and with that money buy or build a new one in Utah. You'll have friends there. You've known many of the members from our branch who have already gone. I'll be there with my family. The move will almost be like getting boots refitted."

"In what way?" William asked.

"Instead of replacing the whole boot, you just tear off the old, worn-out sole and replace it with a new one. You still have the same look and feel on the upper part; it just feels different when you walk."

"Yes, but it will hurt until it gets broken in," William said.

"Well, perhaps that wasn't the best analogy," Thomas said.

"Sounds about right to me," William replied.

"Point is, after you've got it broken in, you wouldn't choose anything else. It becomes your new comfortable, and you start to like it. Besides, the Lord wants us gathered into one body so we can strengthen each other, build Zion, and be free from persecution."

"Maybe it *is* time for us to join with the Saints in Utah. Little William will be five next year. I'll talk it over with Johanna."

"You're a good man, William. I'd better be getting along now."

As he rode Destiny home, William thought about how he would broach the topic with his wife. When he got home, he put Destiny in the stables. He greeted Otto and Rupert as they put away their tools for the day then headed into his house.

As the family sat around the dinner table, William said, "Brigham has called for all the Saints in the United Saints to come to Utah."

"I heard. It has come up in every conversation I've had with the sisters of the Church in the last few days," Johanna said.

"I think now might be a good time for us to join them," William said.

"Maybe we should wait a few years. The children are still young for such a long journey. And our neighbors and friends are so nice."

"Most of our friends have already decided to go west," William said.

"I know, but . . . it just doesn't feel like the right time."

"Maybe we should pray about it; the Lord has never led us astray before."

"Maybe we should," Johanna said.

~ * * * ~

December 12, 1851

William, Johanna, and Brother and Sister Wrigley sat in William's front room enjoying bacon, a fresh loaf of bread, and jam as they discussed the news of the day.

"The worst report was published in the paper. It was about the Utah Saints and the government officials, reporting on why the officials fled Utah," Sister Wrigley said.

"Why would they flee Utah?" Johanna asked.

President Wrigley was holding the newspaper. He looked up. "I guess they just didn't understand the Saints. They probably went in expecting bad things based on preconceived notions and looked for that in the Saints." He then read from the paper:

> The two judges and the secretary sent to Utah have just come to St. Louis on their way to Washington, DC. They brought back the $24,000 that was sent with them to give to the territory governor and turned it in to the Treasury officials here in St. Louis. They also brought back the seal that was made for the territory.
>
> They are saying that the Mormons held the United States and its laws in contempt the whole time they

> were among them. They are also saying that they found on every hand dishonesty, immorality, and the enforcing of their leader's mandates under threat of death. They claim that they feared for their lives and dared not stay there any longer.

William gripped the arms of his chair. "There is no way the Saints are what those officials described,"

President Wrigley shook his head. "Jedediah Grant and John Bernhisel came from Utah to represent our side to President Fillmore. They are saying that the character of the three officials was unbecoming of what one would expect of dedicated public servants. They said they offered hospitality and friendship to the officials but got scorn and belligerence in return."

"People are listening only to the squawk of those federal officials," President Wrigley said. "And those who used to be friendly to us are turning against us."

Chapter 49
The Wagon

The following week, William sat at the dinner table with his family, stuffed with Bessie's good cooking.

Johanna asked, "How has work been going lately?"

"Business has dropped significantly, and folks who used to be friendly to me are now being very rude," William said. "It all started after those United States officials that returned from Utah sent out their report to the public. For the first time in my memory, the people in St. Louis have suddenly turned against us, just because we're Mormon."

Johanna nodded. "I have seen the same thing. Folks are friendly, but as soon as they learn I'm Mormon, they get cold toward me. I guess it was bound to happen. It has happened everywhere else the Saints have been. Probably won't be long before they start trying to drive us out, like they did the Saints in the western end of the state."

Johanna stared off into the distance thinking, then turned to William. "William, maybe it is time for us to join the Saints in Utah."

"I reckon you're right. We can start getting ready and gathering supplies, then leave as soon as the snow is gone in the spring."

~ * * * ~

William put an ad in the papers to sell his store. He took from the store what he thought he might need for their trek west. He then went to look for a wagon that could take him and his family across the plains, but everything he saw seemed too small or too basic.

William approached the man selling wagons. "None of these wagons seem suitable. You know where I can go to get a wagon made to the specifications I need?"

"If you want a higher-end wagon, there is a former slave by the name of Hyrum Young who purchased his freedom. He has become well known for producing higher-end, quality wagons. Be prepared, though; it will cost you for that kind of wagon."

"It may be just what I'm looking for. Where can I find this Hyrum Young?" William asked.

"He has his shop set up down at Independence. You could take a steamboat. It'll get you there in two days. It's right along the Missouri River," the shopkeeper said.

William tipped his hat. "Much obliged."

~ * * * ~

William let Johanna know of his plans to go to Independence to get a wagon.

"Are you sure it's safe? That's where all the trouble started when they drove the members of the Church from the state."

"I'm going to do business, not preach religion. I shouldn't have any trouble," William replied.

William got on the next steamboat to Independence. He decided to save money and ride on the lower deck. He had taken his six-shooters for protection and $550 in a pouch tied to his belt.

As night fell, William found a place on the lower deck to spread out his bedroll. It was far enough away from the livestock and cargo that the smell wouldn't bother him but was still under the upper deck in case it rained. He took his money pouch from his belt and stuffed it in his vest. He put his revolvers and belt under the blanket roll he used for a pillow.

The constant bobbing of the boat made it difficult to sleep as it made its way upriver. William didn't know how long it had been since he laid down, but he thought it had probably been a few hours. He lay there with his eyes closed, thinking about what kind of wagon he might buy for his trek west.

As he lay there, he felt a hand reaching into his vest. William quickly pulled one of his revolvers from under the pillow and pointed it at the would-be thief. The light of the moon shone down on the face of a teenage boy, who looked frightened when William sat up with his revolver pointed at him. The intruder was so surprised, he stumbled backward, tripping over another person who was sleeping nearby. William kept his revolver out and threatened the boy. "You'll get a ripe beating if I see you again."

The boy scrambled away into the night, dodging over other sleeping passengers as he went.

William lay back down. It was now more difficult for William to fall asleep, but after a few more hours he eventually did.

The next day passed uneventfully. William saw the would-be thief again through the crowd as he disembarked. He had thought to track him down and let his parents know what he was up to in the night. But he needed to hurry and find the wagon maker.

William inquired around town. It turned out there were several wagon makers, but only one was a former slave. When he got to the wagon shop, he saw a black man behind the counter and figured that must be Hyrum Young.

"You the owner here?" William asked.

"I'm just tending the shop for my master."

"Your master?" William said in surprise.

"Yes, Hyrum Young," the man replied.

"You're a slave? To a former slave?" William asked.

The man didn't say anything. Behind William a voice boomed, "Is there a problem here?"

William turned around and saw an older, tall, muscular black man.

"No problem. I've come to purchase a wagon. I've heard of your reputation for making quality wagons. That's what I need. You're Hyrum Young?"

"That's me. We pride ourselves in making the best wagons in the state. What kind of wagon are you looking for?" Hyrum asked.

"I want a wide wagon that is capable of holding about twice as much as regular wagons. One that looks nice and will make it through mud and mires without breaking."

"Our wagons are built to withstand the worst mires. I think I have what you're looking for. Follow me, Mr.—"

"Chestnut."

"This way, Mr. Chestnut."

Hyrum took William into the yard full of wagons of every style and variety. They stopped in front of a wide, cherry wood, varnished, covered wagon. It had a perch to sit on and large, spoked wheels wrapped in iron.

"This is our best model, but it is one of the more expensive wagons we sell. Not only does it look nice, it is roomy and functional; the wood underneath has been reinforced with iron rods. It's made from Cherry wood. You could take this thing to California and back and it would last the whole way. This model is $250."

"If you can add cushioned upholstering to the bench and a lockbox that is permanently attached to the wagon, I'll take it," William said.

"Those additions are fairly expensive. That will add another $50 to the price."

"Done. When do you expect to have it ready?" William asked.

"Likely will take at least two or three days to get it done. Tell me where you're staying, and I'll send a messenger to fetch you when it's ready. I'll need a $100 deposit to start the work."

"You said the upgrades would only be $50," William said.

"You can think of the other $50 as insurance. I'm taking this one off the market so I can make the additions you've requested. If you decide you don't want it and I have other buyers come by that would have bought it, that puts me out some money."

"I'm definitely going to buy it, especially with those upgrades," William said.

"All the same, to start working on it I'll need $100 up front. You can pay the rest when you inspect the work and take possession of the wagon."

William pulled out his money pouch and counted out $100. He handed it to Hyrum. "I'll look forward to seeing the finished product. I'll likely be staying at the Hawthorn Inn."

William had decided it would be worthwhile to book passage on a steamboat so he could leave as soon as he had the wagon in his possession. He spent the remaining two days exploring the streets and reading the scriptures in his room.

Word finally came that the wagon was ready. William approached the wagon shop and saw his wagon parked out front. A yoke of oxen was hitched to it. As William approached, one of the slaves looked at him, then went into the building. A short moment later, Hyrum walked out and waved.

"Welcome back, Mr. Chestnut. Here it is, ready for you to inspect."

"Thank you," William said as he climbed aboard. He sat on the cushioned perch and checked for the lockbox. The workmanship was excellent—the best William had seen on a wagon.

"This looks good," William said.

"That will be $350," Hyrum said.

"What? We agreed on $300 total, and I already gave you $100."

"Yes, we did. That is still the price at which I am selling the wagon. However, I assumed you would want a team of oxen to pull the wagon. Unless you brought your own team . . ."

"No, I didn't. I kind of figured it was all included in the original price."

"Oh no, Mr. Chestnut. We never did discuss oxen in our deal, but seeing you came on foot I assumed you would be purchasing a team."

"I suppose I will. So, it's $150 for the oxen?" William asked.

"Yes."

William pulled out his money pouch and counted out the money. "Your name is very interesting. Have you ever heard of Brigham Young or Hyrum Smith?"

Hyrum held up his hand. "Wait, are you a Mormon?"

"Yes."

"You can keep your money. We don't serve Mormons here. Good day, Mr. Chestnut." Hyrum turned and walked back toward his store.

"Wait! I've already paid you $100. You can't back out on our deal now!" William said.

Hyrum turned around, anger evident on his face. "That was a retainer, which means I get to retain it if I don't sell you the wagon. Which I'm not about to do. Now, if I'm not mistaken, there is still an extermination order in place that says you can be killed or driven from the state. If you want to hang around here, I know a sheriff who will be very happy to execute either of those options. It will be better for you if I don't see your face again. Now good day... Chestnut." Hyrum spun on his heel and walked back into his building, slamming the door behind him.

William stood there in shock. He had never been spoken to like that in his life. He wasn't sure what his next move should be. He wanted to go back in and tell the man off, but the threat Hyrum made invoking the extermination order gave William pause.

He thought that the law just might be against him in these parts. It was only seventeen years ago that the Mormons were driven from this very area. William was not sure that sentiments in these parts had changed much. He had heard about the violence and brutality that this end of the state exercised against the Mormons in 1833 and 1838.

William thought through his options. He really wanted this wagon. It was exactly what he was looking for, and he didn't think he would be able to find another one like it. He made a quick decision and walked to the door. One of Hyrum's slaves was approaching the building.

William rushed up to him. "I'm in a hurry and just spoke to your master about purchasing this wagon. Everything is in fine order, and like I said, I'm in a hurry. I must be on my way as soon as possible. Will you give him this $400 for the rest of the payment? It is $50 more than we agreed on, but you can tell him it's a tip for his excellent service. Please help me untie the wagon, and I'll be on my way."

The slave pocketed the money and untied the wagon from the post while William drove the oxen forward. He guided the oxen straight for the piers.

The steamboat he booked would be leaving within the hour. He wanted to get boarded and on his way before Hyrum could find a law man and start searching for him. He hoped they would check the roads for the wagon first.

William was able to get to the steamboat without incident, though the captain wanted to charge William an extra $10 because the wagon was a lot bigger than most wagons they transported. He didn't have time to argue, so he paid the captain the money. That left him with only a dollar.

As the steamship pulled away from the dock, William saw Hyrum running along the docks with a group of men. He ducked out of sight, and was safe.

Chapter 50
False Start

January 10, 1852

Rupert and Otto sat in the barn. "It's been two years. When are we going to raid the house and move on to the next farm, Rup?"

"I know we've worked here a lot longer than I was hoping. But with the maid and the cook always around, the house hasn't been empty since we started. We've never really had an opportunity like we had at the other farms. But we need to stick this one out until the right opportunity comes. These people are much more wealthy than any other farmers we've ever hit in the past. We could retire after making this hit."

"Whatever you say, Rup."

Just then they heard William call out, "Mr. Howard, Mr. Flint, are you there?"

"We're in the barn, Mr. Chestnut," Rupert called out.

William walked into the barn.

Rupert waved. "We were just taking a break."

"I wanted to thank you boys for all the good work you've done on the farm. I'm afraid we've decided we're moving west and putting the farm up for sale. We'll pay you until the end of March, but after that I don't think we'll require your services any longer."

"That's not fair!" Otto exclaimed "What are we going to do?"

"I'm sorry. I really am. But I will give you a good reference. Perhaps our neighbors the Temblors will take you back into their service. He spoke very highly of you when I talked to him."

"Wait, Mr. Chestnut. I assume that this trip you're taking west is why you bought that big, fancy wagon."

"Yes, that's right," William said.

"You'll want some teamsters to drive your teams and take care of any obstacles you come across on your journey."

"Well, yes. I was going to put out an advertisement in the papers," William replied.

"Otto and I would do a great job as teamsters. Perhaps you would consider us to take you west."

"Do you have any experience as teamsters?"

"We have had plenty of experience. Before we did farm work, we took folks from state to state as local teamsters," Rupert lied. "True, we've never traveled on as great a journey as you're taking, and it's been a while, but it's work that you don't soon forget—and you've seen our work ethic. We'll be just as diligent along the trail."

"Then it sounds like I've found my teamsters. We'll start packing the middle of March."

"Thank you, Mr. Chestnut, you won't regret keeping us on," Rupert said.

~ * * * ~

March 1, 1852

President Wrigley was busy helping Saints get ready for their trek west. He had imported several wagons, as the wagons made in St. Louis were reported to break down all along the trail. He made sure each family that wanted to go had the provisions they needed.

Elder Eli Kelsey and Elder David Ross just arrived from Kanesville with a calling to charter boats for Saints in St. Louis to get them to Kanesville. They would be going back in a few months so they could head out on the trail.

In the winter, it was normal for the Missouri to freeze over. As spring came, the ice would start cracking and be swept away down river. In March, the ice blocks were still flowing down the Missouri, and Elders Kelsey and Ross were having a difficult time finding any captain willing to take their cargo and people upriver—none wanted to fight the large chunks of ice in the river.

Immigrants from England continued to pour into St. Louis. Many of them stayed just long enough to resupply and get moving again, while others stayed longer to get their money built back up. Elders Kelsey and Ross were finally able to convince one of the captains, Frances Belt of the *Saluda*, to take one hundred Saints to Kanesville, Iowa.

President Wrigley and another man approached William. "William, this is Will Camron from Scotland. He arrived last week. He and his family are looking to leave on the next boat to Kanesville, which will probably leave around the end of March, once most of the ice drifts have cleared out of the river. Brother Camron and his two children need a place to stay until then, and I was wondering if they could stay with you until they leave."

"I'd be happy to take them in," William said.

"William, you've been preparing all winter. If you're ready, why don't you go with them? You can wait for us in Kanesville. We'll likely be there sometime in April."

"I do have a buyer for my store, and the sale is likely to be finalized before the end of March. But we haven't got our farm sold yet. We'll need to get that taken care of before we go."

"I can help you sell your land, and I can bring the funds to you in Kanesville," President Wrigley offered.

"I reckon that would work fine. As long as you're willing to do that, I think we can be ready by the end of the month."

"That's great to hear. I'll tell Brother Kelsey to add your name to the list."

At home William introduced the Camrons to his family, then told everyone to start packing. He knew it would take multiple weeks, so the sooner they started, the better.

He let Bessie know they were moving and gave her the option to travel with them, but she decided she did not want to make that trip at her age. William agreed to help her find a new job before they left.

William had secured guns in each corner of the wagon with bullet pouches and powder horns. He then went to the bank and withdrew all the money he had inherited from his father, his own savings, and the money from the sale of his business. He bought a tiny chest just big enough to fit all of it. He put the chest in the lockbox he asked to be built into the wagon and put the keys to both the lockbox and the chest on a string of hide around his neck.

Brother Camron approached William. "I'm very grateful for your hospitality, and I know you're planning on leaving at the end of the month. I'm just feelin' that I should be stayin' in St. Louis awhile longer. Could we stay at your place after you've left?"

"I'm sorry, Brother Camron, but the house is for sale. We intend on locking it up until it can be sold after we leave."

"Just thought I'd ask."

"Don't worry. There is no reason to stay behind. You might as well go while the going is good," William said.

"I suppose you're right," Brother Camron replied.

The day finally came. They tied the three cows to the back of the wagon in a line and drove their dark red wagon to the meetinghouse, where other Saints were gathering for a prayer meeting before leaving on their trip. William rode Destiny while Johanna and the children walked. Otto and Rupert drove the oxen. The Camron family followed William's wagon.

When they arrived at the meetinghouse, they recognized very few of the Saints gathered there. Most of them were immigrants from England and Scotland. After the prayer, William had an uneasy feeling but shook it off, figuring it was probably just the jitters from leaving their familiar home for unfamiliar territory.

Elders Kelsey and Ross were at the prayer meeting, giving everyone instruction on where to go. Brother Camron asked the elders if they knew anyone he could stay with awhile longer, as he had an uneasy feeling about leaving that day.

"We don't really know anyone who has room right now, but don't worry. We've booked a good boat for you," Elder Ross said.

Finally, they all headed for the docks to board the ship. When they got there and saw that the name of the ship was the *Saluda*,

William stopped Destiny and called to Rupert and Otto, "Hold up, boys."

The Camrons, who were following, also stopped.

William and Johanna stared at the name on the ship. Rupert and Otto were also staring at their old ship in shock.

"Is this the ship we're going to be taking up the icy Missouri?" Rupert asked.

"This is the dock number we were given," William said.

"Last time we got on board that ship, we regretted it," Johanna said. "I'll not be boarding that ship again."

Rupert and Otto looked at each other.

"Just because we had one bad experience aboard that ship doesn't mean we will have another," William said. "We are traveling with friends this time; they'll have our backs."

Rupert spoke up. "Excuse me, Mr. Chestnut, I don't mean to intrude or interrupt. But I just thought you should be aware that this ship has a bad reputation for reliability. We might just find ourselves on the banks of the river having to make our way on foot taking that one."

"Or we might find ourselves blown to smithereens," Otto whispered.

Rupert kicked him in the shins and whispered, "Shut up, Otto."

"I didn't catch that last thing you said," William said.

"Oh, I was just talking to Otto. He said he agreed that this ship wasn't reliable."

"See," Johanna said, "even our teamsters know the bad reputation of this ship. You remember how they left a bunch of the passengers on the river bank? I don't want to chance being left stranded. We can take the next boat that gets chartered."

William wondered when they would go if it wasn't now. Then a thought came to him: *In the Lord's time.* Then a feeling of peace spread over him like a blanket.

"You're right; we will hold off leaving for another day. Turn the wagon around, boys; we're headin' back home."

William turned and rode over to the Camrons. "We've decided to wait a little longer before we leave St. Louis. We won't be boarding the ship today."

Brother Camron looked relieved. "Do you mind if we join you?"

"Not at all," William said.

Sister Camron spoke up. "Oh no, I'm not staying one more night in that house. We're getting on that ship."

"Come now, Helen. We should wait. The Chestnuts have been hospitable to us."

"They were very nice to take us in, and I thank you, Brother Chestnut, for giving us a place to stay, but if it's all the same I'd rather be on my way to a permanent home," Helen replied.

"I guess we'll be going aboard," Brother Camron said.

"Suit yourselves," William said.

They said their goodbyes and parted ways.

"Turn it around, boys; we're going back home," William told Rupert and Otto.

"All right!" Otto whooped.

"Let's go!" Rupert said, as he started a wide turn.

They pulled up to the house. William dismounted. "Put the wagon back in the barn but leave it packed. We can do without those things for now."

~ * * * ~

William went to see President Wrigley the next day.

"I thought you and your family were leaving on the *Saluda*," President Wrigley said.

"We were about to, but we felt like we should stay here a little bit longer," William said.

"You're not the only ones. I think the brethren had contracted for 150 Saints to go. I've heard from seven other families that either things kept happening to prevent them from going, or they got there but decided not to board. I think only two-thirds of those who the brethren assigned to go actually got on the boat."

Chapter 51
The Saluda

Captain Belt welcomed the Saints and other passengers aboard the *Saluda*. There was plenty of room, as only about two hundred got on a ship that could hold as many as six hundred with cargo. The ship made its way up the muddy river, its progress slowed as they dodged floating ice chunks.

The *Saluda* stopped several times to drop off and pick up passengers. More than a dozen Saints got off at Brunswick to buy cattle and continue their journey on foot.

The *Saluda* got only as far as Lexington, about 230 miles from St. Louis, before one of the ice chunks damaged the paddles. As the *Saluda* stopped for repairs, some of the passengers thought the delays were becoming too great, so they disembarked to continue their journey on foot.

After a few days, the ice floes thinned out, and on April 7, Captain Belt decided it was time to go. There was a point in the river where the ship had to get around an especially fast current. Captain Belt's attempt to get past it was unsuccessful, and he took the ship back to Lexington. He tried again the next day and again failed to get past the bend.

On the third day, Captain Belt was frustrated at their lack of progress. He decided it would be this time or never. The captain ordered the engineers to fill the boilers to maximum pressure so they could get past the bend.

He pulled the whistle that signaled the engineers into action. The steamship moved steadily upstream. Suddenly its forward progress stopped, and the boilers erupted in an explosion that could be heard for miles. Bodies flew into the air. Some landed on the wharf, others landed on a nearby bluff.

Those who were outside on the decks of the ship were blown off into the water. Those inside the ship were engulfed in flames. Others who were far away from the boilers dove off the side of the ship. Nearby steamboats moved to help retrieve people from the water, and others were able to swim to shore. The *Saluda* sank into the murky waters, taking nearly one hundred people to their watery grave.

~ * * * ~

William put his hand on President Wrigley's shoulder. "What's the matter? Looks like something is troubling you."

President Wrigley looked into William's eyes. "Elder Abraham Smoot just got back. He took the *Saluda* but got off at Lexington. When the boat went to leave, it exploded. Twenty-eight of the fifty

Saints that were still on the ship when it exploded died. The other Saints who had boarded in St. Louis had disembarked along the way; some of them even stayed in Lexington."

"That's awful! Did you hear anything about the Camrons?" William asked.

"The whole family is presumed dead, I'm afraid. There was one poor brother who missed the boat when it left St. Louis, and he caught another steamboat to catch up with it. He caught up with it in Lexington. Right after he boarded the ship, it went out on the water and exploded. I'm afraid it took his whole family. He got blown into the water and survived to be picked up by another passing steamboat."

William gasped. "That's terrible!"

"Elder Smoot said he had a bad feeling about it from the beginning, and even told Elder Ross that he shouldn't book passage. But Elder Ross was attracted by the low price they were offering and got it anyway."

William glanced down. "We'll be headed out ourselves in two more weeks. It gives you pause when you hear about things like that happening. Makes me think more seriously about just making the journey overland."

President Wrigley shook his head. "If you did that, you would be traveling across those plains to the Salt Lake Valley in two feet of snow. Besides, it's pretty rare for a boat to blow up like that. It does happen every now and again, but you have a better chance of catching cholera than getting blown up by a boat."

"You're right. I've ridden on steamboats as long as I can remember and haven't ever had an issue like that," William said.

Chapter 52
Getting Ready

April 9, 1852

A conference of the Saints was held in which Thomas Wrigley was released. William Gibson was sustained as the new conference president.

The day after the conference, the Chestnut family, the Wrigley's, and many other Saints boarded multiple steamboats with their supplies, animals, and wagons.

Winter Quarters awaited their arrival. There they would organize into companies and head to Utah. William and Johanna opted to pay the lower cost and ride on the lower deck of the steamboat, since they were charged extra for the larger wagon, three milk cows, two oxen, and Destiny.

Sarah yanked on William's pant leg. Her face was scrunched tight. "What if I slip and fall into the water?"

"I'll hold tight to you so that you don't," William reassured her.

Ann grabbed her mom's leg. "What if the boat blows up on the river like the Saluda?"

Otto smiled at her. "Don't worry, We'll make sure you're protected the whole way."

Ann nodded.

There were multiple stops along the way, and it took several days, but the journey to Kanesville was largely uneventful. When they arrived in Kanesville, they met a man who assigned them two cabins at Winter Quarters for them and their teamsters. They were ready to go, but stayed there for several months until the companies could get organized.

~ * * * ~

Thousands of Saints had gathered to Winter Quarters on both sides of the river. Thomas Wrigley came to see William as he sat tending a fire.

William waved at Thomas. "Any news?"

Thomas nodded. "Ezra Benson arrived a few days ago and created twenty-nine companies with the Saints who are here. There are more than five thousand of us who will be crossing the plains this summer."

"We're fairly anxious to go. Are there any companies leaving before the summer?"

"There are a few, but they are already full. Your family was assigned to the William Morgan Company. My family was assigned to the James McGaw Company. Maybe we'll run into each other on the trail."

"That would be nice," William said.

Thomas threw a stick into the fire. "I'll be glad to leave this place. Last night I spent the evening in the company of a man by the name of Samuel Adair; he'll be with the Benjamin Johnson Company. He recently buried two of his older children, a newborn baby, and his wife. She died from childbirth complications. He has seven children to care for now. One of them he recently adopted."

"It's hard to see how he could have the will to stick with his plans to move across the plains so soon after a loss like that," William replied.

"I think keeping busy is the only thing that's keeping him going. When I was with him, he was fixing the wagon wheel of a member of his company," Thomas said.

"There is definitely plenty of work to do if you go looking for it," William replied.

"Indeed, there is. If I don't see you on the trail, my friend, I hope to see you in the Salt Lake Valley." Thomas shook William's hand and pulled him in for a hug.

Thirteen companies had already left that season, and William Morgan announced that his company would be leaving on June 22. James McGaw would be leaving two days later. Two other companies would be leaving about the same time.

While they waited, William went to a local store that had been created to help outfit the Saints. He bought more supplies and food for the journey, as they had eaten some of what they had brought waiting for their company to be ready to leave.

Chapter 53
On the Trail

William Morgan had his entire company in a large lineup. Each wagon was inspected and deemed travel worthy or had to make adjustments to be ready. They each certified they had brought enough food for the journey. Then they were told to move out and wait for the rest of the company with a group of the other approved wagons. The whole experience was hurry up and wait, hurry up and wait again. Their company had more than one hundred people in it, thirty-three wagons in all.

After the first week of travel, cholera swept into the camp, getting many sick and causing several deaths. William made sure they stayed well away from anyone with symptoms.

With such a big body of people, the moving was slow, as everyone had to be ready before leaving any location. There were a few times when they came to creeks that were flooded. They had to wait several days for the water to go down before they could continue.

One bright morning, dark, ominous clouds could be seen rolling in from the north. There was no room in the wagon for shelter, so William, Rupert and Otto took out a large dresser and an end table. The furniture was left on the prairie, and the family got in the wagon for shelter while Rupert and Otto continued driving the wagon forward. William continued riding Destiny.

The rain came hard and fast. It pelted the men as they continued along the trail. After several hours, the rain had finally stopped, but then the wagon stopped moving also. The wheels were up to their axles in mud. The wagon train got ahead of them. William tied Destiny to the oxen, and Otto got behind the wagon to push. The wagon creaked as it moved forward. They were able to get another twenty feet before the wagon got stuck again. This time the wagon wouldn't budge, even with Destiny's help.

"Let's wait out the rain. Then we can unload it. It should be easier to push if we lighten the load."

The rain finally stopped, and everybody got out of the wagon to help unload. The children played in the mud and got covered from head to foot in it.

They were able to get the wagon out of the mud hole with all the adults helping. Then they got back to pushing and hauling the wagons forward. Everyone was muddy and tired by the time they cleared the mud holes. After they went back for their things and repacked the wagon, everyone was exhausted.

"We lost the wagon train," Johanna said.

"The James McGaw Company was two days behind us. Either they'll catch up to us, or we'll catch up to ours in a day or so," William said.

Johanna and the children got back in the wagon, William untied Destiny from the oxen, and they continued their journey forward.

As the day wore on, the ground dried up, and the oxen picked up their pace.

"I'll ride forward to scout out the trail and see if there is a good place to stop for lunch," William said.

About two miles ahead of his wagon and after cresting a hill, William spotted a company of about a hundred Indians in the distance.

Three Indians on horseback came riding toward him as fast as their horses would carry them. William figured it was too late to run. If he got killed now, it would be his recompense for killing Okara, who turned out to be a better man than he. William was ready. He sat stoically on Destiny.

The three Indians surrounded him. Two of them had full chieftain headgear with eagle feathers down to their belts. The third had war paint on his face and was bare-chested with two necklaces hanging around his neck. A tomahawk hung loosely at his side. He had a bow and an arrow nocked to the string, resting comfortably in his hands.

"Why you come, white man?" one of the chieftains asked.

William did not see hatred or malice in their eyes. He held up his hand. "I come in peace and brotherhood. I have read a record of your noble ancestors and have much respect for your kind," William said.

"Follow us," the Indian said.

William followed them for several miles and eventually arrived at the Indian campgrounds. He was led into the heart of their camp. Hundreds of men, women, and children were dressed in hides and skins from animals. Teepees were set up in large clusters that made a circular pattern, with the biggest teepee in the center of the camp.

William was led to it and noticed that it was decorated with a painted red sun.

As he entered, he saw a circle of old, wizened Indian warriors sitting cross-legged on large, fur rugs around a fire. Each one wore a headdress like the chieftains who escorted William into camp. They identified themselves as Sioux chieftains and asked William to sit; he sat cross-legged on a fur rug that was provided for him.

One of the older Indians spoke in a strange language that William did not understand. Another responded to him, then another spoke. Finally, they said something to the man who escorted William into camp. He nodded and turned to William. "What brings you to our land?"

"I am seeking a new home in the Salt Lake Valley."

The Indian translated to the men in the circle. They responded and the Indian standing next to William said, "You are from the Mormon tribe?"

"Yes. I have great admiration for your ways."

The Indian translated, and they talked among themselves some more. Finally, the one who translated said, "You are accepted by our leaders. Mormons are good. You will now smoke peace pipe with us." One of the Indians in the circle pulled out a long, ornately decorated pipe. William looked at his translator. "But I don't smoke."

The Indian responded, "You no smoke pipe, you do us a great dishonor. You will be treated as enemy."

"I didn't mean to dishonor your ways. I will smoke the pipe," William said.

The pipe was lit, then passed around the circle. When it was William's turn, he put the pipe to his lips and breathed in the smoke. Then he started coughing violently. The chiefs in the circle smiled and laughed. The translator then said, "You are accepted by the tribe."

William left the tent and was allowed to return to his family.

By the time William got back, they were already stopped and eating lunch. He explained where he had been and what had happened to him.

"You're very lucky," Otto said.

"I have been most of my life. In fact, I named a horse *Lucky*. But on reflection, I'm starting to think my luck has been less luck and more divine providence."

"Whatever," Otto scoffed.

"You boys don't believe in God?"

"Why should we? He's never done anything for us," Rupert said.

Johanna dropped her jaw and looked at William.

"Have you ever asked Him to?" William asked.

Rupert was silent for a moment. "No, I haven't. I've done pretty well figuring things out on my own. With the things I've done in the past, He wouldn't help me anyway."

"You'd be surprised. God turns away no man who wants to draw closer to Him, even one with a sin-filled past," William replied.

Rupert squirmed. "Well, we're glad you made it back."

"The Lord protected me and helped me know what to say to be safe. I'm glad to be back. But now that they consider me a friend, we'll all be safe from them."

After lunch they got the children loaded back into the dark red wagon and continued their journey.

As the wagon rattled on through the long, sun-dried day, the ground started to shake. A large herd of buffalo stampeded in their direction.

"Get out your guns, boys; here comes dinner," William said.

Otto and Rupert got their rifles out of the wagon and went to stand alongside William. The herd turned and was now running away from them. William spurred Destiny forward, and Otto and Rupert ran after him.

William stopped twenty yards from the herd and took aim. A buffalo dropped on the first shot. William figured that animal would provide plenty of meat for them for the next few weeks, so William sat and waited for the herd to clear away. Otto and Rupert caught up to William and started shooting into the herd.

"No need to keep shooting. I already got one," William said.

Rupert and Otto kept shooting and ran closer to the herd to get better shots.

William called after them, "I said, I already got one. We can't eat more than that. Stop shooting!"

Rupert and Otto kept going and started killing multiple buffalo, whooping and shouting every time one fell.

William rode Destiny closer to them and shouted again. "What's wrong with you two? We can't eat this much. Quit killing the buffalo!"

Otto swung his gun around and took aim at William. As soon as Rupert saw what he was doing he slapped his gun down. "Not yet," Rupert whispered.

William jumped behind his horse and aimed his gun at Otto. "What do you think you're doing pointing a gun at me?"

Rupert spoke up first. "You'll have to forgive him, Mr. Chestnut. He was just excited. He never would have pulled the trigger. Isn't that right, Otto?"

"No, I never would have shot at you, Mr. Chestnut. I heard you yelling, and I couldn't quite make out what you were saying. I thought maybe you were being attacked by a buffalo."

William lowered his gun. "Then why did you take aim at me?"

"I don't know. I guess I just wanted to make sure you were all right, and I forgot to put my gun down."

William walked around the other side of Destiny.

"Why did you two keep shooting all those buffalo, even if you didn't hear me tell you to stop? You had to have known there was no way we could eat that much."

"We were just havin' fun; there's so many of them, what does it matter if we kill a few more?" Rupert said.

"First, it's wasting life. From now on we kill only what we intend on eating. Second, it's wasting our bullets. We likely won't be able to get any more until we get to the Salt Lake Valley. We need to preserve them for when it really matters."

"Mr. Chestnut's right, Otto. We'll save our bullets for when it really matters," Rupert said.

"Come help me skin and butcher one of these bison," William said.

"Oh, no, We don't do that kind of work. We're teamsters. we only drive your team of oxen. We aren't being paid enough to do extra work."

"I see," William said. He looked at the dead bison laying on the ground. He counted five, including the one he killed. "What was I thinking?" he whispered to himself.

William wondered if he had made a mistake by hiring these two to help him and his family across the plains. But now it was too late; he was stuck with them, and he figured he ought to make the best of it. He still needed the help.

William swallowed his anger. "Well, how about I give you $60 more than we agreed on to help hunt and clean wildlife we come across along the way?"

Rupert smiled; that was much more than he was expecting. "That's very generous of you, Mr. Chestnut. Thank you. I think that's an agreeable arrangement."

They skinned and cleaned one of the buffalo, cut the meat off the bones, then hung as much as they could to dry on the sides and back of the wagon. The buffalo was good eating in the following weeks.

For most of their journey thus far, they had followed the Platte River across Nebraska. Rupert and Otto were good at catching fish and occasionally caught some when they stopped for the night when they wanted something besides buffalo meat.

They caught up with the William Morgan Company. William Morgan approached them. "If you want to remain part of our company, you need to try to stick with us. Everyone in this company has duties, and you can't help us if you're always lagging behind."

"We ran into some difficulties with our wagon. I didn't see anyone coming back to help us. You took the company and left us behind," William replied.

"If you would have stuck with our company, we would have noticed and helped," William Morgan replied.

"We were doing our best," William said, raising his voice.

"Well, try a little harder," William Morgan replied, with a heated voice.

William practically yelled. "If you're going to leave us behind every time we get stuck, maybe we don't want to be part of your company."

Raising his voice even higher, William Morgan replied, "If you don't want to be part of our company, there are thirty others on the trail. You're welcome to join any one of them."

"Maybe we'll do that," William hollered.

After a few more days of travel, many of the companies on the plains had caught up to the William Morgan Company. All around were hundreds of wagons and livestock and people walking and riding across the plains. William rode around to see if he could find his friend Thomas Wrigley in the James McGaw Company. He finally found them and rode back to his wagon.

Rupert and Otto were guiding the wagon through the open prairie. Johanna and the girls walked. Little William was nestled away in the wagon, sleeping.

~ * * * ~

Johanna could see that her daughters looked miserable. There wasn't much for a seven-year-old and an eight-year-old to do on a long, boring journey like this. Johanna felt bad for them. Then a thought occurred to her. "Here, let me show you a game you can play with a string."

Johanna got a long length of yarn out of the wagon and tied the ends together to make a large circle. She wrapped the string around her hands several times. "All right, Ann, pinch the inner strings together and wrap the others around your hands."

Ann wasn't getting it, so Johanna gave Ann the string and wrapped it around her hands and showed Sarah how to pick it up. "See, it makes a new pattern," Johanna said.

The girls were excited. Johanna taught them how to pass the string back and forth. Each time it was picked up, the string formed a new pattern. This kept the girls busy until they stopped for camp.

William caught up to them. "Don't unpack anything yet. Come, guide the wagon this way. I've found the James McGaw camp."

That drew a few grumbles from Rupert and Otto, but they followed him.

The McGaw Camp had twice as many people and wagons as the Morgan Camp had. By the time the Chestnut wagon arrived, the others had already formed up in a circle. William asked Rupert to park the wagon alongside the circle of wagons; he then dismounted and tied Destiny to the wagon. They walked into the circle of wagons and found the Wrigley family.

As soon as Thomas found William and his wife, he greeted them. "William, Johanna, it's so good to see you. How are you doing? How have you fared on the trek so far?"

"We're surviving. We've had a few challenges along the way, but we're making do."

"Good; come and sit by the fire. How is the Morgan Company doing?"

"They're camped not too far from here. I've had a disagreement with Captain Morgan, and we left his company."

"Well, you're welcome to travel with us. I don't see any reason why one more wagon would make a difference. I'll go talk to Captain McGaw about it."

"Thank you, Thomas," Johanna said.

James McGaw was hesitant to take on another family for which he would be responsible. Thomas and William talked him into letting William trail behind the company and fend for themselves so they wouldn't take from the stores of food that belonged to the company.

"You're welcome to come along with us under those conditions. You won't be a part of the company, but you can travel with us," Captain McGaw said.

"Fair enough," William said.

Chapter 54
Samuel Adair

June 23, 1852

Samuel Adair had just finished plowing his plot of land. He had seeds for carrots and corn and was also planting potatoes and onions. He would not get to harvest any of it, but he knew that others who came to live in his cabin after he left would be able to enjoy the fruits of his labors. After having lost six years and one wife in this state, he was finally ready to make the trek to Utah.

A man approached Samuel. "Hello, Samuel."

Samuel waved at him and continued planting. "Hello, Brother Gardner."

"Getting your crops in, I see. How are your preparations going for our trip west?"

"I believe I'm ready," Samuel replied.

"How's your wife doing?" Brother Gardner asked.

"She has been a great support to me, especially after losing my first wife, Jemima, and the baby in childbirth. Though I'm afraid she has changed her views on wanting to move to Utah. We've separated, and she'll remain here."

Brother Gardener's eyebrows shot up. "When you married her, it was all she could talk about."

"I know, but that was three years ago. Now she doesn't want any part of it."

"So, what are you going to do?"

Samuel took in the western horizon. "The prophet has called us to move to Utah, and that is still my intent."

"What about little Joshua?"

Samuel stared at the ground. "She won't part with him. He's the only one we had together. He'll stay here with Nancy."

"I'm concerned about your seven children not having anyone to watch after them when you are attending your duties in the camp."

Samuel looked into Benjamin Gardner's eyes. "You needn't be. The older ones will help take care of the younger ones, and we'll get by just fine."

Benjamin nodded. "If you're confident you can handle the trip, I won't stand in your way."

"Listen, Benjamin, I know as the captain of our company, you're concerned with those who might lag behind, but you needn't focus your efforts on my family. We'll do our part and won't slow down the wagon train in the slightest."

"All right, Samuel. Let me know if there is anything I can help you with before we leave."

"I'll be first in line tomorrow when we cross the Missouri," Samuel said.

~ * * * ~

Samuel put his oldest sons, John and George, in charge of driving the wagon. The two youngest, six-year-old Jemima and eight-year-old Rufus, could ride in the wagon. The rest—fifteen-year-old Permelia, as well as Samuel Jr. and Samuel's adopted son David, who were both twelve—would all have to walk.

The next day started by crossing the Missouri, which was just short of half a mile wide. Samuel loaded his wagon onto a flat boat and set off.

The company had about 150 cattle with them, and they trudged into the river. After crossing, the company progressed slowly to allow time for the cattle to feed.

The first night they camped, Benjamin Gardner approached Samuel. "Samuel, how's your family getting along?"

"No problems yet." Samuel said.

"That's good to hear. Samuel, I would like to call you to be on our hunting team. We want to keep all the cattle for starting a herd in the Salt Lake Valley. Any antelope, deer, or bison you can hunt for the company will be a great help. We'll have plenty of milk with all these cows in our company. Any meat you can get for us will make the trip much more bearable."

"I can do that."

"Thank you, Samuel. Let me know if there is anything I can do to help you and your family."

Samuel preferred hunting to watching over the cattle. Chasing down and shooting live game seemed more interesting than chasing down straying cattle. As they traveled along the trail, a large herd of buffalo was spotted, and the hunting party was deployed. Samuel got about five on his own, and the other hunters got two or three each. They got about as much buffalo meat as they needed to feed the company for most of their journey.

About mid-June, the company came to a river that was full of quicksand. Any animal, wagon, or human that stopped moving for even a few seconds started sinking.

Benjamin Gardner stood at the bank of the river as Samuel approached the water. Benjamin called out, "This is the Loupe Fork River; there is quicksand along the bed of the river, so make sure you keep moving. Anything standing still will sink into the sand."

Samuel turned to his sons who were driving the wagon. "John, George, did you hear that? Make sure the wagon keeps moving, or you'll get stuck in the quicksand."

"Got it," John called back.

Samuel urged his horse across the river. When he got to the other side, he turned around and saw the wagon in the middle of the river with its wheels buried almost to the axles. Samuel rode back into the river.

"Why did you stop? The wagon's stuck now!"

"It was the stupid oxen, Pa; they wanted to stop to get a drink," John replied.

"I'll go get some help," Samuel said.

Samuel urged his horse back to the bank, but it didn't move. The horse had sunk into the sand and was stuck.

Samuel dismounted, and dug the sand away from the horse's front leg. As he dug, he started sinking and had to get up and move to prevent himself from getting stuck. Benjamin stopped the flow of traffic across the river when he saw the predicament and got a few men to help the Adair family get out of the quicksand.

They first focused on the horse, working one leg at a time. They got some large, flat rocks from the bank they could put under the freed feet to give the horse purchase. Finally, the horse was freed and was led to the opposite bank.

Some of the brethren had gotten themselves stuck up to their knees in the quicksand in the process of helping to free the horse. They had to be helped out of the sand as well.

After getting the horses freed and out of the river, they were led back and reattached, but they were unable to move the wagon.

Two extra yoke of oxen were detached from other families' wagons waiting on the bank and were attached to the Adair wagon. The power of the combined oxen, horses, and the brethren pushing at the wheels was enough to pull the wagon free of the sand and out of the river.

After the extra oxen were returned to their owners, the flow of traffic across the river continued.

A big camp of wagons was parked in a circle formation, as was the custom of most companies on the plains to serve as protection from outside raiders. Benjamin sent a rider out to find out which company it was and found out it was the Bishop W.W. Eames Company—and he learned they had some people infected with cholera in their camp.

When Benjamin called for them to stop at noon for lunch, the Eames Company passed them.

That night as they camped, cholera attacked a few of the families in camp. One sixteen-year-old in the Hunt family died before the night was out and was immediately buried.

The next day they passed a wagon from the Eames Company. They were burying Bishop Eames, who had died from cholera. Seven miles later, they passed another wagon from the Eames

Company. They were burying Bishop Eames' wife, who had also died from cholera.

The cholera took its toll on the Benjamin Gardner company. Over the next week, cholera took fifteen more of the company. Samuel helped bury most of them along the trail. After two weeks, the cholera finally abated.

Every day they made good progress except on the Sabbath, when they rested and held meetings. As they reached the fork in the Platte River, they decided they could make more progress and move faster if they split into two companies. They divided into two camps and continued their journey.

It wasn't too many more weeks before they passed Fort Laramie and caught up to the James McGaw Company. There were many in the two companies that knew each other, so they stopped and camped with them. Samuel didn't know any in the James McGaw Company, so he decided it was a good time to go hunting. On his way out, he noticed a fancy, dark-red wagon that looked out of place among the smaller wagons. He guessed it must belong to someone who was wealthy.

The area was a great spot for the cattle to graze, so Benjamin Gardner decided to keep his company there a few days to graze the cattle while the James McGaw Company moved on ahead of them.

When they started going again, Jemima pointed at a valley that stretched out in front of them. "Look, George, the ground is moving." The ground looked like a black, bubbling blanket covered it.

"That's not the ground, Jemima. That's a huge herd of buffalo!"

The herd came right into the wagon train. Guards had to be deployed to keep them away from the wagons and cattle. After a few more days of travel, the buffalo cleared up, and a decision was made to split the company again as the places they could find to camp were not big enough for large herds to graze on.

The following week as they were stopped at noon for lunch, a group of Cheyenne Indians approached their wagon train. They were in full war paint and seemed hostile.

"Get your guns ready," Benjamin called out.

Every man pulled out his guns, loaded them, and stood to meet the oncoming party. Benjamin stood in front.

The Indian leading the party said, "You come peacefully to our lands?"

Benjamin responded, "Yes, we do. We are on our way to the Utah Territory. We are just passing through."

"What proof have you of your peaceful intentions?"

"Excuse me while I discuss this with my men." Benjamin turned around and called the group into a huddle. "Put your guns away, but keep them loaded and easily accessible. Go and fetch the fiddles, and ask your children to come out and dance while we play the music."

Benjamin turned back to invite the Indians to their merriment. Samuel returned to his wagon and approached his children. "I need you to go out and dance with the other children for the Indians."

The children danced. The Indians laughed as they watched and seemed very pleased. Some gifts were presented to the Indians, who then went on their way.

The next day they came across a wide rolling creek. It looked too dangerous to cross, so they threw in some large logs, brush, and dirt, filling the creek up enough for the wagons and animals to cross.

As Samuel went out to hunt that night, he encountered a bunch of prairie dogs. He was able to get many of them, and he returned to camp with quite the feast on his stick. They turned out to be quite tasty, though some refused to eat them because *dog* was in the name.

September was full of warm, clear days, and the nights were cool. After several days they arrived at Fort Bridger, and camped on the west side of Black Fork. The next day the company traveled twenty miles up Aspen Hill and experienced their first mountain snowstorm.

Too cold to sleep, Samuel got up early, checked on his children to make sure they were all covered up, then walked through the snow-blanketed ground in search of wood to start a fire. As he walked through the camp, he noticed the pen they had constructed the previous night to keep the cattle in was empty.

"The cattle have escaped!" Samuel hollered. "Get up! Get up! The cattle are gone!"

Men emerged from their tents.

Benjamin organized four search parties, one for every direction. Samuel was assigned to the group headed south down the mountain. They searched until noon, when they finally found the cattle down off the ridge where there were only spots of snow.

Two hours later, they were on their way and came to Bear River, which was at a much lower altitude and had no snow. They decided that would be a good place to camp, but it turned out to be a chilly night.

After overcoming a muddy trench and an overturned wagon on the morning of September 26, they entered Echo Canyon and had their noon meal at Cache Cave.

Samuel thought it might be a good time to go hunting again, as they were low on their meat supplies. He took his gun and headed southeast into the valley on his horse.

Samuel spotted some antelope in the distance and dismounted from his horse and tied it to a tree. He moved slowly toward the animals. When he got close enough that he thought he could hit them, he took aim at the largest one. Just before he was about to pull the trigger, he had a strong feeling to leave the antelope. He lowered the gun but then shook the feeling, thinking the antelope were too good to pass up. He raised the gun again, and the feeling came back even more forcefully than before. He lowered his gun again.

"You must be some righteous antelope," he said, turning around and walking back to his horse. As he remounted, he felt compelled to continue his hunt to the south.

He rode south for a while. Not seeing any other animals, he felt he had made a mistake leaving the antelope. Then he remembered the strong feeling he had and continued riding south. As he crested the next hill, he spotted a stray cow wandering through the sage-brush. As he studied the cow, his jaw dropped. He couldn't believe what he saw attached to it.

Chapter 55
Finding Home

August 14, 1852

After having traveled roughly five hundred miles in seven weeks without seeing a civilized man or building, the Chestnuts came upon Fort Laramie. There they were able to do some trading. Most of the companies had stopped for only one or two days to rest and get additional supplies. The Saints filled up the fort and many more camped outside its walls.

James McGaw decided that one day at Fort Laramie was enough. The company crossed the Platte River the next day and camped four miles from where they forded the river. The Benjamin Gardner Company had caught up to them. As a lot of people from the two companies were old acquaintances, they camped with them that night, though the Benjamin Gardner Company wanted to stay another few days, as it was a good spot for feeding the cattle they had brought with them. There was no reason for the James McGaw Company to stay, so they went on ahead.

There were more days of rain and getting stuck in the mud. Captain McGaw came back to check on the Chestnut wagon regularly and used his own horse to help pull them out of some of the mud holes they got stuck in.

Tensions rose between the Chestnuts and their teamsters when they got to some lakes covered with saleratus, which had the appearance of ice. They had set up camp and Rupert and Otto had taken the animals to drink the saleratus water. Two of the milk cows and Destiny had gotten to the water first and died. They stopped the other animals from drinking as soon as the first three started reacting to the poison in their bodies.

When they went back to camp and explained what happened, William did not take the news well. He kicked himself for not taking care of Destiny personally. That horse had been with him so long, he already missed her.

"You should have been more careful with my horse," William said.

Rupert curled his lips and tightened his fists. "If it weren't for us, you would have lost the entire bunch and been left with nothing to pull the wagon."

"If I hadn't let you take my horse, it would still be alive."

Johanna intervened. "William, there is no way they could have known the water was poisonous."

That ended the debate, but William never apologized for getting after them for killing Destiny.

William was now left to walk. He missed his horse with every step. Rupert and Otto got lazier with their duties. They slept in regularly and seemed to purposely drag their feet, slowly getting ready for each day's journey. They regularly fell behind the James McGaw Company and caught up to them by the end of each day.

James came and talked to William about his teamsters.

"I'm sorry your teamsters are giving you trouble, but we can't travel on their schedule, or we'll end up caught in the winter snow. We've got to keep our pace."

William nodded. "I understand, Captain. You've been very kind to us. Even though we're not officially part of your company, you've helped us a great deal."

"Do you want me to see if I can talk some sense into those teamsters of yours?"

"It certainly couldn't hurt," William said.

William watched as Captain McGaw approached the teamsters. *There probably isn't a nicer man on the planet than James McGaw. If anyone can get through to those two it'll be him.*

Just then, he heard Captain McGaw raising his voice at Rupert and Otto. The only part William caught was, "Your job is to get this family across these plains, and if you can't straighten up and do that properly, then neither one of you is worth the skin of a fart!"

Captain McGaw rode away. William guessed that his conversation with them did not go as he'd planned.

Rupert and Otto's behavior only got worse, and Johanna started complaining to William. They lounged around after meals and would not pull their weight in getting things cleaned up and ready to go.

William finally had enough. He approached the two after dinner one evening. "I hired you to take care of my family as we cross the plains, and you've slept in, giving us a late start most days, unnecessarily prolonging our journey. If you want to get paid, then you best be getting about your business."

"You sayin' you ain't going to pay us for all the work we done to get you across these plains?" Rupert asked.

"I'm saying that you won't see a penny if you don't start doing your job properly!"

The two teamsters gave each other the slightest of nods, as if some understanding had passed between them. They looked back at William, and Rupert said, "We'll do right by you."

~ * * * ~

One night as they camped, Rupert volunteered to go with Otto in search of firewood. William objected.

"There's no need; there are plenty of buffalo chips to burn in this area."

"Well, I'm sick of eating food cooked over burning dung. Otto and I are going for some wood," Rupert replied.

William thought they were trying to get out of helping set up camp. He shook his head as they walked away.

Once they were out of earshot, Rupert said, "Listen, Otto, I have figured out a plan that will get us out from under William's thumb and will get us all that money we know he must have in that lockbox in the wagon."

"It's about time, Rup. What's your plan?"

"It's not like I haven't been thinking about it. Every plan I have come up with so far would have led to us getting caught. But now I think I have something that will work. But we have to follow it precisely."

Otto stared at him intently. "Well, what is it?"

"First, we'll have to get them alone. We'll delay them in the morning and drive the oxen slowly during the day. We need to get at least a day behind the company. Then we'll take them out."

"All of them?" Otto asked.

"Yes," Rupert replied.

"Even the children?"

Rupert tightened his lips. "We don't want to leave any witnesses. Think about it. If we let them live, they'll start blabbing about what we did."

Otto nodded his head slowly.

Rupert's tactics of delay worked as planned. They had just arrived at a place they assumed was called Echo Canyon from the descriptions McGaw had given them last time they saw him. William was upset they had gotten separated from the company.

"Don't worry, Mr. Chestnut; from what I understand, the Salt Lake Valley is just over that mountain range. We'll be there in the next day or two," Rupert said.

The next morning Rupert and Otto were up early before anyone else had awoken.

Rupert told Otto, "Let's go take care of the parents."

William awoke with a sharp pain in his ribs where Rupert forced a gun into them.

"Get up," he heard Rupert say. Rupert's head was just inside the tent, and William opened his eyes to see the barrel of his gun bearing down on him.

"What are you doing?" William asked.

Johanna sat upright. "What's going on?"

"You're about to find out. Now get up and out of that tent."

William and Johanna got up and left the tent.

Otto and Rupert were standing outside waiting for them. Rupert had the rifle trained on them. Otto had some rope in his hands. "Tie up their hands, Otto. Make it good and tight."

After Otto tied up their hands, Rupert set down his shotgun and drew a revolver. He pointed with the gun. "Now start walking in that direction."

"Otto, you take care of the children while I take care of these folks."

"What is going on?" William exclaimed.

"Shut up! One more word from either of you, and I'll shoot you. Now go stand over there by the wagon."

William and Johanna complied.

"Now throw me the keys to that lock box in the wagon."

William took the keys from around his neck and threw them toward Rupert.

"You're going to rob us and leave us out here?"

"Yes, after you're all dead," Rupert said, smiling.

"William," Johanna exclaimed, her moist eyes fixed on the kids. "They're going to kill the children."

"No!" William hollered.

Two shots rang out. Johanna fell, dying instantly. William fell by her side in a sitting position. He looked at his bleeding chest, the pain seared through his body. He looked at his wife, dead on the ground and heard the screams of his children.

Hate surged into William's heart and yelled out. "No!" He closed his eyes. He didn't want to die full of hate. He also thought of his children and said a silent prayer. *Please, Lord, give me strength. Please save my children.* The pain subsided and a feeling of love flooded into his chest.

William opened his eyes and looked at Rupert. He saw him in a new light and knew instantly what he must do. He knew this wouldn't work unless he was sincere. Rupert advanced on him, William stared into Rupert's eyes. "Rupert Howard, I forgive you."

Rupert stopped and cocked his gun, then aimed at William.

"I didn't ask for your forgiveness. Why would you forgive me when I just shot you and your wife and am going to rob you of everything you own?"

William looked over at his wife then back at his screaming children. Thinking what his children must be going through, a tear rolled down his cheek. His eyes met Rupert's again.

"The Lord loves you, Rupert. I extend that love to you. I forgive you."

Rupert lowered his gun.

"What are you talkin' about? I don't deserve the Lord's love or your forgiveness. Besides, it's already too late for that."

"No. It's not. The Savior's love and our Heavenly Father's love is always with you, no matter what you've done. They still love you. I do too. I forgive you, Rupert. I mean it. I do." With that, William fell down by his wife, silent and still.

A tear rolled down Rupert's cheek. The Chestnut children were still screaming and crying. He wiped away the tear and walked over to where Otto held the children at gunpoint.

~ * * * ~

Otto aimed his gun at the children.

"Ann, Sarah, William, get over there by those trees."

Ann grabbed William. "Come on." Sarah and William were crying; they could see Mr. Howard and their parents by the wagon at the point of a gun.

"You children shut up!" Otto yelled.

They could hear the conversation between Rupert and their parents, and they watched in horror as two shots rang out. They saw the smoke from the gun and saw their parents both fall to the ground. They screamed.

"You all shut up. Now, it's your turn," Otto said, aiming his gun at the children.

"Please don't kill us, Mr. Flint! Please! You said you would protect us!" Ann pleaded, tears falling from her eyes.

Otto lowered his gun. His heart caught in his throat.

Rupert walked up to Otto. "I thought you were going to take care of these children, Otto," Rupert said.

Otto looked at the ground. "I don't have the heart to kill them. They're just children; they can't do anything to us. Let's just let them be."

Rupert replied, "Well, we can't have them following us. They'll tell everyone what we did."

"They're only children; we can't do it, Rup!"

Rupert aimed his gun at Ann.

She cried out, "No! Please!"

William's dying words rang through Rupert's conscience. He lowered the gun. "Fine! I don't have the heart to kill them either. We won't kill them. But we can't take them with us."

"We can't just leave them here, Rup!" Otto said.

"There is a settlement somewhere in that direction," Rupert pointed down the valley. "Tie them to that cow; we'll send it off in that direction. It should get them there."

"How do you know there is a settlement?" Otto asked.

"I saw a trail going off that way when we were gathering wood for the fire last night. It looks well-traveled, which means there should be a settlement in that direction," Rupert said.

Otto tied the children's hands together, then looped the rope through their arms and tied the rope around the neck of the cow. He guided the cow in the direction Rupert had pointed out and sent the cow on its way. Ann, Sarah, and William cried as they were pulled along beside it.

Chapter 56
Desert Wanderers

September 25, 1852

Sarah was heartbroken. She had just seen her parents killed in front of her eyes and was certain she was going to die with her brother and sister tied to the milk cow that was leading them through the desert. William never stopped crying after he saw his parents gunned down. Ann had run out of tears and did her best to take care of her siblings.

Whenever Sarah or William tripped, Ann helped them stand again so they didn't get dragged over the ground by the cow. They had been walking for hours, and their legs ached.

The cow finally stopped when it came to a grassy field and started eating. William started crying that he was hungry. Ann told him to lie down under the cow and she would try to squirt some milk out of the cow into his mouth. But no matter how hard she tried, the milk would not come out of the cow's udders. She squeezed harder, which prompted the cow to jerk forward. Ann fell backward, and Sarah was able to pull William out from underneath the cow before it could trample him, but they both fell to the ground.

All three children started screaming as they were dragged along by the cow. Rocks and brush scraped against their legs and arms. The cow slowed down, and the three of them were able to stand up again. The cow finally stopped when it came to a stream to get a drink. All three kids cupped their hands and scooped up the water and drank.

Ann took advantage of the water and started washing off her scrapes and bruises as best she could. She started washing William, but he fought her and screamed, "Quit. Leave me alone. Stop it. That hurts."

"Stop struggling. Help me, Sarah." Ann said.

Sarah grabbed William, but he continued to fight them.

They finally got William all cleaned up, and Sarah was about to wash herself when the cow started moving again. She got pulled over and dragged through the water. Ann was able to help her stand up before the water got too deep.

Ann had to lift William as the water came past his chest; she was afraid he would drown.

The cow finally stopped to graze, and the children got to rest, though they didn't dare sit for fear the cow would take off walking again. When night fell, the cow stood still. Ann, Sarah, and William huddled together to keep warm. The night was cold, and the children started shivering. The cow laid down, and they leaned against it for warmth. The girls kept William between them so he wouldn't freeze.

The next morning, the children awoke shivering. The cow stood up, as did Ann. She looked down at Sarah and William. "Get up you two, unless you want to be dragged across the ground again."

Sarah was so tired. Her eyes blinked open.

William muttered, "Leave me alone."

The cow started moving.

"Hurry," Ann yelled, as she helped Sarah to stand.

When she reached for William, he fought her. He didn't want to stand, but with Sarah's help, Ann got him to his feet. They started walking.

"I want Mommy and Daddy!" William cried over and over again.

"Stop it, William!" Ann said.

As the day wore on, the cow continued walking. The rising sun burned into their skin. Around noon, the cow found some shade and sat down. The children collapsed onto the ground. Their legs ached with exhaustion.

Sarah rubbed her legs. "I want to die."

"Don't talk like that, Sarah! We need to say a prayer, and Jesus will help us," Ann said.

"How is He going to help us?" Sarah asked.

"I don't know. But I know he will," Ann replied.

She folded her arms and started praying. "Heavenly Father, please help us. We're so tired and hungry and hurt, and we don't know what to do. Please, please, please help us. In Jesus's name, amen."

After Ann finished her prayer, she looked up and saw a man riding on horseback toward them.

Sarah's eyes widened. "He answered your prayer!"

The cow had continued walking, and Ann and Sarah jumped and hollered as they were pulled along. "Here! Please help us! Here! Here!"

The man caught up to them and stopped the cow. He untied the children.

"Thank you!" Ann said.

"How did you three end up tied to this cow, wandering through the desert?" the man asked.

Ann broke down, unable to hold the tears back anymore. The man held Ann, trying to comfort her. When she had calmed down enough, she started to speak. He listened as Ann told their story in between sobs and described the gruesome murder of their parents. She explained they had been wandering the desert tied to the cow for the last two days.

"That is horrible! What are your names?"

"I'm Ann, this is Sarah, and that's William," Ann responded, pointing to her siblings.

"I'm Samuel Adair. Don't worry, I'll take care of you from now on."

Samuel put the children on his horse, tied the cow to the horse, and headed back to camp.

~ * * * ~

Sarah sat by Jefferson's bedside, unable to hold back her tears as she finished telling her story.

Jefferson got up and gave her a long hug. "I'm sorry you had to go through that. I never knew."

Sarah stared at the wall. "It's hard for me recount my past. Most of the time I try to forget because the memories bring so much pain."

Sarah looked her son in the eyes. "My father knew it was not worth it to hold on to the anger. It never is. I hope you can see through his experience how much love and forgiveness can change the hearts of others. You might give it a try with your stepfather."

She grabbed his hand. "You'll never change him and how he treats you until you change yourself first."

Jefferson looked down for several long seconds, twisted his mouth, then came to a decision. "All right, Ma, I'll try harder to get along with Jean. I promise."

"Thank you, Jefferson," Sarah said. "Remember, we have the Lord's promise that charity never faileth."

To be continued . . .

What happens to the children?

Find out in *Reclaiming Love,*

Volume Two of

The Trial and Triumph Series

Thank you for reading Grudges and Grace!

If you enjoyed this book, **please leave a review on Amazon.com**.

I would love to hear your feedback.

Thanks so much!!

~ BJ Salmond

Author's Note

William and Johanna Chestnut are my wife's fourth great-grandparents. I came across their story as I was working on making a five-generation picture chart for her family. Sarah Mary Chestnut was the last picture on the chart that I didn't have. In searching for her picture, I found this story.

The known/true parts of this story are that William and Johanna bought a big, fancy wagon and left Missouri bound for Utah in the 1852 migration of Saints. They are not listed with any of the pioneer companies that came across the plains. The Chestnuts arrived in Echo Canyon, Utah, late in September 1852, just before the William West Lane Company and the Benjamin Gardner Company got there; Samuel Adair belonged to the latter. There were three pioneer companies three to four days ahead of the Gardner and Lane Companies: the James McGaw Company, the Isaac Bullock Company, and the David Wood Company. The Chestnut family arrived in Echo Canyon between these companies.

William and Johanna were murdered in Echo Canyon by the teamsters they hired to take them across the plains. Their three children—Ann, Sarah, and William—were not murdered, but were instead tied to a cow. The cow was supposedly pointed in the direction of a settlement and was sent on its way through the desert. The teamsters continued on to Salt Lake City with the Chestnuts' belongings. The children were later found and rescued by Samuel Adair, who took them in and adopted them.

Nothing else is known about William and Johanna except the dates and places of their birth, and their approximate marriage date. The major events that take place in the book all happened, though whether William and Johanna were part of those is just a guess. I tried to stay as true to history as I could, placing Johanna and William in those times and places to experience what I thought would be happening around them as they lived their lives. Nearly every character they interacted with in the story, were actual people in history in the correct times and places.

Had their story not been passed down by their descendants, they may never have been known, as any official records containing their names are virtually nonexistent. Much more is known about the highly intriguing events of Sarah's life, which will be the focus of Volume Two.

The picture that started it all

Sarah Mary Chestnut

Characters in this book that are my wife's direct line ancestors:

- William Albert Chestnut (4th Great Grandparent)
- Johanna Nancy Chestnut (4th Great Grandparent)
- Sarah Mary Chestnut (3rd Great Grandparent)
- Jefferson Chestnut Slade (2nd Great Grandparent)
- David Tulley LeBaron (4th Great Grandparent)
- Ester Melita LeBaron (4th Great Grandparent)
- Parley Parker Pratt (4th Great Grandparent)

The story of Johanna and Williams conversion came from the experience of another one of my wife's direct line ancestors:

- Joseph Robinson (4th Great Grandparent)
- Lucretia Hancock (4th Great Grandparent)

Acknowledgments

Special thanks to:

- Christie Powell
- Ramy Vance
- Rebecca Watson
- Susan Mitchell
- Kim Clement
- Emily Beeson

For providing suggestions that helped me to significantly improve the story.

References

Bennett, Richard E., Winter Quarters: Church Headquarters, 1846–1848. The Church of Jesus Christ of Latter-Day Saints. Ensign, September 1977.

Bigler, David L., and Will Bagley. "This Land Is My Land - or Yours." The Mormon Rebellion: America's First Civil War, 1857-1858, 41–50. Norman, OK: Univ. of Oklahoma, 2011.

Brown, Lisle G., 'A Perfect Estopel': Selling the Nauvoo Temple, Mormon Historical Studies, 3/2 (Fall 2002): 61-85.

Buehler, Michael. Dramatic Map and View of the 1849 St. Louis Fire. Boston Rare Maps. Accessed July 13, 2020. https://bostonraremaps.com/inventory/hutawa-st-louis-fire/.

Condie, Gibson. "Saints by Sea: Latter-Day Saint Immigration to America." Liverpool to New Orleans 29 Jan 1849–2 Apr 1849. Reminiscences and Diary of Gibson Condie | Saints by Sea. Intellectual Reserve, Inc, 2000. Accessed August 8, 2020. https://Saintsbysea.lib.byu.edu/mii/account/1576.

David Tully LeBaron and Esther Maleta Johnson: Lest We Forget: Our Family Treasures. FamilySearch. Accessed May 17, 2020. https://www.familysearch.org/service/records/storage/das-mem/patron/v2/TH-904-62779-2110-40/dist.txt?ctx=ArtCtxPublic.

Farmer, Thomas L., Woods, Fred E. Sanctuary on the Mississippi: St. Louis as a Way Station for Emigration, The Confluence, Vol 9, No 2, Lindenwood University Press, Spring/Summer 2018.

Hartley, William G. "'Don't Go Aboard the Saluda!': William Dunbar, LDS Emigrants, and Disaster on the Missouri." Mormon Historical Studies, Spring (2003): 40–70. Accessed August 12, 2020. https://ensignpeakfoundation.org/wp-content/uploads/2013/02/MHS_Spring2003_Steamboat-Saluda.pdf.

Hales, Scott A, Goldberg, James, Larson , Melissa L, Maki, Elizabeth P, Harper, Steven C, Farnes, Sherilyn. Saints, Volume 1: The Standard of Truth 1815-1846. Intellectual Reserve, Inc. 2018.

Helpful Hints for Steamboat Passengers. Frontier Life. University of Northern Iowa/State Historical Society of Iowa, 2003. Accessed August 10, 2020. https://iowahist.uni.edu/Frontier_Life/Steamboat_Hints/Steamboat_Hints2.htm.

Hyde, Orson. 1851 07Jul25 Fri 7_THE MORMONS | Emigration--Return of President Orson Pratt--Misc. New-York Tribune. Accessed July 15, 2020. https://www.newspapers.com/clip/28388077/1851-07jul25-fri-7the-mormons/.

Jenson, Andrew. (1901). Caine, John Thomas. In Latter-Day Saint Biographical Encyclopedia: A Compilation of Biographical Sketches of Prominent Men and Women in the Church of Jesus Christ of Latter-Day Saints, Volume 1 (Vol. 1, pp. 727-730). Salt Lake City, Utah: Andrew Jenson History Company.

Jones, Mike. 1849: We Got This - The St Louis Cholera Epidemic. Lafayette Square. Lafayette Square History, March 29, 2020. https://lafayettesquare.org/1849-we-got-this-the-st-louis-cholera-epidemic/.

Kimball, Stanley B., The Saints and St. Louis, 1831–1857: An Oasis of Tolerance and Security

Mahon, John K. "Missouri Volunteers at the Battle of Okeechobee: Christmas Day 1837." The Florida Historical Quarterly 70, no. 2 (1991): 166-76. Accessed August 2, 2020. http://www.jstor.org/stable/30140548.

Marquardt, H. Michael. Nauvoo Temple Endowment Name Index. Accessed July 7, 2020. https://user.xmission.com/~research/family/familypage.htm.

Platt, Lyman D., Early Branches of the Church of Jesus Christ of Latter-Day Saints 1830-1850, Nauvoo Journal, Vol. 3, Pgs 3–50, 1991.

Press, The Church Historian's. Layne, Jonathan Ellis, Autobiography, 1897, 10–18. - Pioneer Overland Travel, 2018. https://history.churchofjesuschrist.org/overlandtravel/sources/5160/layne-jonathan-ellis-autobiography-1897-10-18.

Press, The Church Historian's. Morgan, William, A Letter September 20, 1852 to Presidents W. S. Phillips and J. Davis, in Ronald D. Dennis, The Call of Zion: The Story of the First Welsh Mormon Emigration 1987, 234-35. - Pioneer Overland Travel. Accessed June 10, 2020. https://history.churchofjesuschrist.org/overlandtravel/sources/5686/morgan-william-a-letter-september-20-1852-to-presidents-w-s-phillips-and-j-davis-in-ronald-d-dennis-the-call-of-zion-the-story-of-the-first-welsh-mormon-emigration-1987-234-35.

Simini. (2019). James Sherlock Cantwell 1813 - 1887 BillionGraves Record. Memories. Retrieved June 09, 2020, from https://billiongraves.com/grave/James-Sherlock-Cantwell/49704

Slaughter, Sheri Eardley. "'Meet Me in St. Louie' An Index of Early Latter-Day Saints Associated with St. Louis, Missouri." Nauvoo Journal 10, no. 2 (2013): 48–108. Accessed August 12, 2020. https://doi.org/https://ensignpeakfoundation.org/wp-content/uploads/2013/05/NJ10.2_Slaughter.pdf.

Tucker, Phillip Thomas. "A Forgotten Sacrifice: Richard Gentry, Missouri Volunteers, and the Battle of Okeechobee." The Florida Historical Quarterly 70, no. 2 (1991): 150–65. Accessed July 2, 2020. http://www.jstor.org/stable/30140547.

Uncle Dale's Old Mormon Articles: St. Louis, 1844–1849. Accessed May 7, 2020. http://sidneyrigdon.com/dbroadhu/MO/miscstl3.htm.

Woods, Fred E, and Felt, Jonathan C. "An Essex County Man's Silver Cord Nathaniel H. Felt (1816 – 1887)," 2004. Accessed July 2, 2020. https://ensignpeakfoundation.org/wp-content/uploads/2013/05/felt-woods.pdf.

Woods, Fred E, and Farmer, Thomas L. "When the Saints Came Marching In: A History of the Latter-Day Saints in St. Louis." Millennial Press. 2009

Yann Picand, Dominique Dutoit. "Seminole Wars," 2000. Accessed August 8, 2020. http://dictionnaire.sensagent.leparisien.fr/Seminole_Wars/en-en/.

Conversion

Every individual must seek out Gods light,
Obtain a personal testimony of what's right.

Then reflect that light through actions and deeds,
Letting your light so shine, turning down false creeds.

All must be converted to Gods side,
To feel his love and with him reside.

Are you a convert to his light?
Do you live to do what's right?

Can you say your a convert true,
if your not living the way He taught to?

How many drops for you were shed?
Will you continue to let them be bled?

Do you remember why he suffered so?
Or why he taught the way to go?

With an eye fixed on you and me,
He suffered, there, to set us free.

Exaltation and eternal life are offered thus,
To whom repent, endure, and give Him their trust.

Through service and love our likeness is in Him asserted.
Remember, to turn your heart to God is to be converted.

~ B.J. Salmond

Made in the USA
Monee, IL
23 March 2022